ALSO BY ELSIE SILVER

Chestnut Springs

Flawless

Heartless

Powerless

Reckless

Hopeless

Gold Rush Ranch

Off to the Races

A Photo Finish

The Front Runner

A False Start

Rose Hill

Wild Love

A PHOTO FINISH

ELSIE SILVER

Bloom books

Cover design by Mary at Books and Moods

Published by Bloom Books, an imprint of Sourcebooks
P.O. Box 4410, Naperville, Illinois 60567–4410
(630) 961-3900
sourcebooks.com

Cataloging-in-Publication data is on file with the Library of Congress.

Originally self-published in 2021 by Elsie Silver.

Printed and bound in Canada.
MBP 10 9 8 7 6 5 4 3 2

For my husband, Mr. Silver. I love you, but please stop following me on TikTok.

No hour of life is lost that is spent in the saddle.

—WINSTON CHURCHILL

Reader Note

This book contains adult material, including references to PTSD, anxiety, and sexual harassment. It is my hope that I've handled these topics with the care they deserve.

CHAPTER 1

Violet

Did I really just win this race?

Everything around me moves in slow motion. The pointy black ears ahead of me leading to the shiny black mane down the neck that rocks in a steady rhythm beneath me. My fingers tangle in that mane, holding on for dear life.

I look over my shoulder to ensure I actually crossed the finish line. That I didn't just black out and miss a chunk of the race. Maybe there's another lap left? Maybe I've absolutely blown it like the total rookie I am.

But all around me, other horses and jockeys are slowing, pulling up. Pony horses go around us to grab excited racehorses. I even hear congratulatory words coming from my competitors. Which is nice because I have no business being here on a horse like this, winning such a prestigious race.

This is my first race *ever*, and I just qualified for the Denman Derby. That's pure dumb luck. That's unheard of.

I shake my head, trying to clear my thoughts, and the sounds from around me come rushing back in. Cheering from the stands, horn music over the loudspeakers, the number on our saddle pad flashing across the board in the infield.

We really did it.

I flop down onto his shiny black neck, wrapping my arms around him and nuzzling into his sweat-slicked coat. My throat clogs with emotion, and my eyes water as I murmur, "Who's the best boy?"

When I sit back up, we slow to a walk. Once the race is over, he doesn't stay keyed up for long. DD is a big old teddy bear, though he hasn't always been. It wasn't so long ago that nobody wanted to go near him. But his new trainer, Billie, brought him around, and somehow, I lucked into getting the ride on him.

I sit back and give DD some rein as we walk casually off the track toward the winner's circle. I think that's what I should do. Alarm courses through me as I realize I don't really know what to do here. I know my way around Bell Point Park, but I've never won a major stakes race before.

A moment later, Hank, the barn manager at Gold Rush Ranch, is at my side, patting my leg and looking up at me with pure contagious joy. His heavily lined green eyes twinkle with emotion. "Congratulations, Violet. I could not be more proud of you."

I blink rapidly and look away. Hank has that quintessential dad vibe going on. Or grandpa vibe? I'm not sure really. He's old enough he should be retired, but here he is, working on the farm every day like he's some sort of spring chicken.

The smile I return is watery. The reality of everything is sinking in, and it's overwhelming. "Thank you, Hank."

He reaches up and grabs the reins close to DD's bit. "Whoa, boy." He pulls us off to the side under the shade of a tree. "You two just take a moment before you head up there. A few deep breaths to get your bearings."

I could hug Hank at this moment for knowing what I need right now, even though I'm too shell-shocked to realize it.

"Thank you." I smile down at him and then close my eyes to take those deep breaths he recommended.

Until just recently, I was a groom at Gold Rush Ranch, sometimes an exercise rider when my friend and head trainer, Billie Black, would ask me to help. Imagine my surprise when she announced I would be the new jockey for one of the most talented racehorses I've ever seen. One bad race with local favorite Patrick Cassel as jockey was all it took for her to blacklist him and replace him with me.

So I dumb-lucked my way into this and am now certain everyone will notice and call my bluff.

When I feel like I've stopped spinning, I roll my shoulders back and jut my chin out. DD's breathing has slowed, and I can hear him chewing on the bit in his mouth, a sure sign he's feeling more relaxed as well.

Fake it till you make it, Vi. It doesn't matter how I got here. I rode that race, and it wasn't an easy one. DD and I deserve this win, and I'm going to accept it with grace rather than beat myself up about not deserving it.

"Okay. I'm ready."

With a sure nod, Hank clucks, urging DD forward, and we head for the circus that is the winner's circle.

Billie is there, big sunglasses on to cover what I'm sure are tearstained eyes. Vaughn, one of the two brothers who now own Gold Rush Ranch, is there too, arm snaked around her waist possessively.

I can't help but grin. Obviously, something is happening there. I shoot Billie a wink right as she rushes forward to hug DD and me. She blubbers something about loving me and being proud of me. And I'd be lying if my eyes didn't start to sting and water furiously too.

"Thank you for this," I whisper into her mess of chestnut hair as I lean down to return the hug.

Vaughn steps up next, opting for a firm handshake in lieu of a hug. His smile is wide and genuine, his chest puffed out proudly. "Congratulations, Violet. Beautifully ridden."

"Thank you for the opportunity," I say, grinning back like a total maniac. Because seriously, who puts a completely unproven twenty-six-year-old groom on a horse like *this* for a race like *this*?

My eyes dart over as someone else steps up to us just beside Vaughn. I feel my eyes widen as he does and scold myself internally. My poker face leaves something to be desired. This is something I know and still can't control. My feelings are constantly written on my face. Like a big flashing neon sign. And right now is no exception.

The man is clearly Vaughn's older brother, Cole. I've heard plenty about him, mostly Billie ranting about what a dick he is and making jokes about him being a robot, which I can kind of see, looking at him now. Where everyone else is elated—celebratory—he looks downright murderous.

Murderous and delicious.

I don't know if the endorphins coursing through me right now are making me giddy or if being this happy kills brain cells, but I can't look away from the gorgeous man. Even though he's scowling at me, I drink him in like the champagne I can't wait to guzzle when this crazy day is over.

He looks like Vaughn yet totally different. Harder, more imposing. Where Vaughn is tall and lean, his brother is strong and broad. His shoulders push against his suit jacket, like they might tear through it if he flexed hard enough. My eyes trail down to his trim waist and powerful thighs. *Pull yourself together, Violet. You're practically panting.*

When I imagined the reclusive brother who spends all his time at their downtown office, the one who never sets foot on the farm, *this* is not what I envisioned.

"Hi!" I say a little too brightly. *Cringe.* "I'm Violet." I stick my hand out toward him while people and cameras crowd in around us.

He doesn't return my smile though. His shapely lips stay pressed into a flat line, and his gray eyes sear me from where I still sit on DD's back. When his hand wraps around mine, I can't help but realize how big the man really is. My hand and wrist practically disappear in his grip. The warm rasp of his palm starts softly; then he squeezes and steps close to the saddle. His opposite hand rises between us, and he crooks his index finger.

A silent order to move closer.

I feel my heart rattle around in my chest as I lean in like a total sucker. Like a moth to a flame.

I expect him to congratulate me.

What I don't expect is for him to send me reeling into past mistakes.

"Nice to see you again, Pretty in Purple. I almost didn't recognize you with your clothes on."

All the air in my lungs rushes out in an audible gasp as I jerk back away from him.

No.

I peer down at him, scouring his features, feeling all the blood drain from my face as I try to reconcile my memory of a man I've worked so hard to forget.

No fucking way.

There is only one person in the world who would ever know to call me that, who would ever have the gall to say it that way. My cheeks heat as memories from the last year come at me rapid-fire.

That youthful experimentation part of my life was supposed to be a bump in the road on my way to total independence.

That part of my life was supposed to have stayed anonymous and in the past.

When I ghosted him without a word, he was supposed to stay where I left him.

He wasn't supposed to matter to me.

But as I drown in his gray eyes while the circus rages around me, I realize he still does.

CHAPTER 2

Cole

ONE YEAR LATER

I DON'T WANT TO MOVE OUT TO GOLD RUSH RANCH.

I hate it out here. And I'm not just saying that either. It's that deep spark of revulsion in my sternum that lets me know I don't belong here. That inner instinct that kept me alive overseas flares up every time I get near this place. But here I am, hurtling down the highway that will take me straight there anyway. If this were Iraq, I'd turn my truck around and get the hell out of here.

But this isn't Iraq.

It's Ruby fucking Creek, which honestly might be worse. I'm quite sure all they've got is a gas station and a corner store and a bunch of gossipy old biddies. I hate small towns. I hate how friendly they are, that you're expected to stop and make small talk with people you don't know and definitely don't care about. And I hate that everyone knows your business.

Most days, I think I might just generally hate people, but even I don't want to be that far gone. That dark.

I like my privacy. I like my space, quiet and tidy. And I don't like being asked probing questions. All of which I know are going to be tested the minute I step foot onto the family ranch. Vaughn was bad enough, the perpetual little brother constantly nipping at my heels, but now he's engaged to and living here with Billie Black. Also known as the most obnoxious woman in the world.

Don't get me wrong. I'm happy for them. As much as it makes me roll my eyes to admit it, they're kind of sweet together. And Billie is good for my little brother. But the two of them are just so much fucking sunshine and rainbows that you almost need sunglasses to be in their presence. And earplugs. The talking never stops.

I groan just thinking about how little peace I'm going to get at Gold Rush Ranch.

I think about riding along the trails with my dad. I think about the way we laughed together, the way he smiled at me, and his passion for horse racing. How happy he always looked when he saw me up on a horse, how happy I always was to spend time with him. And then, as I make the turn onto the side road that takes me there, I think about *her*.

That's going to be trickier to deal with than the rest. I should have kept my cards closer. I shouldn't have lost control like that. I could have maintained my anonymity. But when I saw the face that's haunted me every night for the past year, the one I'll never forget, all beaming and pure and carefree, I did what I always do.

A PHOTO FINISH

I ruined it.

Pristine white paper, and I purposely knocked ink all over it. Black liquid oozing out, marring the unmarked page.

I've spent an entire year since that race avoiding her at all costs. I dropped an atomic bomb on the girl and then walked away. Very on-brand for me. *You're such a fucking dick.*

My fingers pulse on the steering wheel, and my molars grind against each other as anxiety builds in my chest. I see the Gold Rush Ranch sign swaying on its chains just in front of the manicured tree-lined driveway. I snort. This place isn't a ranch anymore. It's a world-class horse racing facility and a far cry from what my grandparents started out with.

So much history.

I shouldn't be coming out here to this place filled with memories that haunt me and people who don't understand me and never will because I don't plan to let them.

But I promised the board of directors at Gold Rush Resources, the other family company, that I would take the new acquisition we picked up in the next town over and turn it around. I told them I wouldn't come back until it was running a profit. And in this moment, I can't fathom why I'd have made a promise like that.

I pull into the circular driveway and look around at the property. I have to give it to Vaughn; the place is immaculate. The horses, the fencing, the flowers even. He took over a year ago now, and the place has flourished. I hate to admit there's a little part of me that wishes he'd come back to the offices in downtown Vancouver. I kind of like having him around.

Instead, he started a whole new life for himself out here,

and I'm almost envious of his ability to just completely recreate himself while I keep living in the same rut, snuggled up in the mud that spinning my tires has created.

My eyes flutter shut, and I take a deep, centering breath, the heel of my hand digging into my right thigh as I try to find some inner calm. Deep breathing is something my therapist recommended. I told her it sounded like hippie, new age garbage. She just gave me a blank look—she knows me too well. Which means she probably knows I've secretly been trying it, and it's working, so we won't have to talk about it as a coping mechanism again.

Knock, knock, knock.

"Hey, big bro! You taking a nap? I know you're old, but this is a bit much."

If I pretend that Billie Black isn't here, will she disappear? Like an annoying figment of my imagination I can wish away on command?

I pry my eyes open and slowly turn my gaze on her. I give her my best withering look, one that sends most people running. She just smiles back at me even bigger.

Billie barks out a laugh and turns away, waving me along. "When you're back on your feet, Vaughn's in his office."

I already hate working at Gold Rush Ranch.

"You look like you're going to kill someone."

I scowl back at Vaughn across his desk as I flop into a chair. "I feel like I might."

He quirks an eyebrow. "Why?"

"You know I don't like it up here."

"I do. But the new mine is in Hope. Why didn't you look for a place there?"

I scrub my hand across my face. Vaughn has always been so full of questions. I remember him trailing after me asking them incessantly, and with seven years between us, I wasn't much into explaining things like why the letter *c* so often makes a *k* sound.

It seems unnecessarily cruel to tell him I tried every option available to me, only to find there's not much in the way of long-term rentals in the small town. Seems like you either live there or you don't. And I wasn't about to buy a house in a shitty town or stay with the cockroaches at the motor inn just to satisfy my promise to the board.

"This commute is pretty short. You've got an empty office here. Seemed like the obvious choice." That should appease him.

Vaughn smirks. "Just admit it."

I cross my arms over my chest, the only armor I have these days. "Admit what?"

"You missed me."

His cocky grin makes me want to lay him out and remind him who's stronger. Instead, I just glare at him—my default expression.

He holds his hands up in surrender. "Okay, okay. You missed Billie."

This time, I groan and look up at the ceiling. *I love my job, I love my job, I love my job. Working in the spare office down the hall will be* fine.

"You're right. That's not it… Oh! I know." From the corner of my eye, I can see him lean forward on his elbows and steeple his hands in front of his mouth. "You missed Violet."

Suddenly, the sound of my heart beats loud, like an overbearing drum pounding in my ears. It thumps through my entire body. *Why the fuck would he guess that?*

Years of military training mean I can look like I'm not reacting when I am. Which is why I stare back at him and deadpan, "Who?"

His intelligent gaze scans my face, amusement dancing in those eyes that remind me so much of our dad. He got the dark ones, and I got our mother's light ones, and we both somehow lucked into our height. Maybe that's from Grandpa Dermot.

He stands abruptly, and my shoulders drop incrementally when he completely changes the subject and says, "Well, let's get you settled in then."

Vaughn leads me out to the parking lot and steps into his flashy Porsche. He may have given up on wearing suits every day, but he hasn't gotten rid of this yet.

"Why do you still drive this thing? You live in the middle of butt-fuck nowhere on a bunch of gravel roads."

He hits me with his signature boyish grin. "Because it pisses Billie off." And then he slams the door, and I'm left to keep up with him on the back roads. He drives like a maniac.

It's always seemed to me that everything is all fun and games for Vaughn. He's twenty-nine now and still gets a kick out of spraying gravel around the turns.

When we pull up to the blue farmhouse, I have to say I'm surprised. I expected to be relegated to the guesthouse, not the main house. The house our grandpa Dermot built. The house my dad grew up in.

My flight instincts kick in again. *I should get out of here while I still can.*

Stepping out of my black truck, I ask Vaughn, "Why aren't you and Billie living in the main house?"

He fumbles through an overfull key chain. The disorganization of it makes my eye twitch.

"Billie likes the guesthouse. We started out there and just never left, I guess. You'll have more room to storm around in here anyway."

He means the jab to be funny, but the blow lands with some weight. I hate that I come off this way.

When he slides his hand along the door and swings it open, I'm surprised to find the space updated from when I last stepped foot in the house. Light and airy, like it belongs in a *Country Living* magazine. All white and blue and exposed wood. And it smells *clean.* Like properly clean. Clean in a way that I don't think my little brother can achieve.

I lean across the threshold and take a sniff of the lemony scent. Maybe even a little bleach. "Did you hire a cleaner?"

Vaughn just snorts. "No. Billie insisted on cleaning it for you."

I quirk a brow at him as if to say, "Crazy Billie did this for *me*?" But really, my chest pinches at the thought that someone whom I haven't tried very hard to endear myself to made the space this nice for me.

My brother just waves me off and walks into the house. With his shoes on. My teeth grind.

"Apparently, her house was a mess when she moved out here, and she's never let me live it down. Plus, she's been slowly updating this house as a side project. Said it needed a fresh start."

I know he's referring to the fact that our grandparents lived here until each of their respective dying days. I loved them too, but Vaughn and our grandfather Dermot had a connection I couldn't hold a candle to. One he almost blew his relationship with Billie over.

So while this house reminds him of Dermot, it almost painfully floods me with memories of my dad, my idol, who I watched fall from a horse midrace and never get back up. Vaughn was too young when our father died to tie memories of him to this place, whereas every damn thing at the ranch reminds me of him.

I clear my throat, forcing myself off that train of thought. "She's done a nice job."

Vaughn's eyes bug out a bit, like I've shocked him by complimenting his fiancée. *Am I really so bad?*

"I'll let her know," he replies with a funny look on his face. "And, Cole, if you ever want to…I don't know, get a beer or something, let me know. I'd be game for that. You don't have to hole up alone out here."

I stare back at him, seeing the forlorn kid I left behind when I boarded the plane and took off for basic training. I've never known how to apologize to him for leaving, and maybe I don't need to, but feeling like I should has always left me uncomfortable around Vaughn. I'd like to be close with him, but that probably means hashing out things I prefer to avoid. *Pretty sure my therapist's ears are ringing right now.*

Speaking of which, I lift my wrist to check my watch. "I have a call I need to take right away, but maybe some other time." I don't miss the way my brother's shoulders drop as I turn to grab my bags from the truck. *Would it have killed you to say yes to a beer?*

He waltzes out behind me, that easy smile gracing his face again, and I'm momentarily jealous of his ability to recover quickly, the way shit just rolls off him while it seems to stick all over me.

"Catch you later!" he calls out as he slips his shades on and folds himself into his silly little car.

I grunt back and offer a terse wave, feeling acutely aware of how growly I am. How different we are.

With the door closed, I walk upstairs to the master bedroom to unpack, and I won't lie, I'm relieved to find it just as meticulous as downstairs. They painted the room in soft grays and warm whites. It's a little feminine, but it feels fresh. I even crack a small smile when I see the way Billie has turned down the covers and left a chocolate on my pillow. She is truly ridiculous.

I fold my clothes into the dresser carefully and lay everything out in the en suite specifically how I like it. Straight. Organized. And a bit obsessive about placement. Some habits you pick up in the military never leave you.

When my phone rings, I sink onto the oak rocking chair in the corner and swipe to accept the video call. My therapist's small, heavily lined face fills the screen like she's peering through a pair of binoculars or something. The lenses of her bifocals are so thick they look like magnifying glasses over her eyes as she furrows her brow at the phone as though it's performing some sort of sorcery. A stack of silver bracelets jangles on her wrist as she tries to hold it out in different positions.

"Cole, I'm not so sure about this. I don't look good from any angle on this thing," she muses distractedly, poofing her hair with a small wrinkled hand.

"Hello, Beatrice," I reply, not caring about my seventy-something-year-old therapist's *angles*.

She tuts at me as she settles back in her chair. "I've been talking to you for two years. I'm tired of telling you to call me Trixie."

I stifle the shudder that runs down my spine. There's just something about calling a grown woman Trixie that feels wrong to me, and I kind of enjoy ribbing her, to be honest.

One side of my cheek quirks up as I stare back at the screen. Her office differs from every other therapist's I've seen over the years. She sees patients in the comfort of her early-1900s-character home. Persian rugs blanket the old oak floors, plants thrive on stands in every corner, crystals dangle in the big windows, and art from her decades of international travel covers the walls. I swear I can smell the patchouli oil she diffuses through the screen of my phone.

Yes, Trixie Bentham is a funny old hippie. She couldn't be more opposite to me or my family. But she's also the only therapist I've ever had that has gotten through to me. So I keep coming back, because as detached as I might be, I also know I need this therapy. Which is why she agreed to do video appointments with me while I'm out being a country bumpkin.

"Want me to tell you how I'm doing? About how all I see out here are memories of my dead dad?"

She quirks her head and smiles. "I don't know, dear. Is that what you'd like to tell me about?"

Ah, the rhetorical question game. One of my favorites. I just stare back at her, which never works, but I do it anyway.

Except today she cackles, all raspy and amused, pushes her glasses up the bridge of her nose, and whispers conspiratorially, "Have you run into the girl yet?"

"What girl?" I'm intentionally playing stupid.

She laughs again. "The one you can't stop talking about."

CHAPTER 3
Violet

TWO YEARS EARLIER

Am I really about to do this?

I nibble on my bottom lip and let my index finger hover over the mouse. On one hand, this is a colossally bad idea. This could backfire in so many ways. But who am I in the grand scheme of things? A twenty-five-year-old with little to show for herself—except a distinct lack of life experience and independence.

Growing up on a farm smothered by an overprotective dad and three older brothers will do that to a girl.

But now I'm here. On Canada's West Coast. New job under my belt, new place to live, lots of possibilities on the horizon. Now I need to get to know myself. To rack up some experiences and push my boundaries.

I'm not sure why posting a nude on Clikkit—an online forum with millions of users who dabble in a wide range of interests—is that thing, but it seems risky…a little bit exciting…and a lot out of character. Which is what I'm going for. I'm tired of being sheltered. I want to feel exposed and uncomfortable without someone here to leap in front of me.

I want to do something young and stupid. Plus, I'm horny and lonely.

I click the button with force. The pad of my finger slaps against the mouse loudly. I immediately feel myself blush. It starts at my toes and creeps up my body. It pools between my thighs and crawls up over my chest before staining my face with its heat.

I can't believe I just did that.

The image stares back at me. It's taken from above as I lie on my bed. You can't see my face and I'm wearing my panties, so it's not too outrageous. Okay, you can see my small breasts, but in Europe, people go to the beach like this all the time. It's no big deal—or at least that's what I keep telling myself. The warm morning light is nice on my features, and it's sensual. Usually, I'm hard on my body. Usually, I think everything is a little too small, not what I'd consider "womanly," but in this picture…I feel sexy.

So fuck it! Look at my tits, world. See if I care!

I almost immediately consider deleting it. But the new Violet Eaton will not give in to that voice in her head, and my new internet alter ego, Pretty_in_Purple, doesn't give two shits about that voice either.

I slam my laptop shut, shove my feet into my paddock boots, and jog down the stairs from my apartment above the barn at Gold Rush Ranch before I can change my mind.

ELSIE SILVER

★★★

PRESENT DAY

My mental checklist is overflowing as I pack the last of what I'll need into my little Volkswagen Golf. The one with rust patches above the wheel well and the chewed corner of the seat from when my favorite ranch dog was a puppy. The one I packed up and drove away from my family home when I finally set out on my own a little over two years ago. Some people might see a car that belongs in a junk pile. Me? I see my golden chariot to independence. I love this little car and everything it represents.

I stand back to assess everything I've stuffed into the back seat and blow a loose piece of hair off my face. It's the first big race day of the season, and I'm trying—poorly—to keep my nerves at bay. This season is my shot, my chance to prove myself as a real jockey. To prove that my Northern Crown wins last year weren't just a stroke of freshman luck. This job is supposed to be fun. Hard work, but fun. But today it just feels overwhelmingly heavy. The pressure weighs on me like an invisible lead vest. Even getting air into my lungs feels like it takes concentration.

I force myself to take a mental inventory of what all's here and shake my head when I realize what I've forgotten. "Shit. Right. My silks."

How great would that have been? Showing up to the track in Vancouver—which is at least an hour and a half from the farm here in Ruby Creek—without my Gold Rush Ranch silks. The black and gold uniform I wear every single race.

Shaking my head as I march back into the barn, I head down the long hall of offices toward the laundry room at the end. I live in a small apartment above the barn, so I just do my laundry down here. I grew up on a proper ranch, in the dirt and snow, usually with hay in my hair, so the thought of washing all my clothes in the same machines used for the hairy horse laundry doesn't bother me at all.

I'm almost to the door when I hear it.

"Violet."

That voice. The low rumble of it. The threat woven into it. The man behind it. I swear my feet grow roots that shoot out and bind me to the ground. My heart knocks violently in my chest like it's trying to get out and run away. And quite frankly, I don't blame it. I want to get out of here too.

He wasn't supposed to be here yet. I was supposed to be gone down the highway by the time he showed up. He was supposed to be out of my life. I was supposed to have left him behind. Forgotten him.

But I haven't. I've warred with myself, wrestled and fought. Been with other men to prove to myself that I'm fine. But one word out of his mouth, and I seriously wonder if I am. I could run and hide, but that's not how the new me handles this. *The new Violet isn't a shrinking Violet.* That's what I keep telling myself anyway.

Maybe one day, it will feel true.

So I suck in as much oxygen as I can and hold my head up high. I refuse to let this man make me feel small or embarrassed. We have a shared past, but we're both adults. *This will be fine.*

Spinning on one heel, I turn and march back to the office I just passed, the one that has sat empty for years. I stop just inside the doorway, partly because I don't want to go any farther and partly because I'm reeling. All it takes is one look at Cole Harding, sitting behind a desk in a dark suit, spinning the cuff links on his shirt, for me to lose all the bravado I just puffed myself up with. I literally feel it roll right off me like someone has doused me with a bucket of cold water. My body's reaction to him has never been normal, and today is no exception.

The inky hair, the gray eyes, the square shoulders, the sad tilt to his mouth. He crosses his arms under my gaze, and I roll my lips together at the sight. Just the way he moves, so sure and so calculated, drives me to distraction. There's so much power coiled in every inch of his body. A soldier's body.

His biceps are where my eyes land and where they stay. They're incredible. I wonder how they'd look completely bare, how they'd feel wrapped around me. I hate myself for even going there. But I keep my eyes trained on them, because it's less unnerving than looking him in those soulful eyes. Silvery pools, deep and haunted and swirling with so much. The ones full of anger and pain and sorrow. Those are a much bigger problem for me. And for my heart.

"Violet."

He says my name like it's a sentence, a full thought. Like I should know exactly what he means when he says it. But I don't know *anything* where Cole Harding is concerned. I think I actually know less than anything. Other than the hair on my arms is standing up like there's an electrical current running over me, and my stomach is flipping like I just shot down off the high point of a roller coaster. Which is apt, because my history with Cole is nothing if not a roller coaster.

"Everyone calls me Vi." I hate how quiet my voice comes out. I hate the way my name sounds on his lips, too formal and too familiar all at once.

His eyes rove my body, but he doesn't smile. It's not appreciative. It's more like he's assessing me, like I'm a mess that needs cleaning up and he's trying to figure out how. Shame lurches in my gut. Flashes of the way he talked to me once and how it warmed me to my bones pop up in my head, but I do my best to will it away. I've worked too hard at moving on to go down that rabbit hole again.

"I'm not everyone," he says plainly.

I hiss as I suck air in, trying not to sound like I'm gasping for it. Trying not to give away the fact that he's just winded me with his words. Blood rushes in my ears and pools in my cheeks—like it always does. *You look so fucking pretty in pink.* He told me that once, and now it takes every ounce of my strength not to let my mind and body wander back to that day.

"What do you want, Cole?"

His eyes flash, and his body goes rigid right as his jaw ticks. Like somehow I'm the one who's annoying him when he's the one who called me in here. He could have kept his mouth shut, and I'd have been none the wiser. We could have avoided this entire encounter.

"I just want to make sure that we're on the same page. That we can continue to stay out of each other's way while I work out here. That you can keep things"—his eyes slide down my body and then back up—"professional."

Professional. Nothing between us has ever been professional. He's seen me naked, trampled my heart, and then showed back up out of nowhere with nothing but cool looks and mocking words, and now expects *me* to keep things *professional*?

Indignation flares up in me over the fact that he feels entitled to dictate how I should conduct myself. Like I don't come up against enough of that in this industry as it is. It's a sore spot, and he should know. I spent long nights telling him about my childhood. About how I struck out on my own. And now he's going to waltz in here and talk to me like *that*? No way.

"Let me be clear, Cole." This time, I don't let my voice waver, and I don't stare at his biceps. I stare right into his steely eyes. "This is *my* place of work, and I am nothing if not professional. The way you're talking to *me* right now? It isn't professional. So I'm going to continue doing exactly what I have been for the past year, and *you* can stay out of *my* way. Think you can manage?"

His body snaps back slightly, and his eyes go wide. Like he didn't see that coming. Didn't see *me* coming. And he lashes out at me for it. I see the flash of insecurity on his face right before he spews his words back at me. And it's that hint of sorrow that takes the bite out of them.

"Pretty in Purple was so sweet. What happened?"

I shake my head at him sadly. Because when it comes down to it, that's what I feel when I see him, when I think of him. Sad.

"Seems like you mistook Pretty in Purple for a doormat."

I look at him just long enough to see the forlorn look on his face, the crack in his cold exterior, before I turn and walk away. The spear to my damn heart. Golddigger85 is just as lost as he was before, just as complicated. Just as broken. And I've already decided I won't tolerate the way he lashes out. *We all make choices.* That's what he told me once, and he wasn't wrong.

It's why I moved on. It's why I disappeared without a word. It's why this awkwardness between us now is on him, not me. My head knows exactly what choices to make where Cole Harding is concerned.

But my heart?

It's not so sure.

CHAPTER 4

Violet

"COLE MOVED IN TODAY."

I shove my foot into my boot harder than necessary, grunting as I do, and then busy myself polishing it with the rag from the step stool beside me. Basically, I'm trying to ignore Billie, who is grinning at me like a maniac.

"You're not going to say anything?"

I side-eye her and shrug. Because the answer is no, I'm not going to say anything. Billie Black, my boss and the head trainer at Gold Rush Ranch, has become one of my best friends over the past year. And I've come to know her well. She's like a bloodhound with a scent, she's smart and intuitive, and anything I say she'll stock away in her crazy memory vault until she unpackages it and extrapolates her data. And then she'll figure out how I know Cole.

Which means I won't be able to look her in the eye without turning fire-engine red.

"Nope," I say, popping the *p* sound as I stand up in front of our tack stall and reach for the black and yellow Gold Rush Ranch silks.

"Viiiiii," she moans, "this is *killing* me! It's been a year. I saw your face that day. What did he say to you? Give me something."

I feel the light sprinkling of heat crawling up over my chest. She is relentless. "Okay. We met online a couple of years ago. Chatted a bit."

She rubs her long fingers over her chin as she regards me. "Like some sort of veteran pen pal thing?"

"Something like that." I wave her off. "Now leave me alone. I need to go weigh in and get in the right headspace if you expect me to win."

"Okay, okay. Come find me when you're done, and I promise I won't ask about this again." She waggles her eyebrows as she stands to leave. "Until after the race."

I roll my eyes as I walk down the barn alleyway toward the track offices. Toward the Bell Point Park winner's circle. The very place where Cole Harding waltzed back into my life.

I remember sitting up on DD's back, overwhelmed by our qualifying win, when a man who was clearly Vaughn's brother approached me. I remember thinking he looked like an ominous storm cloud hovering over such a bright and joyful celebration. I remember the way his huge hand engulfed mine, the heat of it, the weight of it, as he crooked a finger for me to come closer. And I remember the warmth in my body evaporating and all the sounds around me fading to white noise when I leaned down to hear him say, "Nice to see you again, Pretty in Purple. I almost didn't recognize you with your clothes on."

Just recounting the memory makes me blush. But I am also still agitated by the way he took one of the happiest moments of my life and tainted it with *that*. The way he threw it in my face when he knew he had the upper hand.

You see, Cole Harding knew exactly what I looked like. What every inch of me looked like. And I still had no idea who he was—a real sore spot for me—until that moment.

Turns out he's my boss's boss, Billie's future brother-in-law, and now he's moving to the one safe space I've created for myself over the last couple of years. A place where I can be a successful and independent version of Violet Eaton with no one coddling me. I'm not the same girl I was two years ago when I responded to that message. And what happened between Cole and me? It's never going to happen again.

I don't think my heart could take it. And definitely not my pride.

Which is why I pasted a wobbly smile on my face and told him to go fuck himself before sitting back up and forcing myself to enjoy the win.

When I accepted his chat request, I didn't expect to spend months getting to know the man. And when I ghosted him in that chat room a year later, I didn't expect to ever come face-to-face with him. Me anonymously pushing my own boundaries and living a little turned out to be a whole lot more. And now my entire house of cards is about to come crashing down around me. Because he's here, at the ranch, threatening that buffer that I've tried so hard to preserve.

I keep my head down as I get prepped for the evening race. I may have a Northern Crown win under my belt, but I still feel like the new girl on the block, inexperienced and out of my depth. I still feel stuck in the mindset of living at home under the watchful eyes and overbearing involvement of my dad and three older brothers. I still feel like a little kid who doesn't belong.

Once I've weighed in, I head back to DD's stall and shove my headphones in my ears. A little Shania Twain never fails to get me in the right headspace. Reminds me of my childhood.

Before I became the in-house rider at Gold Rush Ranch, I was a lowly groom. A girl who moved out to British Columbia from her small-town home in Alberta with not much more to show for herself other than a good work ethic and a lot of desperation to pave her own way.

The thing is I liked being a groom, but I've always wanted to be a jockey, and I lucked into the right body type to pull it off. Sometimes, I miss the quiet moments that came with working behind the scenes. Those times when it was just the horses and me. It's why I still live above the barn in my tiny apartment up that long narrow flight of stairs. I like walking through the stables at dusk, hearing the quiet munching on hay. I like taking care of my own horses. I like the soothing rasp of brush bristles across their coats rather than the loud buzzers and speakers as I blast through mud, trying to make it across the line first.

So I try to create those quiet moments for myself. And this prerace ritual has become part of that. No one bugs me—Billie makes sure of it—and I get a bit of time to go inward and just be with my horse.

Right now, that horse is DD, our little black championship-winning stallion, with long legs and an intelligent disposition. Once I've put the finishing touches on his grooming, I lead him out into the bright sunshine—something we don't see much in Vancouver in April. This area brings a whole new meaning to *April showers bring May flowers*. At this time of year, we pretty much live in a mud puddle, so even though it's sunny, the track is wet.

When DD's hooves clop loudly onto the asphalt road that leads down to the track, Billie pops up, seemingly out of nowhere. She's always ready and waiting for me. We talked strategy earlier in the day, so at this point, we can just walk together in a companionable silence.

She comes to stand beside me, bends down, and cups her hands behind me, ready to give me a leg up. "Up we go, Tiny Soldier."

I feel my cheek twitch; Billie's terms of endearment that reference my size never end. Where she's tall for a woman, I'm petite, and where she's curvaceous, I'm...well, flat as a board.

I drop my knee into her waiting hands, and she hefts me up into the tack, gives my knee a squeeze, and sends me on my way. The rest of my journey into the starting gate is a blur, as usual. The pony horses, the stewards, the other jockeys and horses around me,they all blend together, and I focus on DD and getting us to that finish line safely and quickly. When our pony horse steps up, the rider gives me a friendly nod. The pony rider is completely different from a jockey. They ensure we get to the gate safely, like a security blanket for a nervous horse. An important member of the team.

At the gates, he sends me off with a "Good luck."

DD is a great stallion, reliable and smart, talented beyond compare, but claustrophobic. And when they close the gate behind him, I feel him coil up like a ball of energy, like an elastic pulled back too far, ready to explode out of the small space.

This is where my vision narrows. All I see is what's between his long pointy ears. The rest of the world seems to go soft and blurry as we both settle into our focus.

Until I hear a voice that sends a slithering sensation down my spine, "Hey New girl."

I ignore Patrick Cassel. He's one of the most sought-after jockeys in this area. He rode DD in one race last year, but he defied Billie's instructions on how to ride the race, and well…let's just say that didn't end well for him. Now he's on Gold Rush Ranch's blacklist—we all basically pretend he doesn't exist. And when he sees Billie coming, he promptly turns and walks the other way.

Looks like that level of avoidance doesn't apply to the quiet little blond though.

"Dinner after this, and I might let you win. What do you say, Princess?"

I try not to shudder at the thought. Patrick is slimy and entitled and makes me feel like I have bugs stuck under my clothes. Based on Billie's retelling of their encounter, he's condescending and sexist to boot. I want nothing to do with the man.

"I'm pretty sure princesses only kiss frogs in fairy tales, Patrick," I mutter. "I'll pass."

And before he can say anything, the bell rings, and the gate flies open. DD and I are off, and that interaction with Patrick disappears from my mind as we thunder down the track, staying toward the back of the pack through the first turn. Exactly where the little black horse likes to be.

I stay low and light on his back, mostly letting him do his thing. This horse was bred to run, and he loves it. When we push out of the clubhouse turn, everything is going according to plan. Now is where we move up.

Until I feel a dark bay horse move in beside me. From the corner of my eye, I see Patrick Cassel's lime-green silks. As he pulls ahead, I try to ignore him and reserve my focus for DD.

Until he shouts over the pounding of hooves, "Time to learn a lesson, little girl."

My instincts shift into overdrive as I watch his hands move ever so slightly to change his path. Dread courses through my veins. And before I have a chance to react, he's cut us off sharply, bumping DD's shoulder with his harsh angle, killing our forward motion. And on the slippery footing, the results are disastrous.

With his head and neck already slung low and legs stretched out in a gallop on a slippery track, DD stands no chance.

I feel our motion shift downward, and before I know what's happened, DD and I are both down in the mud.

A PHOTO FINISH

★★★

"I'm going to kill him." Billie paces at the bottom of my hospital bed. "Like, literally murder him."

I'm in too much pain to react much to her meltdown. My leg is swollen like a tree trunk, and they won't give me any painkillers until they have time to look at my X-rays and MRI scans. Like you need a medical degree to confirm that it's fucked up.

"You need to tell Vaughn that I love him and to get the bail money ready. Because I'm going to tear Patrick limb from puny limb."

A ragged sigh escapes my lips as I look around my room. The walls are that signature pale mint color, a color I imagine they produce solely to paint hospital walls, and all I can smell is that harsh, sterile scent that permeates every single hospital I've ever been in. Which is a lot because my brother Rhett is a walking disaster. A rodeo prince with no fear. And even though I'm a year younger than him, I was always the one stuck playing caretaker at the hospital while he was treated for one injury or another. It was the only way my dad could run our farm and keep us afloat enough to take care of the four of us.

So I *hate* hospitals. I don't care about Patrick. But I am worried about DD. He came down on my leg but didn't walk off without a limp either. I scrub my hands over my face and force a deep breath into my lungs.

It could have been so much worse.

"Any word from Mira on DD?" Mira Thorne is our

friend and our newly hired farm veterinarian. She takes care of all the horses in the Gold Rush Ranch program, both at the track and at the farm.

Billie nibbles at her lip nervously now and shoves her hands into her pockets, obviously worried about our boy too. "She said he's fine" is her quiet reply. "She'll call as soon as she knows anything more."

"You should have gone with her."

Billie rolls her eyes. "And what? Left you all by yourself? Mira's got this."

I let my lashes flutter shut and sink back into the lumpy pillow. It's like they want you to be uncomfortable in the hospital. With my eyes closed, all I can see on the back of my eyelids is this entire season swirling down the porcelain bowl with a loud flush. My chance to prove I'm good at this rather than just the girl who got the ride on one of the world's most exceptional racehorses and struck gold.

This fucking *sucks.*

"Okay, Miss Eaton." A middle-aged man with a white coat over his slacks and dress shirt breezes into the room. "I have good news for you today."

I furrow my brow. Nothing about today screams *good news* to me.

"The imaging we had done tells me that nothing is badly broken."

I stare at my black-and-blue leg. It looks pretty broken. "Are you sure?"

He laughs good-naturedly. "Very sure. There's a lot of

bruising. Soft tissue trauma in the knee. And a small fracture in your fibula."

I continue to stare at my leg, still not fully convinced that it's not totally shattered.

The doctor takes my silence as an opportunity to keep talking. Looking down at the clipboard in his hands, he continues, "No surgery required. But you need to take it easy for at least a month. Crutches at the start, at least until the swelling goes down. Try to keep off any stairs. And definitely no riding."

I snort. *Yeah. That's not going to happen.*

"Miss Eaton, I'm serious. I know how athletes can be. But if you fracture the bone further or tear something in your knee, you will require surgery. And the rehabilitation timeline for that is much longer. You're lucky it's not worse. Don't squander that."

Lucky?

Billie steps in now, no doubt reading the look on my face. "No problem, Doc. I'll keep her on the straight and narrow."

The man barely looks at Billie. Instead, he raises his eyebrows and inclines his head toward me, obviously seeking some sort of affirmation. I wave one hand in the air dismissively before crossing my arms. He won't know what I do once I leave this place.

"Got it," I mumble, dropping my eyes and sighing, feeling more than a little chastised.

"Good. Let me grab you some painkillers, and then we'll get you discharged."

I force my cheeks up into some semblance of a smile, too sore and pissed off to do much else. I'm ready for some pain relief and my own bed. He turns on his heel and strides out of the room.

"Don't worry, Vi. We'll find you somewhere comfortable to stay."

"What?" I look at Billie, confused.

"You're not doing those crazy stairs up to your apartment right now. And back down?" She shudders. "I don't even want to hear about it."

"Okay, Mom. Where are you planning on putting me then?"

Billie scrubs her face, clearly stressed, even though she's trying to play it cool and hold it all together for me.

"I'll get Vaughn to stay with his brother at the main house, and you can stay with me at the cottage."

"In the love shack?" I blurt out just as a nurse walks in with a small white cup and hands it to me.

"The love shack?" Billie looks confused as I eye the two pills in the paper cup, toss them back, and then chase them with the water from the table beside me. I almost spit it back up. City water tastes all wrong.

"Yeah. I'm not staying at the love shack and splitting you two up."

"Is that what you call our house?" she barks out, clearly amused.

I can't help but smile now. She and Vaughn are living in some blissed-out bubble. "Billie, that's what everyone at the ranch calls it."

She blows out a tired breath and drags her hand back through her chestnut hair. "I'm not gonna lie. I kind of love that. You're still staying with me though. Vaughn will survive."

"Billie, there's not even a bathroom on the main floor of your place."

"Shit." She looks instantly deflated. "Right. Okay...why don't we move Cole into your apartment and let you take the house. Just for a few—"

Yeah, that can't happen. "No. He's not going in my apartment. That's *my* space."

"Okay then, Violet. What's your solution here? Wanna go back to Alberta for a few weeks? Stay with your dad? Or I don't know..." Agitation seeps into her voice. "You gonna go live at the farmhouse with Cole? Because there's a spare room and bathroom on the main floor."

I can tell that she's joking. But that's looking like the best option at this current juncture.

Yup, today is just full of good news. I'm so *lucky*.

CHAPTER 5

Cole

I GROAN AS I STARE AT THE SCREEN OF MY PHONE. AM I REALLY about to try this again? It's so fucking pathetic. I'm so fucking pathetic. Just because I've decided I can't show myself to anyone doesn't mean I don't still want things.

And the photo is so…ethereal? I don't know. I could get lost in it. I can't look away from it. It's so different from living in my head. Light pink nipples on flawless pale skin. I imagine running the palm of my hand up her body, right up the centerline from belly button over sternum, before coming to rest on her throat and thumbing those pouty, soft lips.

The way they'd part as I rasped my thumb over them, the little sighing noise that would escape past them.

It's been way too long, you old perv. You're getting hard just imagining touching a woman's lips. The ones on her face, no less.

Not to mention a girl who looks like that isn't going to be interested in me and what little I have to offer her.

But what the fuck? Why not? What have I got to lose? I look around my lonely West End apartment. The place is basically a shrine to a grown-ass man who's let every opportunity for the past several years slip through his fingers. A living shell.

I haven't even tried to be better. To get past my hang-ups around my body. To do more. I want all the things. The white picket fence. The 2.5 kids. The wife who kisses me with a little tongue every morning when we part ways. But I haven't done shit to get there. And it's probably too late for me now.

It's just me, myself, and my protein shakes. And my creepy fucking internet persona. Might as well embrace it.

My thumb taps the message icon, and I quickly type before I can change my mind.

Golddigger85: I have a proposition for you.

Then I walk away and get in the shower to wash away how fucking dirty I feel. But I can't stop thinking about that creamy skin sliding against my own. I imagine running my tongue up the inside of each thigh. Really taking my time to taste her, to feel her writhe beneath me. My hand curls around my cock, but I pretend it's her pillowy lips, opening up wide for me. Wrapping around me. Her cheeks hollowing out as her silky blond hair bobs in a steady rhythm while she sucks me off. Then she'd look up at me. Fuck, *I love that. Big wide eyes and my dick in her mouth.*

I wonder what color her eyes are as I spill myself against the cold tiles.

For a moment, I wish I wasn't alone.

Something that I'll never let happen.

★★★

"Hey, big bro." Billie stands under the yellow glow of the porch light above my front door, hands on her hips, and blows a strand of hair off her face. I don't know what she's doing here. But I know I don't like it.

It's 11:00 p.m. on a Saturday night. Is this what people do in small towns? Invade each other's privacy? I'm about to ask her as much when I see another set of headlights turn down the driveway. Vaughn parks beside her truck, and I notice now that she's left the back door open. A shadow shifts inside, and I lean forward a bit to peer past her.

"Is someone lying in your back seat?" I ask.

She glances over her shoulder. "Oh. Yeah."

My eyes shift back to hers. "I don't like you enough to help you bury a body."

Billie grins, her teeth coming off a little vicious in the dark of night. "Fair. I won't come knocking once I kill Patrick Cassel."

"Patrick?" I ask, confused, as Vaughn bounds up the stairs. I already hate Patrick's smug ass. If I had to help her with a body, it would be his. Maniacal laughter streams out of the truck, pulling me away from that thought. "You guys, what the fuck is going on?"

"She might actually kill him, you know?" a hysterical voice cackles out of the dark back seat.

"Is she okay?" Vaughn asks, slightly breathless as he comes to stand beside Billie.

"Yeah, yeah. She's just really high," Billie replies casually.

My teeth grind. This is so like them. Talking a lot but saying nothing at all.

"You. Guys," I bite out. "What. The. Fuck. Is. Going. On?"

"Patrick Cassel took Violet and DD down tonight, and her leg is all mangled."

Adrenaline courses through me as Billie's words process in my head. If I didn't already hate Patrick Cassel, I would now. I see dirt. I hear hooves. I taste bile. I rub at my leg anxiously.

"What do you mean, *took her down*?" My molars grind against each other as I'm transported back in time. To another day entirely. To a seventeen-year-old boy watching his dad ride a race he'd never finish.

"Cut her off and bumped DD's shoulder. It was muddy." Billie sniffs. Her voice sounds brittle, and I don't miss the hand that my brother snakes around her waist.

I feel like I could suffocate on my tongue as I forge ahead. "And can you elaborate on what a 'mangled' leg means to you?"

Vaughn's eyes dart up to me, going slightly wide. Usually, that means my tone is too brusque. Trixie is always asking me how I think other people perceive me. I keep telling her I don't care. She just ignores that and tells me to look at body language for clues. I think this wide-eyed look might be one thing I'm meant to watch for. Vaughn doesn't like the way I'm talking to his fiancée.

"Hairline fracture on her fibula and a strain in her knee. It's mild, but she's kinda beat-up. Recovery won't be that long. A month if she's lucky."

I force a deep breath down into my lungs, willing them

to fill and empty evenly so that I don't start gasping with the ache of my memories. This could have been *so* much worse. I've seen worse. I was seventeen when I waved goodbye to my dad, my idol, as I clung to the railing at Bell Point Park. I watched him load up into the gates. I cheered and whistled and yelled until I was sure my voice would be hoarse the next day. I watched him closing in on the lead horse. I saw the grin on his face. And then I watched him go down. A simple trip and the crush of his mount's body over his. I watched the horse get up and gallop away, its eyes wide with terror.

I watched my dad's still form on the dirt track. I willed him to get up. But he never did.

This could have been so much worse.

"Is she okay?" I keep my voice cool, but even I can hear it brimming with rage, pain that's had years to fester.

"Yeah," Billie replies. "But she's not supposed to do stairs. Which means she can't get up to her apartment above the barn. We were going to let her stay at our cottage, but the bathroom is on the second level, and the whole place is pretty small for three people..." She trails off, shooting big wide eyes up at me like a little kid who's about to ask for something they're not supposed to have.

I guess this is body language that I can read as well. This look has *pleading* written all over it—seen it before. I'm just not sure why she's giving it to *me*, other than to irritate me and make me want to put Patrick in a choke hold more than I already did for the stunt he pulled last year.

So I fall back on my default expression. I stare blankly

at my brother and his fiancée, not sure what it is they're expecting me to do or say here.

Vaughn groans and drags a hand through his hair. I don't miss him mutter something about me always making things difficult. *The feeling is mutual, little brother.* "Can Violet stay at the farmhouse with you? There's a spare bedroom and bathroom on the main floor. It'll just be a few weeks."

They can't be fucking serious.

I keep my fists shoved under my biceps, hoping that if I look angry enough, they'll both back off and come up with a different solution. My chest rises and falls heavily as my agitation grows, snaking out into every joint and muscle. They both just keep looking back at me expectantly. Like puppies.

And no one likes a guy who kicks puppies.

Violet bursts out laughing in the truck. She's laughing so hard she can barely breathe, let alone get her words out. I can hear her gasping for air between guffaws. I often wondered what her laughter would sound like. A year of talking and then another of forcing myself to recall her dainty little face… I didn't imagine the hyena howl she's currently emitting.

"I told you guys he would never go for this," she blurts out. "Look at his face!" She dissolves into another fit of giggles. "I *know* him. This will never fly!"

Okay. I need to put a stop to this. Now. The last thing I need is Mr. and Mrs. Bigmouth knowing my personal business. And the path of least resistance to ending this interaction is… *Fuck my life.*

My legs move before I process what I'm doing. I shove

myself between Billie and Vaughn and approach the truck. Violet is laid out across the back seat, feet toward me and back propped against the opposite door. Her leg is wrapped in a plastic walking cast and is supported by rolled-up horse blankets. Her pupils are dilated, and fat tears of laughter stream down her muddy cheeks.

"Hey! It's Butterface!"

I growl as I reach into the truck. "Violet. Shut up."

She throws her head back and bursts out laughing again. Like spilling our personal history is the most hysterical thing in the world. *Comedy gold, everyone.* My jaw pops under the pressure of my bite. All I can think about is getting her away from prying eyes and ears, so I lean in and reach for her waist. I don't miss the way my hands wrap almost the entire way around her as I pull her across the leather seats toward me.

When I slide my arm under her knees, she winces.

"Are you okay?" I rasp so only she can hear me. I should have been more careful with her.

"A bit sore." Her glassy eyes gaze up into mine unsteadily, wide and lost and so fucking pretty. My lungs constrict at the sight of her, the girl I haven't been able to shake.

Never mind Billie. *I'm* going to kill Patrick Cassel.

I move slowly now, less agitated and more concerned, and wrap my other arm around Violet's narrow back. She feels small and vulnerable against me, and for all the times I let myself imagine meeting her, it was never like this.

Her head lolls drunkenly into my armpit as she announces, "Isn't he so strong!" One tiny fist knocks against my bicep. "Look at these arms!"

I blink once, slowly, working hard at keeping my cool as I carry her limp body up to the front porch. No one this small should feel this heavy. I fight the dread crawling up my spine, the memories of carrying my friends' limp bodies under the cover of darkness. The weight. The dry heat.

I take a deep inhale of the thick, humid air to remind myself where I am. "What the hell did they give her?"

Billie pulls a small orange container out of her back pocket and offers it up. "I don't know, but they probably should have given her a child's dose instead."

I just grunt. I'll look at it later. "I've got this," I bark as I push past them and into the old farmhouse with Violet held firmly against my chest.

"He's so romantic!" Violet giggles, and I roll my eyes. In the past, Violet was one of the few people I actually enjoyed talking to. But that girl is definitely not here right now. This girl is high as a fucking kite.

"Violet, are you okay with this?" Billie looks concerned, but I kick the door shut behind me, right in her face, done talking about this.

"Isn't he rude?" Violet shouts back through the closed door. "All those times you complained about what a dick he is—"

Now it's Billie's turn to shut her up. "I'll bring you your stuff in the morning, Vi!" Billie calls back. "If you need me, just call!"

My cheek twitches. Take that, *sis*.

"Don't worry about me, B! I told you. I know him!"

A deep sense of dread fills me. All I can see is my privacy

slipping away. A part of my life that was always meant to be kept separate is now going to be sleeping in the bedroom below me and probably blabbed about with my brother's fiancée. Which will inevitably get back to my brother. Never mind the fact that I've been pining for her—a girl I've basically never met—for the last couple years.

Nothing good can come from this kind of forced proximity.

I groan as I carry Violet to the spare bedroom, feeling my meticulously organized life slipping through my fingers like fucking sand, and I haven't even been in Ruby Creek for twenty-four hours. This place is cursed. It took my dad down, and now it's going to take me down too.

The room is dark, but the spare bed is already made. Like it's been ready for her this whole time. Like this is some sort of huge cosmic joke.

Leaning down, I gently place Violet on the bed, not wanting to hurt her. She's even more beautiful than I remember, soft and feminine and soothing without even trying. Getting to know Violet was like discovering a medicine I didn't even know I needed.

"Why are you staring at me?" she asks quietly from where she's sprawled, her voice not so giddy anymore.

"I'm not," I grumble, jumping back into action, not wanting to talk. I pull a pillow from the headboard and prop it under her braced knee, how I know it feels best. When I lean over her to pull the covers down, I sneak a look up at her face, something I've avoided doing since that first day I saw her at the track, but I can't seem to stop staring now.

It's like the mere sight of her has short-circuited my brain, opened the floodgates to me gawking at her like some sort of slack-jawed Neanderthal.

I expect those almost too-big blue eyes to be staring back at me, but her long lashes are casting shadows over her high cheekbones, and her heart-shaped mouth has fallen just slightly ajar, shallow quiet breaths whispering past her lips.

Knocked right out.

Which means I can really look. I stare at her openly—every line, every angle, every heavy rise and fall of her chest—my eyes adjusting rapidly to the low light filtering in from the living room, knowing she won't catch me now.

Is her breathing too light? Too slow?

I lean in closer to listen, a little concerned with how hard these painkillers are hitting her. Another thing to worry about. *Just what I need.*

Shaking my head, I leave the room. How did I get roped into this? I should pay someone to run the new company and head back into the city. Fuck the board. I'm a thirty-six-year-old man who can barely take care of himself. I need a woman to take care of like I need a fucking hole in the head.

Back in the kitchen, my hand shoves at the tap, making water shoot out as I reach up to grab a glass from the cupboard above the sink. The water out here stinks. Vaughn swears it's safe. Something about no added chemicals like in the city, but one of the first things I'm buying tomorrow—provided this water doesn't kill me first—is a flat of bottled water.

Turning to walk back to the room, I see my phone light

up on the counter. Missed calls from Vaughn and Billie litter the screen. Must have missed those while I was working out. Before this all went to shit. I stare at my phone so much all day for work that I like to turn it to silent in the evenings. Then no one bugs me.

Except now.

Apparently in Ruby Creek, if someone doesn't answer their phone, it means you show up at their door.

I swipe my phone off the counter and flick through my notifications. Most recently, there's a text message from Vaughn.

Vaughn: Billie is really worried about Violet. We can work something else out going forward. Just bear with me for tonight. And take good care of her.

I roll my eyes. You'd swear Violet was a child on her deathbed or something. Is this level of micromanaging normal for adults?

Cole: Tell Billie that Violet is a perfectly capable adult. I'm sure she'll figure something out for herself when she's awake and not high as a kite.

I'm not even going to dignify his implication about me taking care of her with a response. Does he think I'm not capable? I don't know when Vaughn became so totally pussy-whipped, but it's definitely new.

I toss my phone back down onto the counter, trying

some of that deep-breathing shit Trixie is always going on about, and head back to the spare bedroom with the glass of water I poured for Violet.

I set it on the bedside table, letting my eyes trace over her sleeping form again. Soaking her in, warring internally over how I should feel about this. About *her*.

There's a part of me that wants to crawl in beside her, to hold her and watch her all night. To run my fingers through her hair. Make sure she's okay, ease the tension in my gut, and assure myself that she's really all right. But the other part of me knows she wouldn't want that. That it would be way over the line, especially considering how we ended things.

So I walk out of the room, leaving the door slightly ajar, and sink to the floor against the opposite wall. "Only for a little while," I mutter to myself, shaking my head as I settle in to keep watch.

Deep down, I know that's not true. I know I won't be able to walk upstairs and leave her tonight. But I've been lying to myself and everyone else for years.

Why stop now?

CHAPTER 6

Violet

Holy shit. This is a lot of messages. I scroll through them, blushing as I go, feeling glad I already promised myself I wouldn't respond to anyone. I'm only here to look.

Hey, baby… Hey, honey… I'd like to suck on… Don't be nervous…

Jesus. Who knew there were so many pervs in the world? I can't even read them all. It's too much.

I spent all day busting my butt at the ranch, trying to forget the fact that I put a naked picture of myself, titled "(25F) New and nervous," *on the internet. Since I've finished, I've come up to my little apartment, made myself some macaroni, and pretended my laptop doesn't exist. I even watched an episode of* Gilmore Girls *that I could barely focus on before I finally caved and opened the browser.*

This forum has tens of thousands of subscribers. How forty-seven of them found me and sent a message is beyond my comprehension. I wring my hands as I imagine what these men have been doing while they look at my picture. This was a bad idea. Very poorly thought-out.

A notification for my forty-eighth message pings in the top right corner of my screen. And out of morbid curiosity, I click it.

Golddigger85: I have a proposition for you.

I nibble at my lip. This message isn't like the other ones. What's just one message? It wouldn't be so bad, would it?

Plus, I'm too snoopy to walk away from an open-ended statement like that. What would the proposition be? I flex and release my fingers over the keyboard, itching to type back. If the person says something terrible, it's not like I'm obligated to respond.

Ah, fuck it. I'm going for it.

Pretty_in_Purple: Oh yeah?

I see the dots pulsing on the screen, showing that they're typing. My knee jiggles rapidly, tapping the wooden bottom of my too-small table. Is this person writing me a novel?

Golddigger85: I'm looking for someone I can pay to send me exclusive photos (like the one you posted) or do live videos with. I'll send you $2,000 US every two weeks, and we'll talk 2–3 times a week for 20–30 minutes. I'll give you directions, and you follow them, within reason of course. But I stay completely anonymous. Take your time to think about it. No pressure. Your photo is lovely.

I rear back. Daaammnnn. What the hell? *What a bizarre and clinical proposition. As good as an extra four thousand dollars a month sounds, there's no way I would do this. It's not that I consider myself above it; it's more that the whole thing completely defeats my goal of not living under another person's thumb. I don't want to follow another person's directions. Even as I try to do the conversion to Canadian dollars in my head.*

Pretty_in_Purple: Why?

My cheeks heat. I should just say no. But now I'm intrigued. I have questions.

Golddigger85: Why what?

Pretty_in_Purple: I don't know. Why me? Why do this? What's the point?

Golddigger85: Do you always ask so many questions?

Okay. Sore spot. Maybe I wouldn't like being interrogated about my sexual preferences either.

Pretty_in_Purple: Probably. I'm not going to do it. I'm just curious.

Golddigger85: Why did you post your photo if it makes you nervous?

I think about walking away right now. I don't owe this guy an explanation. But being forward and direct with someone I don't know from Adam just feels easier.

Pretty_in_Purple: Because I wanted to feel nervous. It's totally out of character for me, and quite frankly, I've been living in a bubble. This seemed like a good way to pop it.

Golddigger85: In that case, I do things this way because I'm quite fond of my bubble. Of my private identity. I work a lot. I don't have time to date. I like things done a certain way, and this ensures that. It's worked well for me in the past. I chose you because I liked the picture. You look natural. Real. That's what I like.

I feel my cheeks pink a bit at the compliment. The man may be a total stranger, but his words still land in a way that makes me feel soft and gooey. It's been too long since you last had sex, Vi.

Pretty_in_Purple: Well, thank you for considering me?

Golddigger85: Are you going to think about it?

Pretty_in_Purple: Probably not.

He doesn't respond after that.

I want to open my eyes, but they feel so heavy that it's

borderline not worth it. I try to pry them open; I really do. But they're just so. Damn. Heavy. I give up, sigh, and roll over.

Pain lances through my body. From my toes all the way to the tops of my ears. I'm like one big ball of pain. My eyes shoot open easily now as I gasp, "Ah! Shit!" and opt to stay exactly where I am, flat on my back.

I squeeze my eyes shut and focus on breathing through my nose. If I don't move at all, nothing hurts. The perfect solution. Except with my eyes closed, images flash through my mind. Patrick Cassel. The mud. DD. *Oh god, DD.*

The stream of consciousness won't stop. We went down. My leg. The hospital. The drive back to the… My eyes snap open, and I look around the unfamiliar room. "Mothereffer."

Cole Harding.

I groan and pull the covers up over my face as I sift through my hazy memories, dying a little inside when I get to the one where I openly commented on his biceps. How am I going to face him after *that*? We were doing so well at pretending the other doesn't exist. It was the perfect solution. That strategy has been an absolute success for a year now. I hoped we could just continue it, even though he was going to be living out here. That was my plan. I like having a plan.

But now it's trash. Because I'm sleeping in his house, and my season is down the toilet.

I'm pretty much living my nightmare.

I shake my head at my misfortune and click my tongue against the top of my mouth, trying to get some saliva happening in place of the dry, cottony feeling. I need a drink, and I need to brush my teeth. Looking over at my bedside table, I see a full glass of water. I want it so badly that I decide it's worth moving. Even though I feel like one huge bruise, I shift myself over and up to lean against the headboard. It almost takes my breath away, the weight of the pain pressing in on me. It's everywhere, and it throbs.

But when I put that glass against my lips and taste that first drop of water, I know it was worth it. No pain, no gain. But seriously, where are my painkillers?

I want to stay in hiding. I don't want to face Cole with his stupid, handsome scowl and big biceps that do funny things to my stomach. It's not fair. I'm all broken, and now I'm supposed to face off with the man I've been avoiding for a year.

The universe is cruel, but this full body ache I have going on is worse.

The allure of painkillers is stronger than my desire to hide out in the bedroom all day to avoid Cole, so I slowly flip my legs over the side of the bed, gasping a little as I go, and then hobble out into the main living space on my walking cast, wincing with every step.

I limp to the kitchen island, hoping to see a bottle of painkillers somewhere. It doesn't even look like anyone lives here. Everything is sterile, every countertop perfectly clear, not even a wallet and keys tossed down or a water glass left behind. Maybe he left? My heart soars at the prospect. That would be ideal. Then I'd be able to have a full-blown meltdown about not being able to ride for a month by mys—

"Why are you up and walking around?"

Cole's cool voice is like a spray of frigid water against my back. Shocking and unpleasant. It leaves me breathless. So I freeze, not wanting to turn around and look at him. Because I know what I'll see. And I hate that I'll like it. *Just focus on his lack of personality and you'll be fine. Don't be a baby.*

I turn rigidly, slowly, while keeping one hand on the counter. I basically prop myself up. I need something to hold on to if I'm going to look him in the eyes again. Intelligent eyes, like granite almost, a mosaic of grays and silvers, rove over my body as though he's measuring me to see what size box he'll need to pack me in to ship me off.

"I…I need some painkillers."

Cole snorts and crosses his arms. He's standing in the front entryway of the house, door flung open and sun shining in from behind him. The way its rays wrap themselves around his brutish form makes him look like a glowing silhouette. He reminds me of a solar eclipse, and I know you're not supposed to look at those. It's *dangerous*.

I turn my head away, blinking and trying to find some equilibrium. Trying to focus on the throbbing in my leg that, in his presence, has dulled to a low thrum because my body is focusing on all the other feelings he brings up. Embarrassment, sadness, longing. I hate that he can still do this to me, so I concentrate on the pain, trying to pull it back up and wrap it around myself like a shield. I want to feel better, but I don't want it to be because I'm looking at Cole Harding.

This is living proof that the man is a drug I can't resist. But I dropped the addiction once before, and I'm stronger now. I'm on a different path, one he can't join me on.

There would be far too many complications. Even more than before.

I pinch my shoulder blades together and jut my chin out. "Where are they, Cole?"

"In the cupboard above the fridge."

I turn to hobble away from him, wishing I were wearing something other than a pair of too-big sweatpants that say *Vancouver* across the ass and an oversize T-shirt with an orca whale across the chest. I traveled by ambulance to the hospital, and needless to say, my clothes were mud-soaked. And this sweet little getup is what Billie bought for me at the gift shop. *At least it's clean.*

I stare at the fridge, and then I look up at the cupboard above it. Did he intentionally put the drugs somewhere I wouldn't be able to reach?

"I can't reach that," I grit out through clamped teeth, intentionally not looking at him. My composure is fraying rapidly, and agitation mixes with dread. *A whole month of this. Maybe more!* Now that they've given me the chance, all I want to do is compete. Win. Prove myself. Not take a month off to live in the same house as Cole Harding.

"I know," he says simply without a trace of humor in his tone. *Jerk.*

My head snaps toward him, and I feel my eyes widen in their sockets, my lips rolling against each other almost painfully. I *hate* feeling coddled like this. "Take them down. Now."

He's leaning casually against the doorframe, still staring at me coolly, but now his eyes are focused on my lips. Not exactly jumping into action to help me, which is even more infuriating. Being made to feel helpless is the worst feeling in the world, and men have a bad habit of doing it to me. I don't know if it's because I'm small or quiet, but it fires me up. My dad and brothers did it to me without even realizing that putting baby sister up on a pedestal was some real patriarchal bullshit. Even if they meant well, it wasn't doing me any favors, and it's ultimately why I struck out on my own. But Cole…he's just doing it to be a dick. To make a power play. And I loathe it with every fiber of my being. I won't stand for it.

"I don't know how Vaughn turned out to be such a gentleman when you turned out to be *this*." I wave my hand over his body dismissively, watching his eyes flare and his jaw tick as he clamps his teeth down. "I'll get them myself." I take one limping step toward the big farm table, planning to drag a chair back to the cupboard and stand on it to reach the medicine.

But before I can even get there, he says, "Violet. Stop."

When I look up, he's taking sure strides across the airy farmhouse and rounding the opposite side of the island before he comes to stand beside me. At what must be six one or six two, he can, of course, easily reach the cupboard.

He pulls the small orange pill bottle out from where it sits, surrounded by what looks like a bunch of bottles of vitamins and supplements. I crane my neck to see what they might be, trying to read the labels, before I blurt out, "Grab yourself some happy pills while you're up there."

He turns to me slowly—almost too slowly—before

placing the painkillers on the butcher block island. I expect him to slam them down, but his movements are soft and quiet—a little unnerving if I'm being honest.

Just because I spent a year writing back and forth with the guy doesn't mean I know his mannerisms. In fact, I know little about him. He was never forthcoming, and I've realized, in the aftermath of permanently logging out of my account, that he mostly just played along with a lonely young girl who needed someone to talk to. And to get off. *Once.*

"If I'm going to live out here, I might need to invest in some."

Was that…a joke? I honestly can't tell. I peer up into his face, scouring his features for some trace of humor and finding none. What I find is a fine white scar that cuts through his thick right eyebrow and points up to his hairline. Something I've never noticed before because I've never really had the chance to admire him up close. And I am admiring him, because he's flipping hot. The kind of man who has been—as they say—designed by women. Rugged and harsh, masculine to his core. He looks like he could manhandle the hell out of a girl. A thought that makes my pulse race.

"I'm sorry. I know this… We…" I fumble around with my words, feeling a blush stain my cheeks. I look away, out the front window toward the green hills, and take a deep breath. This can't be my reality for the next month; it just *can't.* "I can understand why you wouldn't want to live with me. I'll find somewhere else to stay for the next little bit."

He turns away to grab a glass. "Go sit down."

I want to tell him to take a hike, but sitting sounds really appealing, and I decide this isn't my hill to die on. Not today anyway. Not when all I want is some water and some pain relief.

I move gingerly around the island, knowing I'm supposed to use crutches but not knowing how I'll do that when my ribs and shoulders hurt the way they do. Once I've heaved myself onto the simple wooden stool at the counter, I watch him turn the tap on and fill the glass.

I try not to look at his ass, but I fail. It's not sweatpants weather, but he's wearing them anyway, and wearing them well. Tapered at the ankle and snug around the waist. When he faces me again, I roll my lips together and pull my hair over one shoulder so that I can run my fingers through it.

I swear he lifts the glass and sniffs it before saying, "Here," and sliding it across the island toward me. His hand engulfs the glass. It looks like a child's cup in his grip.

I take the water once he's completely let go, not wanting to risk a brush of his fingers against mine, and then reach for the bottle of pills. I read the directions on the bottle. It says two pills every six hours. "I think I'll go with one," I mostly mumble to myself.

"Probably a good idea."

My eyes flash up to his. *Dick.* Now I want to take two just so he doesn't get the satisfaction of seeing me do what he says.

I twist the top off roughly and toss the lid down on the counter. "Didn't really ask your opinion, did I?" I shake one out onto my palm and toss it back into my mouth.

"Nope. I'm just here to provide the biceps," Cole

deadpans, and I freeze. The bitter taste of the chalky pill dissolving on my tongue fills my mouth as I glare back at him.

Embarrassment flares up in my chest, and I force myself to choke back some water before whispering a quiet "I'm sorry" as my eyes dart around everywhere but in his direction.

"For what?" He leans back against the edge of the opposite counter and stares me down like he's trying to incinerate me on the spot. His gaze is...unnerving.

But I don't want to let him know I think as much, so I sit up tall and flatten my hands out on the wood counter. "For last night. I wasn't myself. I just...don't like being told what to do."

A smirk graces his full mouth now, and his look flicks from cool disinterest to something else as his eyes roam over my body, leaving a trail of heat in their wake. "That's not how I remember it."

My fingers pulse around the glass of cold water. *Do not throw this at him. You're an adult. Walk away.*

"Like I said." I glare at him now, pushing to stand and trying not to wince, keeping my voice as even as possible. "I'll be out of your hair before you know it."

And then I turn and hobble back to the safety of the spare room. I want to mope in private.

CHAPTER 7

Cole

I HEAR MY PHONE BUZZ BUT PUSH THROUGH MY FINAL SET OF DEAD lifts before picking it up.

Pretty_in_Purple sent you a message.

Maybe the girl changed her mind? Probably not, and I don't blame her. I feel greasy, like I need a shower after every time I send a message like that. I know I sound like a sleazebag, and I hate that. I also know there are creeps on the internet, and I like to think that I'm not one of them. But this arrangement works for me. It ensures me the privacy I want and provides me the companionship I crave.

Sort of.

I swipe the notification open.

Pretty_in_Purple: How many girls have you done this with?

Good god, does this girl have a lot of questions.

Golddigger85: A few.

Pretty_in_Purple: So...three?

Golddigger85: Something like that.

Three dots roll across the screen as she types, and then her message pops up.

Pretty_in_Purple: Guess they didn't stick around for the conversation.

I can't help but chuckle. She's not wrong. I've never been accused of being a great conversationalist.

Golddigger85: No, they stuck around because I talked them into the best orgasms of their life while I watched.

The dots roll and stop. Roll, stop. I wait a few beats before they roll again.

Pretty_in_Purple: Oh.

Golddigger85: Yeah. Oh. Still not interested?

Pretty_in_Purple: In internet orgasms? No, I'm good. I manage those just fine on my own.

I groan. The thought of the pale silky skin in that photo, what's hidden beneath the pretty pink panties, wedged just slightly between the lips of her pussy. The thought of her fingers slipping beneath the triangle of lace.

I adjust myself in my sweats. It's like this girl is totally clueless about how sexy she is—something I like even more.

Pretty_in_Purple is a tease, and she doesn't even know it.

I shove my AirPods into my ears angrily. I've already worked out today, but I'm going for another one. I dig my thumb into my quad muscle and drag it down, trying to relieve the building soreness. Exercise is the only coping mechanism I have for whatever this feeling is. Trixie would tell me to give it a word, but talking about your feelings isn't really part of what the military drummed into me as a special operator.

So with no gym in sight, I run. I do push-ups. I do sit-ups. If I can find some bricks or something, I could probably wrangle myself some weights. The gravel crunches under my feet as I hit the back roads; the air smells fresh and unfamiliar, like the silty rocks down at the cool river that runs through the property. Like the snow that hasn't quite melted off the top of the Cascades, even though it's already April.

I tell myself I miss the smell of exhaust and the sound of car horns blaring that I usually face when I'm downtown. But I think I might be lying. It's hard to tell anymore. What I know is that movement is a gift, freedom that we can never take for granted. Your body, no matter the shape or size, is a workhorse that does incredible things for you. Simple things that you don't even realize until you can't do them anymore.

Which means I also know that Violet is feeling trapped

by her injury. Maybe she doesn't even realize it yet. But I do. And rather than being wise and understanding about it, I was…me.

After she stormed off, I went and got a step stool out of the storage shed so that she could reach that cupboard, even though I'm pretty sure the damage is already done. She thought I'd do that to her intentionally, so I'm going to go out on a limb and guess that I'm not in Violet Eaton's good books.

I pump my arms and run faster, eating up the ground beneath me, breaking into a sweat. Even I want to run away from my personality.

How can I make this up to Violet? I know I don't owe her anything, but the truth of the matter is she's the closest thing I've had to a friend since…I can't even remember. Hilary and I were certainly never friends. We were rich-kid fuck buddies. And then I was a soldier getting ready to deploy. And then we were engaged.

And when I came back for good? We were poison.

I stewed in that poison for *years*. I scoff at myself as I round the corner onto another completely unidentifiable road. *Nice try, old man. You're still stewing. You're saturated.*

Violet doesn't deserve to be tainted by my bullshit. She didn't ask for any of this, and it wouldn't kill me to make her life a little easier after hurting her feelings. Because I *know* I hurt her—not intentionally—but I couldn't give her more. I couldn't give her what she wanted. I wasn't brave enough to take my clothes off in person, let alone on a video chat. That night she told me to take over, to tell her what to do, it was *hot*. So fucking hot. Hotter than any other time I'd done it, probably because we'd gotten to know each other. Her trust meant something to me in that moment. I was feeling things for Violet that I couldn't put my finger on.

But that was all it was: a moment. For me anyway. So the least I can do now is not be a dick to her. I haven't even been trying to. It just always comes out that way, whether or not I want it to. And usually, I don't care how I'm perceived. It's beneath me. I can try to be helpful though. It won't kill me, and Trixie would definitely approve.

My breaths come out in huffs, and I hate to admit it, but my body is tired from my first workout. The midmorning sun is hotter than I expected this far inland, so I stop, linking my hands behind my head to stretch out my chest as I turn around slowly, taking in the heavily treed ditches. All the leaves are a vibrant, almost neon green at this time of year. All fresh and new before they grow bigger and take on a darker shade.

With a deep sigh, I force my body into action. Mind over matter. And feeling tired doesn't matter. So I carry on, forcing myself to run back even though I'd rather walk.

As I hit my stride, Violet's face flashes into my mind. The one she made when she realized she couldn't reach that cupboard. The pink stain on her cheeks. The way her round blue eyes sparked like a live wire. The stupid sweatpants she was wearing all rolled over to fit her tiny waist. The evil part of me wants to laugh because she looked like a scrubby little Tinker Bell stomping her foot, but the good part of me absolutely cringes. I didn't mean to do that. I didn't even think of it. I just put the pills where they belong, with the rest of my vitamins and supplements. I didn't need the counters cluttered with random shit.

I run harder until I feel my lungs and quads burn. Until my mind goes blank.

I don't need my *life* cluttered with any of this shit.

★★★

The minute I walk in the door, I see Violet scowling at me from the stool where she sat earlier. Her mouth is moving, but my music is so loud in my earbuds that I can't hear her. It's kind of glorious if I'm being honest. I'll have to remember this trick for later.

I remove them, holding one hand up to stop whatever tirade she's going on about right now. A bead of sweat trickles down between my shoulder blades as I calmly ask, "What is it you're going off about?"

Her bottom lip pouts out, and her shoulders drop on a sigh. Agitation flows off her in waves. "There's no coffee in this place."

"I know," I say, removing my shoes and placing them on the shelf before wandering into the house for a glass of water. "Coffee is a crutch. It tricks your body into thinking you have energy."

Her knuckles go white from gripping the counter so hard. "I want to be tricked. No. I *need* to be tricked." She slides off the stool gingerly. "I'm going up to the barn to get coffee. I need to figure out where I'm going to stay," she rants on, "because out of everything wrong with staying with you, the fact that you don't have any coffee is the most offensive."

Hands on my hips, I groan and tip my head up to the ceiling. "Violet."

"A crutch. Is that some sort of pun about my mangled leg?" she continues, hobbling away.

"Violet."

With her back to me, she tries to slide her foot into the flip-flop she got dropped off here in and mumbles something that sounds an awful lot like, "So fucking high and mighty."

So I opt for something that might actually get her attention. "Nice sweatpants."

She spins on me so fast you'd never know how injured she is. "Are you kidding?"

I cut her off. "Violet. I'll take you to get a coffee. I need to get some groceries anyway."

Now she just blinks at me, her expression straddling the line of rage and disbelief. When her dainty chin drops in a terse nod, I move near her, grab my keys off the hook, and usher her out the front door.

"Do you want your crutches?"

She takes the front stairs awkwardly, with one leg set straight in the cast, and leans against the railing to accommodate the motion.

"No." She almost growls at me. "You going to lecture me about that too?"

"Nope." I jog down the stairs and head to my black truck, leaving her behind. "You're an adult, and you know your body best."

I swing the passenger-side door open and wait there.

Violet regards me suspiciously as she walks forward, clearly still sore. "What are you doing?" Her tone is accusatory.

"Holding the door open for you." I honestly almost roll my eyes. *So many questions.*

She sort of grunts as she approaches the truck, assessing how she'll tackle getting in, and if she doesn't ask for help, I'm not going to give it to her. She's made that much abundantly clear. If I learned anything about Violet from the year we spent corresponding, it's that she's stubborn. I gave her almost nothing, and she kept badgering me, coming back for more, until it forced me to relent a little bit. She wasn't put off by my persona back then.

And don't I know it. She scrambles into the truck. It's not graceful, and I end up getting an eyeful of her round ass with *Vancouver* printed across it as she pulls herself up into the cab. My fingers pulse at my side, itching to reach forward and give her a boost. Watching her struggle makes tightness twinge in my chest.

When she's finally seated, I slam the door and round the truck, getting into the driver's side and firing the engine up so that we can get this over and done with. As I peel out of the driveway, I don't miss the way she reaches up for the oh-shit handle, like she doesn't even trust me to drive her down a gravel road.

It grates on me that she thinks so little of me now. I'm fairly sure that at one point, we were on good terms.

When we hit the main road, I chance another look at her,

but she's turned her head away as she looks out the window, gazing at the green fields whipping past as I speed down the road. Her hair has a silvery quality to it, like a cool sunlit stream trailing down her back. Complete with mud from her fall, but I don't think it would be a wise thing to bring up when we're already on such tenuous footing.

Plus, I kind of like it. Violet just walked right out the door in hospital sweats, no makeup, and with mud in her hair because she wanted coffee. She didn't spend hours primping to go out in public, and she still looks beautiful. She's feminine, graceful, elven almost.

I remember noting that about her hair when she sent a shot of her head with bird shit on it. "Got a big old dose of good luck today!" she said.

The memory makes my cheek twitch. At the time, it made me laugh, and then it made my chest ache. I still can't remember the last time I smiled like that. She had literal shit in her hair, and all she could do was laugh and comment on the good luck it might bring.

That is a glass-half-full kind of attitude I can only aspire to. But I didn't need to knock her glass over in the process. That was just a dick move. I don't want to be a dick. I want to be *better*.

"You don't need to move out." I break the silence abruptly and stare out the windshield, hard, like there's something interesting out here in the middle of a field. Spoiler alert: there's not.

I feel her eyes on me even though I'm doing my damnedest not to look her way. Her gaze pierces me like a tattoo gun. A sharp needling sensation, followed by warmth that flows deep.

"You don't want me there though."

I sigh audibly and pulse my fingers around the leather steering wheel. What I don't want is all the feelings she stirs up in me. I don't want to have to look at her every day and wish I could touch her or let her touch me, because it's pure torture wanting something that you won't let yourself have. "That's not true."

Her head tilts as she regards me. "This is a weird situation. It's awkward. You're mad. I get it."

I don't need to respond to that. We both know she's right. Weird and awkward don't even begin to cover it. The girl I solicited anonymously on the internet to send me nudes became my pen pal and friend. (I never told her that.) She ghosted me, and now she works for my brother at the family ranch.

It's fucking bizarre is what it is.

Am I mad? Yeah. I'm mad at myself.

"I'll stay out of your way. Short of going home, I'm not sure where else to go. You won't even know I'm there."

I somehow doubt that, but deep down, I also don't want her to leave. It's a relief to not be alone all the time. "Okay."

"Okay." She sighs, relaxing back into the leather seat with a small smile on her shapely lips.

She's only quiet for a few moments. It seems like our tenuous peace treaty has paved the way to her inquisitive side.

"Why Golddigger Eighty-five?"

I try to act casual, but I'm not sure I'm ready to talk

about that. About what happened between us. It's too… well, it still fucking hurts. So I try to play dumb, praying she might drop it.

"Huh?" I grunt distractedly as we turn onto the main street of Ruby Creek. It is literally called Main Street. One sad little street in a place that seems to be stuck in some sort of time warp. A bar, a coffee shop, a grocery/liquor/hardware store, a bank, and a few other stores line each side of the road. You can drive farther and have access to everything you need and more, but this is Ruby Creek. Not a single thing has changed since I was a child. *That's* weird.

"The screen name."

I can see her peering up at me from my periphery.

"Why'd you choose it?"

Why is the speed limit so damn low here? I want this to end.

"Because I run a mining company. We dig for gold. I was born in 1985."

"Huh." She taps her index finger against her lips, a loose piece of platinum hair resting against her rosy cheek.

"Why 'huh'?"

"It just sounds like you're after money or something. You know, like the Kanye song. It's kind of funny."

I try so hard not to smile, forcing my mouth into a straight line. For some odd reason, the name made me chuckle when I created the account. Now all it does is remind me of her.

"Why'd you pick…your name?" I ask, not wanting to say the name out loud.

She flushes and looks away at the stores as we roll past them. "Purple is just kind of my color."

I only look at her for a moment. It's all I can stand before blood rushes between my legs. But as I turn my eyes back to the road, my mind fixates on that blush. The memory of the way she blushed for me. *More like pretty in pink.*

My god. I need to get the hell out of this truck.

Finding parking is easy, so I pull into an angled parking spot in front of the Country Grind, the local coffee shop. Violet has her door open and is sliding out before I can get over to her side. I hear her whimper and then gasp when she hits the ground. I cringe. *So fucking stubborn.*

I stride up to the entryway and hold the door open instead of picking her up and carrying her.

She limps past me with one eyebrow up. "This gentleman's act is cute."

Cute? I can't remember ever being called that. *Distant. Grumpy. Creepy* even. I shake my head and follow her in.

"Hi, Macy!" Violet says.

"Honey!" the curvaceous redhead behind the counter booms back. "What have you done to yourself?"

"Oh, this?" Violet nibbles on her lip as she looks up at me where I stand beside her. "Minor spill. Nothing major. I'll be back in the tack in no time."

"Oh, baby," the middle-aged woman continues, "let me get you a cookie and a coffee. That will help. What about you, darlin'?"

These pet names. They're brutal. Thankfully, Violet

jumps in and rescues me from this line of questioning. Or maybe she rescues Macy from me. Who knows?

"Oh, never mind him. He doesn't believe in coffee."

Macy looks genuinely horrified as her hand falls across her collarbone in mock shock. Her eyes rove up and down my body appreciatively, making me squirm, before she holds one hand up beside her mouth and leans into Violet conspiratorially. "There are certain flaws I'm willing to overlook for a man like that."

Violet gasps out a small giggle, and her porcelain cheeks instantly pink *again* as her eyes shoot up to me nervously, visibly as uncomfortable as I feel inside. I just stare at them like I'm bored, wondering if they're done yet. I hate it when people look at me too closely; that's why Vaughn is the face of the family mining company.

"Tough cookie, that one!" Macy cackles and then turns away, busying herself preparing Violet's order.

Crossing my arms, I look around the place, taking in the rustic decor. An older woman sitting with a newspaper smiles at me, her skin crinkling around her eyes when she says, "Good morning."

I carry on with my assessment, hating to admit that there is a certain charm to the place, when I feel a poke in my ribs and glance down to see Violet's furrowed brow looking straight up at me.

She whisper-scolds me, "She just said *good morning* to you."

I lean down toward her. "I know."

"But…you just ignored her."

"I don't know her." I don't like small talk. Or strangers. Or how small-town people don't know how to mind their business. If I don't invite that type of behavior, my time here will be less irritating. I've established myself as unapproachable before, and it really doesn't take long to accomplish if you offend people thoroughly enough.

Violet's bottom jaw drops open like I've just said something shocking. "You have better manners than that, Cole Harding. You've been opening doors for me all morning."

"Are you scolding me?"

She crosses her arms and raises one eyebrow at me in challenge. Her hip juts out as her slender arms fold beneath her breasts, and I focus on the mud in her hair so I don't sneak a peek at how her stance might press them up.

Her body still haunts me.

"Do I need to?"

She nods.

I groan inwardly while outwardly smiling in a way I'm sure looks more like a wild dog showing its teeth as I turn back to the woman at the table. "Good morning," I say clearly before turning back to Violet, whose eyes are dancing with amusement.

She rolls her lips together like she's holding back a laugh before she hits me with a full, blinding smile. A genuine smile. "Was that really so bad?"

All I can think is that I can't remember the last time someone looked at me like *that*.

CHAPTER 8

Violet

Yesterday, he stopped responding after I turned down his offer for…whatever he does. Watches you masturbate while he calls all the shots?

Sounds bizarre. Then why are you squeezing your thighs together just thinking about it?

How does he even know he'll be attracted to me? Or I him? Why would anyone do this with a stranger? Is this guy really some sort of orgasm magician?

I pull my phone out, determined to get to the bottom of this.

Pretty_in_Purple: Why does anyone sign up for this arrangement?

I throw my phone down on my bed and get dressed for the morning, trying to work out why I'm so fixated on figuring this out when it has no bearing on me. It's not like I'm going to do it.

When my phone buzzes, I practically throw myself across the bed to grab it. Smooth.

Golddigger85: Still thinking about me, huh?

Pretty_in_Purple: What if I'm a total butterface?

Golddigger85: Butterface?

I roll my eyes. Who doesn't know that saying?

Pretty_in_Purple: But-her-face. You liked my picture, but what if I'm a total butterface?

Golddigger85: I wouldn't expect you to show me your face.

Pretty_in_Purple: Okay, Captain Literal. What if you're a total butterface? Maybe faces matter to me. I don't think I'd like showing the goods to some nameless, faceless person on the internet.

Golddigger85: Are you sure about that?

Arousal zings through me, pinging around in my pelvis as I imagine myself doing what he's asking. Touching myself on camera. What would his voice sound like? A shiver runs down my spine as my thumbs hover over the screen of my phone. I'm not sure, but I'll never tell him that. I'm just sex-starved. That's all.

Pretty_in_Purple: Yes.

Dots roll across the screen as he types back, and then a photo pops up on the screen. A selfie.

Golddigger85: Okay, what about now?

I tap the photo and take in the manicured dark scruff on the man's perfectly square jaw. He's wearing a hat that shadows the top half of his face, obscuring what sits above his straight, pronounced nose. I can't even see the color of his eyes, no matter how close I zoom in. It's dim wherever he is and almost looks like a basement or something.

Probably where he keeps all the bodies.

As I zoom back out, my eyes snag on his mouth, almost a little too shapely for the strength of his other features. He has nice lips, that perfect bow shape on the top one. And as I let my fingers fall away, I realize he has lots of nice other stuff too, because he's not wearing a shirt. A strong neck, with a pronounced Adam's apple. Big round shoulders, the bulge of one bicep visible where his arm is outstretched holding the phone. The shot cuts off before I can get farther down his chest, but I can see the sprinkling of hair and a line between his pectorals.

My mouth goes a little dry. Golddigger is cut. And suddenly I feel awkward. Flustered. So I deflect, just like I did when my brothers would start inquiring about boyfriends.

Pretty_in_Purple: Even a butterface looks good in a hat.

Golddigger85: You saying I look good?

I exit the app quickly and shove it in the back pocket of my jeans.

That's not a question I want to answer.

★★★

"Okay, spill." Billie leans forward, shoulders to her ears, with a mischievous look on her face. "What's it like living with the beast?"

Billie and Vaughn live in a cottage on the opposite side of the property, and it is the epitome of cozy. Open concept, exposed wood, big loft bedroom. It's small and simple, but they love it, and it suits them perfectly. Plus, there's a paddock right out the door where she can keep her horse, DD, close by. He's fine. The fall stung him, and he was a little jumpy afterward, but he's healthy—thank god. Billie says he's not racing until I'm ready to go again, so we'll make up for lost time then, even if it means running races closer together than we might otherwise. In the interim, he's happily enjoying some downtime and training with his favorite rider, Billie.

I can't hold a candle to what the two of them have. I'm just lucky he lets me hang on for the ride now and then and that Billie is way too tall to be a jockey.

She's been harassing me about coming over all week. She plied me with wine, and now we're on glass number three. And *this* is why. I finally gave in because it's Friday, and I'm bored of reading the steamy romance novels she left on my front porch. And now *this* is what I get.

I roll my eyes and mutter, "Snoopy bitch." She just laughs, and I ask, "Does that make me Belle?"

"I don't know. Are you going to have a snowball fight and fall in love with the big brute?" She cackles like it's the most ridiculous thing in the world, and I try not to cringe. If you'd have asked me that same question a year ago, I'd have sighed like a lovesick teenager and gone on dreaming about meeting Golddigger85 one day. I was so certain I was special to him, not just another girl he met on the internet, or I never would have taken it that far. Cheek-burning levels of far.

So imagine my surprise when he reminded me I was just that. My heart aches more at the memory than I like to admit. He hurt me, and it was all my doing. I asked for more than he could give.

I shake my head and take a sip of the red wine Billie poured for me, tucking my mixed feelings down behind the big crystal bell. Hopefully.

"I've barely seen him all week. He works long hours. And I have nothing to do, so it's not like I wake up early."

"That's not true. You came and hung out at the barn with me a few days."

"In a chair with my leg propped up on a bucket. Where I was forced to watch everyone else have fun while I sulked on the sidelines."

Now it's Billie's turn to roll her eyes. "Think of it this way. You're one-quarter of the way through your recovery. That's not so bad!"

I glare back at her where she's curled into the corner of the big plushy couch opposite me, legs tucked underneath herself, looking comfortable and carefree. I've been trying to put my best foot forward, to stay positive, but I must confess…I'm floundering. I'm bored. I'm sad. And I'm feeling a little resentful—angry, maybe. This was supposed to be my season to prove myself.

"You okay, Vi?" The skin between Billie's brows pinches together.

My breath rushes out of my body on a huge sigh. "Yeah."

She's not buying it. "What's wrong?"

I don't want to stress Billie out. I don't want her to worry about me, and she's such a mother hen that I know she will. "Nothing," I say, pasting a fake smile on my face.

She stares at me, hard. I hate it when she does this. It's like she's digging through my brain without permission. "Did Cole do something?"

I look down and snort as I trail my index finger around the rim of my wineglass.

"Violet," she whines, "are you ever going to tell me what's up with you guys? I'm trying to be a grown-up about it, but it's literally killing me. Being a grown-up is really hard."

My eyebrow pops up skeptically. "You look fine to me."

She groans and looks up at the wood-beam ceiling.

I roll my lips together again, weighing my options. I could talk about Cole, or I could talk about my intense level of sadness and disappointment and probably start crying. For once, talking about Cole feels preferable.

I take a big swig of my wine. Liquid courage.

"Okay, Cole and I met on the internet."

She hunkers down, leaning forward slightly, like a little kid getting ready to listen to a campfire story.

"On a…um…" Oh god, saying this out loud is harder than I thought.

"Dating website?" she prods.

I almost laugh. The thought of Cole on a dating website. "No, more of a…um…forum?"

"Okaayyy." Billie looks confused now, and my cheeks heat.

I just blurt it out and get it over with. "A forum where people post nudes," I say quickly before shoving my wineglass in my face again.

Her brows knit together. "Cole posts nudes on the internet? If he weren't my future brother-in-law, I wouldn't be averse to see—"

"No, I did."

Billie's feline eyes bulge out as she chokes on her mouthful of wine. With one hand across her chest, she gasps for breath. "You?"

I nod.

"My sweet little Vi?"

I go beet red. Head to toe, I'm sure. I hear a click but can't look away from Billie.

"You posted naked pictures of yourself…on the internet?"

And somehow, because I have the worst luck in the world, this is the moment that Vaughn waltzes in through the front door.

He looks at Billie and me, his dark features intentionally blank, and holds his hands up in the air. "I was never here."

"It was one picture! One time!" I announce to the room, trying to clarify myself and cringing so hard at the thought of people I know and respect finding this out about me. Billie is one thing. But Vaughn? *Ugh.*

"I heard nothing!" he calls back a little too brightly as he heads upstairs. "And even if I did, I'm all for women taking charge of their sexuality!"

I rest my head against the back of the plushy couch and groan. Maybe the cushions will swallow me whole? Envelop me into the down stuffing so that I'll never have to see anyone ever again.

"Sorry." Billie winces. "He went to Hank's place to go over some stuff. I thought he'd be gone longer."

I close my eyes, pretending I can rewind time to about five minutes ago, when my dignity was still intact.

Billie pats my knee. "Don't worry, Porn Star Patty. Your secret is safe with me."

A strangled noise lodges in my throat. I still refuse to look at her.

"Come on, Vi," she laughs. "Want me to tell you some crazy sex stories to even the playing field? Because Vaughn can—"

"Please don't." I hold one hand up to stop her.

"Okay, then stop being a baby and tell me the rest. You posted the picture…and?"

I hear the shower turn on upstairs, and I figure I'm safe to spill for a few more minutes.

"He contacted me." I decide that even if I don't really owe Cole anything, I don't want to betray his confidence with the details of that first message. His offer of payment never struck me as anything other than honorable. A fair exchange for a product—almost clinical, really. Like it made him feel better about what he was asking. And the more I got to know him, the more I realized it was exactly that as well as a way to maintain his precious distance. Something I went and threw a wrench into.

"And we ended up talking." She waggles her eyebrows. "As friends." Her shoulders droop in disappointment. "For a year."

"What! A year?"

I nod.

"What did you even talk about?"

I run my free hand through my hair. What *did* we talk about? It was mostly me asking questions or monologuing. But he always responded, and when I thought he was bored or tired of talking to me, I'd pull back, only to see a message from him pop up a day later, like that was his threshold for when he'd reach out. Something I took to mean more than it obviously did. Sometimes, we'd watch a movie at the same time and type back and forth about it. It was companionship in the most basic sense of the word.

"Everything and nothing," I say, because it's true. We talked about books, television, current events, our families in vague generalities, but we never talked about specifics. Shared nothing that might give our identities away. It was always entirely anonymous.

"So you guys never…" She holds her hand up in a rolling motion, implying *stuff*.

I bite down on my lip and look out the window into the dark rainy night. "Once."

"Once." Billie grips her wineglass with both hands, sitting up cross-legged now and nodding, like I'm telling the most fascinating story in the world.

I steel myself, wanting to get this part over with as quickly as possible. "Yes. Once. And it was very one-sided. Which resulted in the end of our...whatever it was." I feel so hot that I'm sure you could fry an egg on my cheek right now.

"What do you mean one-sided?"

Agitation roils around in my gut. This part still bugs me, no matter how hard I try to get over it. Embarrassment is tough to hurdle. "I mean, things got carried away one night. I ended up losing all my clothes on video because I thought I trusted him enough to do that after a year of corresponding. Had the best orgasm of my life. And then Cole refused to reciprocate. He left his screen black the whole time and said he would never partake. All things he had told me in the past. I just thought..." I shake my head with a sad laugh. "I guess I thought I'd be different. Turns out I wasn't. I deleted the app and never talked to him again. Until the qualifier last year when he figured out who I was."

From upstairs, I hear, "Ow, fuck!"

"Were you eavesdropping on us, Vaughn Harding?" Billie shouts to the open loft bedroom while I look around for a spot to dig a hole and crawl deep inside it.

"Nope!" he calls back, popping the *p* with surety. "Just stubbed my toe."

"I hope it hurt!"

I groan and scrub my hand over my face. "Okay, that's my cue to leave." I set the wineglass on the oak coffee table in front of me and push myself up, feeling pretty used to the walking cast now. I can't get out of here fast enough.

"Vi," Billie says with a breathy giggle, "don't worry about it. He won't say anything."

I know that what she's saying is true. Vaughn is a good guy, an honorable one. But that doesn't mean I'm keen on him knowing about my sex life. About his brother's sex life.

Good god.

Cole. I should probably tell him about this minor mishap. Just in case. I can already imagine the blank expression he'll give me, the way his jaw will tick as he crosses his arms.

I limp to the door, and Billie follows. "Let me drive you home."

I'd come here with her after hanging out at the barn all afternoon, which also means I have no independent way of getting home.

"No, you've been drinking. I'll walk."

I hike my bag over my shoulder and slide my good foot into the rain boot I wore over as Billie holds the front door open for me.

"Let Vaughn drive you home."

"Ha!" I bark out a laugh. "I think I'll pass on that for now. I need a couple days before I can look him in the eye again, thanks."

"You sure?" She nibbles on her bottom lip nervously. "It's raining pretty hard."

I reach into my bag and pull out a small umbrella. "I'm all set. It's not that far."

Billie doesn't look convinced, but she doesn't stop me either—something I appreciate. I don't like being babied, and I don't need people treating me like porcelain because I have an injury. My brothers would have been back up on a bull with a tiny fracture like this, and here I am wallowing around like a wounded princess.

I step out into the dark, damp night and sigh. Raindrops pelt the top of my umbrella, the pinging sound loud all around me. The smell of dirt and rain permeates the air. It smells fresh, like new growth. The perfect night for a walk to clear my mind and cool my cheeks.

Walking was a bad idea. The heavy April rain has washed away all the charm of the night rather quickly.

My leg hurts, I'm cold, and this shitty little umbrella leaks. If I wasn't been such a wuss, I would have just accepted the ride from Vaughn. What's a five-minute drive for him is more like a twenty-minute walk for me. Probably longer with my limp. And I'm not even halfway.

"Motherfucker," I mutter as I hobble down the gravel road in my stupid walking cast—which is also not waterproof, which means my sock inside is getting soaked. And cold. I rarely swear, but now and then, a situation warrants it. This situation is one of those. This night is one of those. Actually, this week is one of those.

Tears sting at the backs of my eyes. The bridge of my nose tingles. I'm not a crier, and this isn't an unmanageable situation. But right now, everything feels heavy. Like more than I can bear. My career, my leg, my personal life. Sometimes being an independent grown-up is exhausting.

I stop and stare up at the sky, trying to force a deep breath into my lungs, but my frustration wins out, and I end up screaming to no one at all, "Fuck my fucking life!"

Which is right when headlights turn down onto the road, illuminating me like the Broadway actress that I am not, like the universe is just dying for someone to witness my meltdown or splash me as they drive by. But when the truck gets closer and slows, I realize I recognize it. A window rolls down, and a thick forearm shoots out, waving me forward.

"Get in!" Cole shouts.

I feel like under different circumstances, I would say no. But at this moment, all I feel is intense relief. Like I don't even care who's here to save me as long as I'm being rescued.

He reaches across the front seats and throws the door open before I even get there. A simple gesture, but I still feel like I could hug him for it. I fold down my umbrella and haul myself up into his big truck, hating how high off the ground it is but loving how dry and warm it is all at the same time.

I say nothing as I slam the door and buckle myself in. I can sense that Cole is looking at me. I can feel anger radiating off him in waves, like when you sit too close to a space heater. But I don't care. I just drop my head back against the headrest, close my eyes, and sigh, suddenly very exhausted.

"Are you *trying* to make your leg worse?" His voice is precise—I can hear his military background in there. He sounds authoritative, and I like it. It's not a question so much as a demand. It reminds me of the night we went too far.

"Thank you for picking me up" is all I say back, instantly feeling a little dopey. Wine, cold, and strapping yourself in on an emotional roller coaster will do that to a girl, I guess. And I assume Billie is behind this—something she'll pay for later.

He just grunts and drives. I sense him moving around beside me and squint from under my lashes to see what he's doing. One big hand reaches over to my side of the dash, and I watch his heavily corded forearm flex as he presses the seat warmer button for me. Is he worried about me being cold? I follow that arm up to his fingers as he rotates the knob to maximum heat, not missing the way his veins bulge over the top of his strong hand.

Everything about Cole is hypermasculine, something my body can't help but gobble up, even though my mind screams at me to ignore him. His body, his features, his *voice.* God. His voice. All deep and gravelly. He could make a killing as a phone sex operator if that was still a thing. And if he ever said more than a few words at a time.

As a pen pal, he was been slow to come around. But in real life? He was like squeezing blood from rocks. Next to impossible to get talking.

Which is why I don't bother making small talk. I let my eyes close and revel in the heat pumping out of the vents all around me. If he's not going to talk to me, I won't waste my energy talking to him about what may have come to light at Billie and Vaughn's house. *Want my trust? Earn it.*

When the truck finally slows and comes to a stop, I open one eye and peek at him. He's staring at me, completely closed off but staring at me nonetheless.

"Stay there," he clips out in that bossy voice.

I'm too bone-tired to argue, and I watch from under heavy eyelids as he hops out of the truck. He may have upset me, but I'm not above watching the way his jeans stretch across his ass and thighs. The man is huge, a wall of muscle. He could crush me if he wanted to.

A shiver runs down my spine as he rounds the front of the truck and opens the passenger-side door before announcing, "You're going to let me help you out of here."

I roll my head along the headrest to look back at him, quirking one eyebrow in response. That wasn't a question.

He crosses his arms, widens his stance, and glares at me. He looks like a bouncer at a club, about to deny me entry. A small hysterical laugh bubbles up out of me at the mental image. But Cole doesn't join in. He continues glaring at me, his mouth set in a thin line, his eyes burning across my skin, threatening to set me alight—like the strike of a matchstick.

Ugh. I need to drink less wine. *And have an orgasm.*

"Okay," I whisper, my voice small and unsteady. My leg really hurts. Not like it did last weekend, but walking around a bunch probably wasn't my best-laid plan. So I flip my legs out to dangle off the seat. I look like a little kid trying to get out of here. "'Why does your truck need to be so big?"

He ignores me as he steps forward. "Why do you have to ask so many questions?"

"You compensating for something?" Yup, that's the wine. I feel my cheeks heat at my boldness as I watch his jaw tick.

I expect him to plop me down on the ground, but he growls and scoops me up in his arms, one slung underneath my knees, the other right across the strap of my bra.

"Oh." I breathe out. "Okay."

He takes long, ground-covering strides toward the house, like he can't wait to drop me. I can feel his biceps bunching against the side of my breast, and with the golden cast of the porch lights, I can admire the definition in his arms, thickly corded and hard. *No wonder I commented on them before.*

I expect him to drop me on the front porch, but he keeps going, crouching slightly and easily snaking the hand from under my knees out to twist the door handle. I know I'm light, but the man isn't even struggling. At all. He kicks the door open and carries me in. I peek up at his face, the harsh slashes of his cheekbones, his heavy brow, the stubble across his jaw.

"What's the scar on your eyebrow from?"

His eyes shift down at me like I'm an irritating child.

"From my time overseas," he says.

I know that means during his time in the military. Something must have happened if that's all the explanation I'm going to get, and now I feel horrible for even asking. It's not my business. I feel like I crossed a line.

"It suits you. I like it," I say, trying to smooth things out. Except I'm sure that was a dumb thing to say by the way he's looking at me, those gray eyes pinning me in place. His chiseled chest rises and falls in a more pronounced fashion, and his breath fans across my throat as he regards me intensely.

That look only lasts a moment before he deposits me on the couch gently. Then he steps away quickly, like I might be on fire.

CHAPTER 9

Cole

I woke up to a message from Pretty_in_Purple. It said, "Good morning, Butterface," and I laughed. For the first time in a long time, I laughed. It felt foreign in my mouth, and I looked around like someone might have seen.

Except I'm alone. I'm always alone. It seems like this is how my life will be. I think it started out that I wanted it that way, but now I'm not so sure. I'm smart enough to know what people say about me…the recluse who runs the family company and is a total dick.

The role comes to me naturally, but I think I'm tired of it. Tired of my own company. Tired of the same fucking thing every fucking day.

I write back. I'm not funny or witty. I don't know what to say. So I just say what I'm thinking.

Golddigger85: Take off your clothes.

She replies a few minutes later.

Pretty_in_Purple: You first.

Yeah. That sure as shit isn't happening. Just the mention of it makes me nervous. I say nothing back, but a couple hours later, I check our chat again and reply this time.

Golddigger85: No chance.
Pretty_in_Purple: Guess we're stuck talking. We could be pen pals!

Pen pals. That's so far from what I had in mind when I first messaged this girl. How old is she?

Golddigger85: No.
Pretty_in_Purple: Come on! I'm lonely. You obviously are too. Let's just be friends.
Golddigger85: Why am I obviously lonely?
Pretty_in_Purple: Do I really need to answer that?

Touché, internet girl. And no. Please don't rub my nose in how pathetic I've become. "Does having a pen pal make me more or less pathetic?" I ask myself out loud as I rub a hand over my stubble and stare at the screen.

I would ask her, but that involves admitting I think I'm pathetic. I refuse to go there. Deflect. Redirect. That's what I'll do.

Golddigger85: Maybe I'm just a control freak.

Pretty_in_Purple: Maybe you're both?

I snort. Touché, internet girl. Tou. Ché.

★★★

I'm getting mighty tired of carrying Violet out of a truck. It's like she has no regard for her own well-being. At least this time, she doesn't feel limp in my arms.

I rip open the freezer and pull out one of my ice packs, agitation lining every movement. I was already annoyed when I walked in after a long week of working at the clusterfuck that is our company's new investment to find her shit *everywhere.* Water glasses abandoned around the house, shoes tossed carelessly by the front door, dishes piled in the sink, and a sweatshirt draped over the back of a chair almost made me go nuclear.

I'm the bachelor. I'm supposed to be the messy one. But instead, I have a twentysomething-year-old living in my space, a now world-famous athlete, who can't put simple things back where they belong. My feet stomped on the worn hardwood floors the entire time I cleaned up the place. Not what I felt like doing on a Friday night, but then I don't know what else I'd do in Ruby Creek.

With the ice pack in hand, I grab a water bottle from the fridge and walk back over to Violet. "Here." I hold the water out to her before I come to kneel by the couch.

I undo the Velcro straps on her air cast as she crinkles the plastic water bottle and regards me curiously. "What are you doing?"

"Getting ice on your leg so that you can get on a horse again one day." The mere thought of that sends a lance of anxiety through my chest, but I push it away. This is her journey, not mine.

"Did you know that plastic water bottles are bad for the environment?"

My god. She really doesn't stop with the questions. I don't respond, which she apparently takes as a sign that she should keep talking.

"They don't decompose. Instead, they end up in the oceans—"

I roll my eyes. Has she tasted the tap water here? "Why did you try to walk home on a leg that you know you're supposed to be resting?"

I know something is up. It was my job for years to sense when something was off.

Violet is ranting about water bottles, and Billie acted weird on the phone. The strained, tittering laugh when she suggested Violet might need help seemed panicky. I could feel the unspoken words, the tension.

She rolls her lips together nervously, and her crystalline blue eyes go wide. They only look brighter next to the pink blooming on the apples of her cheeks.

"Why are you blushing?"

"Now who's the one with all the questions?" she replies with fake bravado. A little tremor in her voice gives her away. The woman is an open book. No poker face to speak of.

"Violet," I scold her, pulling the cast away to assess her ankle below the hem of her leggings. Swollen. My teeth grind.

Her sigh comes out loud and ragged, her voice a little too quiet. "Okay. I just needed to get out of there. I didn't think it through."

"Why?"

Her eyes dart away, and I cup her heel delicately, the smell of her vanilla body cream in the air as I press the ice pack to her swollen leg. She hisses and gives her attention back to me—which is what I was going for.

"I'm just..." Her voice quivers, and she strokes her fingers through her golden locks. Her tell. She does it when she's nervous. "You know. Really disappointed. Really bored. Really...choked up about the current state of my life. I didn't want to talk about it."

She pauses, and I sit back on my heels, moving my hands down onto my thighs to listen, not wanting to touch her any longer. Her eyes are sparkling with unshed tears. I could tell that she was crying earlier, just like she's close right now.

"So I told them about us instead," she rushes out, looking at me pleadingly. "I'm sorry. I'm so, so sorry."

I go still. Stuck in place.

"I swear it was all just really general."

"*Them?*"

She flinches at the bite in my tone, and I'm instantly filled with self-loathing. "Okay. So I really only told Billie. I didn't know Vaughn was listening."

My skin crawls with embarrassment, like that feeling when you have a bug inching its way up your spine but can't quite reach it. My leg aches, like it often does. This was never supposed to happen. My sex life was supposed to stay perfectly compartmentalized on the internet where no one gets to see me. Violet was supposed to stay firmly removed from my real life. She was never supposed to crop up as a mainstay in the family business.

Panic courses through my veins as I see my perfectly laid facade crumbling. Just one little crack in the corner is going to lead to more questions. When one brick falls, the others will follow, torn down by questions I don't want to answer.

I know I'm fucked up. The last thing I need is everyone around me knowing too. And this bombshell is more than I'm equipped to handle. I get up woodenly, not saying a word, and walk away.

That's enough of this shit for one day.

The phone is silent for several beats, and then it fills with a raspy, maniacal cackle. "The woman is *living with you*?" Trixie gasps out, making me bang my head back against the brass bars of the bed frame. This place is like a fucking dollhouse.

"I don't pay you to laugh at me, Beatrice." I pay her because I *need* her. She's the first call I made this Saturday morning when I woke up after a shitty, fitful sleep. A sleep full of dreams about all my deepest, darkest secrets being spilled to the world. Dreams about Violet's naked body spread out before me. Dreams I can't afford and don't deserve.

"And she told your brother and future sister-in-law about how you both met?" She may not be laughing, but I can still hear the amusement in her voice.

"Yes," I grumble.

"And then she told you?"

"Yes."

"Well, you can't fault the girl for her honesty."

"I think I would prefer a little dishonesty in this case."

"Oh no, you don't need any more of that in your life."

I look out the big window across the vast field toward the barn.

"Why don't you let me—"

My eyes snag on something in my periphery. I jump out of bed and take a few hops over to the window, gripping the crown molding with one hand. *Why the fuck is there a horse in my yard?*

"I gotta go. I'll call you later." I hang up, but not before I hear Trixie say something about not being at my beck and call.

I get myself ready, throwing on the same T-shirt as yesterday before heading downstairs and out the front door, straight to the paddock that has been sitting gloriously empty until now. I eye the scrawny brown horse inside and then notice the paper rolled and shoved into one ring on the halter that's slung over a hook.

I pull it out, confused and annoyed.

> *Hey Vi,*
>
> *I know this isn't how you saw your year going. I know setbacks are frustrating. So does Pipsqueak here. Do you remember her from*

a couple of years ago? Apparently, she was a preemie foal that was touch and go there for a bit. Anyway, she's two now, and she's a fighter. Small but mighty, just like you.

I know you can't ride right now, but that doesn't mean you can't work. I'd like to see what she's got. Mind getting her started for me?

Love,
Billie

No. No fucking way am I living with Violet *and* with a horse. I'm not above admitting this is thoughtful of Billie. I can't fault her for that. For me though? This can't happen. I turn and storm back up into the house, note in hand.

The door slams behind me. "Violet! Get up!" My voice is sharper than I intend, but my life is completely out of control, and I'm panicking. That ends now.

I hear a small squeal from the other side of her door, followed by a thump, and I instantly feel like a dick for not keeping my cool. When the door opens, she's already dressed and pulling an earbud out of her ear. "What? What's wrong?"

I shove the note at her as if it will clearly explain what's wrong. Violet takes it from me, one dainty hand reaching out to remove it from mine. Her eyes are wide until she recognizes the writing, and I watch her feelings dance across her face. She's so expressive, it's like she could tell me a story without saying anything at all.

Tears spring up over her irises, usually the color of the sky and now more of an indigo as they darken with emotion. Her long lashes blink rapidly, as though she could sweep the tears away with them. One side of her perfectly heart-shaped mouth tips upward sadly. And then slowly the other side pops up to match. The smile is small, but the impact on me isn't.

I feel like a little boy again, one who just fell off the tire swing and winded himself, the thud of my bones against the packed ground rattling through me. My breath is caught somewhere beyond my reach.

Violet doesn't even look at me though. She doesn't see my struggle. She just limps over to the front window, pressing a hand to it like a child at the zoo, like she's never seen a horse before. I watch her body from behind. Her round ass, the taper of her waist, the slender curve of her neck beneath where all that pale hair is piled up on her head in a loose bun.

"What's the issue?" she asks quietly on a deep sigh without looking back at me. Her spaghetti-strap-clad shoulders go from tight and high to slowly dropping, like the tension is melting right off her and flowing away on a warm, gentle current.

And I know.

I know at this moment that I don't have it in me to make her get rid of the horse. After watching that physical reaction, how could I? I'm not a cruel man—not intentionally anyway. Everything Violet feels is so plain to the naked eye, particularly to that of a man who's spent his entire adult life reading people and situations. If there was something that could soothe me the same way that Violet relaxed at the prospect of having some plain brown horse to play with, I would have done it.

And I would have resented anyone who tried to stop me.

Instead, I just resent myself for being stuck in a rut. Something I don't want for Violet. Because no matter what she thinks, the days I spent messaging with her were some of my brightest in recent memory.

She turns to look at me over her shoulder, her wide blue eyes full of emotion, her cheeks flushed with excitement. Life courses through her so vividly and almost tangibly—like I could reach out and touch it, bottle it up and drink it, or just keep it, possess it, knowing I have the option to consume it whenever I want. Money can't buy this brand of vitality. This is bone deep—soul deep. She shines like the sun, golden and bright.

What a man like me wouldn't give for *that*.

"No issue," I say huskily. "I'm just not taking care of it. That job is all yours."

Violet tilts her head almost imperceptibly. "Who knows, Cole? You might come around."

I cross my arms and widen my stance, wanting to make it clear to her that I'm serious. Although I'm getting the sense I don't intimidate Violet as much as I thought. She's tougher than she comes off. More resilient. "I don't like horses," I say plainly, pinning her with a serious look, choosing to leave out the part where my most vivid memory of them is watching my father fall to his death beneath their hooves.

Her body jolts ever so slightly, like I've just slapped her.

And then a gentle smile spreads across her mouth. "We'll see about that."

She looks far too knowing for a woman her age. She's looking at me like *I'm* the project rather than the scrawny horse in the yard.

I'm already dressed for a run, so that's what I do.

I turn and run.

CHAPTER 10

Violet

I'm pretty sure my surly pen pal, Golddigger, has become one of my only friends. We've been talking daily for a few months, and I've grown accustomed to it. I'd even go so far as to say I look forward to it. Some days, I wake up and fire off a message to him saying, Good morning, *or something equally chipper. And other mornings, he messages me first. Like today.*

Golddigger85: Hi.

My lips tip up at the one-word note. He's not a big talker—this much I've learned—yet he's always there. He always writes me back. If I were annoying him, you'd think he'd stop responding. I think he needs this as much as I do.

The quiet, grumpy vibe is just part of his charm, and I take it to mean he likes me enough to keep me around. So I always write him back too. Otherwise, all I do is work at Gold Rush

Ranch from sunup to sundown. New girl on the farm means no clout, no seniority—grunt worker. And I like it. No one treats me like I need coddling. They throw me in the deep end and expect me to swim.

Pretty_in_Purple: Good morning, Butterface. How was your sleep?

Golddigger85: The usual.

I know what that means. It means he didn't sleep well. He's told me he wakes up a lot. He's also told me he's a veteran, so I assume those two things connect. I haven't asked because he hasn't seemed like he wants me to, and I've come to know that Golddigger is an intensely private man. That he likes my… Do you call what we have company? *I don't know. He likes my reliability but isn't about to tell me his deepest, darkest secrets. Which is fine. I don't expect him to.*

But it doesn't stop me from sharing about myself. I think he likes that too.

Pretty_in_Purple: I had a great sleep. Like a baby. I work outside all day, so by the time I get back to my apartment, I'm beat.

Golddigger85: I don't remember what it feels like to sleep through the night.

I wince. Sounds like my brother when he came back from Afghanistan.

Pretty_in_Purple: I have a brother who had a hard time sleeping for a spell.

Golddigger85: How did he fix it?

I roll my lips together at his question because I don't know the answer to that.

Pretty_in_Purple: I'm not sure he ever did.

Golddigger85: Reassuring, thanks.

Oh, jeez. I need to flip this script.

Pretty_in_Purple: Have you tried masturbating before bed? That always helps me.

The dots roll and stop.

Golddigger85: You offering to lend me a hand?

"Ha!" I bark out a laugh into the quiet room.

Pretty_in_Purple: A for effort. Never gonna happen.

This is our running joke. But the more I get to know him and feel comfortable around him, the more I wonder… Would it really be so bad?

I don't know where Cole went, and I don't care. The only

thing I can focus on is the little bay filly eating her hay quietly outside my front door. She's small, yes, but the way she's built is all correct. Ideal, really. Billie has such a good eye for horses, no doubt she picked up on that too.

I hobble over to the front door and sit on the wooden bench in the front entry to slide my good leg into my rubber boot I kicked off as Cole carried me in through the front door.

Again. Except this time, I remember it clearly. The way his hands gripped me, strong but gentle. The lines of his abs as they rippled along my rib cage while he held me close. The sheer power of him as he carried me through the rain effortlessly.

Every point of contact like a tease.

I wanted him before I ever knew he looked or felt like *that*. I wanted him even when I knew he'd never want me back. When he was just an avatar on my screen. *Stupid.* And that is something I've come to terms with. Something I've moved on from the day that I vowed to never look at our chat again. And I haven't. I never logged in again. I deleted the app. Were there messages there waiting for me? Did he wonder where I went? Or did he just assume my silence was a dismissal? I'll never know because I'll never check.

Having a soul-consuming crush on a stranger on the internet was a phase. And I closed the door on that phase of my life. I pushed my boundaries. I tried something new. And it's done.

I'm in a whole new chapter. Older, wiser, more independent.

I chuckle at myself as I head out the front door toward the paddock. Living with the man and falling asleep thinking about the hard lines of his body doesn't exactly scream *wise* or *independent. Great work, Violet.*

"Hey, pretty girl," I coo as I approach the fence.

Pipsqueak's head snaps up, but she doesn't startle. She just flicks her ears toward me with a joyful look on her dainty face, not the least bit perturbed by my arrival. In fact, when I get close enough, she forgets about her hay completely and comes to the gate, eager for attention. Not unusual for a horse that has probably been handled extensively for her entire life because of health complications.

As soon as I reach the gate, she drops her head over the top post and nuzzles into me like she's demanding a hug. Her warm, damp breath flows over the light hairs on my forearms as she snuggles her face into my embrace.

A genuine laugh bubbles up out of me. It's like she thinks she's a puppy. Her eyes flutter open and closed happily as I stroke my hand over her broad forehead, right over the bright white star in the middle of it.

I love this horse already. I don't even care if she runs well. This kind of contact is therapeutic, and once I can be sure the gesture won't bring me to tears, I have every intention of thanking Billie from the bottom of my heart for knowing this is what I needed. Horse therapy.

She was always rambling on about DD being her therapist. Maybe Pipsqueak can be mine?

"What do you think about that, Pip?" I ask, rubbing my cheek against the firm round plate of hers, basically bunting her like a cat. But I don't even care. Once a horse girl, always a horse girl.

The smell, the dust, the rasp of her ungroomed coat—it doesn't bother me at all. It comforts me. My very own little paper-bag princess.

Excitement at the prospect of her makeover courses through me, and when I look down near the gate, my eyes catch the pink grooming box that Billie left out. It's loaded with every brush and spray I could need. Hoof oil even. Did Billie pack up the trailer to get her here? Or walk over? I decide I don't care about that either. "You ready to hit the spa, girl?"

Pipsqueak snorts and gives her unruly black mane a shake. As close to a nod as I'm going to get. I grab the handle of the box and let myself in through the gate. I don't bother putting the halter on her. If she wants to walk away, she can. For now, we're just getting to know each other. No pressure.

I start with a big rubber currycomb at the top of her neck, brushing in tight circles and watching all the dust and loose hair come up to the surface as I work my way down to her shoulder. When I get to her withers, she sighs and lets her eyes fall shut, like she's getting the best massage. I continue, getting lost in the rhythm of the circular motion and working my way around her body.

By the time I get to the other side of her, she's so relaxed she has one hoof tipped and resting on the ground casually. She is *loving* this. And so am I. I'm completely blissed out. Zoned out.

Which is why I jump when I hear a car pull up. I turn to

see the old blue truck, the one Hank got from Dermot and has kept running. It always warms my heart the way this place has stayed in the family, the way Dermot and Ada's legacy has tied everyone together—even when things got turbulent.

"Hey, Vi!" Hank hollers as he steps out, looking a little stiff. "How do you like your present?" His grin is infectious, all the lines on his face deepening around twinkling green eyes. Hank is wise and kind and comforting, and I've come to love him over the last couple years we've spent working together. He's been a surrogate father to Billie since she was a teenager, but I feel as though he's taken that role over with the rest of us at the farm as well.

"Like? I don't like my present. I *love* her!" I beam back so wide that it almost hurts my cheeks.

He reaches back into the truck and pulls out a bouquet of pink tulips before marching over and holding them out to me over the fence. "Sorry I haven't checked in on you since your accident. I've been getting regular updates from everyone else but didn't want to crowd you."

Taking the flowers from him, I hold them up to my nose and inhale that fresh grassy smell, the hint of honey. "Thank you for the flowers. And don't worry about it. I haven't been the best company."

Pipsqueak does the same, running her nose over the soft petals curiously.

Hank doesn't push the subject; instead, he just chuckles and reaches a firm hand out to pat the filly. "She's a funny little thing, isn't she? So curious about the world. I'm quite fond of her myself."

I sigh contentedly before looking back up at the man. "Me too. I think we're going to get along well."

Hank nods as he presses his elbows into the fence. He looks over at the blue farmhouse, a flash of sadness streaking across his features. "How are you getting along with Cole?"

How am I getting along with Cole? We communicate mostly in grunts and glares. We ignore the awkward vibe between us. I try not to stare at his body as if it's a cold drink on a hot day. It's basically torture. So I just settle on, "He's no Pippy."

Hank barks out a laugh. His head tips back, and his chest rumbles. "That he's not. He reminds me of Dermot. The kind of man who would do almost anything for the people he loves but hard to get to know. Strong. Silent. Sensitive."

Sensitive? I almost laugh. If we're going with *s* words, I pick *surly.* But my dad always told me that if I have nothing nice to say, it's best not to say anything at all. So that's what I do. I say nothing and just give Hank a small smile.

But I'm not fooling him. I can tell by the look on his face.

He tips his head back toward the house. "You know his dad grew up in that house?"

I look at it too. I know his dad died in a tragic racing accident but not much else. "I didn't know that, no."

Hank nods. "I think it might be hard for him to be out here, even though he'd never admit it. I'm sad about your leg, but I'm glad he's not alone. It's hard not to worry about all you kids." He chuckles good-naturedly. "May not have had any of my own, but I feel like you're all mine anyway."

My chest pinches at the thought of the ghosts Cole

might live with, and my eyes sting thinking he could be as sensitive as Hank is saying. Maybe I've been misinterpreting him this entire time? I blink and change the subject, trying to keep my mind from focusing on the puzzle that is Cole Harding. "Didn't want any kids?"

He smiles sadly. "I'd have loved to have kids. Guess it just wasn't in the cards."

"Good thing we're all here to fill in for you then," I say with a wink, trying to lighten the mood.

Hank gives my shoulder a quick squeeze. "I'm lucky to have you all. But I won't bother ya. Just wanted to drop the flowers off and see your smiling face. If you need me, you've got my number. Take care of the boy, will ya?"

I smile and roll my eyes. The *boy* can take care of himself. "Thank you for the flowers, Hank." I limp out through the gate, wrap my free arm around his torso, and give him a quick squeeze. "Don't be a stranger."

"Deal," he says as he strides off with his signature wink and grin, firing up the old truck.

I wave back at him as I enter the house to get the flowers in a vase of water. I set them on the counter. They really are pretty, and they bring some much-needed life to the place. And then I head back outside and get back to brushing Pippy's fuzzy coat.

I feel more than hear Cole arrive back from his run, like a low-pressure weather system blowing in. I only peek at him before I realize it's not a good idea. His shirt is damp with sweat, clinging to his body in an almost erotic way, and his cheeks are flushed pink, making him look younger than I now know he is. It's probably too warm to be running in sweatpants, but that's not my business. He has a mom. And every other thought I have about the man is distinctly un-mom-like.

I bite down on my bottom lip to distract myself. Our eyes meet briefly before I turn back to Pippy, focusing on using a soft bristle brush now to sweep all that dirt and dander away. Cole and I say nothing to each other, and that's fine by me. He's probably still mad about my big mouth—and I can't blame him for that. I betrayed what little trust I owed him. Something I feel bad about but have no idea how to fix.

I can only fix what's right in front of me, so I focus on the ratty-looking little filly and promise myself I'll clean her up as best I can. My arm aches with the elbow grease I put into her, but by the time I'm done, she looks...better.

Standing back to admire my handiwork, I prop my hands on my hips. Maybe she's not shiny yet, but I thinned out her light bay winter coat, and I'm sure it will glow bronze once I get her on a better feeding regimen. Her four white socks are actually white now rather than gray, and her hooves are shining with the moisturizing oil I've applied. She's going to be a work in progress—after all, she just got pulled out of a back field—but I feel accomplished. Hopeful.

And for the first time in the last week, I don't feel quite so sorry for myself.

I'm sitting on a hay bale facing Pippy when I hear the door slam behind me. I've spent all day outside, and it's not even that nice out. Heavy clouds and the smell of impending rain permeate the thick air, making my skin feel almost damp. I don't care. It feels like one of the best days in the world to me.

Pippy's head pops up at the noise, and I turn around to see Cole in a fresh pair of sweatpants and a T-shirt. The image of him all sweaty flashes into my mind unbidden and almost instantly makes me blush. *Am I ever going to outgrow this reaction?*

"Where are you going?" I call out, trying to be conversational. I'm not an idiot. I know he was on the verge of telling me we weren't keeping a horse at the house. I don't know what changed his mind, but I thank my lucky stars he did.

His gait looks stiff as he hops down the stairs, and at my question, his body goes still, his head rotating toward me as his mouth twists into…I'm not sure. Maybe it's supposed to be a smile.

"For a run."

"Again?" I know running is good for you. To a point. It's never been my cup of tea, but two runs a day seems excessive.

"Yes. Is that a problem for you?"

Okay. We're grumpy again. This man needs one of those happy pills I bugged him about. "No," I venture carefully. "I'm just… Well, I'm in a great mood. Wanna grab a drink instead?"

His entire body turns toward me now, and his hand gestures between the two of us as he says, "You and me?" Like it's the most horrifying prospect in the world.

"Am I so bad?" The words spill out on a laugh.

Cole visibly winces, apparently not quite prepared to laugh with me just yet.

"I don't know." His hands rest on his narrow hips as he looks around himself on a sigh, like he's searching for an escape route.

"Come on," I pester him, because this man needs a little pestering. He reminds me of my oldest brother in that regard. Too serious for his own good. "I know you're old, but we'll be back before your bedtime. Before dinner even. It's..." I pull out my phone to check the time. "It's four o'clock. That's happy hour."

He just stares at me.

"Which means you have to be happy." I try to hold back the smile at my own cheesy joke, but I'm failing.

"Violet."

"Yes?" I bat my eyelashes with exaggerated innocence.

"Calling me old *and* grumpy is your plan to make me happy?"

Okay, jokes really fall flat around here. "Come on! I want a drink and to be around some other humans rather than locked up on the ranch. I'm feeling a bit squirrelly. If you don't come, I'll go on my own."

"Yeah? You going to drive with a big walking cast on your right foot?"

"No." I smile slyly. "I'm going to walk."

Cole groans and looks up at the sky like he's hoping some aliens will come whizzing by and beam him up out of this conversation. If they needed a magnificent male specimen, I could see why they'd choose him. "Give me five minutes."

"For what?" I quirk my head.

"To change into something appropriate."

I bark out a laugh. "Cole, have you been to Neighbor's Pub before?"

"No," he says with a slight wrinkle in his nose.

"Okay, well, you don't need to change. It's very casual."

He grunts at me and walks back inside, only to return a few seconds later with his keys. Our drive down the country roads is quiet but not tense like in the past couple of weeks. I almost feel like we've settled into a sort of companionable silence. Or at least on my end. Yes, we have an awkward history, but we're working with it. Plus, I'm only going to be living at the house for a couple more weeks. Once I get the all clear, I'm outta there. We can go back to pretending the other doesn't exist.

"Turn here." I point to where the old pub sits, rustic and full of character—just the way I like it.

I'm so excited that I bounce a little in my seat as I look out the window at the dark painted exterior with a big flashing sign over heavy oak doors and a parking lot patio lit by outdoor lights strung up over picnic tables.

"This?" Cole asks skeptically as he pulls up and looks at the building.

I haven't been off the farm in what feels like forever, and he clearly doesn't share my excitement. Which I don't get. Isn't he bored too? That's what running twice a day says to me: bored.

"Are you scared?" I grab the handle and crack the door. His head flicks instantly at the sound.

"Don't get out," he huffs before hopping out his side and rounding the front of the truck in what looks like only a few long strides.

The man is so big and authoritative, I feel a flash of nerves as he storms over to me. He's got that law enforcement vibe, like I might be in trouble for something. I squeeze my thighs together at the thought of being in trouble with Cole. It wouldn't be so bad. *You're so sad, Violet.*

"What's that look for?" he asks, standing before me now, one hand holding the top of the open door, stressing the rounded lines of his bicep against the sleeve of his T-shirt. It looks like it might unravel under the strain, especially when I take too long to answer, and his fingers squeeze the door harder, making that bulge grow right before my eyes.

Eyes that go wide and then snap back to his stormy face. The harsh slashes of his cheekbones, the square jaw covered in stubble that would rasp against my…

"Violet."

I startle. "Yeah? Yeah! Nothing. Let's go." I look toward the back of the truck, feeling my cheeks burn from the rabbit hole I just let my brain go down. Such a bad idea.

He doesn't even ask this time. His huge hands slide across my ribs and wrap around my waist. I thank my lucky stars I'm wearing a loose cable-knit sweater that hides the little goose bumps dotting my arms. Everything about him is so… almost aggressive that the gentleness of his touch never fails to startle me. I don't think I imagined the careful way he lifted me out of the truck that night Billie brought me to his house or the way he held me close and quietly asked if I was okay.

"You smell like a horse." He grunts as he places me gently down on the ground and yanks his hands back to his sides. His reaction to touching me is not quite a match for the memory I just lost myself in. "Let's go."

I watch his broad back ripple beneath the fitted T-shirt as he walks stiffly toward the front door of the pub.

Obviously, he *really* needs a drink.

CHAPTER 11

Cole

Golddigger85: Do you live near your family?

I SHAKE MY HEAD AT MYSELF. THIS IS MY PATHETIC ATTEMPT AT making conversation. We've been talking for several months now, and I'm not oblivious to the fact that she's been carrying most of the conversation. To be frank, I'm not sure why she sticks around.

I give her almost nothing, and she keeps coming back. Most people have friends because they enjoy their company. I have this friend because knowing she deserves better reminds me how badly I'm failing. I'm a fucking masochist, and I can't even stop myself.

Every time she's chipper and sweet, I feel more like a shit bag. But I can't walk away from her. I live in the shadows, and she's like this ray of light that brightens my day. I'm so fucking greedy.

Pretty_in_Purple: No. I moved to get away from them.

I don't want to pry, but that sounds brutal. So I settle on:

Golddigger85: Oof.

Pretty_in_Purple: Haha. No. That sounds bad. I love my dad and brothers. And they love me too, just a little too fiercely. Like...smother me fiercely. And in a small town? Forget it. I couldn't put a foot wrong or stay out too late. Even dating was brutal. They were constantly meddling, even when I was old enough to handle myself. So I had to get outta there. Fresh start. Fresh me. Naked on the internet was a step for me. Tragic as that sounds. They would HIT THE ROOF. But I did it anyway. Once. I'm good now.

Golddigger85: You showed them.

Pretty_in_Purple: Something like that.

Golddigger85: What about your mom?

She takes a few moments to type even though I can see that she's seen the message.

Pretty_in_Purple: She died having me.

This is why I don't try to make conversation. The fuck am I supposed to say to that? My thumbs hover over my phone, and I feel my heart rate increase, pounding against my ribs. I know a thing or two about dead parents. I settle on the most cliché thing I can think of.

Golddigger85: I'm sorry.

Pretty_in_Purple: Ah. Don't be. People get all weird around me about it when the fact of the matter is I have no frame of reference for what I missed out on. I had a good childhood. I was well loved. I mean, I am well loved.

She's so forthcoming. So honest. I have the sudden urge to spill my dad's whole story. About that day. About watching it happen and about how my life was all downhill from that moment. It would feel so good to get that off my chest, to say the words that have solidified and gone stagnant there. Like when you don't quite swallow that pill, and it's just sort of lodged there in your throat.

But I don't.

Nobody wants to hear about my shit, and I don't want to scare her away.

This place is terrifying. I've seen some scary shit, but Neighbor's Pub might top that list. Who puts carpets in a pub? I watch my feet as I walk into the dim bar, and I swear I can feel them sticking slightly to the carpet with each step I take. I peek over my shoulder to make sure that Violet isn't entirely stuck to the flooring.

Instead of frowning at the interior, I see a small smile touching her lips as she looks around the place. With her silvery hair still in a big bird's nest and her petite body swallowed by an oversize cream sweater, she looks altogether too bright to be in such a dump. But based on the look on her face, she doesn't seem to agree.

"Where do you want to sit?" I ask her, eyeing the dark wooden tables suspiciously.

"Keep going. There's a table at the back beside a fireplace."

In a few more steps, the table—small and round with two mismatched captain's chairs and a tacky green and brown stained-glass light dangling over top of it—comes into view.

I huff out a laugh, disbelieving that I'm actually doing this. "Trixie would love this place."

"Who is Trixie?" Violet asks, coming to stand beside me.

"My therapist," I blurt out before I realize what I'm saying. *Motherfucker.* Since when do I overshare? What else am I liable to blurt out around Violet? I'm getting comfortable around her—which is a problem.

"Cute name. I like it," she says cheerily before charging ahead and grabbing the seat that faces the front door.

That's it? No questions or interrogation? I expected judgment about being in therapy. Instead, she makes an offhand comment and sits down. Right in the seat I prefer. My PTSD is mostly under control these days; it's the image of a lump on the track and hooves pounding past it that keeps me up at night now. It's taken years of hard work, but my deployments don't haunt me like they used to. I still like to assess the room though, see my way out, know if there are threats looming. I hate the idea of having my back to the room, the danger it could put me in. The danger it could put Violet in. I know I'm not in Iraq anymore, but these are the things that stick with you. The training that sticks with you. You're never *just* a civilian again.

I sit down stiffly, feeling all wrong about what I'm doing but not wanting to reveal any more than I already have.

"How ya doin', hon?"

I startle when two plastic menus are tossed down on the table between Violet and me.

The waitress beams down at me, and I lean back in my chair, gripping the armrests, as I grind out, "I'll have a water."

Violet gives me a flat, unimpressed smile, a silent scolding for what I'm sure she sees as inappropriate behavior. Chastising I don't need or want—which is why I prefer to spend my time alone. Less explaining. Fewer expectations to fall short of.

Her look brightens as she smiles up at the waitress. "I'll take a Guinness, please." Her eyes dart over to me briefly before adding, "And thank you. Never mind my friend's manners."

"Sure thing!" The girl darts away, and I glance over my shoulder to watch her head back to the bar and get our drinks.

"A Guinness?" I ask Violet. I expected her to order a margarita or at least something that came with an umbrella in it. Not a thick dark beer.

"Yup." Her eyes dance with amusement. "Not what you would have guessed?"

I check over my shoulder and reply absently. "No."

"I grew up on a ranch with a single dad and three older brothers. Once I could drink, beer and whiskey were the only options in the house."

One side of my lips tips up. "You don't strike me as a whiskey girl."

Violet smiles shyly. "You might be surprised then."

I look back up at the bar, wanting to make sure I'm not startled by the waitress again. I can feel my pulse jumping in my wrist—I can see it even.

"Want to switch seats?" Violet leans across the table. She asks so quietly that I almost don't hear her.

"What?"

She pushes her chair out and stands. "Switch seats."

I want to say it's fine, but the truth is I'm utterly relieved by the prospect. Now she's standing beside me, looking down and waving her hand like she's shooing me out of my seat. So I go and don't ask questions. I just let myself accept the way I'm feeling rather than beating myself up about it. Trixie would approve.

"Better?" she asks as we both settle into our new chairs.

I look away like it's no big deal. It is. Not a single person in my life has ever picked up on anything like this before. On my nervousness around adjusting to civilian life. On how I avoid pieces of garbage on the ground, just in case. My refusal to let anyone else drive. I liked to think I didn't have post-traumatic stress disorder. Instead, I would say the military trained me to be ultracautious. Trixie didn't agree.

"Yep." I look away, feeling a little…I don't know. Vulnerable maybe?

"My brother is a veteran, you know."

"Really? I didn't know that."

She winks playfully, but her tone isn't a match. "You never asked."

That blow lands. She's right. I asked almost nothing about her personal life in the year we spent corresponding. It started out that I didn't care to know. And then it turned into me knowing that if I asked, I would care. But I cared anyway. I kept telling myself that people don't fall in love on the internet. They don't develop *real* feelings. But looking at her now, I feel sure that what I'm feeling is pretty damn real. And it's also a pretty damn terrible idea.

"Do you know Billie calls you G.I. Joe?" she blurts out, obviously trying to fill the space.

I can't help but laugh at that. A low, deep rumble that feels warm and unfamiliar in my chest. Billie is a funny duck, and her ranting has come to seem endearing to me. "I can totally envision her calling me that."

Violet laughs, her eyes all wide and shocked looking.

"What?"

"You…you just laughed. I don't think I've ever heard you laugh."

My head quirks as I lean in a bit. "I laugh."

Violet crosses her arms and leans closer across the small table. "Did it hurt?"

My lips twitch. But I don't want to give her the satisfaction of making me laugh again. Mostly, I want to thank her for ditching the veteran talk. For not looking at me with pity. For just throwing me a fucking bone without starting the Spanish Inquisition into my past.

But I don't. I shake my head instead.

"Get a drink." Her eyes are twinkling now.

"Beer is fattening."

Violet busts out the most unladylike snort. I had no idea someone so small and dainty could honk like this. And then her face is flaming as she slaps both palms over her mouth and dissolves into a fit of giggles.

I stare back at her, trying to look unimpressed, even though her amusement is contagious. Even though she's so fucking beautiful that it hurts.

"I think your abs will survive to see another day," she gasps from behind her hands. And then she clamps them down harder over her mouth, and her eyes bulge out of her head, like she can't quite believe she just blurted that out. She looks *mortified.*

And I can't help it. I laugh. A genuine laugh. It erupts from me like an animal that's been caged up for too long. Like a racehorse shooting out of the gate.

I watch her face transform from embarrassment to pure glee. The look on her face? It heats me from my core. Like a spark on dry grass that sends flames dancing across arid land. Fast and out of control. After all, wildfires are dangerous.

The waitress finally makes her way back over. You'd swear this place was packed, and she had to collect my water out of Ruby Creek itself. She slides Violet her dark frothy beer just as Violet quirks one eyebrow at me.

"I'll..." Ugh. Am I about to get roped into this? "I'll have one of what she's having."

I'll work out twice tomorrow.

I barely feel the waitress's hand land on my shoulder.

Unsolicited touching is something that would normally annoy me, but right now, looking at the woman across from me, I hardly even notice. I vaguely hear her say, "No problem, hon."

Violet presses her lips together so hard it must hurt, except she doesn't look in pain. She looks like she's going to break right open and beam at me and is trying not to. She looks like she did that day after she won the Denman Derby qualifier. *Happy*. And for once, I don't want to ruin it. For once, I don't want to lie down and bask in my own shit.

Right now? I want to enjoy it.

But not *too* much.

"What? The water in this town is poison. Have you smelled it?"

Violet nibbles on her bottom lip and shakes her head at me.

"I'm only having one."

She nods.

"*What?*"

"A girl could throw her panties right in your face, and you wouldn't pick up on it, would you?"

I rear back. Why would a girl throw her panties in my face?

She takes a small sip of her beer, smiling knowingly into the creamy top of it as she does. "Our waitress. She's into you. Didn't you notice?"

My eyes shoot up over Violet's head to look back at the bar, and—sure enough—the girl is staring straight back at me as the bartender places my Guinness on her tray. I didn't notice because my mind has been fixated on the same girl for two damn years.

I roll my shoulders back and sit up taller, feeling a little less comfortable. “I don’t think so.” Eyes on me, even appreciative ones, have a way of making me squirm. I’m terrified that if someone looks too close, they’ll see what I’m hiding. *You’re half the man you were when you left.* That’s what Hilary said to me that night. That’s the sentence that’s stuck with me, that’s made me want to hide myself away.

But when the girl comes back to drop my beer off, she winks at me and taps my hand lightly before departing. And I almost can’t believe it myself. “Women are never into me,” I grumble as I look down at the carpet.

Violet leans back in her chair with her eyebrows pinched together and points at me. “She is.”

“No chance. I’m too old.”

She snorts. “You’re not.”

I finally look up and shrug. “I have to be at least ten years older than her.”

“You’re ten years older than me.”

“And?” I take a sip of the malty black beer and sigh inwardly. It tastes so fucking good. I can’t remember the last time I let myself enjoy a beer without worrying about taking optimal care of my body.

“It didn’t seem to bother you with me.”

I freeze, placing the pint glass back down. I don’t have that much experience with navigating women and their feelings, but I know a field full of land mines when I see one.

“That was—”

She cuts me off before I can finish what I wanted to say to her, waving me off with her hand. "Don't worry about it. How's work going?"

Work. I can talk about work.

"It sucks. We bought a company full of fucking idiots."

"You're a regular ray of sunshine, you know that? I think your swearing might be worse than Billie's." She pulls her good leg up onto her chair, resting her socked foot on the edge and bending her knee. Looking supremely comfortable—a way that most people don't look in my presence.

I groan and scrub at my stubble before taking a long pull of my drink. "People swear in the military, Violet. This is why Vaughn is the happy shiny face of the family company." I spin my glass in my hands. "And the new company? It's just disorganized. Financials are a mess. Safety standards are fucking terrifying. Nobody knows what they're doing. Basically, there's a reason we got a rock-bottom deal on the place."

She shrugs. "I'm sure you'll turn it around."

My cheek twitches at that. "How can you possibly be sure of that?"

"I don't know. You just don't strike me as a quitter."

I grunt, mind racing with what she could mean by that statement. How much does she know? Maybe she saw my last messages? The ones I tried to delete, but the damn app wouldn't let me. The ones I sent when I realized she wasn't coming back. That I'd fucked up beyond repair. I wanted to be mad at Pretty_in_Purple for ghosting me, but when it came down to it, I couldn't blame her.

I'd leave me too.

I clear my throat, not wanting to go down that rabbit hole during what has otherwise been a surprisingly enjoyable outing. I also don't want to think about the bouquet on the kitchen counter. About some shmuck bringing them to her, doing nice things for her, when I've done nothing but be growly and awkward in her presence. I see red at the prospect. The truth is I don't know how to act around Violet, how to handle the feelings she pulls up in me. Feelings that make my dick twitch and my possessive side rear its ugly head.

So I change the conversation to work. The number one conversation boner killer next to the weather. "How about you? What's the plan for everyone's favorite jockey?"

Violet looks around the room in response, and I wonder if maybe she didn't hear me. I'm pretty sure the country music playing isn't *that* loud.

"I don't know." Her tongue darts out, wetting her bottom lip as she looks back at me. Her entire body heaves with the weight of her sigh. "I'm kinda pissed off, you know? Last season was like a dream come true. Like I just fumbled my way into this once-in-a-lifetime situation. Billie. DD. Hank. Just the whole thing was so...*perfect*."

I nod, remembering a time when my life felt the same. The perfect family. The perfect girlfriend—according to everyone else. My future set in stone and paved in gold. And then my dad died, and everything went to shit. I let it.

"But I still feel like I need to prove myself. The other jockeys..." She gestures down at her leg. "They obviously don't like me. I waltzed into those wins. I didn't earn them. I *want* to earn it. I don't want to be coddled and set up for success. I've had that my entire life. I want to struggle and come out better on the other side. You know? I want to prove that I can overcome and still be the best. And only for myself. I need to know that I can do it. My success so far just feels..." Her face squishes up, and her eyes go distant as she searches for the word. "Incomplete. And now I'll be behind. I'll have lost fitness, hours in the tack." Her shoulders droop, and she looks down into her beer like she'd like to drown herself in it.

"I can help you work out."

Her head flicks up. "Really?"

"Sure." That's an offer I shouldn't make, but I can't stand seeing her look so downtrodden over an asshole like Patrick Cassel. "There's lots you can do that doesn't include using your leg."

She blinks rapidly at me, as if she thinks I might be some sort of illusion. And to be frank, I can't quite believe myself either.

"Okay," she breathes.

"Patrick is going to pay for that move he pulled."

Violet rolls her eyes. "That's what Billie keeps telling me. It's under review right now. But who cares? He's out there riding, and I'm here. Doing"—she waves a hand over the table—"this."

My mouth quirks up in response, the odd smile feeling more natural every time I do it. I double tap the table with my fingers as I lean back with my pint in hand and shrug. "This isn't so bad."

★★★

It's dark out and pouring rain by the time we leave Neighbor's Pub.

"Wait here," I say to Violet as I duck and run to the truck.

No point in both of us getting soaked. I jump in, turn the key, and hear it roar to life as I immediately drive to the front door to pick up a very confused-looking Violet.

She pulls herself in awkwardly and wipes away a drop of rain from the tip of her nose. "You didn't have to do that."

I shrug, pulling away from the bar. "I know." But I'm in a good mood, and I wanted to. I'm internally shocked I had a great time tonight. I even ate chicken wings in that questionable establishment. They might be the death of me, but I must admit they tasted pretty good. I hardly go out anymore. I mean, nobody asks me, but I don't welcome the invites either.

My mom drags me out for coffee now and then, which always strikes me as a way to soothe her guilty conscience rather than to spend time with me. I let her do it anyway. Vaughn got pimped out on her dream dates with country club girls, and I got awkward coffee dates with Mom. As far as I'm concerned, I got the better end of that deal.

She went off the rails when Dad died, lost herself in the bottom of a martini glass for a while—or so I hear. Something she hasn't forgiven herself for, obviously. I wasn't here for that part. As soon as I could, I put a ring on my girlfriend's finger—because that seemed like the right thing to do—and then enlisted. I joined the army and got the fuck out of Dodge. I stayed in for twelve years and kept myself safe and unscathed until the last month of that final tour.

Then an already numb existence went blank. Flatlined. But tonight, I've felt the odd blip of a beating heart, like maybe I'm not entirely down for the count after all.

"Thanks," Violet says quietly. "That was fun."

"It was."

Her smile is shy as her focus moves away into the distance. I wonder who else gets to soak up those smiles when I'm not around, and it makes me irrationally jealous. Enough so that I say, "Nice flowers you got today."

The moment the words leave my mouth, I hate myself for even saying them. I shouldn't care if some guy is bringing her flowers. And I definitely have no right to be jealous about it. But I'd be lying if I said it hasn't been niggling at me all evening.

Her lips roll together like she's trying to clamp down on an even bigger smile. "Yup. Hank is a sweetheart."

"Hank?" Now I officially look like a psycho. The longest-standing friend of our family brought her flowers, and I'm acting like a possessive tool about it.

"Mm-hmm" is all she says. But I can hear the trace of humor in her voice. Like she sees my comment for exactly what it is.

My fingers flex on the steering wheel, and we fall into an awkward silence. Where conversation flowed pretty easily in the dingy little pub surrounded by the hum of local regulars in for their daily happy hour and the twangy music playing through the cheap speakers, it feels more strained in the quiet of my truck. Like there's too much left unsaid between us. It's too intimate. Too dark.

Too much.

I nod and retreat into the silence as we travel down the dark side roads back toward the ranch. When we pull up to the house, I shoot Violet a look that garners me an eye roll. But she doesn't move to jump out of the tall truck on her own.

The minute my door slams, the brown horse whinnies loudly to me from her gate, looking like a drowned rat. A happy drowned rat with her ears all flicked forward.

I ignore it and jog around the front of the truck, yanking the passenger-side door open to get Violet out before I get totally drenched. The rain beats steadily across my shoulders as I look down at her in the dimly lit cab. Each drop feels like a pinprick on my skin as she looks up at me without turning her body. She hesitates, like she doesn't quite want to face me. Her blue eyes darken somehow in the low light, going almost indigo, and her hair looks more golden in its shimmer. I watch as her tongue darts out across the seam of her shapely lips.

We stand in limbo, her in the dry warmth of the truck, me out in the rain drinking her in like I've been stuck in the desert, parched.

My body pulses in time with my heart as she spins herself toward me slowly, one hand on the handle and the other on the edge of the seat, lifting the cast gingerly. I run a hand over the top of her injured leg to hook my palm behind her knee and pull her closer. She shivers, like she's cold, so I slide my eyes back up to her face. "Are you—"

She cuts me off this time. "Thank you again for tonight. I know you don't like me. But I still had a good time with you."

My chest fills with heavy air and self-loathing as I step in and feel my knees bump against the truck, my waist centered between her slender thighs. My fingers lock onto the back of her knee as I ask, "Why would you think I don't like you?"

Violet looks over toward the horse, avoiding my eyes, stammering as she does. "I…I…" Her sigh is a harsh emptying of her lungs through that distracting heart-shaped mouth. "Because I ghosted you? Because I'm in your house? Your life? I'm not stupid—I know I'm invading your space. I know you like your privacy. I'm an inconvenience. I can tell you don't like me. And you know, really, that's my issue. It's not my problem if people don't like me. Not really. But it bugs me, you know?"

I almost want to laugh at the absurdity of the statement. She thinks I don't like her? *If she only knew* is what runs through my head as I lean in closer.

CHAPTER 12

Violet

Pretty_in_Purple: Cats or dogs?

These are the questions I've resorted to asking to keep Golddigger engaged. I can't figure him out. Some days, he seems talkative, and other days, he's quiet and withdrawn. On those days, I usually let him be and then wake up to a message from him the following morning.

But tonight, I've cracked a bottle of wine by myself, and I want someone to talk to. The ranch has been launched into turmoil, and they finally hired a new trainer. And she's awesome. I tried to play it cool around her, but I'm pretty sure I just got all quiet and weird.

Either way, I'm excited. Because my days just got a lot less lonely.

My phone dings, and I snatch it up.

Golddigger85: Pussy.

My cheeks flare. Now and then, he throws out something super sexual. Something that makes me squeeze my thighs together and wish we were more than just avatars to each other. I wonder what his voice sounds like. What his mannerisms are. Does he have an accent? I wonder what color his eyes are. Does he do this with other girls every day too?

That last one makes my chest pinch uncomfortably.

I spend a lot of time imagining the details of Golddigger's appearance, trying to piece him together with the few puzzle pieces he occasionally drops. Mostly, I imagine his muscles.

Every man I've been with has been lanky and boyish, but based on that one photo of him, that's not the case here. I've had nice boyfriends. I've had nice sex.

But I'm tired of nice. What I really want is for someone to manhandle me. Cross that consuming type of lust off my bucket list.

Pretty_in_Purple: Huh. Never would have guessed. How many of those do you have on the go?

Golddigger85: One. I'm a solo pussy kind of man.

Pretty_in_Purple: Oh really? What's her name?

Golddigger85: Not sure. All I know is that she looks good in purple.

Pretty_in_Purple: Okay. Sorry. Innuendos aside. Are you meaning to tell me I'm the only girl you chat with on here?

Golddigger85: Yes.

Pretty_in_Purple: Why?

Golddigger85: Because talking to you uses up all my free time.

I read that sentence over and over again. Coming from anyone else, it wouldn't sound sweet. But coming from him, well, I can't help but smile and stifle a laugh on a sip of wine.

Golddigger likes me.

He leans in closer and glares at me, big fat raindrops rolling down his masculine face. His gray eyes bore into me from underneath thick lashes and then skim down to my mouth. He looks mad, like every muscle in his body is held taut. Like a predator coiled and ready to strike. But I haven't been afraid of him before, and I won't start now.

I keep rambling to fill the space. "Don't worry about it. Billie has talked to me about this too. Not everyone is going to like me, and that's *fine*." I edge forward to turn myself so he can lift me down the way he has in the past. The way he demands. But his hand pulses on my leg before lifting it higher and dragging me toward him. And I don't resist. We're like two opposite ends of a magnet, naturally drawn to each other.

His waist takes up all the space between my thighs. I almost lose my balance or swoon—I'm not totally sure which—but I let go of the handle above me to catch myself, my palm landing in the middle of his hard chest to brace against him.

His opposite hand shoots forward and captures my chin, the pad of his thumb pressing gently on the cleft there. The intense gray eyes scouring my face freeze me in place. He's so close I can feel his breath fanning down across my throat. His cologne wraps around me like a comfort blanket, all spice and cinnamon and warmth.

"You are not an inconvenience." His voice is rough, low, a growl. "Anyone who doesn't like you is an idiot. Do you understand me?"

I nod, feeling a bit breathless at his nearness. At his words. The way he overwhelms me. The way he's holding my thigh.

My fingers grasp at the fabric of his T-shirt, not wanting him to pull away. Wanting him closer. Even after everything.

I angle my face up at him, watching the shadows play across his features. The glow of the headlights highlights all the prominent ridges and sharp lines. His jaw ticks as he stands frozen, staring me down. But somehow the meaning behind that glare has transformed. I'm not sure what it is, but it's different. The flicker of desire reflected from my own eyes, maybe. Because I would have to be a blind idiot to pretend I don't want Cole Harding. I've wanted him for years—before I knew what he looked like—when he was just a faceless avatar providing a lonely girl company. The friend I needed as I set out in the world. The hand giving my bike a push as I took off on my own for the first time.

"Okay," I whisper, blinking once to give my eyes a rest, even though I don't want to take a break from looking at him. And holy hell, am I glad I opened them back up in time because his stony gaze goes straight to molten lava as he lifts that thumb from my chin and rubs it across my slack lower lip almost possessively.

The rumble that breaks free of his chest is like a shot of electricity to my core. My entire body tingles, goose bumps and intense awareness shooting out through every limb. Emboldened by his touch, I reach up with my spare hand and run it across the scar that cuts through his thick brow. I trace the raised tissue and hear his sharp intake of air as I trail my fingers over the line, reveling in the feel of his skin under my fingers, of his hands on my body. The leg he has nearly wrapped around his waist. The way we're just *almost* lined up perfectly. The soft pattering of rain around us. It's like we're frozen in time, in this tiny bubble of curiosity. Because that's what I see on his face now.

And it makes me brave. I fist his shirt tightly between my fingers and yank him to me, wanting to feel the swell of him against my thin pants. I sigh when I do, right as he groans, right as he drags that thumb across my lip again.

Jesus. I like that.

I lift my good leg and wrap it around his other side, wanting him closer. Our heavy breaths mingle wordlessly between us in the cold, damp air. His eyes devour me, confusion written all over his face now. I don't even want to think about what's written on mine as he hikes my thigh up higher and presses himself against the apex of my thighs, making my eyes flutter drunkenly. Pure lust, I imagine.

I let my other leg trail down the back of his, rubbing against him right as he rocks against me. But then he freezes and steps back abruptly, holding me at arm's length, panting into the night air, his breath like steam rising between us.

I want to launch myself back at him. I want to beg him to keep going. But I know Cole isn't the type of man who bends. I know he's complicated. I know he has rules. Rules that he doesn't break.

"I'm sorry." His voice cracks as he sets me down gently and brings his trembling hands back down to his sides.

I'm sorry?

Everything that was hot goes cold. Cold with dread. I shake my head. I've been here before. This is so like him—so like *me*. To let myself get carried away where he's concerned. To think something is there when it's not.

I can't even look at him as I feel myself go bright red. I send up a silent *thank you* that it's dark out as I stare out at Pippy's paddock. And like she knows this moment needs to be broken up, she whinnies. Long and loud and shrill, like an alarm bell that makes us both jump.

"Can I take your truck for a minute?"

Cole shakes his head as if to clear it, trying to keep up. "What for?"

"I need to run up to the barn and get her a rain sheet. She's getting soaked. No blanket. She doesn't even have a shelter in there."

He steps back quickly, putting space between us as he looks over at the little filly. "Horses have survived for years without waterproof coats."

Frustration surges up in me, fueled by our interaction. Fueled by my embarrassment. I can't be this close to him right now. "Can you just throw me a fucking bone and not tell me what to do?"

Now it's his turn to stare back at me wide-eyed. Dropping an f-bomb always does that to people. When you don't use the word much, it certainly packs a different punch.

He holds his keys out, looking adequately chastised and more than a little shocked. *Good.* I swipe them and walk away to the other side of the truck, leaving a motionless Cole behind me.

"Drive carefully, please." His voice is all gravel with a pleading tone to it.

I snort and continue to the driver's side. At least he knows better than to get in my way. My legs propel me, even though my head is spinning. It's like that night at Billie's. I just need to get away. And my new horse needs a blanket. I start the truck and pull out of the driveway, only sparing Cole a glance as I drive past where he's still standing like a statue in the rain. He looks shocked, and I don't care.

I need some fucking space.

Bang. Bang. Bang.

I peel my eyes open and look at my clock. It looks bright out. Ten a.m. I never sleep this long. But then, I hid out at the barn for a while, trying to get my bearings before coming back to the house and hanging with Pippy, who is now privy to some of my deepest, darkest secrets, including the fact that Cole still gets under my skin.

Once I tracked down a small enough rain sheet, I drove

back to the farmhouse. With my left foot. It was a short, slow drive, and my left foot worked fine, though it's definitely not something I plan to make a habit of. Sitting on top of the fence in the rain, I stayed with Pippy until I was soaked and cold to the bone. She rested her chin on my lap, like the dog she obviously thinks she is, and let me braid her forelock. The best company I could ask for as I grappled with whatever the hell happened between Cole and me in the rain last night.

I genuinely thought he didn't like me. And I assumed the attraction was one-sided. But the rock-hard bulge in his pants that he pressed against me told another story. I just couldn't reconcile the cool, removed man I know with the person he was last night. None of it makes sense. Laughing, the odd reluctant tip of the lips, and then the way his hands gripped my body. The way I melted for him.

Bang. Bang. Bang.

The noise finally registers. Is that the door? I roll out of bed and strap the walking cast on my leg. I almost feel like I don't need it anymore. The pain is gone, as is most of the swelling, and only the yellow remnants of the bruising remain. After grabbing my robe from the back of the door as I head out into the main living space, I move toward the front door, hoping I don't run into Cole on my way.

When I yank it open a crack, because I don't feel like I'm appropriately dressed to be answering the door, I'm met with Billie standing on the front porch with her palms cupping her eyes like blinders.

"What are you doing?"

"Open the door, Porn Star Patty."

"Ugh." I groan and tip my head back. "It was one picture. One time!"

She pushes the door and shoves herself through frantically, almost tripping in the process. "Holy shit. Let me in already. And close the door!"

"What's going on?" I'm so confused.

"I'm trying not to check out my future brother-in-law. You're going to need to put up some sort of neon sign on the driveway if he's going to waltz around shirtless like that. Smoke signals would be effective too."

Wait. What? It's my turn to almost trip pushing past her, but I'm going in the opposite direction—back out the door. And holy *hell*. She's not joking. I swallow hard and feel my mouth go dry.

Cole is just outside Pippy's paddock, unloading lumber and setting up sawhorses, and he is gloriously shirtless. His body ripples in the bright sunlight. No rain today; instead, it feels hot, damp, and muggy. Apparently, Cole is a "sun's out, guns out" kind of guy. And irritated as I am with myself for last night, I'm not about to complain.

"Like…couldn't he just put some shorts on and call it a day? A glass of cold water does wonders to cool a person down."

I look over my shoulder to see Billie leaning against the wide-open doorway. "I thought you weren't looking."

"I'm engaged to the love of my life, not blind."

I laugh. That's so Billie. Turning away from the mouth-watering masterpiece on the front lawn, I usher her back into the house.

"What do you think he's doing out there?" she inquires, now moving to watch out the front window.

I roll my eyes as I head to the kitchen. "You're such a perv, B."

"I know." Her eyebrows waggle as she walks to the kitchen island and starts making coffee like she lives here too. "Go get dressed. I'll make some coffee. I don't know what kind of internet-sex-nudist commune you two are starting, but I'm not here for it."

I look down at myself. "I'm wearing a robe."

"What's underneath?" she asks before she hits the coffee grinder, effectively cutting me off.

Okay. She has a point. I turn and walk to my room. Cutoffs and a T-shirt so old and broken in that it's almost see-through are my picks. Perfect for a lazy Sunday. All I have planned today is spoiling Pippy and practicing some basic groundwork with her.

By the time I've brushed my hair and teeth and twisted my hair up into a bun, Billie has a cup of coffee ready for me on the counter.

"Okay." I slide up onto a stool and wrap my hands around the old clay-work mug. "Why are you here banging on my door and absolutely not checking out your fiancé's brother?"

Before she can answer, the front door swings open again. "Can we have our coffee on the front porch?" Mira, our veterinarian and the other member of the girl squad, waltzes in like she owns the place.

"We just came to visit our favorite little Por—"

"Billie," I warn, widening my eyes at her and knowing exactly which new nickname she's going for. Not that I wouldn't tell Mira. I mean, she probably would have been a better choice to confide in anyway. Cool and collected, the woman is almost impossible to get a read on. It took me a while to figure out that she's actually nice. It's just hard to tell with Mira. She keeps her cards close. So yeah, I should have told her instead.

"Oh, Vi. You should see the pictures I send Vaughn."

I clamp my eyes shut and let out a dramatic sob. "Billie!"

Mira, all shiny black hair and intelligent almond-shaped eyes with a smirk on her face, raises one shapely brow without inquiring and pours herself a cup of coffee before changing the subject completely. "How's Pipsqueak, Vi?"

I sigh, and I'm sure hearts pop up in my eyes. "So good. The best. Exactly what I needed." I shoot my gaze up to Billie and quietly add, "Thank you."

Her hand lands on my shoulder, and she gives it a firm squeeze. "Don't mention it." Billie seems like she's joking around all the time, but you'd be a fool to underestimate the size of her heart. She knew exactly what she was doing when she trailered that filly over here for me.

"When you get her going, let me come check her out a couple of times. Just make sure she's doing all right. No soreness or breathing issues."

I nod and sip my coffee, watching Mira meander over to the front window again.

"Come to the races tonight. You need to get out. Leave the farm. See some humans, not just the cyborg you live with."

"He's not so bad," I snap, a little more defensively than I intended.

Billie rears back a little, letting the corners of her lips tip up as she silently mouths *Okay* before adding, "That's good, because you'll have to catch a ride with him. Mira and I are heading down there for the early races right after this little visit."

I glance down at my coffee cup, trying to hide the pink stain I feel spreading across my cheeks. I hate how easily I blush; it's so blatant. I can't pull a fast one on anybody because I blush like a teenager at the drop of a hat.

"I think he's..."

I look over at Mira's form as her head tips to one side.

"Building your horse a shelter?"

"What?" I almost shout. "No chance." But I also don't want to go look. If she's right, it will confuse me even more about where I stand with Cole Harding.

Billie hustles over to the window, peering out beside Mira. They look like two snoopy old women watching the hot pool boy.

"He is! He's right in the paddock. Vi, come look."

All my joints lock up as I try to wrap my head around what they're saying. There's just no way. Cole hates horses. He wouldn't do that for Pippy. He couldn't even understand why I wanted to get her a blanket last night. Why would he go get wood and spend his spare time building her a shelter?

"Oh. He sees us."

"How can you tell?" Mira asks, neither of them looking away. No shame.

"See?" Billie points out the window. "He's scowling at us."

"Huh. I wasn't looking at his face, I guess." Mira waves at him, like this is perfectly normal.

I groan. "You guys. Time to go. Out!" I march over to the front door and swing it open.

They don't argue; Billie cackles, and Mira winks at me knowingly. *Mothereffer.* They're both totally onto me.

"See you tonight?" Billie asks as she pulls me into a bear hug.

"Yeah, yeah. I'll be there," I reply as they file out like little kids in trouble.

Billie keeps her head down as she heads back to her truck, but Mira gives Cole a long and thorough once-over before grinning at me over her shoulder and giving me a discreet thumbs-up.

I roll my eyes and blush all at once.

As they both pull out, I finally spare Cole a glance from where I stand on the front porch and feel my heart stutter as I watch him duck between the fence posts with a drill in his hand. He's like every construction worker porno I've ever watched rolled into the perfect package. And the fact that Pippy is following him around happily is just the cherry on top. When he stops to look down at the setting on the drill, the little filly wraps her neck around his side and sniffs the tool.

He gives her an absent scratch under her chin, and I almost implode. Hot guy with a horse? It doesn't get better. He walks over to the boards, and she follows on his heels, observing, like she might learn how to make a shelter if she focuses.

"What're you doing, girl?" he grumbles as he reaches down, and I can't help the quiet swooning sound that bursts out of my throat.

Not quiet enough though. Because Pippy hears.

Her head shoots up, and she bobs her head in my direction with an ear-piercing whinny. *Little traitor.* Her signature hello just threw me right under the bus because Cole stands up, looks over his brawny shoulder, and pins me with those gray eyes.

"Hi!" I shout a little too brightly, not knowing what the normal thing to do here is. I've had the odd relationship over the years. More since leaving my overbearing dad and brothers behind, but nothing with the intensity of whatever this is. Whatever last night was. Nothing where I feel like a mere look from the man might make me burst into flames.

"Hey," he says a little cautiously.

My inclination is to run and hide back inside the house. But that's not the new me; that's not how adults handle this kind of situation. *Fake it till I make it.*

I force myself to walk toward him and try even harder to keep my eyes from roaming his body. I mean *seriously.* The guy is ripped, so it's hard not to stare. I guess that's what working out multiple times a day gets you.

When I get to the fence, I rest my arms against it. "What are you doing?"

One hand on his hip, he holds the drill up to me like I've just asked the most obvious question in the world. "Building a shelter."

My brow wrinkles as I hear him confirm what Billie and Mira guessed. "I thought you hated horses?"

"I don't hate horses."

Pippy snorts and bats her eyelashes at him. Another one down, apparently.

"Okay. You said you don't *like* horses."

"Yup." He grunts as he turns his back on me and crouches down to line up two boards. "But I like you."

And then he silently gets to work while I stand there watching him. Dumbstruck.

CHAPTER 13

Violet

Golddigger85: Like a full-blown cattle ranch? You're a farm girl?

I'm lying on my bed, in pajamas, chatting. As usual. I just told Butterface that I grew up on an honest-to-God ranch, and he seems horrified.

Pretty_in_Purple: Cowboys, lassos, and rodeo, baby.
Golddigger85: What about whips?
Pretty_in_Purple: More of a spurs and chaps kinda gal.
Golddigger85: Jesus. You should be careful talking like that.

My cheek twitches. If he can say suggestive things, I don't see why I can't do the same.

Pretty_in_Purple: Why is that?

Golddigger85: I have a vivid imagination.

I nibble at my lip and consider my next move. He's in a good mood. I think he's even flirting with me. It makes my chest feel all fluttery.

I laugh and look up at the ceiling. Sad, Violet. I've got that new-love-interest, giddy feeling over a stranger on the internet. I'm too old for this. I know better.

Pretty_in_Purple: Tell me more.

Oh god. I shouldn't have said that. I roll up onto my knees and stare down at my phone screen like I'm waiting for big news when really, I'm just watching those dots roll across the screen as he types. I wonder if he's lying on his bed doing the same thing as me.

Golddigger85: Turn on your camera, and I'll tell you in detail.

Jesus. My finger hovers over that little video camera icon. What would it be like to just throw caution to the wind and do it? Could I handle it? I don't know anymore.

Pretty_in_Purple: No chance, Butterface.

My response sounds resolute. But I'm feeling anything but. I'm confused. Tempted. Horny. Instead of giving in, I pull my favorite toy out of my bedside table and pretend I said yes.

★★★

I look around the expansive owner's lounge at Bell Point Park. As a farm girl from Alberta turned groom turned brand-new jockey, this isn't somewhere I've been privy to until now. Usually, I'm covered in horse manure and sweat down in the stables. And to be honest, I think I prefer that.

I put on my nicest dress, and I still feel like I'm out of place. One ballet flat, one walking cast, and a pretty, flowy floral dress that's perfect for a hot day and maybe less so for the amount of icy air-conditioning pumping into this room.

"Here." Cole comes to stand beside me by the tall windows and holds out a drink with an umbrella in it. I don't miss the way his cheek twitches when I look up at him.

Now we're joking around? Cole Harding gives me whiplash. Cold and agitated. Hot and handsy. Friendly and joking. How many versions are there? And why do I like them all?

"Cheers," I say with a small chuckle as I take the drink and clink it against his glass of water.

I have no clue where we stand right now. I spent all afternoon grooming Pippy in the sun. Practicing picking up her feet. Throwing brushes over her back so she gets used to seeing something out of the corner of her eye when I eventually swing a leg over instead. It's probably time for me to get some tack down at the house so I can mess around with trying the saddle and bridle on her. Because she is downright unflappable. Everything is just a fun game for her. Nothing startles her. Even Cole, drilling and hammering away on her shiny new shelter all day, didn't bother her.

In fact, she often went over there to check out her new digs and to give his elbow a little nuzzle. And I pretended not to see when he'd swipe a wide gentle palm over her forehead.

Doesn't like horses, *my ass*.

I have yet to meet a better judge of character than a horse, and Pippy wouldn't be hanging around him if he gave off that vibe. As much as I hate to admit it, she might even like him more than me.

Or maybe he just needs her more than I do.

A thought that makes my chest ache.

"Do you usually watch from up here?" I ask, trying to make conversation and fill the awkward void between us.

I sneak a look up at him. The bump of his Adam's apple bobs in his throat as he opens his mouth to answer me without returning eye contact.

"I don't—"

And then I see a perfectly manicured hand slide over the shoulder of his suit jacket.

"Cole." A woman's light feminine voice comes from the opposite side of him as she pulls into view, standing just a little too close to be a passing acquaintance. She's petite, like me, but that's where our similarities end. She's dripping in expensive jewelry, and her perfectly painted red lips are a match for her sleek hair. "Long time no see."

Cole shifts toward her, essentially blocking me out of the conversation by covering my body protectively with the bulk of his. "Hilary."

I can tell by the way he's holding himself—shoulders rolled back, neck held high, chin tipped up proudly—that all traces of the humor from before have dried up almost instantly in this woman's presence. Over the past few weeks, I've been privy to what Cole looks like happy and relaxed.

And this ain't it.

His knuckles are white around the glass in his hand, and I see his opposite one clenched into a fist at his side. His tells may not be as blatant as my flaming face or bulging eyes, but this is what Cole looks like when he needs rescuing. I can see that he's struggling, and suddenly I'm feeling very protective of him. I put my drink down on the table beside us as I step around his broad frame. My hand slides over his fist, and I push my fingers between his tense ones. They both look down at me, equally surprised by my appearance. But where Hilary looks irritated, I feel Cole's hand soften in my own and hear the breath that rushes out between his lips in relief.

"Hi. I'm Violet."

She stretches one hand toward me politely with a fake smile plastered on her face. "Violet. I've never heard of you before. But what a pretty name. I'm Hilary."

I almost snort, because I've spent enough time around my brother's past girlfriends to know fake nice when I see it. To know words laced with venom when I hear them. Hilary isn't fooling anyone with her polite act, and I know she's not fooling Cole by the way his hand pulses around mine.

I return her false tittering laugh with one of my own. "Well, that's too funny because I've heard *so* much about you!" I haven't, but my guess works.

Her face clamps down almost instantly as her eyes shoot up to Cole, seeking some sort of invite to stay but not finding any. "Well, it was nice seeing you again. It's been too long."

She rests her hand on his bicep, and I want to rip it off. White-hot jealousy shoots up my throat. Instant nausea. And instant self-loathing. I have absolutely *zero* claim to this man, yet here I am getting my panties in a twist over someone touching his arm with a familiarity I envy. *Pathetic.*

He nods sullenly as she turns and walks back across the room. We both watch her go, hand in hand, my gut churning with a deep sense of dread.

"I need some fresh air," I squeak as I set my sights on the door and dart away. Or as close to darting as I can muster with this damn walking cast. I'm so beyond ready to ditch this thing and get back to my life. My job. My focus. This hiatus is messing with my brain.

I sigh in relief as the stairs out of the godforsaken building come into sight. I need to be down on the ground with the dirt and the noises and the beer-drinking gamblers. I don't belong up there.

One more set of stairs comes into view as I round the corner. Except the exit is not clear. Far from it.

"Fancy meeting you here," Patrick Cassel drawls with a stupid, smug smile on his face.

I recoil but jut my chin out and keep walking, deciding the best way to handle a child is to ignore their attention-seeking behavior.

"Shame about the cast."

"Mm-hmm," I say, keeping my eyes peeled on the door

ahead, on the bright white sunshine pouring into the dark landing, shining like a beacon on where I can get away from both Cole and Patrick.

But then his arm shoots out in front of me as he grabs the railing at the base of the stairs to block my forward motion.

"Trying to leave so quickly?"

"Move your arm, Patrick." I glare back at his manicured features and too-thin lips made especially ugly by the snide look on his face.

"Most new girls on the scene would bend over backward to have my attention. Forward too." He winks, and my skin crawls.

I know that this kind of shit happens behind the scenes. The sex. The drugs. The drama. And it's part of why I prefer hiding out in Ruby Creek on the ranch. I don't want to be down at the track every day catching whatever ride I can with whatever trainer I can. I *like* my bubble.

"Move. Your. Arm."

"You might enjoy yourself, and I might give you a little more space the next time I pass you out there."

My throat goes hot with rage. It's one thing to think he cut me off on purpose, but to hear him confirm it is something else entirely.

But a dangerous voice takes over my train of thought from behind me. "Nobody enjoys fucking you, Patrick. Now move your arm before I remove it completely."

I turn my head to look over my shoulder and find Cole standing at the top of the stairs like some sort of dark avenging angel. He often looks grumpy, but right now, he looks downright deadly. All those years in the military have scored every hard line in the body that stands over us. He looks relaxed. *Too* relaxed. Like this is an easy default mode for him. And Patrick, idiot that he is, doesn't pick up on the danger at all.

He *laughs*. "Harding Senior. Nice to see ya, buddy."

I don't even spare Patrick a glance, mostly because I can't tear my eyes off Cole. He looks like he could tear the other jockey limb from limb, and I'm alarmingly turned on by the prospect. I know they know each other from some intertwined family business, and Cole had him ride DD at his debut race, which went poorly. I also know Cole is not looking back at Patrick like they're friends.

"We're not buddies," Cole bites out. "You're a slimy little fuck who I would love nothing more than to set straight. If you think that episode with the whip hurt, you have no clue what you're in for. What I'm trained to do."

Patrick, who is clearly missing some sort of survival instinct, scoffs at him. "Dude. You're not seriously worried about this barn brat, are you? Our little conversation is just part of how things run around here. There are loopholes to working your way up in the world. Violet just needs to learn them."

"Touch her, and I'll kill you." Cole's voice is downright arctic.

Patrick just smirks in the face of the threat. He steps right up to me and defiantly places his spare hand on my shoulder. Like I'm too simple to understand his implication—like it's perfectly normal to talk about another person like they aren't even there. Like touching a woman without her permission is acceptable.

From the corner of my eye, I see Cole spring into motion, but not before uncontrollable fury lances through me. My season is in the toilet thanks to this sleazebag, and the realization makes me snap. I do to Patrick exactly what I'd have done to one of my shithead brothers when they picked on me too much.

I knee him right between the legs. Hard. And then stand back to watch him double over in pain.

"Serves him right," Cole says from behind me, surprise lacing his tone.

His hand lands on my shoulder, but I shrug it off. I don't want anyone touching me right now. I feel angry and scared and like I just narrowly missed what could have been a very scary encounter.

"Are you okay?"

I press my shaking hand against my chest to feel my heart racing there, to feel my ribs heave as I struggle to catch my breath.

"Let me help you."

His voice is soft, but I don't want this side of him. I don't want to be coddled. Especially not by him. It makes me feel things I shouldn't. And Patrick? I want to get as far away from him as possible.

"I'm good." I take that final step onto the landing, striding around a groaning Patrick, desperate to get out that door and away from whatever that was.

The worst part is, deep down, I want Cole to follow me.

CHAPTER 14

Cole

I'm way too attached to Pretty_in_Purple. It's beyond my comprehension. A fucking internet pen pal. And I live for her messages.

Some nights, we type back and forth until I drift off with my phone in my hands. I wake up clinging to the device like it's a fucking lifeline. Maybe it is. Maybe she is.

Maybe that's why I check our chat first thing every morning, hoping she'll have written to me. Anything, even just an emoji from her, is enough to start my day off right.

I thought jerking off to girls on the internet made me pathetic. So what does getting attached to one make me? I only have that one photo of her saved. I should be tired of jacking off to it by now.

But I'm not.

And beyond that, I imagine meeting her in real life. I imagine holding her, whispering my deepest, darkest secrets into her ear and then feeling her arms wrap around me as I slide inside her.

It's gone beyond wanting to fuck her to... whatever that would be. I've gone so far as wondering if she's with someone in real life. So fucking pathetic. Of course she is! She's sweet and she's beautiful—what guy in his right mind wouldn't want that? But it doesn't stop me from sending a message asking her.

Golddigger85: Any lucky guys in your life these days?

She takes a long time to respond. It's the middle of the day. I know she's working. I'm supposed to be working too. But here I am, obsessing over a random internet girl. Agitation builds inside me, something I take out on a few low-level employees like a total dick. Like a kid who can't control his emotions.

When my phone finally pings a few hours later, a deep sigh surges out of me. I flop down in my leather office chair and lean back as I pull my phone out of my suit pocket.

Pretty_in_Purple: Only one.

My brows squeeze together, and my forearms go tight. I knew it.

Golddigger85: Does he know about me?

Pretty_in_Purple: I don't know. Does he?

I rear back as I do some mental gymnastics to figure out

what she's just implied. My chest puffs up a bit over a girl I've never met and never will.

Does she mean me?

I have no idea where Violet went. All I know is that I got a text saying she had a ride back to the farm. But she's still not here. So I'm just sitting on the porch step, nursing another tumbler of scotch, with the brown horse staring back at me like I owe her something. Attention, food, who knows. It's getting unnerving.

I can't believe I'm letting a fucking horse make me feel bad.

As if I don't already feel bad enough. I wanted to follow Violet when she took off, and I started out that way until I saw she was heading straight for the track—not for the stables. Then I pussied out.

The track is such a dichotomy for me. The place that holds all my best and worst memories. On one hand, I grew up there. My dad was a popular and successful jockey at Bell Point Park. We spent a lot of time there together. On the other hand, I watched him die on that track.

The booth up top is the perfect compromise. Trixie's idea—exposure therapy. A removed view, no sound of pounding hooves, no crackling loudspeaker, none of the triggers that take me straight back to that day. Never mind the war, *that* day is my tipping point.

I know Violet doesn't want anyone taking care of her, but goddammit, I wanted to. I wanted to grind Patrick to a pulp and then whisk Violet as far from him as possible. The sight of his hand on her shoulder made me see red.

I shake my head.

I almost combusted on the spot. I almost turned into the soldier that I haven't been in six years now.

Which is exactly why Violet is a weakness I can't afford. I've worked too hard to combat my outbursts and my down days, the ones where I can't even muster the energy to smile. Against all my best instincts, even when I know I'm nothing but a hot mess where she's concerned, I wanted to be there for her. To chase her down and fix things for her. Which is a terrible idea. Colossally stupid.

And exactly what she doesn't want.

I want to call Trixie, but it's too late to be doing that. I hang my head in my hands and mutter to myself, "Good work, Harding."

The horse nickers from across the driveway and bobs her head at me with a long blink of her thick lashes. I can't help but chuckle. She is relentless. No quit in that one. I leave the tumbler on the deck and walk across to the fence where the horse is waiting.

She's kind of hard not to like. Her ears prick forward at my approach, and her head rises just a little taller in excitement. I swear if she had the right kind of tail, she'd be wagging it.

"Hey, girl," I whisper, running my hand down her neck and feeling the heat of her exhale against my stomach as she nuzzles in.

She's the first horse I've touched since my dad died. I've barely allowed myself to admit this, but it feels good. Therapeutic maybe. The soft prickle of her coat under my fingers… I wonder if I'm having the same tactile experience that my dad might have had when he was still alive. If I'm feeling the same thing as he did once.

Her excited whinny every time I pull up to the house almost makes me smile, and the way she followed me around quietly while I worked out here earlier made me feel…I don't know. Worthy of attention.

Like maybe I could be likable after all.

I walk down to the corner of her paddock where there is a stack of square hay bales under a blue tarp, and she follows. Lifting a corner of the tarp, I pull a flake off the top bale and inhale the dusty, grassy smell as I carry it back over to her feeder.

The hay is all over my suit, but I don't care. Material shit hasn't mattered to me in years. I guess that's why I live in a small and dated condo in a four-story walk-up in Vancouver's West End neighborhood. It's a clean place to lay my head at night while I go through the motions of my day-to-day schedule. My days of feeding into my mother's elite lifestyle died along with my engagement to Hilary.

I'm leaning against the fence, listening to the horse's contented munching, lost in a memory, when lights turn down the driveway. I recognize Billie's truck, but it's too dark to see inside.

Violet jumps out and lands on one foot, obviously not wanting help to get out anymore after I dry humped the hell out of her last night.

I cringe internally at the memory. Thirty-six going on sixteen, apparently. Next thing I know, I'll be asking her to play just-the-tip.

Which is a terrible plan. Because like I told her, I like her—and I shouldn't. I like her as more than a friend, and that's all we can be. I haven't touched a woman in years, never mind had one touching me. I haven't let anyone get close enough. It feels insurmountable now. Pathetic as it sounds.

But after two weeks in the same house as Violet, it's all I can fucking think about.

"Hi," she says shyly as she walks over to me. "What are you doing out here?"

"Just feeding the horse."

Her head tilts imperceptibly. "I fed her before we left."

The brown horse's black globes for eyes flit up momentarily like she knows I'm a sucker for giving her more. Then she gets back to grinding her teeth and shoving the hay around. She looks happy, so who cares?

I just grunt and continue to stare at the little horse, expecting Violet to leave. Instead, she comes closer to the fence, a full post length away from me, and leans against it. I can feel her gaze on me, like hands roaming over my body—soft and searching.

I don't want to look back at her. To see that pale blond hair shining in the moonlight, those wide indigo eyes boring into me, so full of unasked questions. I don't want to think about Patrick's hands on her, the way he cornered her, the things he said to her. He deserved the extra twist I gave his arm, the threat I whispered in his ear before I headed back upstairs. He deserved a lot worse than that.

And Violet? She deserves a man better than me. More

honest than me. A hell of a lot more available than me. But the more time I spend around her, the less I care and the more I want.

"You sure you don't like horses?" Amusement infuses her tone.

I scoff and keep staring at the brown filly.

"Not even a liiiittle bit?" She holds her thumb and finger up with little distance between them.

My cheek twitches, and I sigh, feeling the tension in my shoulders drain out to nothing. "Okay. If I had to like a horse, it would be this one."

"Ha! I knew it."

I shake my head. She looks far too pleased with herself. I shouldn't give her any more ammunition to run with, so I clear my throat and change the subject. "Are you okay? I didn't know where you went."

The victorious smile on her face melts off, and now it's her turn to look away from me. "Yeah. Just needed some space. I don't know if you noticed," she chuckles sardonically, "but I don't really belong up in the skybox."

What? "Why not?" I ask, genuinely confused.

Her eyes roll as she continues to focus on the horse. "You saw me in there. I'm a different breed, Cole. I'm not a Hilary, and I don't want to be."

"Thank fuck for that," I mutter as I look down between my arms, which rest on the top of the fence. We stand in silence, so much still left unsaid. "I was engaged to Hilary. When I was younger."

Violet's body goes rigid as she turns her entire frame

toward me slowly. She says nothing, which I take as her giving me the opportunity to keep talking.

"We dated in high school. Our families ran in the same circles. It was...easy. It made sense to me. And then my dad died, and nothing made sense anymore."

I chance a look at Violet, who is standing stock-still, like I'm a wild animal she might spook if she moves or says anything. And it must work because my lips keep moving.

"I proposed, and she said yes. Everyone was happy. And then I enlisted, and everyone was distinctly *not* happy. But I didn't care. I needed to live in another world for a while. So I left. We'd write to each other and see each other when I was home, but...well, let's just say distance didn't make the heart grow fonder. And one tour turned into one more, which turned into one more. And I kept putting off the actual wedding. I always wonder if maybe I knew subconsciously that she was a bad idea. That she loved the image of me more than anything else..." I trail off thoughtfully, looking down again. Another age-old wound that still causes phantom pains. I press the heel of my hand in against the indent just below my thigh, something I've found that helps when the burning sensation strikes.

"At any rate, when I finally came back for good, I wasn't the shiny perfect husband she hoped to have anymore. So that was that."

"Because you came back with PTSD?" Violet's voice is brittle, a current of anger lacing it.

I scoff as I stare back at her. "Who doesn't? But nah, I'm sure I was grappling with that before I even enlisted.

Apparently, watching a parent die as a teenager can do that to you. Or that's what my therapist keeps telling me. I guess I'm double fucked up."

She rolls her lips together, searching for the words, and settles for moving closer to me and resting her arms exactly as mine are.

Her forearm is so petite next to mine. She elbows me gently, not a shred of pity in her tone. "I think we're all a little fucked up in our own way."

I just hum my agreement. She's not wrong.

"I mean, you're clearly *a lot* more fucked up than I am, but..."

My eyebrow quirks up at her, the small smile playing across her face right now making me join her with a grin of my own.

"Okay, Pretty in Purple."

She groans dramatically and drops her head. "Am I ever going to live that down?"

"Probably not," I chuckle.

"You know I've spent the last year terrified you'd tell someone or out me somehow? Fire me even."

All traces of humor drain from my body. "Why would you think that?" I ask, standing up straight. "I'm the one who should be embarrassed."

She still doesn't look up at me. "You just seemed so angry when you approached me that day at the derby." Her tongue darts out over her bottom lip. "You're like...my boss's boss. I just didn't know what it all meant. I still don't."

Irritation courses through me, not with her—with myself. "Violet, look at me."

She peeks up at me from beneath the dark fringe of her lashes.

"No. Stand up and look at me."

She does it almost instantly, and the depraved part of me gets off on it. I'm transported to that night when she did everything I told her to. Even when it made her cheeks go bright pink. My cock twitches, and I berate myself internally. *You're really fucked up, bud.*

She tips her head up and rolls her shoulders back with fake bravado. I can tell she feels vulnerable; it's written all over her face.

"I'm sorry I did that. But you need to understand that I will never, *never* tell anyone. That will forever be between us…and apparently Billie and Vaughn."

She winces visibly at that part.

"I'm not angry with you. I'm angry with myself."

"Why?" she asks, pure confusion on her face.

"I don't even know where to start with that question. It feels like I've been furious for a very long time at nothing in particular. And definitely not with you."

Did it hurt when she disappeared from our chats? More than I ever imagined. But could I blame her? No. Wanting me would be like choosing a vial of poison to quench your thirst. A slow and painful way to get dragged down into the dark. And no one wants that. Not anyone sane. I know I'm damaged goods, which is why I like to keep my relationships at a safe distance. Fenced off. Something Violet wiggled her way under over the course of a year.

I run one hand through my hair and look away, not

knowing what else to tell her. What I do know is that I'm tired of lying. Tired of obscuring the truth. Presenting myself as someone I'm not. Tired of hurting the people closest to me—or those who get as close as I let them. The ones who don't scurry off when I growl and bark at them.

She steps in closer to me, tilting her head to catch my eye again, seeking some sort of connection. One I'd rather pretend we don't have. It's less intense that way.

"Why are you angry with yourself?" Her voice is gentle, and her small hand snakes out and latches itself on to mine. Her dainty fingers wrap around my wrist, like she's feeling for my pulse point. The one that's pounding under the pads of her fingers. The one that riots every time she comes near or touches me. The only woman that's touched me like this in...a really fucking long time. The only one I've let get close enough to try.

And maybe it's that. That she's somehow poked and prodded at me enough that she's broken holes into my shell that are big enough for her to slide in and get at all my dark, sensitive spots. Or maybe it's just the fucking scotch. But I decide right here and now she deserves the truth. Even if it makes me feel nauseous to say it out loud.

"Because I scared away the only real friend I've had in—" I scoff. "Well, maybe ever."

Her thumb rubs in reassuring circles on the back of my hand. She's calm, like water lapping at the shore. Gentle and even, continuous, and I can't help but want to lie down in that shallow water and let myself get lost in the rhythm.

Violet soothes me. Even if she might be the most oblivious woman in the world.

"Who is that?" Her eyes are wide and shocked, scanning my face for more information.

I chuckle. Serves me right to say it out loud. "It's you, Violet."

"Me?" Her thumb stops moving, and her lungs empty on a gasp.

"Listen…I'm sorry." I reach out and touch a lock of pale gold hair that has slipped across her cheek.

"You're sorry?"

I groan. "Are you trying to rub this in?"

"No!" One hand falls across her chest in shock. "I just… You considered me your friend?"

Her eyes twinkle in the dark of night. With the light of the moon, everything around her is more of a dark blue than black, deep and sparkling, like the river I can hear faintly running behind the farmhouse. The moon's glow highlights her features in the most alluring way. I should tell her she's so much more. The thing that got me out of bed most mornings. My bright spot. My sunshine.

I run my thumb along the highest point of her cheekbone, watching the way the light plays up the coarseness of my hand against the silkiness of her cheek. Such a contrast between the two of us. Dark and light. Rough and smooth. Big and small.

The things I want to do to her. I shake my head, silently scolding myself for even letting myself go there. She's young, driven, bright—full of promise.

And I'm the opposite in that regard too.

I lean down toward her, hand cupping her lower jaw, and press a gentle kiss beside her mouth. "I still do."

I hear a sharp intake of air from between her lips when I pause there. I want to swallow that noise and taste her mouth. Claim it. I want her to never kiss another man again. But that's not practical. Not realistic.

I'm all about the realities of life. I know them well. And the reality with Violet is that as badly as I want her, I'm not sure I'll ever be able to open up enough to take that chance. Especially not with what she does for a living. The fact of the matter is I've worked too hard on my mental health to put myself through that kind of agony. Falling in love would be bad enough. Falling in love with a jockey would be downright impossible.

I gasp and sit straight up in my bed, blankets tangled around my legs like I've been kicking or maybe running. Running from my past, most likely.

I can feel the perspiration soaking the back of my shirt, can feel the strain in my lungs and the burn in my leg. I flop back down and run my hands over my face, scrubbing at the stubble there. Feeling myself so I know that it's real, where I am, that I'm safe. It's been so long since I had a dream like that, one that takes me back overseas. There were so many bad days, so many gruesome ones. But only that one stands out.

I remember the sun. The way it beat down on my dark

uniform, the way I'd sweat under my heavy kit. The way you could gasp for air, trying to catch your breath, but all you'd get was hot, stifling oxygen and grains of sand. It would coat your tongue, scrape your throat, and stick in your nostrils.

It fucking sucked. But not so much as dragging your friend's body away from a blast. Checking his pulse, shouting at him to wake up. No, that was the part that sucked the most. That's the part that has my hands shaking right now.

The survivor's guilt. Why him and not me? *Why him and not me?* If I had a penny for every time I've asked myself that exact question, I could probably end world hunger.

A light knocking on the door snaps me out of the memory.

"Cole?" Violet's voice sounds small and uncertain. *What is she doing up here?* "Are you okay?"

"Yeah." My voice cracks uncharacteristically, so I clear my throat, not wanting to sound as choked up as I am right now. "Why?"

"Can I come in?"

My heart pounds hard in my chest, trying to silence my mind. My rules. It's too dark. Too quiet. She's getting too damn close. And my heart wins out. "Yeah. Yeah, sure." I pull my sheets over myself, lifting the duvet to use as an extra layer of coverage.

I see the shape of her as the door creaks open, a dim silhouette of the body that has consumed me for the past two years.

"I heard you shout," she says quietly.

I sigh, giving in just a little bit. I hate sharing this part of myself. This broken part. It's why I like my solitude. I don't need to explain my shit to anyone when I'm alone. "Sorry. I didn't mean to wake you up."

"It's okay," she whispers, taking a few small steps into the room. "Are you all right?"

A sad laugh escapes my lips. "Probably not." Because it's true. Some days are good, some aren't. Mostly they're good now. Lonely, but good…or good enough. But am I all right? I doubt it.

She doesn't press any further. The questions and inquiries don't come. She just says, "Do you want me to stay with you?"

And before my head even catches up to the question, my heart seizes hold of my vocal cords, forcing a raspy "Yes" from my throat.

With no hesitation, her feet pad quietly toward me, and she crawls onto the mattress, lying down on top of the covers a short distance away. I feel her proximity like a tug on a fishing line, like she's latched herself on to me and I can't get free. I could struggle, I could fight it, but she's hooked in. And I'm not even sure I want to get rid of her anymore. I'm not sure I want to hide myself from her anymore.

I'm not sure of anything anymore.

Except that when she reaches out to squeeze my hand, I squeeze back. And that when I wake in the morning after one of the best stretches of sleep in my life, I'm sad that she's already gone.

CHAPTER 15

Violet

Golddigger85: What are you doing?

I SMILE AS I WALK UP THE STEPS TO MY APARTMENT OVER THE BARN. It's been a tiring week. DD had a bout of colic after a bad race, and now Billie and Vaughn are acting super weird around each other. I feel like the kid whose parents are going through a divorce, like I'm tiptoeing around them both. Basically, I'm relieved to be alone in my space for the night.

Pretty_in_Purple: Just getting home now.

Golddigger85: You work too hard. Your boss must be a dick.

I chuckle as I walk in the door.

Pretty_in_Purple: I have great bosses. But I am beat.

I strip off my sweaty, dust-covered clothes. Everyone thinks horse racing sounds so glamorous. They think enormous hats and mint juleps, not wood shavings in your jeans and dirt under your nails.

Golddigger85: Want me to help you relax?

I shake my head as I walk naked to the shower.

Pretty_in_Purple: No, thanks. I've got a hot shower for that. Be back soon.

The response comes out so quickly I don't even have time to put my phone down.

Golddigger85: Are you telling me you're naked right now?

A smile touches my lips. Poor Butterface and his one-track mind.

Pretty_in_Purple: Yes.
Golddigger85: Fuck. Let me see.

I ignore that last message and step into the shower, my mind suddenly fixated on him and his offer. Something that has been taking up more and more space in my head. Something that's becoming more and more tempting with my total lack of consistent sex life stowed away on this farm.

My hands roam my body, slippery with soap, and I let myself imagine that they're the hands of the man I've talked to every day for almost a year. The first person I talk to in the morning and the last one I talk to before bed.

That counts for something, right? I may not know him, but I do feel like I trust him. A tiny voice inside my head yells, "Naive!" *but as one palm slides over my breast and the other trails down between my legs, I feel emboldened.*

And when I get out of the shower, I grab my phone and snap a photo before I can change my mind.

I'm going to kill Cole Harding.

"One more," he barks at me like I'm the one in the army here.

I'll definitely kill him—as soon as my arms stop shaking. And as soon as I stop daydreaming about his lips so close to mine. The scrape of his stubble against my cheek. The sheer power of his body as he towered over me that night a week ago.

That's right. It's been one week since Cole Harding called me his friend and kissed me on the cheek, and I'm a bumbling mess around the man. One week since I crawled into his bed and held his hand in mine like I had a right to. Every touch, every look, every gentle word, it's like a slow-motion reel that won't stop playing through my mind. I'm so far gone, it's not even funny.

Things were awkward before because we left so much unsaid between us, and it's awkward now because I can't stop thinking about banging the guy. Doesn't help that he's been *nice* to me. Like…normal nice. He's still quiet, but he doesn't grumble so much. He's even cooked me dinner most evenings this week. Like he wants to take care of me. He said he was sick of watching me eat mac 'n' cheese. That I'm an athlete, and I need to treat my body like one.

Which is why I'm here, on a yoga mat in the living room, working out with him.

Riding a horse feels natural, but *this* does not. This feels like torture. Double torture because it's obviously physically exhausting, but being this close to him is emotionally exhausting too. Every nerve ending stands at attention. Every time a warm palm lands on my body to position me, goose bumps race out over my arms. My breathing hitches. My stupid cheeks turn pink.

It's like every part of my body is in a competition with the others to out me as a total goner for the surly soldier who is currently nudging my hip bone with the tips of his fingers.

"Don't let your core sag. Your lower back will get sore."

I do the last push-up from my knees before flopping down onto the floor, feeling like a beached whale who's given up on life. Given the choice between moving and death, I choose death. After an entire week of working out with Cole Harding the super soldier? I. Choose. Death.

I hear the rumble of his deep chuckle from above me. "That wasn't so bad, was it?"

"It's been nice knowing you," I reply as I pant into the floor.

He laughs again and drops a palm onto the center of my

back, rubbing up and down, his hand catching on the strap of my bra.

"Are you sore?"

"Not if I don't move."

"Dramatic," he grumbles as his hand moves again, fingers pressing in and massaging my aching muscles.

"Oh god, yes," I murmur, resting my chin on my forearms and letting my eyes flutter shut. His hands always feel good on my body, but this? This is ecstasy.

I hear a quiet grunt, but he keeps massaging me. His fingers move to the right places every time. Like he knows exactly which spots to hit.

"Where are you sore?" His voice is thick. It sends a chill down my spine.

"Everywhere."

"Violet."

He cups one of my elbows and flips me over so I'm flat on my back and forced to look up at him where he kneels beside my vulnerable form. I stare at his broad shoulders and biceps filling out his T-shirt in a way that just isn't fair. At his throat, which bobs as he swallows and looks down at me. At his eyes, which are locked on me like I might be his last meal.

Am I imagining the look on his face? The rise and fall of his chest?

"Where are you sore?" he repeats his question.

Transfixed by the sight of him kneeling over me, oozing raw masculine power, I lick my lips. It's like a shot to my core. What I wouldn't give to watch Cole Harding move above me with *that* look on his face.

"My neck and shoulders," I squeak out, trying to play it cool and failing miserably.

He leans over me, the sheer width of him casting a shadow over my body as his hands slide across my collarbones and rub at my shoulders, digging in so hard that it almost hurts, an ache that blooms into a burn that blooms into pure consuming heat.

I close my eyes, not wanting to watch him anymore. Not wanting to see the harsh look on his face though I can still smell him. That faint clove scent mingling with my perspiration and baby powder deodorant. The whoosh of his exhale feels like a cool breeze across my dampened sternum. My yoga shorts and tank top suddenly feel sticky and altogether too tight against my body, like they're constricting around me and stealing my breath.

I try not to focus on the caress of his hands on my bare skin, the flutter of his fingertips, the overwhelming press of his body looming over mine. But I can't. Even closing my eyes isn't working. He's *everywhere*, smothering me, weighing me down. It's like I'm suddenly being suffocated by him.

I can't breathe around him.

"Okay, that's enough!" I push up onto my elbows, breathing hard. "I can't do this anymore," I say as I look down over my body, noting the way my nipples have pebbled through my unpadded sports bra.

His eyes follow mine, those gray irises going molten as they scour their way down and land on my breasts. They momentarily flick back up to my lips, causing my tongue to dart out nervously. Any words I could say die in my throat as I peer up at the man I've fantasized about for two years, who is currently looking at me like he might have the same fantasy.

"Violet."

"Yeah?" My voice is weak, breathy.

Cole leans closer, inhaling deeply as his mouth hovers near my throat. "Tell me you don't want me to touch you."

My heart stops. Lurches. Freezes. I look up into his eyes, so full of uncertainty and longing. So tortured. So *pained.*

I search his face, looking for some clue as to what he really wants me to do here. A hint, a tell, *something.* But that military training is shining through, so I opt for the truth. "I'm not a very good liar."

A strangled growl tears free from his chest, right as his head drops down onto my body. I feel the tip of his tongue trail up the center of my sternum, sending a jolt of electricity straight to my core. My vision goes fuzzy, and my head spins. I fall back flat on the mat. *Is this really happening right now?*

Cole devours me like a man starved—like an expert. His lips dust kisses over each collarbone as the tips of his teeth scrape against my skin, followed by a soothing swipe of his tongue.

"Tell me to stop." His voice vibrates across my skin, spraying goose bumps out in its wake.

I whimper and run my hands through his thick hair, wanting to keep him close. Wanting him to keep going and never stop. "Cole..." I trail one trembling hand down over his neck, fisting his T-shirt at the shoulder and pulling him in.

He slides his hand up to cup the base of my skull as his thumb presses softly to the very top of my throat, holding me like it's his right. His body looms over mine, mouth moving up toward the hand that grips me. He nips gently just beneath my ear, and I arch up into him, my back coming up off the ground, my nipples rasping across his hard chest, wishing he was lying right over me so that I could grind up into his length again.

"Tell me," he whispers into my ear.

"Don't stop" is my pleading reply.

His teeth trail across the line of my jaw, his lips hovering close to mine. So, so close. I can't tear my eyes from them. I want to watch this all and commit it to memory.

"What are you doing to me?"

I can feel his breath on my lips, smell the mint on his breath. I want to taste it too.

It seems rich, him saying that, when there hasn't been a day in the last two years when I haven't thought of him. When my fingers haven't itched to log in to our chat and ask him an innocuous question or beg him to give me another one of those mind-altering orgasms.

I've *missed* Cole, and I've only dreamt of this. His lips on me, his hands roaming freely, while I turn to putty beneath him. I want so much more.

"We need to stop."

My eyes flash open as his mouth hovers just over mine, soaking up words that make little sense. Inches apart. So close and yet so far away. He pulls up and sits back on his heels, panting. His hands shake with the strain of holding himself back as he scrubs them across his face.

"Okay," I huff out. "Why?"

"Because I don't do this."

I'm breathing like I just ran a hundred-meter dash. "Do what?"

"Physical contact. Relationships. Any of it."

My eyebrows knit together. "Like…at all? Ever?"

"Not for…a long time. Years." He trails off as he stands, and the enormity of his confession hits me like a wrecking ball. *Years?* "Not since…"

He doesn't need to finish that sentence. I already know he means since Hilary. My throat burns with jealousy. Sad, pathetic jealousy. Such a wasteful and pointless emotion.

"I'm sorry," he adds as he turns to walk away stiffly toward the kitchen.

I stay here on the mat, trying to get my bearings and figure out what the hell just happened. He didn't seem hung up enough on Hilary to be pining for her to this extent. In fact, he didn't seem to like her at all. But…*years?*

What the hell am I missing?

★★★

My cast is finally off. The follow up X-rays were all clear, and the first thing I did after getting that go-ahead was march over to Billie's house and get on DD.

I wanted to gallop.

To feel the wind against my cheeks and have my shirt billow out behind me as I hunch down over a horse's back. To let the rhythm of his hooves and strong legs move beneath me like the drumbeat that gets stuck in your head. The beat I've been marching to since I was a little girl.

I've been good. Rule abiding. I stayed off the horses, even though I didn't want to. God knows there are plenty of riders out there who wouldn't have. Without Billie and Cole in my face, I probably wouldn't have either.

So I went out for a breeze around the practice track. And now I can't stop grinning. Or wanting to ride. I would get on every horse in that barn all night long if I could. Who cares about Cole Harding licking my chest when there are horses to ride? Who cares about the brush of his stubble or the sound of his ragged breath? Who cares about the fact that I let my hands wander in the shower while I recalled it?

Not. Me.

Now I have a *good* reason to avoid him. I can officially move back into my apartment. I can drive again. With my doctor's blessing that is. My first race back is in a couple of days. I can finally get my career back on track and stop obsessing over a man who is complicated beyond what I'm equipped to handle.

He's not my project; Pippy is. And I'm determined to get ahead with her as well. I pull my old Volkswagen Golf up to the farmhouse, feeling light for the first time in weeks. Like I have direction. That's what horses are for me. Purpose. There's no finish line. It's never good enough. There's always more. After each line I cross, I just want to keep pushing harder toward the next one, the next horse, the next win. It's *consuming*.

When I step out of the car, Pippy—sweet thing that she

is—whinnies her hello at me. I pull my favorite saddle out of the back seat and walk to her fence, slinging it over the top board to rest.

"Hey, sweet girl," I murmur as she speed walks toward me, her dainty little head swinging with each enthusiastic step.

Once she's close enough, I glide my hands over her cheekbones, one on each side, and plant a big loud kiss on the tip of her nose. Her soft lips flap around near my neck as she does whatever this is. With most horses, I'd think this might lead to a quick nibble, but not Pippy. With her, it almost seems like a gentle kiss.

"You're a little weirdo, you know that?" I run my hand down her neck to give her withers a quick scratch, right at the base of her mane. She stretches her neck out and twists her head, enjoyment written all over her. "That's the spot, huh?"

I chuckle at how expressive she is. And as I stand back and take her in, I can't help but notice how different she's looking in just a few weeks. She's shed her spring coat and, as I suspected, is getting that bronze shimmer her coloring lends itself to. I've pulled her mane to a perfect straight line down her neck, and she has her first pair of horseshoes on. The farrier fascinated her. All the smoke, all the noises—none of it fazed her.

I can't tell if she's goofy or just totally bombproof. She might not have the regular competitive edge we look for in a racehorse, that eye-of-the-tiger vibe. But only time will tell.

Maybe she's smarter than I'm giving her credit for. Maybe she's an evil genius. After all, she brought Cole around. He thinks he's playing it cool, but I've seen him. I don't know what kind of special operator he was, but I think he's out of practice because I haven't missed that he throws her a couple flakes of hay every morning before doing some sort of jail yard workout in the driveway with tires and bricks.

I know he keeps a bag of carrots in his truck and gives her one after work every day. It's no wonder she practically runs to the gate when he pulls up. I've even spied him late at night, leaned up against her fence, holding a rubber feed tub full of the omega-3-rich feed I've been giving her, stroking her forelock while she chows down.

Basically, the man who swore he doesn't like horses—and who said he wanted nothing to do with Pippy—is feeding her three times a day. And try as I might to not find it endearing, I do. *God*, I really do. It makes my chest pinch and my core throb. That little bay filly has softened him up, and I'd be lying if it didn't almost make me jealous.

Things have been *awkward* since our last workout. Friendly but strained. Bordering on sad. The way he looks at me, talks to me…it's different.

I shake my head. I've never been boy crazy. Horse crazy, yes. But boy crazy? Nah. And I will not start now. Especially not with one so impossible to break through to.

I turn to grab the saddle and look at her. "What do you say, Pippy? You ready to take your maiden voyage?"

I swear she bobs her head in response, and I roll my eyes as I get to tacking her up. She's been the easiest horse I've ever started so far. Even at home in Chestnut Springs as a kid, I worked with young horses on my family's ranch, and not a single horse has *ever* been as easy as Pippy.

I cinch the girth, and she stands happily in place. She's not even tied up. Plenty of horses would walk away, but not her.

I've spent the last several days lying across her back with my stomach on the saddle so I could easily slide down if things went sideways. But she hasn't flinched. I think I even noticed her eyes flutter shut one time when I stayed there a bit longer, just to see what she'd do.

Fall asleep is apparently it.

So here I am, sliding the metal bit into her mouth—another thing that didn't faze her at all—ready to get on an unbroken two-year-old with a freshly healed leg and no one here to help. At the back of my mind, I know it's not the smartest idea, but it feels right. It feels like my moment to revel in freedom.

The sun is setting, the birds are chirping, and the cool mineral breeze off the river feels refreshing after an unseasonably hot day. I realize I'm happy. Happier than I've been in a long time. I have the perfect amount of distance from my dad and brothers—who I love but were smothering me. I have the job I've always dreamed of. Friends. My independence. My *body*. Something I will never take for granted again. Just being able to walk barefoot is such a gift, such a blessing.

I lift my boot into the iron hanging down Pippy's side, pressing down onto it twice to be sure that she's prepared for me. And then slowly, so slowly, I lean across her and swing my leg over her back, letting myself sit on the leather seat of the saddle. Her ears flick out to the sides, like a little donkey, and I feel her back go slightly tense as I settle into the seat.

But any tension in her is momentary before she turns her head and neck to nibble at the toes of my leather boots. Right back to her goofy, in-your-pocket persona. Like she's been here and done this before.

Even when the crunching of gravel comes down the driveway, she doesn't startle or spook. Her head flips back toward the noise, and she watches calmly as Cole's black truck pulls up to the house.

When he gets out, wearing a suit with the top two buttons of his shirt undone in the most appealing way, I can't help but admire him. I wish I could crack him open and figure him out. *I really need to get back to my own space.*

Pippy whinnies, loud and shrill, and then walks to the corner of the pen, not at all concerned with my presence on her back. Simply happy to see the big grump who's now walking toward us.

"Hey, pretty girl," he murmurs as he reaches the fence and slides a big palm down her forehead.

I know he's talking to Pippy, but it doesn't stop my stomach from doing a flip. He's like the dad who never wanted the dog but ends up being best friends with it. It's like Pippy knows he didn't want her and proved him wrong. She tried extra hard to endear herself to him. To break through that tough exterior.

And it worked.

He looks up at me now, his eyes glowing and something

like wonder on his face. "This is new." His eyes trace down my body, pausing momentarily on my castless right leg. He tips his chin at me in question.

"Got it off today."

"And you're already back up on a horse." It's a statement, not a question, and his voice goes a little chilly.

"Yup. No fracture means no fracture."

"Is this the first time you've been up on her?"

"Yes."

He rolls his shoulders back. "Alone?"

"Yes..." I say, not liking where he's going with this.

"Is that your best plan?"

He had to go there, didn't he? Trying to tell me what to do after I've been perfectly careful and patient for the past month. Now I'm supposed to keep acting like I'm injured when I'm not?

"It's *my plan*. I don't require your approval to get on a horse that I've been put in charge of."

One of Pippy's ears flicks back at me, like she can feel the tension, and then she takes a step closer to Cole, dropping her head over the fence and nudging him.

"Violet."

Agitation courses through me. The way he says my name like I'm a child. *Violet.* Like just huffing my name with that scowl on his face is actually saying something at all.

"No. Don't. Don't *Violet* me. I don't need your permission to do this. I have races this weekend. I'm riding in those too. I have a dad and three overprotective brothers. I don't need another one. You *know* this. So get on board, or get out of my way."

Cole shakes his head at me as he turns stiffly to walk away. I hate that he doesn't say anything.

I hate that I can't provoke a reaction out of him when he does nothing but make me react.

CHAPTER 16

Cole

I BLINK AT THE SCREEN OF MY PHONE AS THOUGH IT MIGHT CHANGE what I'm seeing.

The corner of one long-lashed eye, looking straight up at the camera. Like she might look up at me if she were down on her knees at my feet. Wet blond hair, plastered to small round perfect tits, the valley between them glistening with droplets of water. I imagine one rolling down her body, over her stomach, to the mound between her legs. Getting caught in that small pale patch of hair before dripping right over her clit.

Fuck. What am I supposed to do now? This girl has firmly friend-zoned me for the last year and then drops the sexiest fucking nude I've ever seen. Fresh out of the shower, wet and ready. She took it for me. Without me even paying her. Because she wanted to. And somehow that just hits different.

Golddigger85: Is that an invitation?

Pretty_in_Purple: Yes.

Jesus. My cock twitches, and my pulse thunders in my ears. I swear I look around my condo just to see if someone is going to jump and out and scream about me being punked or something. This whole scenario just seems so fucking unbelievable.

But she didn't send me that picture for me to be a shrinking violet. It's time to play.

Golddigger85: Good. Prop your phone up, swap to video, and kneel on your bed.

The chat is silent for a minute, and I wonder if she's changed her mind as I adjust myself in my pants. Maybe she'll back out. That's fine too. Whatever she wants. But fuck. I hope she wants this. Because I do. To see the real thing rather than imagining her while lying around with my cock in my hand.

Her face fills the screen, and I feel like someone just suctioned all the air out of my lungs and left me on the ground gasping. She's incredible. Fascinating—ethereal almost. Eyes a little too big, cheeks a little too full, chin a little too sharp.

"Hi, Butterface." A small smile touches her mouth, and her cheeks turn the prettiest shade of pink. I love that. She's genuine. She's brave.

She's fucking beautiful. The kind of beauty that makes you stop and stare. The kind of beauty you want to study. I don't draw, but suddenly I'm overcome by the need to sketch her face. Her rosebud mouth. To document her. She's like a porcelain doll.

Yeah. And you're going to fucking shatter her.

I brush my intrusive thoughts aside. I wouldn't. I can be a gentleman. I liked her long before I knew she'd make my heart seize up in my chest. We were friends first.

This is fine.

I turn my microphone on but don't accept the app's request to access my camera. That can never happen. Not only am I probably too recognizable, but I hate the thought of opening myself up again. To be ridiculed and made to feel less than. I won't ever do that again. That took me too low, and I have too much baggage to dip down into that headspace again.

"You are fucking beautiful," I say, hating how gravelly my voice comes out. I sound downright emotional.

She looks away with a quiet "Thank you." Her legs are squeezed together tight, and she holds her arms over her torso like a shield.

"Are you uncomfortable?"

Her eyes roll, and her laugh comes out as a nervous titter before she looks straight into the camera, pinning me with her gaze, crystalline like the water in the tropics. "Of course I am. I've never done this before."

Does it make me a douche for wanting to beat my chest over that? Probably. But I don't care. She hasn't done this with anyone before, but she's doing it with me. My sad, tattered sense of self-worth latches on to that knowledge with a death grip. "What can I do to make it better for you?"

I watch goose bumps rise across her forearms as she rubs her biceps as if that might comfort her. "Turn your camera on." She rolls her lips together, her expression implying that she already knows I'm going to deny her request.

I'm hit with an overwhelming sense of shame that I can't do this for her. The one thing she wants. I just can't. My voice cracks when I admit it to her. "I can't."

One small dip of her chin later, she drops her arms, baring her naked body to me. "Okay. Then talk. You promised me the best orgasm of my life."

My cock jumps again as I watch her mouth make the O *shape that goes with saying* orgasm, *and I pull it out of my pants, gripping it tightly, jerking it a few times. Pretending it's her soft hand instead of mine.*

"Do you have a toy you like?"

Her tongue darts out over her lips, and her voice is breathy as she replies, "Yes."

"Good. Get it out, but don't use it yet. I want to watch you fuck your fingers first."

My palm rasps over my steely length. I'm sure she can hear me fucking my hand while I watch her, but I'm beyond caring.

"Jesus," she mutters as she leans over toward the bedside table, trying not to show too much. Like she's going to be able to avoid that.

"Now lie back on your pillows and spread your legs."

She flushes deep crimson as her legs slowly part.

Holy fuck. *I growl and pump harder at my dick, feeling my balls tighten at the sight. Never has someone looked so perfectly made for me. The teeth digging into her lip, the pretty pink that applies to what's between her legs as well. The only thing that's missing is my come on her tits.*

I wish I were there to touch her. To press her knees wide open and then run my fingers through her wet heat. To feel her pussy twitch and squeeze and go slick around me. I'm panting at the thought, trying to keep myself from blowing already. I need to slow down.

"On all fours. Let me see that tight ass." I watch her raptly. So eager to please. "Good. Now look over your shoulder at me. Fuck me. You are incredible." I say it, and I mean it. Wide blue eyes, slightly parted lips, hair plastered against her cheek, and that perfect round ass. It's almost more than I can take.

I have so much planned. So many positions to put her in. So much pleasure to give her—as much as I can without sacrificing myself. Tonight, I'm going to see every square inch of Pretty_in_Purple's tight little body.

What I don't realize is...I'll never get over it.

Violet isn't at the house. Her car isn't here. All her stuff is gone. I can tell because usually it's all the fuck over the place, and now it's mysteriously not. I even poked my head into her room, and it looks like it did the day I moved in. The only thing of hers that's left is Pipsqueak, who still whinnies loud enough to hurt my ears every time she sees me.

I started out worried when I couldn't find her. I spent all day at work beating myself up for being an overbearing asshole last night. I couldn't help it. The thought of her falling off and getting hurt had me tied up in knots. I know how wrong that can go because I've seen it firsthand.

But now this? It feels even worse. I didn't wanted Violet living in my space. I was annoyed, and it had nothing to do with her and everything to do with the level of privacy

I like. I've grown accustomed to having her around in the last month though. From the smell of the coffee she makes every morning to the quiet murmur of her voice when she calls home every few nights to the random shit she leaves all over the place.

I think I've actually started to *like* it. To crave it. To look forward to it. And now I've gone and been such a dick she packed up and left without saying a thing. *Again.* Not that she owed me an explanation. Her leg is better. Why would she stay anyway? I'm terrible company, and I know it. And once people get to know me, they rarely stick around. Why would Violet be any different?

I've done nothing to endear myself to her. Quite the opposite, in fact. I've acted like a total jackoff and mauled her a couple of times when I couldn't help myself. And then I turned and walked away like the fucking coward I've become. That day on the floor, she basically told me she *wanted* me to touch her. Her blue eyes all soft and alluring. Her soft lips parted, just begging to be kissed.

I wanted her, and she wanted me, and somehow, I still couldn't figure it out.

March into enemy territory? No problem. Face the girl you haven't been able to stop thinking about for two years? No fucking chance.

I am such a pussy.

My fingers dance across the phone in my pocket, itching to call Trixie and ask her what I should do. But I know what she'll tell me. She'll tell me to stop being such a baby and to use my words. Okay, maybe not so colorfully, but still. Trixie is over my mopey self-hatred. I can tell because she recently started pushing me a little harder, cutting into my streams of consciousness with those annoying rhetorical questions that make me reflect on myself.

I hate those fucking questions. I hate how fucking wrecked I am right now over Violet leaving. And I hate how I'm grabbing my keys to march back out the door and confront her about it.

I pull up to the barn, park beside her death trap of a car—one more thing for me to worry about concerning Violet Eaton—and get out of my truck. I march up the stairs to her apartment and knock loudly, probably a little too aggressively.

"Coming!" I hear her call from the other side of the door as I look out over the horizon. The low sun casts a golden glow over the farm. With all the white fences and rolling hills, it's kind of beautiful.

I shake my head. The water out here really must be poisoned. *Beautiful.* I almost roll my eyes, but the door opens, and instead they bug out of my head as I stare back at Violet in tiny cotton short shorts rolled down at the waist and a white ribbed tank top with no bra.

"Did you change your mind…?" She stops talking when she realizes it's me and not whoever she was expecting. "Oh. Hey. I thought it was Billie."

"Hey," I reply, like me showing up on her doorstep is perfectly normal. Except I can't tear my eyes away from her body, from where her nipples have gone instantly hard underneath her tank top. Just like that morning on the living room floor. The sight of them poking through her sports bra sent me over the edge. As if I hadn't been struggling hard enough to keep my instant hard-on at bay every time we worked out, every time I touched her to correct her position or give her a little support. I'd worked out with women in the military. And it had always been just that—working out. Helping a fellow soldier.

But Violet is not a fellow soldier. I don't know what she is anymore, other than firmly entrenched in my life and in my mind.

She must notice my gaze because she looks down quickly, squeaks, flushes pink, and then hides behind the door before narrowing her eyes at me. "What do you want, Cole?"

"You moved."

"Yup. My leg is better. So…"

I blurt out the part that's really bugging me. "You didn't tell me."

Her head quirks slightly as she grips the door in front of her like it's a shield. "Didn't know I needed your permission."

"You don't. I just…" I groan and run a hand through my hair, lost for the right words. I just what? *I want her to come back.* "I was worried. I didn't know you'd left or where you were." I cross my arms and look down at her. "I was worried. And you left your horse behind."

I watch her face soften as her eyes scan me, framed by the pale blond waves that spill down over her shoulders. The golden sunlight tints her eyes more of a turquoise color tonight; they're a like a mood ring—constantly changing.

"Okay." She nods. "That's fair. I'm sorry I didn't say anything. Friends don't do that to each other."

Friends? After I sucked my way up her chest and came close to totally losing control and fucking her bare on the living room floor, she's referring to us as *friends*?

"Want to go on a hike with me tomorrow?"

"A hike?"

"Yeah. I'm ticking things off my bucket list. Time to take life by the horns again. Sasquatch Mountain is one of them. Billie is too scared to go with me."

I raise one eyebrow, having a hard time imagining Billie Black fearing much.

"She thinks the Sasquatch might be real. You know, because of all the 'sightings,'" Violet clarifies, holding one hand up to do air quotes.

My cheek tries to tug itself up a bit at the thought of finally having something to bug Billie about.

"I'll go. I know the mountain well."

"You do?" Her voice perks up at the prospect.

"Yeah. I know a good trail and lookout. I used to run it when I was trying to get fit for the military. Should only take a couple of hours."

"Okay!" she says brightly, looking so happy I almost smile back at her before turning away.

"I'll pick you up when I get back from work." I wave over my shoulder, both wanting to stay near her and to get away from her as quickly as possible. I feel happy too, and it's throwing me for a loop.

Maybe I didn't run her off after all.

★★★

"You're late."

"Pfff." Violet waves me off as she climbs into my truck after making me wait for fifteen minutes. She wasn't even done working when I pulled up at her place. "It's just a few minutes."

I imagine myself trying to tell a superior that in training and cringe. "If you're not early, you're late." And being late in the military can cost lives. Violet doesn't live with these pressures, these memories.

She straps herself in and slaps her bare thighs with excitement, ignoring me entirely. "Let's go!"

Of course, she has to wear those tight fucking shorts again. The ones that leave absolutely nothing to the imagination. They hug every curve, including that tight round ass I'm dying to put a handprint on. Something she probably wouldn't like—I'm sure Hilary only pretended to. She did a lot of pretending though. Until she didn't. And her truths cut like a knife. She left me with wounds I wouldn't let heal. Wounds I pry open every morning when I look in the mirror and every night when I get ready for bed.

"I'm so excited!" Violet gushes as she looks over at me. Wearing that sports bra again too. This woman is a walking, talking memory. "You look hot."

My arms stiffen on the wheel as we head down the road toward the nearby mountain. *What?* My eyes dart off the windshield in her direction just in time to see her go beet red and look all flustered.

"I mean your clothes! It's warm out! The pants!"

She's scrambling to undo calling me hot, and I can't help but laugh at how awkwardly she's covering it up.

"Ugh." She drops her head back on the seat and throws an arm over her eyes. "Every time you laugh, it's *at* me!"

I chuckle because it's true. "Yeah, but I laugh with you more than I've laughed in years."

Her arm drops, and her head rolls in my direction as she looks at me. Really looks at me, like she can see right in through all the shields I've erected. All the walls, all the protection, it all goes to shit around Violet, and I'm thinking that might be okay. Maybe she wouldn't be disappointed if she found out I wasn't whole.

"That might be the nicest compliment anyone has ever given me," she says sincerely.

I just grunt back, not sure what to respond with. I've shocked myself into silence, and we drive the rest of the way just like that. In a companionable silence.

When we pull up and walk past the little wooden sign that says, *Lookout This Way*, the silence continues. I lift one arm, ushering her onto the narrow path ahead of me, something I almost instantly regret, because all it gives me is a completely uninterrupted view of her ass in tight shorts, the bottom crease of each cheek taunting me with every step.

I've done this path a million times, but never with the added challenge of a raging hard-on.

"This is beautiful," she says, slightly breathless with the strain of climbing straight uphill.

"It is," I reply, mostly breathless from trying not to stare at her ass but figuring out that even her ankles turn me on. Everything about her is driving me to distraction. The way her calf muscles flex with each long stride. The way her ponytail sways as she walks. I've spent a lot of time thinking about Violet, wondering who she really was, what she was doing, if she's ever read those messages, if she found someone else to chat with online—or maybe even a boyfriend in real life. But obsessing over her body this way is new to me.

"How much farther?" She looks back at me over her shoulder with some stray hairs plastered to her damp temple, her cheeks flushed—not with embarrassment but with life. With the rush of a new experience, a new place. Violet is *living*, and fuck, does it look good on her.

It makes me want to live too. To stop being such a hermit. To take risks, make friends, maybe even leave a vitamin bottle on the counter now and then—because who the fuck cares if everything is in perfect order all the time?

Life is messy, something I know *well*. But when did I decide that the solution to that was to stop living?

We're so close to the top now, and I can't wait to see what her face looks like when she gets to see the lookout over the lake.

But I hear a loud snap. And I fucking crumple.

CHAPTER 17

Violet

He wasn't kidding about the best orgasm of my life. The only time I've ever felt so out-of-body is when I'm on the back of a horse with the wind whipping my face so hard it almost hurts. When all you can hear is that whooshing sound in your ears and the hoofbeats that reverberate through your bones.

Except this time, it was my heart beating and my blood rushing. Rushing to every delicious spot. Responding to every direction he gave me—coming to life for his words. For his attention.

Can you fall in love with someone you've never met? Never seen? I spent the day mulling over that question. Because this morning, I was nothing but one big bundle of complicated feelings.

We fell asleep talking to each other. Actually talking. And his voice. His. Voice. It's so deep and commanding. I don't know how anyone could ever deny him anything if he talked to them like that.

Never mind the sound of his heavy breathing, the rasp of his palm against the silky skin of his cock. The odd tortured groan that would slip out when I knew he was trying so hard to keep them in. I could hear him pleasuring himself, but I couldn't see it. And it was so fucking hot.

We weren't even in the same room. I couldn't even see him. Yet last night catapulted itself firmly into the hottest, most unforgettable sexual experience of my life.

I want more. I want him.

I race up the stairs to my apartment, feeling so sure that I can convince him to join me on the video chat. I want to do more than hear his pleasure. I want to see it.

Pretty_in_Purple: I want to celebrate!

Golddigger85: Oh?

Pretty_in_Purple: I just got a HUGE promotion at work. Huge, huge. Like... FUCKING HUGE!

Billie pulled me aside and told me I was the new jockey for the best racehorse I've ever seen. I still can't believe it. I thought she was joking when she told me. Groom to jockey is a gigantic leap. An unheard-of leap. We're going out to celebrate tonight, but I thought I could fit some playtime in with Golddigger first.

Golddigger85: Ha! Congratulations. I've got something huge for you too. ;)

I smile. I bet it is. He looked like a big man in that one photo he sent.

Pretty_in_Purple: Butterfaces usually do. ;)

Golddigger85: You're so mean to me.

I can't help my smile. He's so playful today. Maybe we've turned a corner?

Pretty_in_Purple: I want to be really, really nice to you.

Golddigger85: Oh?

Pretty_in_Purple: Let's video chat again.

Golddigger85: Greedy girl.

I swear it's like I can hear him chuckle. The sound of it in my head makes my chest flush with the memory of last night.

Pretty_in_Purple: I am. I want you on there too.

The chat goes quiet. He goes from responding almost instantly to silence. Anxiety simmers in my gut. Maybe I pushed him too far?

Pretty_in_Purple: Please?

Golddigger85: I thought we cleared this up?

Okay. That's not the response I was hoping for.

Pretty_in_Purple: I thought you might...I don't know. Change your mind. I thought you might trust me enough to try it.

A several-minute wait again. I pace. I brush my teeth just for something to do.

Golddigger85: Well, I don't. I don't trust anyone. It's never going to happen. Never. I've been very up-front about that from the start of whatever this is.

I don't need him in the same room as me to feel that punch to the gut.

Pretty_in_Purple: Whatever this is? We've been talking to each other every day for a year. How many more years would I need to go? I've always said no to it too.

Golddigger85: We all make choices.

I suddenly feel embarrassed. Deeply embarrassed. He has been adamant from day one that he'd never show me more than that one photo. Yet I somehow convinced myself I'd be the one to change him—that I'd be the exception to the rule.

The realization that I've just been totally vulnerable with a man who would never reciprocate, even though I was naive enough to convince myself he might, hits me like an avalanche. It takes me right out. I compromised my values, my morals—fuck, possibly my career—all because I was horny and hopelessly obsessed with a stranger I met on the internet. The faint taste of bile burns my throat and sours my mouth.

I need a drink. Or two.

Or ten.

★★★

I see the crest of the mountain ahead when I hear a thump and a pained "Fuck!" I spin around to see Cole down on his knees, head bowed with his strong hands splayed out on the dirt path beneath him.

"Are you okay?" I hustle back, instantly concerned about what could take a man like Cole Harding down.

"Yes," he bites out harshly, making me pull back the hand I was about to rest on his shoulder. "Just go to the lookout. I'll be there in a sec."

I glance back up the hill before I recall how Pippy has softened him up by just being relentless in her affection. A strategy I've decided to adopt because, for as little as I know about Cole Harding, I *know* he is starved for attention. I know he has his shields up. I know he's been hurt. And I know no one has stuck around long enough to prove to him he's worth sticking around for. Pippy has taught me that much.

Which is why I moved out. I knew he needed his space, and he needed to see that even without being forced to live under the same roof, I would keep coming back for him. For no other reason than I want to spend time with him. I planned to invite him on this hike. He just made it easier by storming up my steps last night.

"No. I'm not leaving you behind," I say simply. Because I'm not.

"Violet." He still doesn't look up at me. "Please just go."

My heart races. This is weird. "Are you hurt?"

"No."

"Okay. Well, I'm not going." And then he looks up at me with so much pain in his icy gray eyes that I fall to my knees in front of him, feeling the tiny pebbles and grit digging into my bare knees as I come eye-to-eye with him. I watch his Adam's apple bob and his lower lip tremble slightly on a heavy exhale.

"Cole, you're scaring me. What's wrong?"

He presses his lips together again and rolls over to sitting, right in the middle of the path. "It's my leg."

"Okay. So you're hurt. What part?" I crawl around beside him so he can't keep facing away from me and then sit back on my heels. "Want me to check?"

"No, no." His arm darts out across my chest to stop me from moving down to his feet. And then he sighs. An exhausted sigh that lurches out from somewhere deep inside him. A sigh that takes his tall broad shoulders and makes him slump forward in defeat.

A sigh that leads him to pulling up his pant leg roughly, angrily, to show me the black prosthetic hidden beneath his pants. A sock covers his knee and disappears down into the plastic leg.

He points jerkily down at the high-tech-looking appendage and reiterates, "It's my leg."

I nod once, mind racing for how I could have missed this. We lived together for a month, and I never noticed that he's an amputee? What the fuck is wrong with me? And how hard has he been trying to hide it? That had to be damn near impossible. "Okay, so how do we fix it?"

He snorts dismissively. "We don't. It's probably something in the pinlock. I felt it go."

I don't know what that means, but I assume that someone closer to him will. "Okay… Want me to call Vaughn?"

"No," he almost shouts. "He doesn't know."

I widen my eyes as I look back down at the prosthetic. *His own brother doesn't know?* "Who knows?"

"My mom. But there's no reception up here." He looks away from me, avoiding my eyes as he shakes his head. The pain in his body right now—the shame—it almost kills me.

I rest my hand on his broad back, feeling his muscles ripple and tense beneath my palm as I rub small circles there. "Tell me what you need me to do."

He grinds his teeth, making his jaw pop as he looks ahead, avoiding my gaze. "You'll have to hike back down and get my spare from the house."

I glance around at the fading light over the peak. "But it'll be dark by the time I get back."

He just grunts and bends his knee, making the prosthetic fall onto the packed dirt with a hollow thud. "That's fine. You can come back for me in the morning."

"What? I'm not leaving you here overnight."

"I've done fine without your help so far. Don't need you to get all sentimental now. It won't be my first time sleeping outside, and Sasquatch Mountain is a hell of a lot safer than Iraq."

He has to be kidding. No way am I going back down there without him. I wouldn't sleep knowing I left him up on a mountain alone. "I know you can take care of yourself.

I'm not worried about that. I wouldn't leave *anyone* I care about behind. I'll hike down in the morning and bring you the spare myself."

"No." He looks at me fiercely, but he doesn't scare me.

A lot of my missing puzzle pieces concerning Cole Harding fall into place. Plus, I already promised myself I'd stick around for him.

"Well, that's just too bad for you," I say, pushing to stand and dusting my hands off while looking around the densely forested path, "because I'm sleeping over with you."

"Violet."

There he goes with that again. I know I'm pissing him off, but frankly, I don't care. Maybe getting angry would be good for him. That blow-your-top-off type of explosion that consumes you but also leaves you with some startling clarity. Yes, that's what Cole Harding needs. Some clarity.

"Let's go." I reach my hand down to him. "I'm a farm girl, remember? It won't be my first time sleeping outside."

After helping Cole off the path, he sits on a log and tells me how to build a lean-to shelter. I know how to build one, but I feel like letting him dictate how I put one together will give him some semblance of control in this situation. Something I don't mind ceding, considering he still won't look at me.

I search for branches, pine boughs, everything I can find to build us a safe spot for the night. Yeah, the day was warm, but it's still May in Canada. It's going to be cold tonight. Something Cole obviously knows based on the way he's had me cover up so much of the space and leave only a small opening for us to get in through.

I stand back, hands on my hips as I blow a loose piece of hair off my face and admire my masterpiece. Twilight is setting in now, and it's cooling off. I shiver at the prospect of how cold I'll probably be tonight.

"Okay, I think that's as good as it's going to get," I say, slanting Cole a curious glance. He's still brooding on the log, the lighter version of him nowhere to be found. It's clear he didn't want me—or anyone else for that matter—to find out about his leg. Like I would care. *That's because you're more interested in what's between his legs.*

"Why are you blushing?"

Motherfucker.

I rub my cheeks. "I'm not."

He pins me with a glare that I assume means he's not buying my denial.

"Okay. Well, I'm heading into Casa del Violet. You know where to find me when you're ready."

I turn toward the shelter just as he lashes out, "What? You're not going to offer to help me get over there?"

Stopping my forward motion, I turn back to look at him. He's sitting tall and rigid now. He's trying to look strong and proud, but his words are insecure and petty. I could take his attitude personally, but I know him well enough to know that tone means nothing where he's concerned. In fact, I usually think it means he's angry with himself, not me. And right now, he doesn't need my pity. He's already drowning in his own.

"Do you need help?" I prop my hands on my hips and tilt my head in question. "Because it strikes me that you're one of the strongest men I know. Presumably, you've been getting around fine for years with no one's help. Am I right?"

He blinks at me, face blank. I think he might be shocked. But I have brothers, and I know when a boy needs coddling—and this ain't it.

"Hop on over when you're ready." And then I leave him. Big tough Mr. I Sleep Outside needs my help? I scoff to myself as I crawl into the dark lean-to, leaves crunching underneath me as I come to sit.

Only a few minutes later, I hear Cole making his way over. He kneels in front of the entryway and crawls in beside me. What felt spacious before his arrival feels downright claustrophobic with his bulk taking up space beside me. Taking up *way too much space*. I feel my heart race at the proximity of him, at the idea that I have nowhere to retreat to. Nowhere to hide from him and the intensely confusing feelings he stirs up inside me.

"Did you seriously just tell me to *hop on over*?" The light is dim in the shelter, but I can see the amused tilt on his shapely lips.

"I..." God, that sounded kind of bad, doesn't it? "I did." Might as well own it. "Seemed preferable to 'crawl on over.'"

The laugh he barks out is so loud that it startles me. Like it leapt out of nowhere and surprised us both with its power. I laugh uncertainly and eye him skeptically. Like...is this okay? Am I allowed to laugh at this? But Cole doesn't seem to have any such qualms. His shoulders shake, and his body curls in, his hands resting across what I know are rock-hard abs. He laughs so hard that when he looks up again, I see his fingertips swipe away a stray tear.

"What the fuck, Violet?" He gasps, still trying to catch his breath. "I never knew that amputee jokes would hit quite like that."

"I'm sorry!" My hand flies up across my mouth.

"Don't be." He shakes his head with a grin plastered on his face.

It's weird. He never smiles at me like that, with true amusement. Maybe the odd peek of contentment or care. But not like this. This is unnerving. This is… He looks downright edible like this. All dark hair and glowing eyes.

"Are you okay?" I venture, because I'm honestly a little disturbed.

He leans back on his hands and looks up at the roof of the shelter. "Am I okay? That's a loaded question. I'm…" He trails off, and I watch his chest rise and fall, his throat move as he swallows, his cheek twitch momentarily, and I feel my core thrum.

The tiniest things he does set me alight—that cheek twitch and the dimple that pops when he does it? Gah! Delicious. Everything about the man is delicious. Dark and chilly on the outside, soft and gooey on the inside. Far too experienced for a girl like me, but so damn tempting.

I lick my lips as I soak him in, staring at him and suddenly not really caring if I get caught.

"I'm relieved," he finally says.

"Relieved?"

"Yeah." He lifts his stump up and drops it back down in explanation. "It's like a weight off my chest that someone knows about this. Keeping it a secret is exhausting."

I mean, no shit.

"How did it happen?"

He sighs deeply and crosses his arms over his chest the way he always does when he's trying not to look vulnerable. "I was so close to finishing my third tour. So fucking close. It's not even a good story. We were outside the wire, no live fire or anything. We drove over an IED. Junior, who was with me, didn't make it. And my leg took the brunt of the shrapnel. There were nails in it. I didn't even realize how bad it was. I got Junior and carried him to safety before it completely gave out on me."

I swallow. That's more detail than I was expecting. "So why keep it a secret? No one would care."

"Hmm. Trixie asks me that too. I tell her it's because of Hilary. She cared."

"I'm sorry, what?"

"I wasn't easy to deal with when I came back. I had a lot of shit to work through, even beyond the amputation. But finding the right prosthetic isn't a quick process. The shape of your stump, it all affects your comfort and the fit. Not to mention the change in balance that comes with it. The phantom pains. We'd grown apart already, and I was a growly motherfucker. But apparently, the physical aspect of my recovery really wasn't working for her."

I feel a chill roll down my spine, like when my brother would drop that fluffy, dry Alberta snow down the back of my shirt. I probably shouldn't press, but he already knows I'm snoopy. "What does that mean?"

"You and your questions." He snorts and then angles a look down at me as if to confirm I'm not backing down. "Okay. Well. When I finally got my body and mind sorted out enough to fuck her, it just wasn't what it once was. She liked when I was aggressive and dominating. But I couldn't be that anymore. Especially because my heart just wasn't in it. At any rate, I lost my balance, everything felt different, and I fell over partway through." He shakes his head, lost in the memory. "Right on the fucking floor. It's where I wanted to stay too. So I decided I was done for the day. It embarrassed me, you know? It more than embarrassed me. It *ruined* me. I barely knew her anymore. And she got frustrated. Had some choice words about me being a *half man* that resulted in the end of our engagement. I wasn't the shiny whole trust-fund baby she latched on to a decade earlier. So that was that. The end."

I imagine Cole, proud and dominating and so fucking broken, fallen on the floor. And then I imagine a woman who professes to love him making him feel anything less than loved in that moment. And then I feel fury. Fury that spews right out of me.

"Okay, so Hilary needs to die." I slap my hand over my mouth. I didn't mean to say that part out loud. But I feel fierce. I feel protective. Like I want to crawl into his lap and use my body as a shield for him from anyone who would talk to him that way—wound him that way.

Cole laughs a sad laugh but doesn't look at me.

“So that’s what you tell Trixie. But what’s the real reason you don’t tell anyone?”

“Picked up on that, did you?”

I can’t stop looking at him. I want to touch him so badly that holding myself back is utter torture. My hands ache to even just hold his forearm, to feel the pulse of his veins under my fingertips.

“I guess I don’t want anyone’s pity. I don’t want to be treated like I’m incapable, like I’m weaker somehow. I don’t want those words, those looks. That’s probably why I liked your crawling joke.”

I turn my body, wanting him to look at me or at least know that I’m looking at him. “You are not weak, Cole. I said you were one of the strongest men I know, and I meant it. Your leg doesn’t matter to me, and if it matters to anyone else, fuck them. They suck.”

His eyes dart around my face as if he can’t quite decide where to focus, and I wish—not for the first time—that I could figure out what is running through that beautiful head of his. I wish I could open it up and rummage around in there. Cole is such a closed book. And even though he’s talked more to me tonight than he ever has, I’m greedy. I want more.

Which is why I’m blindsided by the frustrated growl that tears out of his chest and the hand that darts out to grip my head and pull me to him. His other hand moves to my jaw, cupping my face reverently as he stares down at my lips. Like he’s tortured by them, entranced by them.

I don’t move. I don’t want to break whatever tenuous

hold I have on him right now, sharing whispered truths in the dark. I want him to do it. To devour me. To take a piece of me and keep it.

I want him to want me as badly as I want him.

The smell of him mingles with the pine boughs around us and wraps around me as his chest heaves and his heavy breaths heat my cheeks.

"Do it," I whisper, taunting him. "Please," I add, begging him.

And this time, he doesn't deny me. "Fuck it," he rasps right as his lips descend onto mine. Hard and fast, strong and relentless—just like him.

My hands coast up over his chest and flutter over his throat nervously as he kisses me senseless. I don't even know what to do with my hands. They tremble as I let them trail through his hair while the rest of me turns to putty in his lap.

Everything about Cole is masculine. So powerful. I feel small and inexperienced and so damn hot. I swing one leg over his waist, wanting to be closer to him, and he groans into my mouth as I settle down on him, feeling his steely length grow beneath my ass when I do.

His tongue finds the seam of my mouth as he tastes me, lips moving firmly—like a command to open for him. I rock my hips in response, pretty sure my panties are already ruined just from the skim of his calloused hand over my neck. The way he holds me there, it's consuming, it's...liberating.

He wants me. He brought me to him. I can feel proof of it pressing against my aching core. I grind down again, brazenly riding him and loving the feel of his hands constricting on my body while he teases my mouth so expertly. His hands slip underneath my shirt, tracing the indent along my spine and burning across my skin.

We kiss. A tangle of tongues and hands and moans. We don't rush; we explore. And I sigh into him, a little overwhelmed by how right it feels to be here with him. By how little everything else matters when he takes me in his lap and claims me like this.

I roll my hips again, my mind wandering down a path where we're doing this exact thing but with no clothing between us.

"Jesus Christ, Violet. I'm going to blow in my pants if you keep riding me like that."

His voice is shaky, and I pull back—only slightly—to meet his wild, lust-drenched stare with my own. "Sorry."

"Don't be sorry. Stop apologizing." His eyes take on a faraway look, and he hesitates, fingers fluttering over my body uncertainly all of a sudden. "This is, well, it's just that this is—"

I want to rise up and cut him off. I want to make him stop what he's about to say because deep down, I'm terrified he's going to tell me to stop again. Something I'm not sure my body can take, let alone my heart. "Don't. Just… Can you just not ruin it? Save that for tomorrow. Let me just revel in how hot that was."

I don't want to hear him say that this is a bad idea. That we shouldn't do this. He's already put his mouth on my body and walked away once. I don't think I can bear it again. How many times do I need to get turned away by this man before I learn my goddamn lesson?

This time, I'll beat him to the punch. I kiss him one more time, hard, and then end it there, knowing that now isn't the time or place to push him. "It's fine. Let's sleep."

He regards me silently, a deep wrinkle in his forehead as I crawl off his lap and eye the ground, trying not to think about how many bugs are going to be down there with me tonight before shaking my head at myself. I'm a farm girl. Bugs don't scare me. I flop down, feeling the dirt and pine needles against my bare skin and hearing Cole's heavy breathing from somewhere near my feet.

He eventually lies down beside me. We're not touching, but we might as well be. I can feel his heat along my back and smell that spicy cinnamon and clove scent I always pick up on him, but I can't hear him anymore. His breathing has gone soft and quiet. I'm hyperaware of everything about him, his nearness. I could fold myself into his big warm body and fit perfectly.

I get lost in my head, remembering all those messages we swapped. All those nights I stayed up late talking to him. Saying good morning to him as soon as I grabbed my phone the next day. The dorky jokes we'd tell each other. How were we so compatible for so long only to be so damn confusing now? I know he's not an open book, not a clear communicator, but this not saying anything is driving me insane. I can't tell up from down where Cole Harding is concerned. Do I not live up to his expectations in real life? His dick felt like it was attracted to me, but maybe that's the reaction he'd have to any woman? If he hasn't had physical contact in years, that's perfectly feasible.

Is he really so insecure about his leg he'd keep me at arm's length even now?

I shiver, thinking about the feeling of his calloused palms scraping up my bare back, about how I'd like him to press me down hard with that palm and—

"Are you cold?"

I look down to realize I'm hugging myself and have my knees tucked up tight, and yeah, I am cold. "A little," I confess quietly.

With no warning, his arm comes over me and pulls me back into his body, tucking me against him safely. I can still feel his hard-on against my ass, but I force myself to ignore it, relieved to feel his heat around me.

He surrounds me, chin on my head, arm draped over my ribs possessively, and legs tucked up underneath mine. The perfect fit.

"Cole?"

He sighs audibly. "Yes, Violet?"

"Do you think the Sasquatch is real?"

He doesn't answer. Instead, he pulls me closer and holds me tighter. The feel of him wrapped around my body soothes me, lulls me off into a light sleep where I'm resting but still intimately aware of every part of him. Every point of contact hums with possibility, something I can't quite stop thinking about, something that won't let me drift off completely. Which is probably why I don't miss his quiet whisper several minutes later.

"What I was going to say is that this is perfect."

CHAPTER 18

Cole

WE ALL MAKE CHOICES.

The message that fucking haunts me. What a dickbag thing to say to a girl you care about. A girl who just put it all on the line for you to, what? Jerk off?

I shake my head.

We all make choices.

Don't I fuckin' know it. I should take my own implied advice.

She hasn't messaged me back, but she's seen the message. That was last night, and there's still no message this morning. That's probably not a good sign. Fuck. Leave it to me to ruin the one good thing I had going in my life. The one thing I actually looked forward to in a monotonous, lonely fucking day. Because she was right all those months ago.

I am lonely. Actually, I don't even know if lonely *really covers it.*

I'm numb. By choice. And talking to Pretty_in_Purple was like the one pinprick that was getting through, making me feel something. And I couldn't even bring myself to fess up about my leg, just put it out there in the open. I was too fixated on keeping it secret. Something that doesn't even make sense to me, yet I can't bring myself to change it. Maybe if she'd have known, she'd have been more accepting of my not wanting to go on video. Maybe if she knew I ran a multinational company and couldn't be recognized as the guy jacking off on the internet, it would make a difference.

Maybe she'd understand. Maybe letting someone in on my secret would be a good start? Someone whose face I couldn't see when I told them. The pity. The disgust.

This cloak-and-dagger game I play with my leg is fucked up, and I know it. I never intended to let it get this far. It started out as something I just wanted to process on my own. After all, when I came back from Iraq, I had a lot to process. Apparently, watching your friends get blown to pieces will fuck you up. Never mind coming to grips with losing a limb after spending your entire adult life defining yourself by how physically capable you are. But the longer I went without sharing with anyone, the lower I let myself go. The more I focused on Hilary and her cruel words, the more it just became something I never wanted anyone to know about. The more I believed them.

Hiding it became integral. Like breathing. And now when I think of it, I don't even know why I do it, but I can't quite bring myself to stop. I'm stagnant like a swamp.

I pick up my phone and fire her off a message, determined to fix this.

Golddigger85: How are you?

Smooth, Cole. You've really got a way with words, pal.

After a few hours, she still hasn't responded. She hasn't even seen it. I tell myself she's probably busy. It seems like her job lends itself to long hours without set weekends. But as the day wears on with no response, I get worried. In a year, we haven't gone a single day without at least popping in to say hi or mentioning that things are busy. Not because we owe each other an explanation but because we like each other enough to do it.

Golddigger85: Is everything okay?

Still nothing. I spend the evening closing the app and rebooting it. Uninstall and then reinstall. Hoping that it's a technical error. Technology fucks up all the time. It's probably that.

But when I wake up the next morning with my phone in my hand and still nothing from Pretty_in_Purple, dread takes up residence in my chest. I fucked up, and there's no clear-cut way for me to fix it. Or something terrible happened to her, which is a thought I can't even handle. I'd rather feel like the shithead I am than imagine her injured—or worse.

I can't even let myself go there.

All I want to do is make this right.

Golddigger85: Listen, I think you're probably angry with me. I'm sorry if I hurt you. That was never my intention. I just...I' m complicated. It's a long story. One I'd like to tell you if you come back.

My misery grows with every passing day that she doesn't respond. I feel pathetic continuing to message her. But I can't stop. Talking to Pretty_in_Purple has become part of who I am, a thread leading me back to the man I want to be. A thread I decide I will not let go of. I'll keep going even if she's not here to partake.

Golddigger85: I think I'm just going to keep writing to you, even if you never come back. I need this.

After all, I am exceptional at avoiding reality.

I've held Violet in my arms all night long. It doesn't take a rocket scientist to know that her telling me *it's fine* means that it's not fine at all. But I keep holding her anyway.

I've barely slept. I'm exhausted but also buzzing. Kissing Violet last night was fucking *everything*. It really was perfect. Until she freaked out and shut it down. The way she asked me not to ruin it. It's like she already knows I ruin everything.

And then holding her? Her warm body pressed into mine? It was like clinging on to a teddy bear for comfort. But I've never wanted to fuck a teddy bear.

I'm also freezing, but I couldn't care less, so long as she's warm. She fell asleep quickly, quietly, lulled into a dream world where soft little sighs slipped past her lips, where she snuggled in closer and turned into my chest.

It was heaven. Just holding someone—someone who knows *everything* and doesn't look at me with disgust. I haven't felt that level of relaxation in years. In the middle of a forest, in a shitty little shelter, I'm the most relaxed I've been in years. All because Violet is here in my arms.

Yeah, I'm royally fucked. Because not only do I want to rip all her clothes off and use her body in every way imaginable, I want to cook her breakfast after, make sure she takes her vitamins and works out. I want to take care of her body once I'm finished desecrating it.

What's worse, I want to talk to her. In the dark, in the quiet, I want to let it all out. My dad, my mom, my time overseas. All those stories bubble barely controlled beneath the surface. When that pin on my leg snapped, so did the reservoir of everything I've held in for so long. It came surging up like water out of a dam, and now I'm struggling to keep it in.

Trixie is going to be obnoxiously pleased.

I look down at Violet now, snoring softly, snuggled into my chest with one leg slung over mine. The warm drops of morning light filter through the porous roof of the shelter, speckling her cheeks and hair. Her long lashes cast a shadow, and her lips are a pale shade of pink, the same color as her pert nipples. Something I'll never forget. Violet has *perfect* tits.

She looks small and weak, but if I've learned anything about Violet in the last month, it's that she's strong. So damn strong.

I knew she'd yanked her independence away from her family and set out alone, determined to be her own woman. I just didn't realize how thoroughly she'd succeeded. How intensely herself she'd become. Her confidence isn't loud or brazen; it's subtle and natural, intrinsic almost in how well it suits her. She isn't hard or crass; she's just steadfast.

When our online conversation wasn't serving her anymore, she was done. I spent a year desperately hoping she'd log in and see my last messages. Hell, I still have our chat open on my computer and check it daily. If she would just log back in, she'd know I wasn't done with her. She'd know what I haven't been able to say out loud.

I admired that about her. Envied it. When life didn't go my way, I retreated, but Violet? She kept on trudging. With a smile. Eternal sunshine.

Her lashes flutter before her lids pop open. She looks around the shelter. Mostly she gets an eyeful of my chest as the gears in her head spin. When her chin turns up to look at my face, she startles. Obviously, she didn't plan on me being awake.

"How long have you been up for?"

"A while," I lie. "Hard to sleep with your snoring."

Her face flushes pink as she moves away from my chest. I want to pull her close again, but I don't. I'm not sure how I'm supposed to act this morning.

"I was not." She looks horrified.

"You were."

She scrubs her face with her hands as if doing so will make her cheeks less red.

"It was more like...purring. Like a kitten," I continue.

"Oh god."

"Hey. I'm missing a leg, and you snore like a kitten. It's all good."

Her hands shoot down off her face so fast I can't even react to her pointy little finger jabbing my chest. "Missing a leg isn't embarrassing!" She just went from embarrassed to all fired up in under one second.

I hold my hands up in defeat and roll away from her. "You're right. The only embarrassing thing here right now is your breath."

Her little mouth flattens as her already big eyes widen at me. She sits up slowly, shielding her mouth with one hand, muttering, "Cole Harding, you are such a prick." Once she's brushed herself off, she looks down at me. "Okay. Tell me where the leg is, and I'll go get it. I'm starving."

"Bottom left drawer of the dresser in my room."

She nods before turning away, and my hand shoots down quickly to adjust my cock. The thought of her in my room is not helping with my morning wood. And neither is the view of her ass in those goddamn shorts crawling out of the shelter.

"Make sure you sing or something on your way down. Make noise. Keep your eyes peeled for wildlife. There are bears out here."

"Good god, Cole. What do you think I am? A city girl?"

She brushes her ass off, wiggling it just a little as she does, and within a few minutes, I can hear her singing some god-awful country song about riding a cowboy—completely off tune.

I've made my way back out to the log I sat on yesterday. It's a good log, in the perfect position to see the path. The brush behind me is so thick it would be impossible for anyone to sneak up. I feel as relaxed as I ever would, sitting in the middle of nowhere, missing my leg from just below the knee.

I'm trying not to worry about Violet, but it's not working. I know she's perfectly capable of walking down the mountain, but I can't keep my mind from straying to her. The same way it has for two years.

Zoned out as I might be, Violet clearly has no military training. I can hear her coming from a mile away. How someone so small can be so heavy on her feet is beyond me.

"Got it!" Violet waves the prosthetic overhead like it's a flag, but her movements are jerky. Her face is pinched. Sure, I pestered her about the snoring thing and kissed her senseless last night, but she didn't leave with body language like this.

"What's wrong?" I ask as she approaches me.

She almost flinches as her eyes dart to mine before lowering again. "Nothing." She drops to one knee, swings the backpack off from over her shoulder, and zips it open.

"How is the brown horse? Did you feed her extra? She was probably starving."

"For crying out loud, Cole. She has a name. You can stop pretending you don't like her around me." She shoves a black fleece jacket at me, agitation lining her every movement. "And of course I fed her. Hard to forget with that loud-ass whinny every time one of us pulls up."

I can't help but smile. It really is kind of annoying, yet I look forward to her greeting every day. The soft brush of her lips against my palm when I offer her a carrot. The way she nuzzles her dusty little face against my dress shirt, like she's bunting me. I'm not used to someone being so happy to see me all the time.

"Okay, good. Thanks for the coat."

"I figured you were probably cold." Violet is bundled in a lightly quilted Gold Rush Ranch jacket now and looking... uncomfortable. Nothing like the way she looked this morning or last night, when she straddled my lap and ground herself down on me. What the hell is going on?

"Thanks." I eye her speculatively. "You sure everything is okay?"

"Yup!" she says a little too brightly, popping the *p*.

I'm not buying it, but I also hate when people pry—so I won't.

Instead, I focus on fastening my spare prosthetic. It's not as comfortable as my regular one. It's not customized in the same way, and I know it's probably going to rub my stump. It's definitely not made for hiking.

I look down into it, and my leg aches. My leg that isn't even there. Phantom pains. They're not as bad as they once were, but sometimes the reality that my leg is *really* gone just lands differently. It's like I can feel it there. The pain of the day it was blown off. The pain of my recovery. The pain of my loss.

It rarely bugs me, but shoving my leg into a prosthetic I know is going to be uncomfortable gives me pause.

I shake my head and push it in anyway. No point in crying about it. Gotta get down this hill somehow. With my socks pulled up comfortably, I tie my shoe before looking up at Violet, who is staring at my foot with her brow furrowed.

"Do you have another question?" I ask, half joking.

She sighs, her shoulders squeezing up high and then falling as she does. "No. It's just amazing. I had no idea. I couldn't tell at all—the way you walk, the way you work out, the way you"—she waves her hand over my body—"look."

I bite back a smile. I'm not sure of much where Violet is concerned, but I know she likes my body. I catch her checking me out all the time when she thinks she's being discreet, and relief hits me like a blast of AC on a hot day because she's still giving me *that* look now that she knows what I'm hiding in my pants. Or, well, one of the things I'm hiding in my pants. I almost feel bad I assumed she'd look at me differently, but that's been my experience, hasn't it? I have little else to go on because I've been so busy hiding it from everyone.

"Okay, let's get the fuck off this mountain." I stand and press a little weight onto the prosthetic, feeling it out. It sucks. But it'll have to do for now.

Violet turns and starts walking back down the path. I follow, pretty sure my walk isn't as even in this prosthetic. People would notice now, but as Violet slows to match my pace, she says nothing.

The silence is fine by me.

Only when we pull up to the barn does she talk. "Thanks. See you at the track tonight?"

I wrinkle my nose. "Tonight?"

"Yeah. I'm riding tonight. That's why I've got to get going."

Maybe that's why she seemed so off? Was she focused on tonight?

"Is that safe?" I ask before I can stop myself. But really, she just spent the night sleeping poorly and hiking up and down a mountain to help my crippled ass. Running around at breakneck speeds on a thousand-pound animal being anything short of perfectly alert seems dangerous to me.

One shapely brow quirks up as she crosses her arms back at me. I feel like I'm looking at a small blond elfin version of myself with that pose and facial expression.

"Friends look out for each other, Violet," I grumble at her. I know she doesn't want people telling her what to do, but this is serious.

And she just scoffs, "Yeah. *Friends*," and rips the truck door open before slamming it with nothing more than a wave over her shoulder as she stomps up the stairs to her apartment.

CHAPTER 19

Violet

MY HEAD HURTS, AND I FEEL LIKE DEATH WARMED OVER. I CAN barely move. I'm not sure if it's the copious number of drinks I downed in front of Billie at Neighbor's Pub last night or that I've made myself feel sick over a goddamn internet pen pal.

My stomach roils, and again, I can't differentiate the cause.

I'm so mad. At me. Not even at him. Because he's right. He was nothing but up-front with me about his limitations. About his rules. Yet I barged ahead, thinking I'd be the one he'd change for.

I shake my head and press the heels of my palms into my eye sockets, trying to dull the throb in my head. I can hear my oldest brother, Cade, giving me dating advice—and there was a lot of it—but this bit stands out as exceptionally pertinent right now.

Don't pick a man who needs fixing—or changing—to meet your needs. He either wants to, or he doesn't. And if you need to convince him, he doesn't love you the way you deserve.

I hated the way my brothers meddled in my love life. The three of them practically put me up in an ivory tower, but I guess they knew Mom better than I ever did. They lost our mom and didn't want to lose me too. So instead, they smothered me and drove me away. Because I couldn't stay there. But right now, I ache to go back. A hug from my dad, a noogie from Rhett, an easy smile from Beau, and some deep poetic advice from Cade. Good men, all four of them.

And I'm not sure I truly realized it until now.

I know what they'd tell me this morning, and I know what Billie told me last night.

It's time to move on. I deserve more. I deserve better.

I delete the app from my phone and go lie on the floor of my shower, where my quiet tears blend and wash away with the spray of lukewarm water above me.

The sounds of the track filter in around me as I tack Brite Lite up. It's my second year riding her, and she's a solid racehorse with a good head on her shoulders and a fair number of wins under her belt. But today, the pretty gray mare is antsy. Just like me, raring to go, right back where I was a month ago. I shove my earbuds in and get to work on zoning out, humming to try and soothe her nerves as well as mine. Except where I usually play the race through in my mind, I'm instead replaying the last twenty-four hours.

The walk down the mountain and subsequent drive home were quiet. Awkward. I didn't know what to say to Cole, and my mind was so busy piecing it all together that

I couldn't have come up with small talk to fill the space anyway.

When I went into his room to get his leg, I tried not to take my time looking around, but I did a little bit. I'm only human, okay? And it doesn't matter. The place is military clean. Everything laid out just so, everything spick-and-span clean. I wondered if he polished the floors with a toothbrush like you see in the movies, but I couldn't even bring myself to ask him that.

Because when I shoved the sticky drawer closed on the dresser that was home to his spare prosthetic, it moved the mouse next to the laptop plugged in on top. The one that was still open. The one that was open to our chat. Our messages from over a year ago were sitting right there, looking me in the eye.

And I was very, very human at that moment. Because I couldn't look away and definitely couldn't stop myself from scrolling through. I wondered why the hell he would have our chat still open on his laptop when I haven't responded to him in a year. Until I came face-to-face with my answer.

Golddigger85: How are you?

Is everything okay? Listen, I think you're probably angry with me. I'm sorry if I hurt you. That was never my intention. I just...I' m complicated. It's a long story. One I'd like to tell you if you come back.

I think I'm just going to keep writing to you, even if you never come back. I need this.

Talking to you has been the most healing thing

to happen to me in years. Please respond. I'll reciprocate. Sharing much about myself terrifies me. But I'll try.

I don't think you're coming back. But if you do, my offer stands. I want us, or whatever this is, back.

Sometimes I daydream about meeting you in real life. The things I'd do to you.

I miss you.

He's been messaging me ever since I ghosted him. Even since I moved in with him. Like a diary dedicated to me.

My breath left my body with a hollow whoosh. My heart pounded in my ears.

Tonight, I carried your limp body into my house. I know you're just knocked out from the painkillers, but I felt sick all the same. I've carried limp bodies before, and the thought of one being yours is almost more than I can take. I fell asleep in the hallway listening to you breathe.

Today you talked me into going out for a drink at some shitty little pub. I had the most fun I've had in years.

Today you moved out. I didn't expect it to hurt this badly.

Tears spring up in my eyes just reading them all, each one like a pin in my heart. The most aloof, closed-off man in the world turned my heart into a fucking pincushion with his words, and I don't even know how to tell him.

I am well and truly speechless. I've spent a month in close

quarters with this man. A man who I thought didn't even *like* me, when the entire time, he's been writing me notes. I've been beating myself up over wanting Cole Harding, over going against every fiber of logic in my body that tells me he's just going to let me down again. Embarrass me again. And all this damn time, he's been writing me love notes he knows I'll never see while I try to be his *friend*.

Some girls might swoon. The notes *are* sweet. So sweet that my teeth ache. But I feel agitated. He could have just told me. It's not like we haven't talked about our pasts. Now I feel like a juvenile fool for crushing on him secretly this whole time, tiptoeing around his moods.

If I'd have known he missed me, wanted me, I'd have crawled in his lap and kissed him earlier.

I unbuckle Brite Lite's halter, and she instantly drops her head into the bridle as I easily slide the bit into her mouth. She's usually so polite, but today it's like she chomps down on the bit. Goes after it. Takes it, just like we're going to take this race.

It's time to put the big brooding soldier out of my mind and focus on kicking Patrick Cassel's ass in round two. Brite Lite is ready too. I swear she knows this is a revenge round. A rematch. Us girls have a keen sense for that—especially with tools like Patrick.

We walk out into the bright sunshine, very unlike that soggy day just over a month ago. The conditions are perfect.

Billie slinks out from who knows where with Mira in tow.

"All good? How's Brighty?" she asks, shrewd golden eyes

assessing me like she just *knows* something is up. No one reads a person better than Billie.

No one.

"Yup. Let's do this." I nod, yanking up that competitive spirit that comes with the territory of being the only girl and youngest sibling of four kids.

Billie gives me a well-practiced leg up into the tack before pinching the side of my butt playfully. "Break a leg out there."

"Billie." Mira stares at her, unimpressed. Which, to be fair, is her go-to expression. "Really?"

Billie cackles and walks ahead but freezes in her tracks when we hear a smooth, slightly accented voice say, "Good luck out there today, Miss Eaton."

Stefan Dalca. The other big player in the horse racing scene out near Ruby Creek. Everyone thinks he's sketchy, and Billie hates his guts after he tried to bribe Vaughn into selling DD. Which would have been a huge mistake. Not only because the ranch would have been without our championship stallion, but Vaughn would have been without Billie.

"Dalca, you piece of..."

I sit up poker straight, a little worried that Billie might go off. She's a bit of a live wire that way, but Mira steps in front of us and turns her unimpressed expression on the suit-clad man in question.

"Stefan, walk with me." She crooks a finger and heads in the opposite direction without even looking back. Like she just knows he'll follow.

To his credit, the usually perfectly curated man looks a

little shaken. He tugs at the lapels of his suit jacket and clears his throat before spinning on his heel and striding away.

Billie makes a gagging noise, and I giggle. I know how much she detests the man, but I'm thinking he should be a little more scared of Mira at this current juncture. Billie might be the unpredictable firecracker of the three of us, but Mira is smart, cunning, and wily. Billie you'll see coming because she'll burn it all down around herself to take you out. But Mira? I think you'd be down for the count before you even knew she was there.

Tonight, I am going to channel my inner Mira. Sweet and quiet Violet isn't here right now. Patrick Cassel is going down in the only way I can take him down.

On the track.

★★★

I pull into the driveway and park right in front of Pippy's paddock. I couldn't sleep because I was too excited about my win. Too high on adrenaline. So I snuck out of the barn apartment, slid my feet into a pair of sandals, and threw a long cardigan over my floral sleep shorts and matching tank to keep the chill out. It's dark out now, past my regular bedtime, and I hoped to keep my arrival on the down-low, but she's pretty much a guard horse at this point, sounding the alarm as soon as I pull up.

Little traitor.

"Hey, sweet girl." I jump out of my car with a pocket full of peppermints and head her way. "We won tonight. Left everyone else in the dust. It felt so damn good." She nickers and rubs her lips against my pocket, homing in on the minty smell. I pull one out and let her chomp away at it. White foam forms on her lips from the chalky candy. "I was going to go to bed, but I couldn't sleep. Figured I'd come celebrate with you."

I peek up at the darkened farmhouse before I shake my head at myself. *Cute, Violet. Pretending you're not here to spy on Cole. Pretending thinking about him and wondering where he is isn't what was keeping you up.*

I still don't know what to make of what I read on his laptop. I have even less of an idea of what to say to him. I'm half in love with the man, and the other half wants to shake some sense into him. He's so damn broken, so full of fake bravado.

Everyone sees cool, calm, and collected. Emotionless. I think I might have at one point too. But now all I see is sad. Closed off. Lonely. I'm scared he'll break me, but suddenly I'm more scared I'll break him. Loving him feels like a big responsibility.

"Violet?"

The sound of his voice sends a thrill down my spine. Deep and gravelly, a tad sleepy sounding.

I turn slowly to take in his dark form on the front porch of the little blue house. "Hi." I let my gaze trail over that perfect triangular upper body, strong thighs. "Did you see my race?"

"No, sorry. I didn't make it down."

Disappointment lurches in my chest. I wanted him to be there. "Did I wake you?"

"Yeah, but it was time."

Huh? I walk closer to the porch and realize he's only wearing formfitting boxers and a T-shirt. "Did you sleep all day?"

He runs a hand through his hair. "Yeah. I was pretty tired."

I come closer, gripping the porch railing. "I thought you were joking about my snoring keeping you awake."

He laughs. Deep and smooth. Like honey. And I want him to drizzle it all over me and then lick it off.

"It wouldn't have been safe for both of us to sleep. I kept watch."

"We could have taken turns!" I hate feeling helpless, hate that he didn't even bother to include me in that decision. "I don't need you to coddle me. I'm perfectly capable of taking care of myself."

He pins me now, his gray eyes sparking with fight. "That's what you keep telling me. But, Violet, letting me help doesn't make you weak. It just means I care. I know you don't *need* me, but I want to be there for you. Let me care for you in the only ways that I can."

"Is this where you tell me that's what friends do?"

He swallows. I watch his throat bob as his intelligent eyes regard me carefully. "No."

That one word. He doesn't say more, but he doesn't need to. It's his confession.

My tongue darts out to wet my bottom lip as I gaze up at him, his body towering above me, just a few steps away. I swear the air between us heats by the second—like I can feel his energy from several feet away.

"I saw the messages," I blurt out. "On your laptop."

He blinks a few times, but his face stays predictably blank. He shows so little emotion sometimes. It's almost impossible to get a read on him. But when he turns away from me and limps back into the house, I feel enough emotion for the both of us. Walking away, *again*.

I boil over. Fiery hot. Jilted, frustrated, *tired*. I storm up into the house I called home for a month, hot on his heels as he makes his way through the living room.

"Would you just talk to me already!" I shout. It comes out louder and more forceful than I think I've ever talked to anyone in my life. My cheeks heat, and I initially feel a little bad. It's out of character, but I am so done with not saying anything to each other. I like quiet, but this is beyond. Cole is downright uncommunicative.

He turns, jaw popping and the veins in his arms pulsing with tension, all highlighted by shadow with only a floor lamp shedding dim light in the corner. His hands fist and then let go as he raises his voice right back, shouting, "What do you want me to tell you? I never open up to anyone. You think everything between us just started and finished with a photo for me? Like it was easy for me to lose you? To not know if you were okay? To miss you so much it physically hurt? You broke me!"

His words wind me. My chest empties, hollow and throbbing with the weight of his confession. Both my hands creep up over my chest, my fingers wrapping around the base of my throat to stem the growing flow of nausea. *He missed me. I broke him.*

"You broke me first," I whisper. But the admission feels loud in the quiet room. Like I shouted it at him.

His smile is pained as he looks up at the ceiling. "You're not broken. You're perfect. And I'm a shitty fucking patchwork quilt. I've spent years picking up the tattered pieces of myself, every life event, every heartbreak, and slowly stitching it all back together. But I'm not good at sewing, Violet."

His eyes find mine across the room, raw and anguished. All I want to do is wrap my arms around him, but I'm stunned into stillness with his next words.

"And now the edges are starting to fray. I'm coming apart at the goddamn seams, and you're the one holding the thread that could undo it all." Cole groans and runs a hand through his already disheveled hair, agitation and heartbreak lining every limb. "Don't you get it?" His eyes are wide and pleading now as he shakes his head. "You have the power to completely unravel me, and I *hate* feeling like that."

I can feel my pulse jumping in my throat as I stare back at him, swallowing audibly under the weight of the responsibility I'm feeling. "I promise not to unravel you, Cole. It wasn't easy for me either. You hurt me. Being that vulnerable… I need to know what this is between us, once and for all."

His chest rumbles, but the tone is different. And when his eyes pin me in place, he says, "I'm not good at talking. I think I should just show you."

And with that, he grips the back of his shirt and pulls it off over his head, his smoky gray eyes not leaving mine for a single beat. His thumbs hook into the waistband of his boxers, his eyes still homed in on mine.

"What are you doing?" I pant out, suddenly feeling breathless and completely immobile, entirely unable to look away from his body in the warm glow of the darkened room.

"Evening the playing field. You need to know what this is between us? It's fucking everything."

My breath catches in my chest as he pulls his boxers down. My lips part on a sigh, and I stare at him like a total voyeur, dumbstruck. *Is this really happening?* Watching him undress before me. My mind is blank. I feel like I'm having an out-of-body experience.

He kicks the boxers off, and I watch his cock swell under my gaze. Thick, long, and veined, and growing harder every second I spend staring at it.

"Staring is rude, Violet."

My head snaps up to his face, and I bite down on my bottom lip, feeling my body pulse and my pussy go slick. "Sorry."

A smirk flits across his mouth. "No, you're not."

He's right, of course. I've never been less sorry in my life.

"Tell me what to do next."

"What?" My heart beats in every limb, right into the tips of my fingers. They itch to touch him.

"You read the messages." His voice is like gravel. "I told you I'd reciprocate. Tell me."

I feel like my throat could close on me. Like I could choke on all the things I want to say to him. How the hell am I supposed to do this? This man—this Adonis—naked before me. His length is rock-hard and jutting out in my direction now.

Knowing what I know, watching him undress in front

of me, it's the ultimate in vulnerability. The ultimate in trust.

I take a step closer, tongue darting out to wet my lips. "Fist it."

His hand wraps around the thick base of his shaft as he says, "Fist what?"

I have a hard time dragging my eyes up to his face. "Your cock." Excitement coils at the base of my spine at my boldness. I've thought a lot of dirty things about Cole over the last couple years, but saying them out loud feels foreign.

I take another step, wanting to get a closer look. He's so well-endowed. It matches everything else about his body. Strong and thick and tempting.

My voice comes out as a hoarse whisper. "Now stroke it. I want to watch you stroke your cock."

His hand slides slowly over the silky skin of his cock, and he looks down briefly, causing one lock of dark hair to flop down over his forehead. He looks disheveled and completely at my mercy. Utterly delicious. My heart aches in perfect unison with that spot between my legs.

When he looks back up, eyes meeting mine, I know I'm a goner. His cheeks are pink, his eyes are wild, his body is tense, and all I want to do is touch him. To make him feel good.

"Cole." His name spills from my lips like a prayer.

And then I shrug my cardigan off and let it pool on the floor around my feet along with the rest of my inhibitions.

CHAPTER 20

Cole

My chest seizes as her sweater drops to the floor. Her flowery little pajamas leave little to the imagination. I want to rip them right off her, to lay her bare right along with me.

I feel so fucking vulnerable. So far out of my element. She knows about me, about everything—that I'm messy—and she's not running.

She's getting closer. Every nervous step she takes is like a shot to the heart. She's not looking at me like I'm pathetic. She's looking at me like she can't get enough. I can't remember the last time a woman looked at me like this, and it's waking up a side of me that hasn't come out to play in a very long time.

I keep my hand moving, stroking myself as she approaches me slowly, like she might scare me off. She has no idea what will happen if she gets close enough for me to touch her though.

I'm fucking done shutting down this thing between us.

"Violet. If you don't want me to completely lose it, stop right where you are."

Her voice is small, and her cheeks are pink. "What if I want you to lose it?"

It's hard to catch my breath when she talks like that. So effortlessly sexy. So innocent. "You don't know what you're getting yourself into."

"Don't I?" she muses with a quirked head. "It's like being small and quiet gives people the impression I'm a prude." She nibbles on her lip, eyes raking down over my body like I'm her favorite snack. "Would it shock you to know I've closed my eyes and imagined being fucked by you for two whole years? You're my go-to fantasy, Cole."

"Violet."

She's not dissuaded. Another step forward. "With my hands. With my toy. With other m—"

"Violet," I bite out. "I don't want to hear about that."

"Jealous?"

I nod because I am. The thought of her with any man other than me tints my vision red. I give my cock a rough jerk in her direction. She's so close now.

A small pleased smile touches her lips. "Good."

"Little minx, it's all fair game if you're going to taunt me like that." And then my spare hand darts out, hooking into the elastic waistband of her tiny shorts, yanking her to me easily.

Her wide, startled eyes stare up at me as she cranes her neck back, and my hard cock juts into her stomach. She repeats herself. "Good."

My heart races. I don't even know where to start. I want all of her. Every square inch. I want to kiss away past hurts. I want to bend her over and give her delicious new ones. I want to watch her come over and over again.

My fingers find the thin strap of her tank top and gently brush it off her shoulder before doing the same to the opposite one. Violet's breath comes out heavy and ragged as I lean down and press a kiss to her cheek.

I pepper them along the line of her jaw, up to the shell of her ear, nipping at her lobe and then smoothing the indent away with a gentle suck before I whisper, "Get on your knees."

She turns her head and kisses me square on the lips. Hard. Both her dainty hands wrap around my head, and her tongue pushes in between my lips. She tastes like mint toothpaste and cherry lip balm. She's fucking delectable, and I can't wait to taste what's between her thighs.

She pulls away, hands trailing over my chest and abdomen as she drops to her knees before me. The sight of her looking up at me with those wide blue eyes. *Fuck.* It's everything I've dreamed of. My cock twitches, and I can't help myself. I reach down and pull her tits out over the top of her tank top, liking the look of her disheveled and exposed on the ground in the middle of my living room.

"So fucking pretty," I murmur.

Her gaze shifts to my throbbing cock, and her lips part as she leans in and licks the drop of precum from the head. And then she fucking hums. Like it's a lollipop. Like it's the best thing she's ever tasted, and I swear I almost blow right here and now.

With one hand on my thigh and the other cupping the back of my knee just above my prosthetic, she slides my cock into her mouth, not once looking away from my face.

I'm not sure what I've ever done to deserve this. I'm not sure I even do. But the sight of Violet on her knees for me will live in my mind until the end of my days.

Her tongue swirls, and her cheeks hollow out as she sucks.

"Jesus, Violet." One of my hands finds her silvery hair, gathering it together so it doesn't impede my view, and the other cups her jaw as my thumb brushes across her cheek. Her head bobs eagerly, gliding over my length, taking me so deep that her nose bumps into my stomach. *What. The. Fuck?* "You are so fucking good at this."

She hums again before pressing a chaste kiss to the tip of my cock. And I lose it. This might be the best blow job of my life, but I need more before I finish.

I give her hair a gentle tug. "Up. In that chair." I nod toward the large armchair beside us and gently direct her there by the elbow.

She moves swiftly and sits down before looking back up at me like a little girl in trouble, her hands pressed between her knees, tits squeezed together between her arms.

"You gonna get shy on me now?" I take a step, wincing at the pain in my stump, but not caring.

"No," she whispers back. "I'll take my shorts off if you take the prosthetic off. I can tell it's hurting you."

I groan. That's a level of honesty I'm not sure I'm ready for. But when she adds, "I'm not wearing any panties," I bend down and get to work peeling the sock down so I can remove it. The minute it pulls free, my leg feels better, but my brain doesn't.

I feel exposed. Completely naked, right in front of the most beautiful woman I've ever laid eyes on. Young. Vivacious. Whole.

"You are so fucking hot." The words rush out of her as she licks her lips, and I realize she's not even looking at my stump. Her eyes are bouncing around my body hungrily, like she can't decide which part she likes best. Pure lust. Pure desire. And suddenly I don't give a fuck about my leg. If Hilary was the poison, Violet is the antidote.

I lean down, resting my hands on the arms of the puffy chair, as I come to kneel before her. She leans back and yanks her shorts down, and when they get stuck around her thighs, I lend her a hand, savoring the feel of them sliding over her skin, of the flex of her calves as I pull them off her feet. And then with one hand covering each of her tiny knees, I open her legs.

So much fucking better in real life.

I slide my palms up her inner thighs, giving her a tight squeeze there before letting one hand continue up over her mound.

"Oh god," she huffs out, looking down at me, at my hands, blue eyes gone dark with yearning.

"Is this what you've been dreaming about, little Violet?" I ask as I hold her spread open for me.

"This…this is beyond."

I can't help but chuckle. "I haven't even touched you yet."

Her hips buck in response, and I beat my chest internally. She's so damn eager. For *me*.

I trail a thumb over her seam, and she whimpers. So I do it again, more firmly this time, parting her lips. "Violet. You are so fucking wet for me."

"Always," she whispers, and I groan at her confession.

Why did I take so long to get here?

I slide my thumb into her up to the first joint, and she sighs, her eyes fluttering shut. She looks so fucking good that this time, I sink two fingers into her wet heat, feeling her stretch around me.

I gaze up at her, watching those perfect pink nipples turning to hard points, watching goose bumps spray over her arms. "I wonder how a pussy this pretty tastes."

Her eyes fly open, just in time to watch me slide those same two fingers into my mouth.

"Jesus Christ," she mutters, watching me with rapt fascination as I savor her.

And then I pull her down toward me and dive in.

CHAPTER 21

Violet

I'M HAVING AN OUT-OF-BODY EXPERIENCE. I'M BATTING SO far out of my league. Cole Harding is so fucking hot. I thought he was from that first day he came storming toward me in the winner's circle. Older. Richer. Better looking. But the sight of his disheveled, inky hair between my legs is something else.

It's primal. It's delicious torture.

The way he wraps his arms around my legs. The rasp of his stubble against my inner thighs. That goddamn tongue.

I feel so small with him holding me open. So exposed. But not like last time. This time he's *here*, and the way he looks at me—dark and possessive—makes my stomach flip.

I moan, making a sound I'm positive I've never made before this moment. A sound that would normally make me blush. But I'm beyond blushing. My entire body is on fire. I'm one big blush.

I roll my hips up toward his face, and he pushes back in harder, devouring me, propelling me higher. Tongue, lips, teeth, everything in perfect proportion. The man is a master.

"Cole…" I tangle my fingers in his dark hair and give him a gentle tug.

He pauses only long enough to pepper a few sweet kisses right along my inner thigh.

"Don't stop."

He chuckles, and it rolls across my skin like electricity. So deep and so private. Every time he laughs with me, shares that pleasure, it feels like more. He doesn't just hand out laughs like they mean nothing. With him, it's a true sign of affection. And I eat it up.

When he slides two fingers into me again and curls them *just* right, I fall apart.

"Cole!" My legs shake as I clamp them around his head, and my fingers twine in his hair, squeezing in time with the pulsing of my body. Pure heat surges through me as my orgasm overtakes me, making my back arch to its limits.

I swear I see stars.

But as I come down, I don't feel boneless. I feel ravenous. I want more. I want to watch Cole hit that high. I want to see him come apart for me.

I want him inside me.

My fingers dig into his toned shoulders, trying to get purchase, but they're clammy and just end up sliding over every muscle. "Get up here. I need you."

He looks up at me from between my legs, lips glistening, eyes wide and dark like coal. "Violet, it's okay. We can go slow." He unwraps his arms and slides his hands up the tops of my thighs, gaze flitting down to my pussy again.

I grab his wrist and pull him toward me right as I lean down and capture his mouth. He groans as my hands roam his shoulders. I can't get enough of his shoulders. Big and round and broad.

Holding him close, I whisper against his cheek, "I think I'm done going slow. I've wanted you for long enough."

With a deep growl, he grabs me as he pushes himself up into the chair and flips our positions. Now I'm straddling him just like I was last night in the forest shelter. Except this time, there's nothing between us, and the length of him is pressing right against me. I can't help but rotate my hips, to slide myself on him, to finally feel his skin on mine.

He stares at his hands wrapped around my waist and lets his gaze trail up over my body. "Lose the tank top." His voice is all heat now. Any hint of uncertainty has fled his tone.

I pull it off instantly, not feeling shy about being completely naked in front of Cole. Not at all. I've been here before. I knew less about him then—less about the type of man he is. Because if I've learned anything in the last month, it's that Cole Harding is a *good* man. Broken and sensitive and so fucking good.

I also didn't have the benefit of seeing the way he's looking at me right now, which is with pure awe. Unadulterated lust. Intense hunger.

"I don't have a condom." He doesn't even look up at me as he says it.

I push up on my knees, hovering over his lap, feeling the head of his cock bobbing against my inner thigh.

"I'm on birth control. I don't care. I want to feel you inside me."

"Jesus Christ, Violet." The pads of his fingers pulse on my waist as he lifts me to line us up perfectly. "I'm going to watch you take every inch," he mutters as he lowers me back down on him.

I feel the stretch, the overwhelming fullness, as I glide down the length of his cock slowly, his fingers digging into me tightly. I gasp with the feeling, with the knowledge that he's really inside me, with the brazenness of his words.

"Good girl. Every fucking inch."

His voice is raw, and my nerves are frayed. I want him to undo me and never put me back together again. We both look down at where we're joined. Nothing between us. Just the two of us. Together.

Finally.

His grip finds my chin, and he kisses me roughly, with so much passion that it winds me. I taste myself on his tongue as it swipes into my mouth, and I move my hips in time with the pace he sets.

Every pass of his tongue matches the swivel of my pelvis. His spare hand roams my body, leaving a trail of blistering heat. I feel every ridge of him, every thick inch, as his hips buck and meet me, shoving his length into me with growing abandon.

We clash. We melt. We heal.

I don't need poetic words or grand apologies from Cole.

That's not the man he is. Just this. Opening up to me like this—loving me like this—it's how he shows me. The phrase *Actions speak louder than words* has never applied to another human more aptly.

Cole Harding wouldn't be fucking me like this if he didn't care about me, and I know it. I feel like a queen writhing in his lap as he pulls his mouth from mine and drags it down my throat and over my collarbones.

"You are so fucking beautiful," he whispers as he captures my nipple in his sinful mouth. His teeth graze, and I hiss. "And so fucking precious." The flat of his tongue soothes the sting. And then he glances up at me, looking completely and utterly blown away. He looks like he's worshipping at my altar in this darkened living room. His hands hover shakily over my ribs. "You are so fucking precious to me."

I can't keep my hands from fluttering over his face, my fingers from tracing that scar that cuts through his brow, as I look back down at him, knowing I'll never want to let him go after this. "Don't let me go this time."

His throat bobs, and I think his eyes might sting, just like mine, as he nods back at me. "I won't."

"Good. Now make me come again."

He moves hard and fast in me, gripping my hips and manhandling my body in the most dominating way. My thighs slap against his as he lifts me and slams me down on his length over and over again.

Perspiration dampens his chest, and his cheeks are ruddy when he puffs out, "Let me see you rub that clit, Violet. Come on my cock."

My hand darts off his shoulder as I lean back a little. I think his words might be enough to push me over the edge, and all it takes is a few slick swipes with my fingers to have me hitting that crescendo again. Heat pools at the base of my spine as my orgasm roars to life.

"Cole!" I cry out just as that spot below my hipbones aches and the arches of my feet cramp up.

I collapse forward onto his chest, damp and spent and completely at his mercy as he pumps into me a last few times, hitting every tender spot as he does.

And with one powerful thrust, he freezes.

He clamps his arms around me, caging me in as he holds on for dear life and pours himself into me.

Chest to chest.

Heart to heart.

★★★

A hot bath has never felt so good. Partly because my body is gloriously sore from the best sex of my life and partly because I'm sitting across from the most deliciously sexy man I've ever known.

After our time in the living room, we were both a sticky mess. Boneless, breathless, sticky messes. I didn't know what to say after sex like that, but I knew his stump was rubbed and sore from the spare prosthetic, so I got up and ran us a bath.

This bathroom has the best deep claw-foot tub. I thought it was big before, but looking at Cole sitting at the other end, it doesn't look so spacious anymore.

Steam wafts up from between us. It smells like eucalyptus from the Epsom salts, which has the added benefit of being good for soreness—and for perfectly clear bath water.

And yeah, I can't stop sneaking peeks at the monster between his legs.

Cole's hands are wrapped around my calves as they rest across his thighs, and his head is tipped back against the tub, eyes closed. I am positively bursting with questions, but I also can't stop admiring his body. It's like a piece of art. A testament to long hours spent healing, adapting, and surviving. Living proof of his strength and resilience.

A goddamned treat.

My eyes wander over his leg, the one that ends just below the knee. The angry red scar at the end of the stump, the puckered skin all pulled together to close off the leg they couldn't save. But mostly I stare at his huge dick. In fact, I have a hard time looking away from it.

Yeah, I'm perving hard, and I don't even feel bad. The man looks like a well-hung Ken doll, and he's somehow magically into *me*. A scrappy ranch rat from a small cowboy town. Scrawny little Violet Eaton.

"Are you sure you haven't had sex in years?" I blurt out, because I can't reconcile this hot, rich, successful older man being interested in me or keeping it in his pants for *years*.

He doesn't look up, but I see one cheek quirk and feel his thumb rub in a circle on my calf.

"I knew you had questions. It's like I could hear the gears in your head turning."

"I mean, *come on*. Look at you. You really mean to tell me

you haven't had sex since—" Ugh. I don't even want to say her name. I'm jealous, and it's so unlike me. "Since what's-her-face took off?"

His shoulders shake on a silent laugh, but he still doesn't open his eyes. "There were a few off the start. Random encounters with a stranger where I wouldn't have to take my clothes all the way off. Like just bent her over and—"

"Okay. I've got the gist."

He chuckles again and peeks one eye open at me and catches me nervously chewing on my lip. He knows I'm jealous, but he doesn't call me on it. He just says, "All that taught me is that I don't like casual sex."

"Okay...but years? You could have anyone you want."

He grunts. Like he doesn't quite agree with my assessment. "Maybe I don't want just anyone. I think I like being in a relationship. It's probably why I rushed into an engagement before. But she didn't want me; she wanted the idea of me. The status." He sighs and sits up straighter. "You..."

My heart lurches in my chest. *I what?*

"You stuck around when you knew nothing about me. Like you enjoyed my company or something—and no one enjoys my company. Not anymore. But you were like a moth to a flame, knowing it would burn you eventually. Beautiful and innocent. And strong. And I was so fucking scared of letting you get too close, of opening up. But you never forced my hand. You just quietly made me need you." He scrubs at his stubble with one hand. "And then you left, and I told myself I was right all along—that everyone leaves me. Until the universe laughed in my face and shoved you right back into my life."

I let out a breathy laugh and blink rapidly, turning his words over in my mind. "It sort of did, didn't it?"

"And then you were just yourself. You didn't miss a beat. You came back for more. Forced me out of my shell. So relentless. So fucking consuming. It's like you've seen all my darkest corners and don't give a shit about them. You're not scared. You don't look at me like I'm tragic. You look at me like we're inevitable."

My throat aches, and my eyes go glassy. I look at him with a watery smile because I don't trust myself to speak. What I don't say is…*that's* what scares me.

We are completely inevitable.

CHAPTER 22

Cole

For the second morning in a row, I wake with Violet snuggled into my chest. She's curled into me like she can't get close enough, little hands grasping at the white T-shirt I'm wearing, fisted into it to keep me close.

I smile, liking how it looks. Liking the thought that she wants me close. Liking waking up next to her, the smell of her on my sheets. Even the purring doesn't bug me. Someone so small and dainty making that noise is just plain charming.

The sun filters in through the windows of the room, casting a sparkly glow over her pale hair. She looks downright angelic. With those pouty, rose-petal lips parted slightly, I can't help but think back to sliding my cock between them, the way she kneeled before me and looked up into my eyes.

I feel myself swell. *Fuck.* That was something I'll never forget. She might have been the one on her knees, but it felt more like I was the one begging. Even this morning, I feel like I should pinch myself. A woman like Violet wants me. And I can't wrap my head around it.

She asked why her, when I could have anyone I want, a comment that still makes me shake my head. I'm a thirty-six-year-old man with nothing to show for my years on earth except a company that was handed down to me and a nice lingering dose of PTSD from a dead dad and a blown-off leg. No house. No friends. No kids. I've always wanted kids, but here I am without a single one of those things on the horizon.

And in walks Violet, every one of those things readily available to her, and she wants what? *Me*? I just can't reconcile it. I haven't even tried to pretend I'm something else. I've been surly and unreachable, and the odd time I've given in to her allure, I've ended up shoving her away like she's nothing.

I realize she might be everything.

The light at the end of the dark tunnel. The sunshine my dark existence so desperately needs.

I can't stop myself from brushing my lips across her temple. She feels so precious wrapped up in my arms right now.

"Hi," she murmurs quietly, nuzzling against my chest.

"Sorry. I didn't mean to wake you up."

"I'm glad you did. That's a pretty good way to start the day."

My heart thunders against my ribs. *Is she serious?*

This time, I press a kiss to her hair and cup the back of her head, still amazed she's even letting me touch her. She's so fucking precious.

"What time is it?" She doesn't even poke her head out of our little cocoon.

I look over at the bedside table. "Eight."

She groans. "I need to get going."

"For what?"

"Into the city. I've got rides today on some of the younger horses early on. And then DD in the stakes this evening. You coming to watch?"

Her voice sounds so hopeful. I swallow roughly. I don't love watching the races at the best of times. But now? After this? Having to watch Violet on a horse, running at breakneck speeds, over the ground where I watched my dad die? It feels impossible. Terrifying.

It feels like I need to call Trixie and confess some shit.

"Sure," I say woodenly as I trail a hand over her slender back, feeling it rise and fall with each breath, something that feels reassuring as I try not to fixate on the thought of her getting hurt out there. Or worse.

She slides a hand over my ribs and squeezes. "I'll be fine."

"I know," I murmur back.

The lie tastes sour on my tongue. I don't know that she'll be fine. I can't predict that kind of thing. The words feel cheap, but I say them because I know they're what she wants to hear.

The traffic heading into the city is obnoxious. I guess after over a month of living out in Ruby Creek, I've grown accustomed to getting anywhere I need to go in mere minutes and without encountering a single other person.

Something I appreciate. Not having people everywhere

all the time is preferable to the noise, the mess, the ant-colony feel of downtown Vancouver. Just a bunch of mindless little worker ants scurrying off to their jobs so they can overpay for rent or—god forbid—a mortgage. The housing market in this city is downright criminal.

I could afford one if I wanted, but it's the principle. A run-down bungalow on a small lot shouldn't cost a person over a million dollars. I've seen how people live in other parts of the world, and the excess of this city grates on me. It's wasteful.

Maybe that's something I've come to appreciate about country living and small-town residents. They live well within their means. Hardworking people who aren't trying to keep up with the Joneses. It's like another world. A smaller, quieter, more real world where people work to enjoy what they've got rather than working to afford something that might impress their friends.

Just a completely different mentality. One I like—that I might align with more than I initially thought.

Since traffic doesn't appear to be going anywhere—on a fucking Sunday afternoon—I decide I might as well bite the bullet and call Trixie. Something I've been avoiding doing because truthfully, I don't know how she's going to react to everything that's transpired.

Have I gone off the deep end? Is this happening too fast? It feels fast. We haven't even talked about what we're doing. Violet kissed me sweetly, deeply, when she left my house this morning and then hopped in her car and drove off.

All she said was, "See you later," and I'm so fucking out

of practice with women that I don't even know what that means.

I blurted out more to her last night in that bathtub than I've said to anyone, other than Trixie, and she didn't run screaming for the hills. So where does that leave us? I feel like a teenager all over again. Can I just leave her a note like I would have back then?

Want to be my girlfriend? Check yes or no.

I scoff as I jam my finger at the screen of my phone and hear the ringing filter in through my Bluetooth system.

Trixie's voice booms through the cab of my truck, making me wince and adjust the volume. "Cole. It's a Sunday."

"I had sex." That should change her attitude.

The speakers are quiet for a few beats. "Real sex? Or internet sex?"

Why does everyone keep calling it that? "Real sex."

She lets out a long whistle. "How was it?"

"Jesus Christ, Trixie. Is that something therapists ask their patients?"

"Ha! I don't see why not. If you're going to call me on a Sunday like I'm a guy friend, then I might as well ask the same questions someone like that might."

I groan. Trixie is anything but your average therapist. Of course, that's actually what I like about her. Sad as it sounds, she's also one of the closest things I have to a genuine friend. And I pay her.

"It was...overwhelming."

"Overwhelmingly...good?"

"Yes," I bite out, feeling uncomfortable even though I'm the one who called her.

"Okay. And where did you meet this person?"

"It was Violet."

I swear I can feel Trixie smile through the phone. She's spent the last year telling me I needed to bite the bullet and reach out to Violet. Say something. *Anything*. Rather than pretending she doesn't exist. That even if it didn't go anywhere, I might feel better just getting everything off my chest.

But I kept putting it off, telling myself I'd do it eventually. All I'd have to do is drive out to the farm and talk to her. But no, instead I hid out in the owner's lounge and scowled down at her during every race she ran. I haven't missed many since I figured out who she was. The one where Cassel took her down, because I was busy moving out to Ruby Creek, and yesterday, when I was just too tired and too sore from our adventure up on the mountain to make it. It felt wrong not being there. Like I've been in this secret relationship with her for the last year that she had no idea about.

Because I have. Writing her in the chat, watching her from the skybox, getting updates from Vaughn, who always eyed me suspiciously as he did.

"I'm happy for you, Cole," Trixie says. Like she doesn't think I've fucked up at all.

"That's it? No words of wisdom? No advice? No scolding?"

She hums. "What would you like me to tell you?"

"I don't know. Something. Anything? She's young. Maybe I'm a creep."

"Is she of legal age? Did she consent?"

I want to feel you inside me, that's what she said, and Trixie knows Violet is well into her twenties. She's only asking to prove a point.

"Yes."

"Then I don't see the issue," she says simply.

"She's just so vivacious. Really going somewhere, you know?"

"And you're not?"

I groan. She always does this. Spins it back around on me.

"I don't feel like I am."

"Okay. And have you asked her how she feels? Do you think that a woman who you've described to me as intelligent and going somewhere would saddle herself down with someone she perceives to be deadweight? What would that say about her?"

My brain backflips to follow her logic. But I see what she's saying. If Violet is who I've told Trixie she is, then she must see something in me I can't see in myself.

She takes my silence as an answer. "Presumably, she knows about your leg now?"

"Yeah." I scrub at my face, remembering how I felt like my world was falling apart two days ago on the mountain. How I felt like I wanted to dissolve into the dirt path to avoid her knowing about it. "My prosthetic malfunctioned on our hike. She knows about it in graphic detail." I spit the last part out, still hating how incapable it makes me feel.

"And what was her response?"

I think back on the hopping and crawling jokes she made and sigh. "She didn't seem to care at all."

"I've been telling you for two years that no one cares about your leg except for you."

I can't help but chuckle as I recall the few times Trixie has told me this. *You're not a special snowflake. Stop acting like one.*

"I guess I needed proof. The universe forced my hand with this one."

"It has a funny way of doing that, doesn't it?"

Traffic crawls toward Bell Point Park as I mull over those words. All the ways I've woven Violet into the fabric of my reality. How inescapable she's become.

"Guess so," I muse. "I just don't want to hold her back."

"But you want to keep her?" Trixie sounds far too hopeful. I almost hate to confess this to her.

"Yes," I reply, because I do. I've avoided admitting this to myself, but it's true. I want Violet as way more than a pen pal or friend and definitely as more than a one-time thing.

"Then don't hold her back. Bolster her up. Be her biggest fan."

All that hope sprouting in the dusty wasteland that is my heart shrivels. Can I bring myself to support her when I can barely stand the thought of her out there on the track? And why the fuck would the universe put her in my path when I can barely stand the thought of kissing her goodbye to go do the very thing that killed my dad?

"And, Cole," she adds, "talk to her."

Right. Talk to her.

★★★

A PHOTO FINISH

I stand in the owner's lounge beside my brother, looking down over the track. It's almost time for the stakes race, and I feel like I might barf. I cross my arms over my chest and squeeze, trying to push the panic clawing its way up inside me back down.

"You look like you're going to kill somebody." Vaughn takes a sip of his scotch and shoots me a playful glance. Always joking around. What must it be like to feel so carefree? I wish I knew.

I just grunt. I'm okay with looking like I might kill someone. It means my poker face is still intact because I definitely don't want to look like I might break down. Or worse, like a lovestruck idiot. And even more, I don't want to talk about my past with Violet now that he knows about it. In fact, I'm a little surprised he hasn't cracked a joke about it yet.

"Gentlemen," I hear from behind me and turn around, coming face-to-face with a man I've never met before. Dark blond hair, crooked nose, expensive suit. He looks like a total chump.

"Dalca," Vaughn says, his voice going chilly after teasing me mere moments ago. "What can I help you with?"

Ah, this is Stefan Dalca. The man who almost took my little brother for a ride. The man who employs Patrick Cassel, the shithead who made Violet fall. I want to kill them both.

"I just wanted to apologize for Patrick Cassel's behavior. He's no longer employed by me."

Okay, I want to kill him a little less now. Maybe just maim him. Break that nose again. "The person you owe an apology to is Miss Eaton."

The man turns his hawkish eyes my way. They're intelligent, scanning—altogether too confident. I don't trust this guy as far as I can fucking throw him.

"I'll track her down." His lips tip up into a sly smile that I want nothing more than to wipe off his face.

But instead, I nod. My days of flying off the handle are behind me. I've got different problems now.

"Good luck today." He sticks his hand out as though I'll shake it.

I look at it and then shift my gaze up to his face. I'm not shaking this guy's hand. All I'm giving him is an unimpressed look. Vaughn does the same.

"Okay. Tough customers," he says with a chuckle before he swaggers away. I can see why Billie hates the guy. She's nothing if not an excellent judge of character.

"Nice. I love it when you go all glacial like that. It's fucking terrifying." Vaughn drinks again with a big goofy grin on his face. "Violet is a braver woman than I am."

There it is. I shift my eyes over to Vaughn, who looks like a kid on Christmas morning, far too excited to see my reaction to that comment.

"And Billie is a more patient woman than I."

Vaughn barks out a loud laugh that has people looking our way as his shoulders shake. "Thank fuck for that," he says, looking back out over the track. "There they are!"

He points toward Violet, sitting atop a shiny dark horse in matching black and gold silks, her champagne hair plaited straight down her back. I feel instantly nauseous at the sight of her out there but swallow it down.

I don't want to be that guy. And I don't want my snoopy little brother knowing that I feel like that guy.

DD prances beside the pony rider that leads them along the track, and I'm glad that someone is there to escort them safely. Some horses are really riled, jumping around, but not the little stallion. He prances along slowly, like he knows he's fancy—perfectly confident. Violet looks that way too. Still and quiet, one hand smoothing up and down the horse's muscular neck.

I shouldn't be nervous about this race. It's not a huge deal. It's a qualifier. But I am. My chest is tight, and I feel like my throat is trying to crawl up out of my mouth.

I cross my arms over my chest again as they load up into the gates. I know DD gets nervous in there because I've heard Violet talk about it. I also know jockeys can get injured in there if things go sideways. My fingers wrap around my thumbs underneath my biceps and squeeze tightly. Maybe if something hurts, I'll be able to get a handle on my anxiety, focus on something else.

The bell rings, the gates fly open, and the line of horses surge out in a mass of pounding hooves and flying dirt. Violet and DD hang back predictably. This is their play, their move.

My teeth grind as I watch her sink into the tack. So in sync, moving in time with the horse as he stretches out underneath her. He's a finicky stallion, but Violet doesn't get in his way. She lets him be quirky and uses it to their advantage, making it a winning feature rather than forcing him to be a type of horse he isn't.

They keep to the back—but not too far behind—down the first stretch. But when they move into the first turn, their focus changes. Violet shifts down lower, pushes her hands farther up his neck, and he surges up through the middle, making his way into the pack.

Exactly where *it* happened. The slip. The fall. The hooves. And a still form in the dirt as the pack continued to head away toward the finish line. Like a man in the dirt was nothing.

It's been *years*, and that image is still burned into my mind. No one stopped. No one went back. In the army, we *always* went back. Even if it was just for pieces.

A gray horse moves out in front of Violet, and I suck in a breath. Vaughn notices, but he doesn't say anything. He just peeks at me out of the corner of his eye. Violet backs off, playing it safe, looking for an opening. And when she doesn't see one coming out of that final turn, she takes him wide. It means they'll be forced to cover more ground.

But if anyone can pull the move off, it's going to be this team. Even I know that much. Murmurs roll through the skybox as she flattens out and pushes her arms at DD while his stride eats up the ground. I know he's not a large horse, not even especially leggy by racehorse standards, but the little spitfire doesn't let that stop him.

It is truly a sight to behold.

As they near the finish line with a wide-open lane, I feel my icy dread morph into something warmer. Excitement. She's about to do it again. And I am so damn proud.

Hard work, sweat, and her fierce determination are

paying off in spades. A little country bumpkin with a no-quit outlook and infallible positivity is making her dreams come true. And I admire the hell out of her for it.

They fly across the finish line, and it's tight with DD and the other horse pretty much neck and neck. To be honest, I can't tell who won, but I don't care. All I want to do is see Violet. I realize in this moment how badly I need her—want her. I want to run my hands all over her body. I need to feel her. To know she's okay. I haven't felt this level of anxiety since right after my discharge, when I couldn't even hear a car door slam without jumping. *You're fucking losing it, man.*

"A photo finish," Vaughn mutters as he shakes his head and jangles his keys in his pocket.

I'm not the only nervous wreck, it would seem, but he stays up here because Billie gets anxious. She doesn't like him in her space when she's working, which is something I can appreciate. Suddenly, I realize I don't know what Violet likes. Would she want me down there? Are we going to be a thing where that's even an option? I'm not sure if I could handle it. What about now? After the race? Do I wait until tonight, back at the ranch? Tomorrow? Follow her around like a sad little puppy dog? *So fucking pathetic, Cole.*

I groan, hating how uncertain I feel about this whole thing. I hate feeling out of control. This is when accidents happen. Missions go wrong. People get hurt.

Hearts get broken.

"I gotta go," I say to Vaughn as I turn to leave before he can see my face. Because as good as I am at hiding my emotions, I feel like they are probably written all over me right now. I don't care about the photo finish results; I just need Violet.

I shoulder through the crowd in the skybox, heading to the exit, down the stairs, out the door, and into the muggy heat. Rather than turning toward the track, I head in the direction of the barns.

I'm going to see Violet because it feels right. And if I think about it too much, I'll let my uncertainty talk me out of it. God knows the woman has put herself out there enough times for me, to get to know me. And I've been a closed-off dick about it, taking far more than I give.

What's the worst that could happen? She tells me now's not a good time? She's busy? Seems to me I've faced bigger disasters for less reward.

I stride into the barn and turn down the row of stalls with the Gold Rush Ranch sign at the entryway. Mira, the vet, is at one stall going through what looks like a big toolbox.

"Where's Violet?"

She turns and looks up at me slowly, like she has all the time in the world. "Excuse me."

"I said—"

"No," she cuts me off, "I know what you said. But you missed saying it politely."

My jaw ticks. What is with all the insanely lippy women at Gold Rush Ranch? Has Vaughn made it a job requirement? Even Violet isn't as mild-mannered as she used to be, which is good. Billie and Mira are good for her. But man, getting called on my shit all the time is tiring. It's like I'm living among a bunch of young Trixies.

I sigh dramatically as I try again. "Excuse me. Have you seen Violet?"

"I knew you weren't as bad as Billie makes you out to be," the black-haired woman singsongs. *Fucking Billie.* "And also no. I imagine she's weighing in. Head out that way, and you'll probably run into her." She points to the opposite end of the darkened alleyway.

"Thanks." I wave as I head in that direction.

She just winks at me. Like she knows I'm a total fucking goner. But as I round the corner, all I can think about is Violet. On her knees. In my lap. In my bed.

It's like she broke down all the walls around me, and now I can't stop myself from spilling everywhere. I'm oozing out all over the fucking place.

When I walk out into the sunlit road, I catch sight of Violet walking toward me, wearing a simple blue wrap dress that matches her eyes perfectly. Her hair is drawn up tight in a bun, and her smile is blinding when she catches sight of me.

"Hey, you!" she calls out with a small wave and a little skip in her step. "I'm so glad you're here! We won!"

And then I go full caveman.

CHAPTER 23

Violet

When I see Cole marching out of the barn, I can't help but smile. When I get close enough to him, I look away. He's so beautiful it hurts. He looks like a storm cloud, dark and menacing and problematic for my panties. But I know better. He's a big puppy d—

I lose my train of thought when he wraps his hand around my wrist and drags me back toward the barn.

"What's wrong?"

He pulls us into the darkened shed row and then straight into an empty stall. When he turns me to face him, he's all steely eyes and hard lines. He prowls forward, and I back away. Not because I'm scared. More because I don't trust myself not to combust under a gaze like that. I can't believe I was about to call the man a puppy dog. My nipples rasp against my bra, and I press my thighs together as I bump into the wall.

I hold one hand up to stop him. "Cole. What's wrong?"

"What's wrong?" His voice is low. "What's wrong is I can't stop thinking about you. And those perfect tits. And that tight little cunt. And those pretty little lips."

I moan and feel my face go pink. He may have been vulnerable last night, but *this* is the Cole I remember. Gruff and filthy and so damn hot. The man who could push me to my limits—exactly where I want to go.

I try to say something, but my lips just open and close like a fish out of water. Like a girl out of her league.

"Do you have panties on this time?" His intense eyes scan me, leaving a trail of sparks in their wake.

I go pure red, from head to toe, and look around us. The stall is lower than the alleyway, with no bedding in it, just rubber mats, and we're pushed up into the corner behind the front wall. No one would see us unless they specifically came into the stall.

I roll my shoulders back and look him square in the eye, refusing to be Shy Violet. I shed that skin a long time ago—at least in my head I did. "Yes."

"Turn around."

"What?" I feel my eyes bug out of their sockets.

"I said turn around."

My blood hums through my veins as I take a shaky breath and turn to face the wooden wall of the stall.

"You drive me crazy. Do you know that?" He steps in close, and I feel his heat along the entire length of my back, his breath across the nape of my neck.

"Good," I reply honestly. "Serves you right."

His breath hisses out, and he finally puts his hands on me, right where my waist nips in. And then he's taking fistfuls of my dress, pulling it up, the hemline tickling the backs of my bare thighs as he does. "I should spank you for talking like that."

I moan and shimmy my ass, brushing it up against the hard bulge at the front of his pants.

"You'd like that, wouldn't you?"

"Yes," I breathe out.

One minute, I'm in my element: galloping toward the finish line, winning a race, waiting on results, and weighing in; the next, I'm bent over and rubbing up on the man I can't stop thinking about, getting spanked for being mouthy. His palm lands swift and sure against the bare cheek of my ass, and I can't help the needy whimper that spills out over my lips. The sting blooms into heat, and I love the feel of it.

Today is a good day.

One of his palms presses between my shoulders, and he kicks my feet apart with perfect authority, complete control. Over himself and over me.

A thrill races down my spine, and I submit under his touch, allowing him to bend me forward. Is it okay for me to be fiercely independent everywhere except when his hands are on me? Because right now, all I want to do is exactly what he tells me and just let go for a little while, to not try so hard for a few minutes. It's addictive. Freeing.

My breath comes in choppy spurts as he lays my skirt across my lower back and hooks his fingers into my lacy panties, dragging them down, leaving them stretched between my thighs. He runs his hands over my ass, giving me an appreciative squeeze. "You look downright edible with a little bit of pink on that ass, Violet." His voice is quiet, but I feel it in my bones. Like his body is speaking right to mine. "But I'll save that part for when I get you home. Back in my bed where you belong."

"Fuck yes" is all I can manage before going completely mindless as he slides a couple of fingers between my legs. I usually feel scrawny when I'm naked, unfeminine, but with Cole's hands on me, I feel like a different woman.

He groans and I shiver as he slides a finger inside me. "You're wet already. Dirty girl. You do like that, don't you?"

"You have that effect on me," I rasp out as I look over my shoulder.

His eyes hold mine, dark and frantic. "Tell me what you want."

I don't even need to think about my response. "More. Always more."

One hand shoots out to grip my chin roughly. His lips crash into mine as he fumbles with his belt and zipper. He shoves his tongue into my mouth. He's not searching or asking—he's taking.

And I'm giving.

I feel the blunt end of his cock slide against my seam and moan into his mouth. Suddenly I'm ravenous. Everything is taking too long. Time is moving too slow. I'm greedy.

I arch my back and push myself on him, feeling him slide inside me. Hard and fast. Just like the kiss. Relentless and unforgiving, that's what we are in this moment. Two bodies joined. Two people running at each other without the sense to stop before they crash.

Our mouths part, and I turn back toward the wall, dropping my head as he slams into me. One of his hands grips my hip, and the other slides firmly up over my back. His calloused fingers hover over my neck, right to the base of my skull, before his grip wraps gently around my throat, essentially holding me in place.

Like I might leave him.

I want to tell him that there's nowhere else I'd rather be than here. But my mind is mush, and my body is burning. The words don't come.

When his hand slides across my hip and over my stomach, he pulls me tight to him, shoving me forward into the wall before his fingers move down and press on the perfect spot. I rock in his arms as his fingers circle, driving me higher and higher. Right toward a cliff. I should know better than to jump from such heights, but I'm past the point of caring.

I leap and plunge right over the edge with him inside me. And he follows. I feel him twitch and go still as he covers my body with his. I sigh when he relaxes over me, his lips replacing his hand at the nape of my neck as he peppers kisses down my spine. His breathing is heavy in my ear.

"That was..." I can't put it into words. Inappropriate? Unprofessional? Super fucking hot?

"Yeah," he replies, sounding just as breathless as me as he leans down to pull my panties up and smooths my dress back down over my bare legs. His touch is warm and reverent as he sets me to rights. And when he spins me around to face him, he kisses me sweetly, longingly.

Cole is a man of dichotomies. Hot and cold. Rough and soft. Intense and relaxed. Confident and uncertain. He's multifaceted. And in the weeks I've spent around him, I've come to realize that I like every facet. Love them? Maybe. But that sounds like the ramblings of a lovesick girl swept off her feet by a rich older man who she's been lusting after for years. And I don't want to be that girl. So I don't let myself go there.

Instead, I kiss him back with all the feeling I can muster. All the longing, the affection, the acceptance—I want him to feel it all. That I'm here for *him*. Just the way he is.

When he smiles against my lips, I wonder if I've succeeded.

"Can I come to your place tonight? Once I finish up down here?" I ask quietly.

He offers me one of those rare soft, panty-melting smiles as he cups my head in his palms and gives me one of his quintessential one-word answers. "Yep."

I let out a giggle as he pulls me into his embrace, wrapping me inside his steely arms, and presses a soft kiss to the top of my head.

Cole Harding is way more romantic than he lets on.

"Open the gate."

Cole stares back at me, bulging biceps twisted together across his chest, legs wide. I chuckle internally. When Billie calls him G.I. Joe, this is what I envision. Army green joggers and a black T-shirt that is being downright abused by his muscles.

Just like I have been for the last couple of weeks. Every time we're not working or in public, we're naked. Together. I like to think of it as making up for lost time.

"Are you sure?" he asks, enunciating his words carefully. I know he wants to tell me no. I know he worries about me riding. I know his father's death haunts him. He doesn't need to have told me explicitly for me to have pieced it together. You can't live in fear of these unexpected tragedies though. And the only way I can prove this to him is to have him hang out with me and *the only horse* he likes. I want him to see the fun—the joy—riding a horse can bring to his life.

I'm sitting on Pippy's back, and he is being a literal gatekeeper. He doesn't want me to take her out into the fields even though I've spent the last couple weeks getting her started in the arena. She's walking, trotting, and cantering under saddle now. The steering still leaves something to be desired, but that will come.

Plus, steering doesn't matter much in a big open field.

"Very sure." I give him my best serious look, trying to instill confidence, though I'm sure I just look like a mischievous child trying to pull a fast one. The fact is, I'm not *very sure*. You can't be sure of anything in life. That you won't die having baby number four. Or on horseback. Or in an IED explosion. There aren't any guarantees. I mean, hell, if someone told me two years ago I'd be the jockey for the world's most popular racehorse, I wouldn't have believed that was possible either.

But here I am. Living. Taking life by the horns. Exactly like I promised myself I would. My dad couldn't stop me, or my brothers, and definitely not Cole. I want him around me for the long haul. And I need him on board if that's going to happen.

He still doesn't look sure, but he unlatches the gate and holds it open so I can steer Pippy onto the driveway. The hills near the barn look so lush and green this time of year. I love running races on the track, but galloping across an open field takes me back to my roots. Back to Alberta's foothills, where I grew up kicking cow ponies across the range. British Columbia is beautiful, but I miss that prairie feeling sometimes. Less polished, more country, endless flatland.

I walk past him as Pippy's ears flick around. Her neck comes up higher now as she looks at her surroundings. She's sweet and calm, but even she can feel that something else is happening right now. That's the biggest question mark with this filly. Is she too mellow to run?

"Good luck," Cole bites out, every part of him tense as he watches me go.

I look over my shoulder, wink, and blow him a kiss, trying not to let myself linger on his ashen face, the way it matches his gray eyes. He looks sick, and if I let myself stare at him for too long, I'll hop off and hold him instead. So I turn my game face to the field ahead of me. Time to find out what this little filly has under the hood.

Once I hit the edge of the grass, I give her ribs a gentle squeeze, urging her into a trot. Her head is still swiveling around, and when she senses we're heading out of her bubble, she lets out an excited whinny.

I wince. Such a pretty horse. Such a terrible sound.

We go down a gentle slope, and then all that's before us is the freshly cut hayfield with a big hill at the end of it—same one that Billie conditioned DD on. In case my brakes fail, my plan is to use that to slow down if needed, like one of those runaway lanes for semitrucks on the highway.

I run the leather reins through my fingers, shortening them, and adjust my feet in the irons, wanting to be as stable in the tack as possible before I let Pippy gallop for the first time. At my change in position, her back comes up, and I feel her haunches go tight. Like she knows what's coming.

When I slip one leg behind the girth and give her a little nudge, she breaks into a comfortable canter, still feeling a little uncertain. Like she doesn't know what I want from her. She's such a people pleaser. It doesn't surprise me at all. It's like she doesn't want to put one hoof out of place.

I move up in the tack, getting off her back, and loosen my elbows, letting my hands float higher up her neck. Her ears flick back in question, so I give her a squeeze with my legs and a firm cluck. She bursts forward almost instantly. And then I smile.

Because I've got a racehorse on my hands.

CHAPTER 24

Cole

Violet stirs in my arms, rubbing herself against me, and my cock instantly stands at attention. But I squeeze my eyes shut tighter, wanting to stay exactly where I am and savor it for a little bit longer.

My mind wanders to the day at the track when I outed myself to her as Golddiger85. I could have said nothing. And she would never have known who I am. Who I *was*. We wouldn't be here. *Together*. My rash decision in that moment has completely altered the course of my life, and for once, I'm not beating myself up about it.

It's been several weeks of sleepovers now. We don't spend any nights apart, and I wouldn't want to anyway. When Violet's with me, I know she's safe, and as much as I hate to admit it, she makes me feel safe too. Someone who knows everything I've been hiding for so damn long and still wants me. Someone who just looked at me like, *Yeah? And? Who cares?*

My leg, my PTSD, my anxiety around horses, she just lets it all be. Like it's my shit to deal with. Shit she's happy to put up with for some godforsaken reason. A reason I can't explain—or maybe I don't want to.

It's been bouncing around in my head lately. That four-letter word. I often wondered if I was in love with this beautiful, sweet, funny woman who kept talking to me for an entire year. Like I had something to offer her—like she enjoyed my company. But now, spending almost every night with her, inside her, it's a thought I can't shake.

I'm definitely in love with Violet Eaton.

The problem is admitting I'm in love with Violet means my carefully plotted-out existence is about to topple. I've spent so many years feeling undeserving of love, hiding myself from the mere possibility of it, that it feels bizarre to think that I might have found it now. With Violet, no less.

My hips push toward her ass of their own volition. I can't get enough. I feel like I'm in my twenties again with her around. Insatiable.

"Good morning." Her voice is warm and dopey as she pushes herself back at me, always equally eager. *Because she* is *in her twenties.*

I always feel weird about our age difference, a feeling that Violet doesn't share at all. Mostly she looks at me like I hung the moon. A look that makes my heart constrict, even if it makes me feel uncomfortable. I've spent so long hiding from view. Having someone admire me as openly as Violet does is a little unnerving.

"Good morning, beautiful," I murmur as I drag my teeth

up the side of her neck suggestively, watching a slow smile spread across the top side of her face. She's practically glowing in the golden morning light. She looks like an angel—my angel.

"I'll play if you go start the coffee."

Yes. Now I stock coffee. I don't know what it is with these women's reliance on the stuff, but it seems to make Violet happy. And I'm all for that.

I sit up and slide my stump into my new prosthetic, happy to have that custom fit back. And so damn fortunate that I can afford the state-of-the-art one I have. I like that Violet doesn't jump out of bed to make her own coffee because of my leg. She doesn't baby me, because she knows I'm perfectly capable. I smile over my shoulder at her, watching her stretch out like a cat in a sunbeam, all fucking pleased with herself.

I hum to myself as I jog down the stairs to the kitchen, feeling lighter than I have in years. I press the button on the coffee machine and then slide some sandals on at the front door, heading out to feed Pippy. The other girl in my life.

A chuckle rumbles in my chest when I open the door. She's waiting at the closest corner of her fence, too-long ears pricked in my direction and nostrils vibrating with the shrill hello whinny she's known for.

I never would have guessed it, but this little filly makes me smile every day. Another thing that hasn't happened to me in years. I pull a few flakes of hay off the bale and toss them over the fence for her, something she completely ignores until I've given her a few good scratches behind the ear.

"More concerned with lovin' than eating, huh?"

Her head twists toward me, and I admire how she's grown into herself. At two, her haunches are still a little higher than her wither, but she's filled out with muscle and a glowing bronze coat. Between her feeding regimen and Violet's elbow grease, she doesn't look like the same ratty filly who showed up at my house a few months ago.

"Guess we've both undergone a bit of transformation, haven't we, pretty girl?"

She snorts and bats her long lashes at me, her eyes like deep black pools. I swear she gives me a knowing look. Like, *Yeah, you fucking idiot. We both needed a fresh start.*

I shake my head and stroll back inside, leaving her to eat but mostly eager to get back to Violet. And when I make it up the stairs to the master bedroom, I go to announce my arrival, "I'm back—" but I stop short when I see Violet kneeling at the end of the bed, golden hair streaming down over her pert breasts, just like that day on the video chat. Except today, she's giving me that heartrending shy but willing look she pulls off so effortlessly.

"Let's try this again, Butterface." Her fingers pulse, squeezing at the bedspread beneath her. "But this time, we don't quit on each other."

My mouth goes dry instantly. "Violet. We don't need to do this."

"No." She wets her lips. "I need you to do this. Rewrite the memory for me. Don't leave me this time."

"I don't think I could leave you even if I wanted to. I'm so fucking sor—"

"Don't. Just tell me what to do."

Every muscle in my body goes taut. This is so fucking hot. She's so fucking forgiving. I don't fucking deserve her. But I'm going to spend every damn day trying. The thought invigorates me.

I start like I did a year ago, "Lie back on your pillows and spread your legs."

And just like the time before, she flushes pink. A whole-body blush.

"You look so fucking pretty in pink," I say as I stalk to the bed, feeling my knees butt up against the brass footboard. And when she lets her legs fall open, I groan. "You're going to be the death of me."

"Good," she says with a slight smirk. A small sign of her strength.

She might be gentle and soft-spoken, but Violet isn't weak. She can't be if she's going to withstand a man like me.

She settles back into the pillows, and I admire her body splayed out before me like an all-you-can-eat buffet. I plan to sample every inch. I let my gaze linger between her legs, glistening already. I can see it, but I want to hear her say it. "Are you wet already?"

Her chest rises on a small gasp as she looks down over her body and confesses with a small hiss, "Yesss."

"Of course you are." My prosthetic clangs against the bed frame, and my cock throbs. I don't know who I'm torturing more here—her or myself. "You love this, don't you?"

She just nods this time, cerulean eyes wide like pools of deep water. Like the river I can hear rushing behind the house.

"Why don't you touch yourself and show me?"

Her hand finds her pussy almost instantly while the other tangles in the sheets below her. Like she's holding on for dear life. I'm transfixed as her fingers trail through her folds, her eyes closing and head tipping back on a moan. Most men would probably be engrossed by what's happening between her legs right now, but I'm staring at the way her elegant neck extends, her exposed throat and the way it moves as she swallows.

"Two fingers in, baby."

She whimpers but follows my directions. I don't miss the way her thighs tremble as she does it though, the way her toes curl and clench. She pumps in a few times, making the most delicious fucking noises as she does.

"Now show me how wet you are."

Her eyes flick open, and her jaw drops. Still so damn shocked sometimes. *Oh, honey…*

Right as she holds her fingers up to show me how wet she is, I say, "Now suck them."

"Jesus…" she mutters, momentarily looking away with a small smile on her mouth. Like she loves it but can't believe she does. It makes me smile too. Until she puts them in her mouth and moans around her fingers.

Fuuucckk.

She giggles, which makes my cock jump painfully in my boxers.

"No toy to play with this time."

"I'm looking at him." She sounds out of breath now. Wet, breathless, and blushing.

I live for this version of Violet Eaton, and I can't wait another minute to dive in. I'm over the end of the bed and crawling toward her, yanking my boxers down and moving straight in between her spread legs before she can get another word out.

"I don't remember this part from last time." She laughs, and it's fucking music to my ears. I'll never get sick of making that up to her.

I'm ready to crawl back into bed and sleep after an early morning marathon sex session with Violet. I haven't had this much sex in, well, probably ever. Unfortunately, we're both gainfully employed and have jobs we need to get to today.

"See you tonight?" she asks, sliding into a pair of skin-tight riding pants that has my mind wandering places it should be tired of going by now. We've been sort of sneaking around for a few weeks. We don't go out. We work and fuck and then talk until we fall asleep in each other's arms. She's met up with Billie and Mira the odd time, but she never invites me to come—even though I know Vaughn is often with them.

I sometimes catch myself wondering if she wants more. I should just ask her. I should take Trixie's advice and talk to her about my anxiety around my dad, the depth of it. Around horses. And the fact that she rides them for a living. But it's so pathetically insecure, I haven't talked myself into it.

At least I'm consistent.

"Of course." I swipe her wet hair off her cheek and cup

her head just below her ear as I press a kiss to her cheek. I love how dainty she feels in my hands. Precious.

We get ready quickly, quietly, running behind after having to take another shower. And when I lock the door behind us, she stops and spins around, launching herself at me, wrapping her arms around my neck and planting a big kiss on me. I'm a little surprised, but I catch up, pulling her close with one arm around her waist and letting the other take a nice big handful of that ass in those tight pants. This is the morning goodbye I've always dreamt of.

And then a throat clears loudly. "Is it weird for me to say that was pretty hot?"

Billie.

Violet laughs, her shoulders shaking as she buries her head in my armpit and whispers, "I'm sorry."

What? "Did you know she was there?"

She nods, her forehead against me, her body still shaking.

I laugh too. It's always contagious with her. I'm also relieved she doesn't seem horrified by being caught kissing me, and I can't help but let my amusement show. "Do you think that if we ignore her, she'll go away?"

Her laugh turns into a loud snort as she wheezes out, "No. Definitely not."

"I heard that," Billie shouts. "Really cute. I came to bring you the farm financials."

I look up as she waves a folder over her head and then sets it down on the gravel driveway.

"But I'm not getting any closer to that house. God knows what kind of filthy shit has been going on in there."

"Billie," I warn, knowing it won't make a difference. The woman has no filter.

Violet chortles in the most unladylike way, squeezing in tighter like if she gets close enough, she can hide inside me entirely.

"I'm leaving them right there." Billie points down before holding her hands over head and stepping away slowly, like this is some sort of hostage situation. "For what it's worth, I'm just glad people will stop talking about *my* cabin being the love shack now. See you up at the barn, Porn Star Patty!"

She grins and winks at me as Violet melts down into my arms. Billie looks far too pleased with herself and, to my surprise, not upset at all. I don't know why…but I expected her to be weird or protective or something. I expected a scolding for scooping up someone so young and normal. I expected Billie, of all people, to see how I don't deserve the woman in my arms.

But she just looks amused.

When she finally pulls out of the driveway, Violet gasps out, "I'm…I'm sorry." She looks up at me with tears of laughter pouring down her face. And I feel like I'm in some sort of upside-down world. Why is no one mad about this? "I shouldn't have done that to you."

"Let me get this straight." I lean back to look down at her with a furrowed brow. "You kissed me on purpose. Because you knew Billie was there?"

She swipes at her face, trying to catch her breath. "Yes. I–I'm sorry. I wanted people to know about us but didn't know how to bring it up or ask you or tell them. I saw her truck there out of the corner of my eye, and it seemed like the simplest solution. We are an *us*, right?" When she says *us*, she peeks up at me from under thick lashes shyly.

I blink at her, scanning her face for some sign that she might be joking. Because in what universe does *this woman* want *me* to be an *us* with *her*? I literally shake my head and count my lucky fucking stars. And then I kiss her hard, hold her to me tight, and show her how badly I want to be an *us*.

"We are definitely an *us*."

I pull up to the farmhouse and close my eyes, dropping my head against the seat. Work was shitty, and that's saying something considering the mood I arrived in. Between hot morning sex and Violet staking her claim on me in front of her friend, I was in a great fucking mood.

I don't feel like I'm getting anywhere with the new acquisition. Which means I'll be stuck out in Ruby Creek for longer, getting things organized and running smoothly before finding someone else to take it over. I wasn't supposed to like it in Ruby Creek. I was supposed to hate it. But I'm not hating it at all.

I don't want to leave because I know Violet won't be leaving. And that agitates me. I spent all day working out the ways we'd see each other once I move back to the city. She can stay with me on the days she races at Bell Point Park, and maybe I can get out to the ranch on the weekends.

But I don't like that option. I want Violet in my bed every night. Where I can see her. Hold her. Keep her safe.

Not an hour and a half down a major highway doing a dangerous job and living alone.

No. I don't like that at all. And what I like even less is the possibility I'm subconsciously making the new business out to be worse than it really is, all so I can stay here. *I'm a fucking head case.*

When I get out of the truck, I expect to hear Pippy whinny, something that usually makes me smile. But today, smiling feels like work. My muscles don't fire right. I feel a cheek twitch, but my body doesn't quite comply. The smile feels half-hearted. Even this horse deserves better.

And anyway, a whinny doesn't come.

I look at her paddock, feeling blue to my bones, wishing I could nap. Sometimes these moods hit me for a day or two. Everything feels heavy, and I feel low—downtrodden. I know I haven't been in touch with Trixie enough for my own well-being. One more thing I can beat myself up about.

I've been so high on Violet in the past weeks, I haven't had time to wallow. She's not here. I don't see her car, which means she's probably with Pippy up at the barn. I'd usually wait for her, but today I need to see her. I'd face Billie's mocking, Vaughn's smirk, and Hank's knowing twinkle if it meant getting to see Violet.

I jump back in my truck and take the road up to the barn. When I pull into the parking lot, I can tick off who will be here by looking at the cars. Everyone is here. Something I'm dreading already. There's a reason Vaughn took up the mantle as the face of Gold Rush Resources. Partly because he's pretty and partly because I hate that shit. Too many people and too much attention makes me feel like I'm an actor up onstage. Fake. With a big bright spotlight on me, highlighting every flaw while everyone stares, slack-jawed and horrified. A man who's killed people, who's watched people die, and who's been handed a multinational company with no experience. That's what I'm sure they must see.

I walk past the offices, not wanting to talk to Vaughn, and head down the vaulted barn alleyway. This facility is so ridiculous. *Ranch.* I snort.

A young man with a wheelbarrow full of dirty shavings gives me a friendly nod.

"Do you know where Violet is?" I ask.

"My guess is down at the track. Saw her and Billie head down there not so long ago."

"Thanks," I bite out, not really wanting to go to the track but wanting to find Violet more.

Back in the fresh air, under the oppressive cover of heavy cloud, I walk down the paved path toward the dirt oval, running the pad of my thumb over the teeth of the key in my hand, pressing it into the soft skin until it bites.

When the path angles down and I clear the stand of trees that gives the track a private feel, I see Violet on Pippy and Billie up on her black stallion. They're chatting amiably, trotting toward the gates at the far end of the track. Vaughn and Hank stand in the covered viewing booth, and I head that way.

I take the few small steps up onto the platform, and Hank turns to greet me, stopwatch in hand. "Cole! Good to see you, son. How you been?"

"Good." I try to muster a smile, but I know it's a sad attempt. Hank deserves better. He's been a mainstay in this town for years. My grandfather Dermot hired him and got him into the horses. I don't know him as well as Vaughn does, but he always gives off that warm, fatherly vibe—the one that makes me squirm with discomfort. The one I miss from my own dad.

"Hey." Vaughn looks me over the way he always does. A tad uncomfortable, like he's trying to gauge what kind of mood I'm in, and I hate myself for making my little brother feel that way. Like he needs to walk on eggshells around me.

I feel like I've sufficiently killed whatever good vibe they had going in here and jerk my chin out toward the track. "What's going on?"

"They're going to try the filly up against another horse, see how she handles the competition."

"Is a stallion the best choice?" My voice comes out steely, and Vaughn raises an eyebrow at me, though this time he spares me the teasing about my "military voice."

Hank steps in. "DD is a mellow stallion and very experienced. With Billie on him, it's the best choice for sure. If she needs to pull him up, she'll be able to. He's got a level head like that."

I try to ignore the anxiety roiling in my gut. I should go back up to the house, spare myself the stress of being here. But I've always been a glutton for punishment, so I stay, forcing myself to face it. Wanting to not be such a royal chickenshit about this.

I'll need to get a grip on this if Violet and I are going to be an us. I watch her and Billie guide their mounts into the slots. No gates are up today; it's just an open lane. I guess that part comes later.

"On your marks!" Hank shouts, his voice booming in their direction. "Get set!"

Pippy prances on the spot, like she knows something is coming. Like she's ready to explode.

"Go!"

As Billie and DD fly out of the gate, completely well practiced, Pippy startles. Her eyes roll slightly, showing the whites, and rather than surging out and running, the little bay filly goes straight up, standing tall on her back legs with her front hooves flailing ahead of her. I watch in frozen horror as Violet attempts to slide her arms around Pippy's neck and hang on. Her stirrups are set too short for her legs to provide any support.

Time moves in slow motion as her mouth sets in a grim line, concentration painted all over her face. I know Violet isn't new to a young horse's antics, but it doesn't stop pure dread from filling my chest.

And when I watch her topple off the back of the filly, I'm running. Down the stairs, across the bank of grass, vaulting the fence, as though I could get there in time to catch her. Billie sees me and pulls up, finally looking behind herself. Pippy lopes toward me, away from the gates, confusion in her eyes. Dirt flies out behind my feet as I scramble across the track.

I feel bile rise in my throat and stop a few meters away from Violet's still form, trapped in my worst nightmare.

I can't be back here again.

I can't breathe.

My vision blurs. The ground sways beneath me. And I bend over, pressing my hands into my knees as I drop my head and try to force my body to work again. I feel like an old car that needs a jump, a spark. I'm too fucking broken to even help her when she's on the ground.

But I can't get my body to cooperate. I heave, one hand coming up over my mouth to hold it in. If she's hurt. If she's dead. It can't happen. I only just found her. I only just found us.

"For fuck's sake!"

I look up just in time to see her fist hit the dirt and her small feet kick the ground like she's having a temper tantrum. And suddenly, I can get air back into my lungs. With a few more steps, I fall to the track at her side, kneeling in the dirt, fingers hovering over her body while tears spring up in my eyes.

Relief. Relief so intense. Like I've never felt before. "Are you okay? Are you okay?" I can't stop saying it. The question pours out of me repeatedly, as though I'm short-circuiting. Stuck on a loop. Suddenly, I'm transported to the dry heat of Iraq and to that day on the track all at once. It feels like I'm breathing sand again. It scratches my throat; it weighs on my lungs. Checking pulses. Ears ringing.

But Violet's eyes aren't dull and vacant. They're clear blue pools, reflecting the puffy white clouds above us. Her expression changes from looking pissed off to looking concerned as she takes me in.

"Hey, hey. I'm fine."

She tries to sit up, but all my first aid training kicks in, and my arms shoot out to hold her down. *What if she has a spinal cord injury? A brain bleed? She could be in shock.* When I watched my dad fall, he never got back up.

"Cole. Let me up. I'm fine. I was just winded."

Her lung could be collapsed.

I feel a nudge against my shoulder and look back to see Pippy standing behind me with a sheepish look on her face, black eyes staring at me with such kindness. Billie is just behind her with a sad look on hers. She's seen how fucked up I am, and now she pities me. *Great.*

"Just take a minute, Violet," Billie says so that I don't need to.

I'm intensely grateful that she's not just throwing me under the bus, telling me to chill out. Instead, she's helping me, something most people don't do. Especially people I've been as growly with as I am with Billie.

"You guys!" Violet shoves my hands off and sits up, frustrated. "If I tell you I'm fine, I'm fine. I don't need to be handled with kid gloves just because I'm the same size as one."

I flop back, sitting on my heels as Violet brushes herself off and comes to stand. She places one gentle hand on my shoulder before offering the other to pull me up.

"Cole. Babe. It's nice to see you. But I'm working right now. I'm coming to your place when I'm done. Billie, let's go again."

Her tone isn't cruel, but it is matter-of-fact. She's not in shock. But I think I might be, even though she's fine. I feel my hands tremble. I feel like I'm having an out-of-body experience. Like every square inch of me is numb.

Except for my heart.

That part of me aches. I can feel it, see it. The damage there, like an inconsequential ding from a rock that quickly splinters the glass and spiders out across the entire windshield uncontrollably. *Ruined.*

I stand and nod, keeping my eyes trained on the ground as I move away from the gates.

"Cole! Wait up!" Vaughn calls after me, but I wave him off and pick up my pace.

I flee.

Everyone saw me freak out. That goddamn spotlight I avoid is on me. *They all know.*

But I can't focus on that right now. My mind is reeling with two thoughts:

I need to be alone.

I can't be with someone who does this for a living.

CHAPTER 25

Violet

"I don't think you should be mad at him, Violet. You didn't see him. He was..." Billie trails off with a faraway look in her amber eyes. They pinch at the sides. "I think it would have made him feel better if you'd have just taken a minute to show him that everything was in working order."

"Why?" We're wiping down our tack together, and I rub the saddle soap–covered sponge over the reins of Pippy's bridle roughly. I'm aggravated. "I'm doing my job. I don't need him here micromanaging me and telling me what to do. Can you imagine if I waltzed into his office and did the same?"

"I know. I *know*." Billie squeezes the water out of her sponge with a loud sigh. "But sometimes, when we care about someone, we make their priorities our own. You didn't see him, Violet. He sprinted. I thought he was going to hurl right on the track. I don't think Cole's priority is to micromanage you—it's keeping you safe. Your safety is important to him. So throw the guy a bone and just, like, wiggle your toes and catch your breath next time before you jump right back on."

"Didn't know you were on Cole's team." I instantly hate myself for saying that. Childish.

"I didn't know you were twelve." Billie arches one shapely brow at me, successfully chastising me without saying more. She squeezes my shoulder and drops a sisterly kiss into my hair. "See you later, tough cookie."

But as soon as she goes, the sentence that runs through my head as I finish my chores in silence is the one about shared priorities. I'm still mulling it over when I pull up to his house, knowing that we need to hash some things out. Because if I'm going to make his priorities my own, he needs to make mine his too.

I'm about to open the door and walk in when nervousness hits me. Was I too hard on him? Snappy? I was miffed I fell off because I wanted to give Pippy the best experience possible, and that didn't happen. I was being hard on myself, and I think that spilled over into being hard on Cole. Based on Hank's and Vaughn's faces, I feel like I might have been harsher than necessary. Unintentional as it might have been.

I opt to knock instead, feeling the distance between the two of us already and not wanting to intrude.

"Come in." His voice is ragged, tired sounding.

I twist the knob and step into the pretty farmhouse. So light and airy, painted in whites and blues. It reminds me of delft pottery—the kind my dad still keeps in a china cabinet in the dining room from my mom's family in the Netherlands. I remember pulling them out as a child, running my sticky little hands over a plate or a bowl and making up stories in my head to go with the scenes painted on the sides.

Cole is in the corner, sitting in the cushy armchair where we first made love, looking like a dark shadow. Pure turmoil. I must have missed how insanely handsome he looks today when I was lying in the dirt. Gray dress pants with a bit of a sheen to them, black dress shirt with beautiful pearl cuff links. His elbows are braced on his knees and his head is dropped, his eyes fixed on where he spins one cuff link near his wrist.

He doesn't bother looking up at me. He's always looking at me like I'm the sun and he's been living underground for years. The way he looks at me warms me to my toes. I want him to look at me like that forever. So this—him avoiding me altogether—stresses me instantly.

"Hey," I say cautiously, unzipping my paddock boots and setting them neatly on the mat by the door. He likes it tidy. *See? Here I am. Sharing priorities.*

He mumbles something in response but doesn't change position.

"Cole? Are you okay?" I pad across the floor, onto the Persian area rug in the living room, and kneel before him, trying to get his eyes on mine, seeking that warmth.

I fold myself onto my knees, butting up against his feet. One flesh, one plastic. I wrap my hands around each of his calves. One flesh, one plastic. "Hey. Look at me."

When he finally does, my heart lurches in my chest. He

looks tortured. Broken. So lost. His eyes are glassy, his longer hair on top disheveled and flopped over his forehead. His face looks more lined than usual, showing our difference in age, the difference in how our lives have played out. Sure, I've had my challenges, but Cole… It's like he got dropped in the middle of the mountains at seventeen and has been forced to survive on his own.

I feel guilty. Like I haven't really wrapped my head around just how much he's been through. I've been so focused on wanting him, on showing him, that maybe I missed seeing just how lost he is. *Has he been pretending to be fine this whole time, for my sake?*

I think back to his nerves around me riding Pippy in the fields, the fact that he never watches any races from ground level, his vocal dislike of horses—save for Pippy, who seems to have completely won him over—and realization dawns on me.

Dropping my head, I kiss his knee. "I'm sorry I scared you. It wasn't my intention. Is this something that's been bothering you for a while?"

"Yes," he says, looking at the ground again. Not touching me back. Zero reassurance in his body.

"Okay." My hands rub up and down his calves, silently begging him to look at me. "We can work on that. Figure out a happy medium. I don't want you worrying about me like this."

"Then stop."

"Stop what?"

"Making me worry."

I chuckle sadly. It's such a sweet sentiment. "Tell me how. I'll try."

I feel his heavy sigh over the tips of my fingers as he finally pulls his head up and looks at me. The sigh is defeated, and so is the look in his eye. "I can't do this."

I lean back, away from him, like he just slapped me. "What?"

"This." His voice has transformed to the cold, unfeeling version of him I started out with a couple of months ago. His defense mechanism. "You and me. *Us.* I can't do it."

My pulse throbs in my throat as I try to keep up with what he's saying. Seems like an extreme reaction to a simple spill off a horse. Not my first. And definitely not my last.

"Why?"

"The riding. The horses. The racing. It's more than I can handle. Day in and day out. Every weekend. My dad died on that fucking track. I'm both drawn to it and repulsed by it. You deserve someone who can be there for you. You deserve someone who will be your biggest fan. And I can't do that."

I reel. First, I'm devastated, and then suddenly I'm furious. "Are you telling me if I found a new job, we'd be fine?"

His eyes shift away and his jaw ticks, like he's too ashamed to admit I hit the nail on the head. I let my hands fall away from his legs and flatten them on the carpet to ground me, breathing deeply and taking in the low-pile threads, the way the dark blues and creams and whites blend. Him and me. Dark and light. I feel like he just plucked my thread right out and tossed me away.

"So you kept this going, pursued me even, *knowing* the

job I've always dreamt of and am finally making a name for myself at would be a deal-breaker for you?"

He groans and runs his hand through his hair, tugging at the ends angrily.

"And now you have the gall to ask me to quit for you?"

He looks at me quickly now, his eyes blazing. "I would *never* ask you to quit for me."

I push up to my feet, shaking my head as I go. "Ask it. Imply it. What's the difference?"

"Violet—"

"No." I hold both hands out to stop him. "Nah. Don't. I don't want to hear it. You've always been clear about your boundaries. And now I need to set my own. I spent a whole year thinking I might be the exception to your rule. That maybe, just maybe, I would be the one to change your mind. Which is stupid, right?" I laugh tearfully, knowing I'm losing the grasp on my control, and move swiftly toward the door. "I'm never going to force you to change, and twice now, you've proven that I'm not worth changing for. Fool me twice, shame on me."

"Violet, please, you have to know it has nothing to do with—"

I spin and stare back at him. One tear spills out on my cheek. "I know, I know. It's not me, it's you. Except it's not. You're so much more than you give yourself credit for. I wish you could see it in yourself. What I see in you? So much strength. So much love. But I can't make you embrace it. That's on you. I don't believe for one second that you don't want us. But you're stuck, Cole. You can't see past one moment of your life. One terrible moment. And you're letting it define your entire existence." I jam my feet into my boots, hating walking away from him when he looks like he needs me more than he ever has before. "When you're ready to make other moments just as important, let me know. This isn't me quitting on you. But I won't wait around forever, Cole. Figure your shit out."

I keep my eyes trained on the door as I say it. My escape route. Because if I look at Cole right now, I'll go back to him.

I'll wrap him in my arms. I'll kiss him.

I'll forgive him.

And that's not what either of us needs right now.

I haven't slept. I haven't cried either. I've just thought. I lay in my bed all night thinking. About Cole, about his scars, his insecurities, his trauma. And about me and mine too. About how mad I am at him and how my heart bleeds for him.

I don't want us to be over. But I need him to be the one to take that step. And if he can't get over my chosen career path, then we weren't meant to be. I'm not folding to make another overbearing man in my life happy anyway. It's not even on the table.

"That's not the new Violet," I mutter to myself, staring into my coffee cup in the staff room, wishing I could hook it up to myself with some sort of IV drip. I should talk to Mira about that possibility.

"Hi, New Violet," Mira says as she marches in, like I

willed her into existence, and grabs herself a mug. She's obviously oblivious to what went down yesterday.

"Funny," I deadpan.

"What was Old Violet like?" She stirs her coffee with a smile on her full lips.

I groan. "Meek. A pushover."

"Maybe you're not new. Maybe you're just growing. Nobody stays the same. New goals, new experiences…they're all building blocks that put a person together. Constantly shifting."

"Are you a doctor of philosophy or veterinary medicine?"

She laughs and takes a sip of her coffee.

"You're in a good mood. What's wrong?"

Her feline gaze peeks over her mug at me as she grins. "I'm always in a good mood."

"You're not usually this talkative."

"Sometimes I learn more by listening."

"You scare me a little bit."

She throws her head back and laughs. "I'm in a good mood because I just came from a meeting with Vaughn and your boyfriend. They're going to be building a clinic here on the farm for me to work out of. Not enough quality facilities around, so apparently they're expanding into their own."

I smile, and it's genuine. I couldn't be happier for Mira. "That's amazing! Congratulations. But he's not my boyfriend."

She scoffs and tops her coffee. "He looks just as shitty as you. Actually," she says and peers at me closely, "worse. The man's got it bad. What did you do to him?"

"What did *I* do to *him*? Why is everyone taking his side?"

"No one is taking his side, Violet. I just know you're strong. And yeah, that man might fill out a T-shirt like it was painted onto him, and he could probably bench-press me, but he's in pain. It's written all over him—even before you guys had your little spat. I diagnose animals who don't talk for a living. He's basically the same thing. Trust me."

I laugh and then look at her seriously. "You think I'm strong?"

"I do. And you shine bright. Bright enough that a man like that might need you to light his way."

CHAPTER 26

Violet

THE FLANNEL BLANKET IS SOFT BENEATH ME, AND THE STARS are bright up above me. Most of the horses have been tucked into their stalls for the night, but we're still lying out among all the paddocks, down by the farthest one that backs onto the fields—the one DD used to be kept in.

"Is this really how you spent your first night on the farm, Billie?"

"Yup. Pass the wine."

The two of them have me sandwiched in between them. Their way of forcing me to come out for a girls' night. When I said I couldn't muster the energy to go to Neighbor's Pub, this was Billie's suggestion. What I didn't tell them was I didn't want to go to the pub because it reminded me of that night with Cole. When he finally softened up a little. When things got out of hand in the truck. That night, over pints of dark beer and chicken wings with a little too much batter, we came to a tenuous agreement. We turned a corner. The next day, he built Pippy her shelter.

"Wine straight out of the bottle and everything?" Mira asks from where she lies on the other side of me.

"Oh yeah," Billie says. "It's not the same with a glass. Less therapeutic that way, I think."

I giggle. "And the bread? You didn't cut it? You just ripped pieces off?"

"I'm fancy like that." Mira snorts in the most unladylike way, and Billie continues, "But it's way more fun with you guys here."

"I love you guys," I blurt out with a light slur.

"Violet, no more wine from the bottle for you," Billie says. "You're just drinking your feelings now."

"Seems as good a plan as any." I put my hands behind my head and continue searching for constellations up in the night sky.

I wonder if Cole is sitting outside looking at the same thing. He liked to sit outside with Pippy when he couldn't sleep. But I haven't taken her back over there yet—something I feel bad about. I left and took the one other living thing he enjoyed spending time with.

"Maybe try eating your feelings instead?" Mira holds a chunk of ripped French bread with a slice of brie on it over my way.

I take a bite right as Mira asks, "Have you seen Cole at all?"

"No," I mumble around my overfull mouth. It's been three days, and nothing. No call, no text, no smoke signals from his house.

"Well, go get on his case already."

"I don't know what to say to him. He told me he can't handle me being a jockey. What the fuck am I supposed to do about that? Quit?" I snort. "Screw him."

I look over to see Mira nodding. "The screwing must be pretty good for you to be this torn up about it."

My mind flashes to his hands on me, his gruff voice, his stubble between my thighs, me bent over in that stall for him. "You have no idea."

"Ugh! Gross," Billie says as she sits up to take another swig of wine. "You guys are both so stupid. He's scared of losing you, and you're scared of losing him. You both need to toughen up and get back to smashing. You're both in a better mood when you do. He's less grumpy, and you're less emo."

I can't help but laugh. Billie minces no words, and it's one of my favorite things about her.

"When I first met you," she says, "I thought you were like Drew Barrymore in that movie, *Never Been Kissed*. Virginal and awkward, but you're more like a secret freak. I respect the hell outta that. Channel that girl, and go make G.I. Joe pull his head out of his ass so I won't have to keep avoiding the offices when I know he's there."

"So this is about you?" I quirk a brow and point at her unsteadily.

"Of course! Everything is about me!"

We all dissolve into a fit of giggles and revel in the lightened moment.

Until Mira ruins it. "Speaking of egomaniacs, Violet, has Stefan Dalca spoken to you?"

My body goes tense at the mere mention of his name. I feel like I sober up instantly. "No. Why?"

"He said he was going to."

"About what?"

"Not my place to say."

Mira is like a lockbox. I know there's no point in pestering her. Where Billie might spill, she won't.

"Just checking," I say.

"Didn't know you and Dalca the Dick were buddies, Mira." Billie swigs again.

"Honestly, Billie. What is with you and the nicknames?"

"Way to deflect." Billie flops back down onto the blanket.

I feel safe between these two women. Coworkers turned friends—best friends. I've never had this before, and it warms me to my core. Without a mom or sisters and living on a ranch, I always felt isolated. Not cool or girly enough to feel like I belonged with other women. But Billie practically plucked me up and told me we were friends, and Mira just slid in. She started out cool, maybe a little standoffish, but we carried on like we didn't notice and now… "Here we are. Sisters from other misters."

I meant for that to be an internal thought, but the other two women don't laugh. They shift closer to me, elbows touching mine, feet flopped over against each other.

I've been numb for the last few days and have thrown myself into Pippy's training. We've got her running the track pretty comfortably after that first blip on the radar. I want to call Cole and brag about her. *My* project. Living, breathing proof I'm not just the lucky blond who got handed a championship horse. I'm an exceptional horsewoman. I want to crawl under the covers and tell him about it. I want his smell to wrap around me and the light dusting of hair on his chest to tickle my lips as they move, telling him about my day as we drift off together.

I want him with me. I want him there cheering me on. I don't *need* those things. But I need him to be mine. And I decide, as I'm lying here with two of the strongest, most accomplished women I know, that I'm going to make sure I tell him. I'm not going to be shy about what I want. I won't make it easy for him to walk away.

Because Billie is right. More than anything else, I'm terrified of losing him. And I'm going to tell him. Even if he can't tell me back.

I walk along the gravel roads with a flashlight in my hand. I'm too inebriated to drive, and I have, once again, underestimated how long the walk is. With every step I take closer to the blue farmhouse, doubt seeps in. And sobriety. Maybe I shouldn't be doing this. Does this make me seem desperate or brave? I can't decide.

On one hand, how many times do I need to tell this man I want him for him to believe me? On the other hand, if I don't lay it out to him in plain terms, face-to-face, I know I'll regret it. If I let this thing we have fizzle without trying, I'll never forgive myself.

Still, my feet feel heavy, like someone put lead in my pink-and-white-checkered Vans. It would be easy to turn around. A relief even. But I made it my goal a few years ago to take risks, to take chances, to *live*. And this is that. Staying true to myself. Or at least the girl I want to be.

I walk up to the house and pause at the base of the few steps that lead to the porch. It's after midnight, and there aren't any lights on. *Great, I'm going to wake him up* and *put him on the spot.* I blow out a deep breath and look up at the sky. A silent prayer for strength.

"Careful. I hear the guy who lives there is a real dick."

I start and spin, eyes scouring the dark yard until they land on his figure, sitting hunched over on the top rail of Pippy's empty paddock. He takes my breath away. His inky hair in the dark almost looks like it's alive above his glowing gray eyes.

"He pretends to be."

"He is."

"He's not."

Cole runs his hands through his hair. It's like he wants me to hate him as much as he hates himself. But I won't.

"You're stubborn," he says as he drops his elbows back onto his knees.

"Yup." I nod my head, struggling for what to say next, aching to rush across the gravel driveway and kiss him, hold him, run my hands over his neck, and tell him how I feel.

"I'm sorry." His eyes look pained as he trails them over my body. He looks uncomfortable.

I give in to my urge to move closer, wanting to get a better look at him in the moonlight. "Sorry for what?"

Only a few feet separate us, and my entire body aches

with the need to touch him. But I don't give in because it would make walking away again that much harder. I'm like an addict. One more hit, and I'll be off the rails.

He breathes heavily for a few beats, and I watch his pectorals rise and fall in his signature black T-shirt. His closet is full of them. Different neckline shapes. Same color. Arranged perfectly on hangers.

"For messaging you two years ago. For being intrigued by all your questions and sticking around when we clearly weren't after the same things. For talking to you. Every day. All night sometimes. For coming to rely on a woman I'd never met to make me feel good. For embarrassing you to save myself. For the way I spoke to you on the day you won the qualifier—not sure I'll ever forgive myself for that one. For being a growly shithead when you came to live with me. For not being able to resist you. For being dishonest. For not telling you things you deserved to know. For not being what you deserve." He stops, panting under the strain of the extensive list he just recited, and looks down. "Fuck. I'm sorry because I fell in love with you somewhere along the way, and now I don't know what to do with that."

I thought I blacked out that day DD and I fell on the track, but that was nothing compared to right now. I sway on the spot, and I don't think it's the wine straight from the bottle.

"You love me?" My voice is high and uncertain. I sound like a child to my own ears. My chin wobbles.

"Yeah." His wobbles too as his eyes meet mine.

"Then get your shit together and start loving me!" The

words burst out of me in a flurry of frustration that even I didn't see coming.

"It's not that easy. I'm..." A tense growl tears from his chest as he looks away. "I'm fucked up, Violet. There's hard work that I need to do. The shit in my head? It doesn't just get better because I want it to."

If he's searching for pity, this isn't where he's going to get it. He just told me he loves me, and he's still dicking around ignoring me? That's even worse than thinking he doesn't care about me enough to make this work.

"Do you want it to? Do you want to get better? Because from everything I've seen, you're pretty stagnant."

"Violet—"

"No. You are. Don't lie to me and pretend you're not. Take the demons by the horns. I don't need you *better*. What is better anyway? That's not a goal. That's not quantifiable. Pick something you can do, and *fucking do it*. I don't need you down at track level. I don't even need you at every race. I don't need you to love horses, but I *need* you to love me."

He starts, gray eyes wide and glassy, full lips rolling together like he's holding words in that he just can't quite bring himself to say.

"I know you see yourself as dark. But you aren't. You're swirling color, all different shades, a mosaic. You're complicated and beautiful. And I'm not quitting on you, so you better not quit on me." The words ring out between us like chimes on a windy day. The silence is heavy, and so is my conscience as I brace myself to put an expiration date on us. "Pippy has her debut race in two weeks. Tell me a plan by then. Or don't. At least I'll know how to proceed with my life."

"You're giving me a deadline?" He sounds borderline offended. Like no one ever lays down the law where he's concerned. Like they're so busy tiptoeing around his shitty moods and broken persona, they forget to treat him like he has responsibilities. Like he's capable of handling pressure. That his actions have consequences.

"Yeah. Two weeks should be long enough for you to decide if you're going to try or not. That's all. Not"—I hold my hands up in air quotes—"'better.' Not healed. Not different. I don't want you different. I want you with your jagged edges and your growly moods." I step forward and let my hands fall onto his knees, feeling the line of muscles beneath my palms. And I squeeze, urging him to look me in the eye. Really look me in the eye. So he knows how serious I am right now. That I mean every word right down to my bones, to my marrow. "I know everyone else has let you hide away. No one has gone out of their way to check on you, to love you. Everyone around you has failed you so thoroughly, given up on you so easily." I shake my head, and tears spring up in my eyes at the injustice of it. It makes me want to fight even harder for him. "I want *you*. But you need to want you too. I can't want you enough for the both of us."

There are no more words to be said between us, and it feels like Cole knows that too. He just gives me a terse nod, one I return before turning and walking away from him for what might be the last time. I walk down the gravel road back to my apartment, mulling that possibility over.

And then the tears finally come.

CHAPTER 27

Cole

I LIE ON THE COUCH AND STARE UP AT THE CEILING. LITTLE rainbows dance across the flat expanse from the crystal prisms hanging in the window. Light and pretty. They remind me of the farmhouse, of Violet.

"Does this actually help? Or is it just something people do in movies?"

"I don't know." The stacked bracelets on Trixie's wrist jangle as she holds a hand up dramatically. "But I will say that I don't think I've ever seen you relaxed enough here to lie down. You can't even see the door from there."

"Maybe I've stopped caring."

She cackles a raspy laugh. "Is that what you're doing? Lying down to die? How very Shakespearean of you. Good thing you drove back in for a session."

I turn my head to glare at Trixie. Sometimes it's like she thinks I pay her to mock me. "You know that's not what I mean."

She smiles back at me, all the wrinkles around her lips creasing in a way that tells years of tales. "Then by all means, tell me what you intended to say."

"I need to figure out how to cope with watching the woman I love get up on a horse and ride away from me. I need to know how to be happy for her rather than terrified she'll never come back."

"Okay. Is this something that has come up between the two of you? What does Violet say?"

I'm grateful she doesn't home in on the *L* word, but it also feels good to admit it. Last night talking to Violet outside, the way she reacted, I don't know why I waited so long. I've loved her from afar for years and never said a thing.

I think she might love me too. She didn't say it. But I can *feel* it. What woman would wait around for a fucking mess like me if she didn't love me?

I think we might love each other.

She makes me feel safe, makes me want to take chances, makes me a better me, and if making someone a better version of themselves just by being there isn't love in action, then I don't know what is.

I want to do that for her too.

"This is where I fucked up."

I chance a look over at Trixie. Her face gives nothing away, and she just sits there, staring at me. She's not disappointed or joking. She's just waiting.

"She fell off a horse while I was watching, and I crumbled. I had a full-on attack like I haven't had in years. In the aftermath, I may have implied I couldn't be with her because of her job."

"And what was her response?"

There's no hint of judgment in her voice. For some reason, I was expecting a scolding for being such a self-centered prick. I'm always expecting people to see the worst in me.

"In much kinder words, she said something along the lines of *fuck you* and *get your shit together.*"

"I do like this woman." Trixie adjusts herself in her seat and watches me thoughtfully.

I can feel the old crone's eyes on me. I can hear the wheels turning in her head.

"Tell me, what do you like about her?"

"What are we doing? Making a pros and cons list here?"

Trixie gives me a look as if to say, *Are you done yet?* I sigh, feeling self-conscious waxing poetic about a girl on my shrink's couch. I'm a walking fucking stereotype.

"Okay. Most of all, I like how driven she is. She hit the road on her own to carve her own path and has worked her ass off to get it. I admire that. She's calm and quiet, soothing, but not a pushover. I don't feel agitated by her, even when she never stops asking questions. She's thoughtful. She lets me have my issues and doesn't look at me like I'm a puppy who's been kicked a few too many times. She just reroutes, like I'm not an inconvenience to her at all. She's just...she's like sunshine on my face. Warm and bright. I feel like I've been living in the shade, in a dark corner, and rather than dragging me kicking and screaming out of it—like so many people have tried to—she's just shifted over a little bit to share her light."

I watch the multicolored dots move across the ceiling from the prisms, the pattern swaying slightly as the crystals do. They're hypnotic.

My voice comes out hoarse. "I don't want to live in the dark anymore."

Trixie looks up at the ceiling too, her neck stretching out above the big wooden beads of her necklace. "Pretty, aren't they?"

I swallow audibly, trying to clear my throat before I say anything. "Very" is what I manage.

"It's fitting, you know. Those crystals in the window are called suncatchers."

I blink rapidly.

"They're good feng shui."

I snort, but Trixie ignores me. She knows I'm not into that kind of stuff but carries on anyway.

"They take the sun's energy and cast it around, breaking up negative energy. Positive light. Healing light. Brightness and color."

I know it's my turn to respond, but I'm too choked up to do it. I just make a gurgling noise. Caught up in what she's telling me without really saying it. What are the chances I message Violet? What are the chances we forge a friendship? What are the chances she ends up working for my family? What are the chances I think of her as the sun while I'm staring up at a fucking suncatcher? Everything about us feels so unlikely yet so fated. After all the bad things that have happened to me in my life, it's hard to wrap my head around the universe shoving a gift like Violet in my face over and over again. But it's too much to ignore.

"You fell in love with that woman's drive. Her passion. Her spark for life. Her *light*. What if, rather than throwing that all away, you became her suncatcher? Take that light and amplify it in every way you can. Bask in it. How wondrous to have found it!" Trixie claps her hands excitedly. "But light is tricky. It slips through your fingers. It's fleeting. It comes and goes. We never get to possess it; you can't hold it in your hand. We just get to enjoy it. And if you can figure out a way to just let go and *enjoy it*, well, Cole, you'll be one of the lucky ones."

Lucky. I've never considered myself to be lucky. My dad, my leg, my engagement, my mental health. Money doesn't matter when everything else around you is shit.

I can't hide the crack in my voice when I respond. "And what if something happens to her?"

"But what if nothing happens to her, and you spend the rest of your life missing out on all that light?"

One voice in my head screams out louder than all the other ones. All the doubting ones. All the hateful ones.

I don't want to live in the dark anymore.

One step I need to take in getting my life back is rekindling some sort of relationship with my baby brother. Trixie only confirmed this for me as our conversation went on this morning. Which is why I'm here, sitting on the front step of his cottage while he's not home, waiting for him to get back. I don't know what I'm going to say to him. *Hey, want to sit down and drink a bottled water while I tell you about how I've been pretending not to be an amputee for the last six years? Cool, right? Super normal, I know, thanks.*

I groan and cross my arms, kicking at a rock before me. I'm frustrated. I'm impatient. I want this all fixed now. *Yesterday.*

I want Violet back now.

How did I let this get so far out of hand?

I'm ready to jump into berating myself when Billie's truck pulls up to the house. *Great. Just what I need.*

"Hey, big bro!" she calls as she hops out, just perpetually in a good mood or something. "Good to see ya."

I eye her speculatively. I thought Billie would be mad at me for the shit I've pulled with Violet. But she's acting totally normal instead. Annoying. She's acting annoying.

"Do you call me that specifically to annoy me?"

Her brows knit together as she approaches the front porch. "No. I call you that because we're going to be family, stuck together until we're old and gray and wrinkly, and I'm going to soften you up eventually. I'm very likable. You'll see."

Her ponytail swings as she stomps past me in her signature Blundstone boots. She enters the cottage saying nothing else to me, leaving me with my thoughts about how she just automatically assumes we'll be family for the rest of our lives. Like it's a fact, an unavoidable truth. I wish I had that kind of optimism where permanence is concerned. Nothing feels very permanent to me most of the time.

"Here." She startles me as she reappears, dropping to my right on the step and handing me a cold brown bottle of beer.

I take it from her and trail my thumb across the condensation forming on the outside. "I don't drink much."

"Be a lot cooler if you did."

I snort. "Dazed and confused. That's me these days for sure."

She chuckles and takes a swig of her own beer, staring out at DD's paddock. The black horse is munching on his hay, swishing his tail happily. A multimillion-dollar pet. I shake my head.

"Beer isn't healthy," I continue, trying to qualify my statement and mostly just change the subject.

She outright laughs now, waving her hand over my body. "Neither is whatever you're doing to your blood pressure right now."

A sigh whooshes from my mouth, and I take a deep gulp of the beer. She's right. Billie is perceptive like that. She's smart. People smart. The kind of smart they don't teach you in school. I remember setting Vaughn straight when he almost blew it with her. She knows right from wrong, and she taught my little brother a lesson in that.

I like them together.

"You must think I'm a real dick."

"Nope." She still doesn't look my way. Thoughtful eyes stare at the hills beyond the paddock, the ones that lead to the barn—to Violet. "I think you're doing the best you can with the shit hand life dealt you. Just like the rest of us."

Okay. That's not what I was expecting. But then, I know

Billie has her own share of family drama, her own set of daddy issues to contend with. Maybe we're more kindred than I ever realized.

She drinks again, looking thoughtful. "The shitty thing is Violet's out of your league."

I just grunt. And then drink. Because she's not wrong about that either.

"The good thing is she's too fucking angelic to see it that way." She inclines her head toward me and holds her beer up in a silent cheer. "So you've got that working for ya."

"Thanks for the vote of confidence, sis." I figure if she's going to dish it out, I might as well give it right back.

Her lips tip up in a small satisfied smile. "What you need to do is level up. It's not about Violet. It's about you believing you're worthy of her."

"You know I pay someone to help me with these types of revelations."

She doesn't miss a beat. "Okay. Cash or check is fine."

I chuckle. I can't help it. I hate to admit it, but Billie is funny.

"What would make you feel worthy of her?"

"That's a great fucking question. I…don't know."

"What's holding you back? This?" She taps her finger to my temple. "Or this?" She taps my prosthetic.

I pause, turning my head slowly to stare back at her. Bright feline eyes regard me inquisitively. "How did you know about that?"

"If you're asking if Violet told me, the answer is no. But I watch people and horses for a living. I think I see things that other people don't. Body language. Tics. Clues. Is a horse scared? Uncomfortable? Where can I diagnose a problem? I'm constantly assessing. And you…you hide it well. But your gait is just a *little* off. You always wear long pants and high socks, no matter the temperature. You massage your leg without even noticing. I put it together a while ago."

"And you just haven't said anything?"

Her nose wrinkles up in confusion. "Why would I say something? First, it doesn't matter to me. Second, it's not my business."

"Does Vaughn know?"

"Nope. You once told him that my secret was a conversation to be had between me and him. And my feelings on this are the same. That's for the two of you to talk about."

My chest caves in a little. "Do you think he'll forgive me?"

She shakes her head absently, looking back at her horse. "Forgive you for what? He's your little brother. He loves you."

My eyes sting with the simplicity of her statement. Like it's the most obvious thing in the world. The most natural. I hate how badly I've failed Vaughn.

"What about Violet?"

"Same question: For what? You plan on breaking her heart?"

I bristle. The thought of causing Violet pain causes me pain instead, like a heavy punch to the gut. Shrapnel to the leg. "Not if I can help it," I grumble.

"Okay, good. So what's the holdup?"

I tap my temple, mimicking the way she did it before.

"Everyone thinks I'm fucked up from the war. But I've worked on that. I've got that part under control, for the most part. It's the sight of my dad falling to his death on the track that haunts me. It's what I see every time I watch Violet race. It's what I worry about every day when I know she's up on a horse. What if it happens to her too? It's the question that plays on repeat in my mind. I want to be her biggest fan in one breath, and in the next, I don't want her on a horse at all. Which I know is a dick thing to admit, but it's the truth. I need to figure out a way around that."

Billie spins the bottle in her hands. She looks like she's completely ignoring me, and she's quiet for long enough that I seriously question if she even heard me blabbing about my feelings.

"Okay. So…are you afraid of losing Violet, or are you afraid of horses?"

"I'm…" My knee-jerk reaction is to say that of course I'm not afraid of horses. I grew up around them. But something stops me as I mull over the question. "No one has ever asked me that before." Am I? Afraid of horses? Does my fear stem from not understanding what she does more than my fear of losing her? *Fuck.* "Can I be both? I used to ride with my dad, and I wasn't scared then, but I don't know anymore."

"Yeah, man. You can be whatever you want to be. Except her number one fan, because that's me. You'll have to fight me for it. But if you don't fight me for it, some other guy will. Is the risk of her maybe, possibly, improbably, one day dying worth having to watch that? The family, the wedding, the babies?" She groans. "Ugh. Violet will probably make the cutest babies."

What. The. Fuck? Leave it to Billie to drop the most devastating emotional truth bombs possible. I feel my cheeks heat and my heart pound. That blood pressure? It's right back up where it started. "No fucking way. No chance. That can't happen."

Billie smiles and leans her elbows back on the step behind her, looking so damn smug. "Good. Ready to put in some work? Because I have a plan."

A Billie plan? I am equal parts invigorated and terrified. As she lays it all out, that terror turns to dread. I'm not sure I'm up to it, but I'm sure as shit going to try. She only stops talking when Vaughn pulls up in his stupid sports car.

"Everything okay? Did someone die?" he asks, looking concerned as he steps out quickly.

I guess from his perspective, it's weird that Billie and I would have a beer together when we're usually like oil and water.

"Everything is great except for the fact that you continue to insist on driving that car out here. You look like a total tool. A hot tool, but still," Billie quips back quickly, earning a sly grin and brow waggle from my brother. As he approaches us, Billie stands and hands me her empty beer bottle. "I need to…uh…go talk to Mira about the construction on the clinic."

Bullshit. She's clearing out so that I have to talk to Vaughn. She saunters up to him, ignoring the suspicious look on his face—apparently, he's not buying it either—and plants a quick kiss on his lips before slapping his ass and continuing to her truck. These two are perfect for each other.

"Hey, man," he says to me as he approaches. "Want another beer?"

I see my micro and macro counts go out the window, but it's not every day you have this conversation with your little brother.

"Sure. Why the fuck not?"

CHAPTER 28
Violet

It's Pippy's maiden race day, and I should be excited. But instead I'm pissed off and a little sad.

I still haven't heard from Cole. It's been two damn weeks, and I *still* haven't heard from him. Billie keeps telling me not to worry about it, and I've asked her a couple times if she knows something I don't. Her answer is always no.

But for once, I hope she's lying to me.

I shouldn't have given him a deadline. I shouldn't have put this pressure on him. I shouldn't have fallen in love with him. But here I am, taking all that frustration out on Pippy's coat, trying not to feed her all my anxious energy and failing miserably. Everyone knows I'm in a mood. Billie, Hank, Mira, Vaughn—they're all ignoring me. Pippy though, she's just stuck with me. And luckily, she's the happiest, most laid-back little horse on the planet. She's like an eternal optimist. I guess when you're born as early as she was, just surviving is an accomplishment, something to be proud of.

I need that optimism to rub off on me because I feel like a storm cloud right now. The good part of that is my killer instincts are in overdrive. I want to win. I want to brutalize the competition. I want to prove to everyone I'm not a ditzy blond. I'm the woman who took a horse that no one thought would race and turned her into a winner.

All Pippy's breezes have been solid lately. Her health is excellent. She's unflappable. But you never *really know* until you get a horse on the track. Sink or swim.

I threw myself into the deep end a couple of years ago, and today it's Pippy's turn to do the same.

"Miss Eaton?"

I start and then turn with a scowl to face Stefan Dalca, who is standing at the entrance to our grooming stall. I have to hand it to him. The guy must have a real pair on him, showing up in the Gold Rush Ranch shed row with how most of us feel about him.

"Why do you insist on talking to me before a race? It's not a good time. Do you know nothing about this sport?"

He blinks at me, looking surprised by the way I lashed out. To be honest, I'm a little surprised too. Do I like the guy? No. But this is out of character for me. *Fucking Cole Harding.*

"I just wanted to come and offer an apology to you."

"You?" I point at him. "Want to apologize to me?" My thumb butts up against my chest.

"For Patrick Cassel's behavior."

I snort and get back to tacking Pippy up.

"I was completely unaware of his behavior, and he's no longer in my employ." When I look up at him, his jaw ticks and he pins me with his green eyes. His hawkish features leave no room to doubt his sincerity. "His behavior on and off the track is not befitting of someone who works for me and especially not befitting of any man I want aligned with me. I'm very sorry for all the discomfort he's caused you."

I could say something snarky. I could throw his sleazy move last year in his face, but he seems serious. He seems… chastised.

"Okay." I huff out a breath as I tighten the cinch around Pippy's ribs. "Thank you for that. I appreciate it."

When I look back at him, he looks shocked by my response. Like he was expecting me to tear into him or something. But that's not me. I don't like holding grudges. I don't like having enemies. I like being on good terms with people, and if I can't be on good terms with Cole, then I can be with Stefan. At least that's something.

"Okay. Well. Best of luck." He holds his hand out to me, and I stop what I'm doing to take it in my own.

"Thank you. Same to you." I see his body relax as I offer him a small smile, like he was genuinely worried about talking to me. It's kind of sweet for a guy who's been nothing but a total snake in the grass.

I let his hand go and turn back to Pippy with a renewed sense of excitement. If someone like Stefan Dalca can come around, maybe Cole can too? The day isn't over yet. But now, it's time to put boys and drama out of my mind. It's time to work, to get down to business.

It's time to win a race.

With all our silks on, we walk out of the barn toward the hitching ring. Billie pops out of nowhere as usual, wearing one of the pantsuits she always dons on big race days, gives me my leg up, and leads me down to the circus that is Saturday afternoon at Bell Point Park. Pippy looks around with interest but not with alarm or anxiety—something that is distinctly not normal for a two-year-old at her debut race.

Other horses prance around anxiously, frothing at the bit, but she just walks her big steady walk with a curious look on her face. It's like she's been here before. Like she's here to teach us all a lesson, and maybe she is. I'm just not sure what it is yet.

When we get to the hitching ring, Billie gives my knee a squeeze and sends me in with a "Go get 'em, tiger."

I'm handed off to the pony horse, and everything else falls away. The noise, the distractions. All I see is what's between those pointy brown ears. My goal lies straight ahead. All I need to do is reach out and take it. Billie and I talked strategy earlier. The basic plan is to take it easy and let her find her footing. This race is practice since it's not a qualifier. It's a test. There is no pressure, except for the heaping piles of it I've put on myself.

After one lap, we load up into the gate, and I can feel Pippy tense up a little bit—finally. Her big ears flop around like windmills on her head, making me chuckle, and I reach down to give her some gentle scratches.

"Good baby. You got this. Everyone ruled you out. They thought you were too small, too weak. We're going to show them though, aren't we? We're going to show them what that rosy little attitude will get you."

And maybe that's my lesson. Positive energy begets positive energy. A winning outlook, that's what Pippy has, and when the bell rings and those gates fly open, I smile. I feel it in my soul.

Pippy is going to win this race.

She drops her head and drives forward, hard. She doesn't hang back and take some space. She doesn't assess the competition. It feels like it's more likely that she'll run them right over if they don't get out of her way.

Gone is the sweet little filly. In her place is a competitor. She drops her head and pushes hard from behind. I try to hold her back a bit. She isn't all that fit yet, and I don't want her burning all her energy down the first stretch. Running flat out from start to finish isn't anyone's ideal game plan. Except Pippy's, apparently.

She takes the bit between her teeth and drags me down that first straightaway. I sit up, leaning away slightly, trying to ease her off. But she's not having it. She is full throttle and flying to the front of the pack. And me? I feel like a little kid on a runaway pony. All that time spent turning and stopping and going, all those little nuances that I thought she had a decent enough grasp on, go out the door. At her practice runs on the farm, she was fast. But not like this.

So I'm left with a choice. Fight with her or let her run the race in a way that feels natural to her. Let her take the lead and show me what she needs.

I barely need to think about it.

I press my feet into the irons, get low on her neck, and let her run away with the lead. She flows through the corner beautifully, and I can't help but smile. Being on a horse with the wind on my face, I feel alive. And based on the way she's not tiring, I'd say that Pippy does too. She uses that final turn to rocket herself into the straightaway. We are absolutely flying, and I'm glad this is a short race, because I don't know how long she can keep this up.

When I chance a look behind myself, I almost can't believe what I see. The other horses have to be at least ten lengths behind us. With a small shake of my head, I press my knuckles into her mane and get low. Might as well make it eleven lengths.

We thunder down the straight to the finish post on an even tempo. I can feel her tire beneath me, but by this point, the spread is so big that it doesn't matter. I don't need to push her.

We sail across the finish line. It isn't even close.

I let my arms slide down around her neck as I press a kiss to her mane and laugh. That was the most bizarre and most fun race of my life. Pippy is a total psychopath.

"You're nuts. You know that?" I sit up tall to slow her a little, scratching at her withers the way I know she likes, feeling my cheeks ache with the intensity of the smile I can't wipe off my face.

I see our pony horse move up out of my periphery, something I'm glad for because Pippy doesn't seem too keen to stop. Hopefully an older, calmer horse will get her head screwed back on right. I'm still looking around as the rider comes up beside us and reaches for the rein. Sad as it sounds, I'm still looking around, hoping I might catch sight of Cole somewhere. Wearing a beautiful suit and that growly look on his face. I love that growly look and the voice that matches it.

I love him.

I should enjoy this win. But I'm pining after a guy I fell in love with like some wishy-washy teenager.

"I knew you'd win," the pony rider says from beside me. But his voice is…

I look over, and my jaw goes slack. Because Cole Harding is on the sturdy quarter horse beside me. He's holding Pippy's rein. *He's on a horse.*

"Cat got your tongue?" He grins, looking so damn proud of himself.

My eyes prickle and fill as I work to pull Pippy up, wanting to slow down, wanting to stop—wanting time to stand still so I can crawl into his lap again. "You're here."

"Surprise."

His smirk is panty-melting. All I can bring myself to do is shake my head.

"Did you think I'd miss it?" he asks with a tilt of his head.

"I…" We slow to a trot and then a walk before coming to a complete stop in the middle of the track while other horses barrel past us to the exit gate. "I honestly wasn't sure."

"Both my girls in one race? No chance."

My girls. "I just…" My mouth moves, but no sound comes out. "It's been two weeks!"

"I know. Learning how to ride again with a prosthetic in only two weeks was almost a full-time job."

I scan his body in the big western saddle. He looks comfortable. "You look good," I say honestly. "How did you pull this off?"

He chuckles. "Billie." Like her name alone explains everything. "Something about horses being therapy. I honestly think she might be on to something."

"You're here. On this track. On a horse," I say dumbly, still having a hard time wrapping my head around it.

He looks around as if soaking in everything—the sights, the sounds, the horses—and a wistful smile touches his lips as he looks back at me. "I am."

"Why?"

"Because I don't want to live in the dark anymore."

My throat constricts, and I wish I could say something, but I'm too choked up. I wipe my eyes and look around us shyly. *That's* what I wanted to hear. Not that he's only doing this for me but for himself.

"Come on. Let's get you off the track."

I nod, letting him give the rein a gentle tug as he leads us toward the gate and the winner's circle. I'm dazed. Elated. *Shocked.*

I watch him ride, and he looks so natural. He said he rode with his dad. It was something they liked to do together. Hit the trails and go on an adventure. I know he hasn't sat on a horse since his father's death.

"How does it feel? Riding again?" I murmur quietly as our horses' hooves clip-clop in unison on the concrete path to the winner's circle.

His Adam's apple bobs as he swallows, peeking at me

from the corner of his eye. "It feels like this is what he would have wanted."

I nod, sensing he's had a bit of a breakthrough, and look back up at the crowd gathering at the winner's circle. It's not quite the frenzy it usually is with DD, but it might be even more satisfying. It might be the best race ever, to be honest.

Cole is about to hop off his horse, but I can't take it anymore. "Stop." I reach out and grab his elbow right as he looks over my way. "Does this mean you're going to try?"

He looks around us shyly, knowing that people are watching now. Probably wondering why the hell I'm having an intense conversation with the rider of my pony horse. He looks at me so sincerely, I swear I feel my heart squeeze in my chest. He reaches out, one hand on my cheek, thumb rubbing like he always does.

"Yeah, Violet. I'm going to try. More than that, I'm going to just fucking do it. Because you? Us? I think we're meant to be. You found me, and I found you. Over and over again. If that's not a sign, I don't know what is."

A big fat tear rolls down my cheek. He catches it and wipes it away.

"I love you, Violet Eaton. I loved you before I ever met you. And god knows, I love you even more now."

More tears fall. I hear murmurs around us, but I don't care. I can't look away from his silvery moonlit eyes. He thinks he's dark. I think he just shines differently. The way the moon illuminates the world at night, soft and subtle. He doesn't shine—he glows. Especially when he looks at me the way he is right now.

And the thought that I could be the one to make this man glow? It takes my breath away. "I love you too," I whisper, eyes searching his, wishing I had more words for him.

He leans down, and his mouth finds mine.

And I opt to just show him how I'm feeling.

I pour myself into this kiss. The pain, the longing, the admiration—I lay it all out, and he soaks it all up. Every hurt, every triumph. He's there, and I know he always will be. His hands on my skin tell me so, his tongue against mine like a promise.

He pulls back and rests his forehead against mine. "Go. Savor your win. We'll finish this off in a stall later."

I giggle and blush at the memory, peeking around us, realizing we've got an audience.

"I'll be right here. I'm not going anywhere."

With one more swift brush of my lips, I turn and walk a very pleased-looking Pippy into the winner's circle, where she basks in the attention and pricks her ears up prettily for pictures. I soak it all up, knowing Cole is right there.

And he's not going anywhere.

EPILOGUE

Cole

ONE YEAR LATER

"Put. Your. Heels. Down. Do you not speak English anymore?"

I swear, if Billie didn't currently have my sleeping baby strapped to her chest, I would jump off this damn horse and give her the noogie she's so desperately asking for right now.

"It's my prosthetic," I grit out instead of, *Fuck you, it's my prosthetic*. I'm trying really hard to not swear so much now that I have another girl in my life. A far more impressionable one. Okay, she's only a few months old, but if I practice now, then I won't have to worry about *fuck* being her first word when the time comes.

Billie rolls her eyes dramatically, one palm resting gently on Lilah's bald little head. "Suck it up, buttercup. If our Paralympic athletes can manage, then so can super soldiers."

My teeth grind, but I push down on my leg as I trot

around the ring, trying to find my center of balance and get that joint at the angle Billie requires. We're not doing daily riding lessons anymore, but we try to keep up two per week. Billie is busy, and so am I, but she never complains. Even if it's at the very end of her day, she'll come out and help me.

I'll probably never admit it to her, but I love Billie. I jokingly call her Little Sis, but the truth of the matter is, that's exactly what she's become. She gave me an ass kicking and then patted my back. And now, I'd say we're friends. *Family.*

"Yup. Now you've got it." Her hand swirls around on Lilah's head.

"She's not a dog, Billie."

"I know." She peeks down at the tiny human strapped in a carrier to her chest and smiles. "But she's soft like one."

I chuckle and slow to a walk, feeling the ache in both my legs from the no-stirrup work she just had me doing. Total fucking masochist. "I thought you didn't like kids?"

Her eyes narrow at me, and she cups her hands over Lilah's ears. "Shh. Don't tell her that. She's the only one I like, but I don't want to hurt her feelings."

Now it's my turn to roll my eyes. "You're a fuckin' piece of work, you kno—"

"Cole Harding. I know you did not just swear in front of our baby." Violet walks up to the fence of the outdoor ring in those tight riding pants I love so much with a teasing smirk on her face. Beside her, Vaughn shakes his head. They just gave a press tour of the newly finished vet clinic, something neither Billie nor I wanted any part of. Cameras. People. Attention. *No thanks.*

"How'd it go, pretty girls?" Billie quips, walking toward them. "Want your baby back, Vi?"

"If you wake her up and ruin my couple hours of freedom, I will kill you." Violet's eyes flash with humor and a smidge of desperation. She's joking, but only sort of. New babies are both wonderful and exhausting.

Turns out Violet got pregnant as soon as we got back together, after Pippy's maiden race—possibly in what's become known as the baby-making stall. Something that makes me cringe every time someone says it. The timing wasn't ideal for Violet's career, something that stressed her almost instantly, but with her doctor's blessing, she finished the season. (Something I spent many hours on Trixie's couch hashing out. There's no finish line where therapy is concerned.) But ultimately it was fine. Lilah was born in our farmhouse in April, and a month later, Violet was back up on a horse. Violet is happy. And that makes me happy.

I think my dad would have loved Violet. He'd have respected her. Just like I do.

"It was great. Vaughn is made for the camera. You should see him. It's like they hit a switch, and he just turns on. All charming and mature."

"I am charming and mature." My brother grins with that playful look in his eye, something I love seeing. It reminds me of when we were kids. A time I can now look back on fondly rather than with bitterness and longing.

"Ehhhh. You're charming…" Violet says, rolling her lips together and going pink at her own joke. *Fuck.* I hope she never outgrows that blush. It makes my dick twitch every time.

Motherhood has changed her in all the best ways. I knew as soon as we found out that she'd be an amazing mom, patient and gentle. I just didn't foresee the fierceness it would bring out in her. It's added a little spunk to her, a little possessiveness that I live for.

I watch Billie and Vaughn sometimes and feel like Violet and I missed out on the fun, playful part of our relationship. But I'm not sure we were ever that type of couple anyway.

"Where's Mira?" Billie asks, only for Vaughn to pipe up with, "Hey! You're supposed to defend me."

She just raises an eyebrow at him and gives him an unimpressed look.

Everyone laughs, even Vaughn.

"She got called out to Dalca's farm." Violet answers Billie's question warily, almost predicting the growl that she emits at the answer. "Billie. It's not about him. It's about the horses. You wouldn't have her ignore a horse who needs help just because it belongs to Dalca, would you?"

Billie sighs and whispers something in Lilah's ear. I already know she's going to get her into trouble once she's old enough. Aunty Billie is going to be a problem.

"Really mature, Billie!" Vaughn laughs at his own joke like a total dork.

I jump off my horse to plant a kiss on my wife's cheek. "Hi, sunshine," I murmur against her skin, only for her to nuzzle in and reply with, "Hey, Butterface. I'm hungry." A nickname that has stuck.

"For dinner?"

She smiles, and her eyes dance with mischief. "No."

And suddenly, I want Sunday dinner over with and Lilah put to bed as quickly as possible.

We all turn together and march back up to the barn to finish with the horses and then head over to Vaughn and Billie's place. Sunday dinner is a tradition that Billie started, and it's now become a regular part of our week.

Especially since I never moved back into the city. I go back weekly, but the ranch is my home. I feel tied to the property in a way I didn't realize I could. It's the family connection, knowing that my grandparents met here. Lived here. Knowing my dad was born here. It feels right to be here. Like part of my feeling lost was just a complete lack of connection to my history—my roots. So that picturesque blue farmhouse is where I want to be, with all my girls, Pippy included. She still lives out front in the shelter I built her. A champion sprinter in the making and also the family pet.

Because we are a family now. In the very traditional sense of the word. In the way that I've longed for. Once Violet finished having her freak-out about being pregnant, I got down on one knee and let her freak out about marrying me. That was a happy sort of freak-out though. We traveled back to her family ranch, to a real cowboy sort of town in the prairies, and tied the knot with her entire family in attendance. They got to see the new Violet, the butterfly that emerged from the cocoon. And judging by the number of farm boys shedding a tear during our ceremony, I'd say they were impressed with her too.

"Hold up. Want help getting your horse put away?" Vaughn walks up quickly from behind me and gives me a quick shoulder shove.

"Dick." I shake my head and laugh at him.

Our talk on the front porch that night about my leg turned into a talk about a lot more. It turned into a pile of beer bottles on the ground and a big old shame spiral and headache the next morning. But it was worth it. Vaughn and I talked about our feelings—something I'm getting better at—and we reminisced. I've never felt closer to my brother, and my regret over pushing him away has slowly ebbed.

"What's for dinner?"

"Lasagna. Billie made it this morning, so the place has smelled like it all day. I'm only going to help you because I'm starving."

I can hear Billie and Violet walking up the path behind us, talking animatedly and laughing airily. Music to my ears. It doesn't even bug me anymore. The talking, the questions, that incessant chatter comforts me. It's the sound of my girl being happy.

"Charming," I say, looking at my brother, who grins happily back at me and claps my shoulder.

"Have a beer with me?"

I sigh. Why did this have to become our bonding ritual? "Okay, yeah." I can't say no. I'm too…happy. Too relaxed, too softened up from reflecting all this light that surrounds me.

I tie up GD, the old gelding I like to ride, and get to untacking him while Vaughn brushes him down thoroughly. I smile as I watch him talking to the horse and doting on him. Our dad would have fucking loved this. To see us like this. At his farm, working together, continuing his legacy.

My throat feels thick at the thought. Maybe he can see us; maybe he knows. Wherever he is. I hope he sees this. I hope he sees us happy.

Violet once said something to me about wanting to earn what she gets. Wanting to struggle and come out stronger on the other side. It's a sentence that changed my perspective. It gave my day-to-day life a purpose. It made me want to come out stronger on the other side too. It made me want to get to the other side, period. To step out of the dark and the mundane and into the light. Life was bitter, and now it's sweet.

I pat GD firmly and pull off his saddle. "Thanks for putting up with me, old man," I grunt as I pat his back. A perfectly golden palomino that Billie found for a novice like me—one with a heart of gold to match and who I jokingly named Golddigger. Who is now the pony horse that leads Violet's mounts to and from each race. And so long as I'm not stuck at work, I'm the one riding. I'm the last one to wish her good luck and the first one to congratulate her. I may not be jockey material, but being out there on the track with my wife—where my dad loved to spend his days and where I'm starting to as well—it's special. Especially when I get a front-row seat to see the look of pure joy on Violet's face as she crosses that finish line.

Win or lose. She's always smiling out there. Smiling right at *me*. Lighting me up.

Because she's my fucking sunshine.

BONUS SCENE

Cole

"Do you, Cole Harding, take this woman to be your lawfully wedded wife?"

Violet looks up at me, head craning to see my face. Her eyes are the same color as the sky, and I can't believe she's about to be *mine*.

After everything we've been through, after the way our roads kept crossing and leading us back to each other…it's almost hard to believe that we're here. Making it official in the way I've always wanted.

I'm still not convinced I deserve her, but when has the world ever given me anything that I deserve? I'm taking her anyway. She's mine. She always has been. I feel like the woman on that IKEA commercial who gets a such a good deal that she acts like she's stealing everything. She runs toward her husband waiting in their vehicle, shouting, "Start the car!"

Start the fucking car is right.

"I do," I reply to the officiant, my voice more gravelly than I want it to be.

Violet beams back at me, eyes shining more than usual, and my heart constricts. I love this woman so damn much that it's almost painful looking at her sometimes. *She saved me.*

"And do you, Violet Eaton, take this man to be your lawfully wedded husband?"

Her head quirks slightly, and her eyes scour my face, like she's committing this moment to memory.

"I—I do." Her voice cracks, and she has to look away for a moment to regain her composure.

I squeeze her tiny hands, the ones she's placed in mine. Along with her heart, her life, her trust.

On one hand, loving Violet the way I want to feels like a heavy burden. On the other, nothing has ever felt more right. I fully intend to spend the rest of my life proving to her she made the right choice—for herself and our precious baby growing inside her.

I stare at her stomach. The swell is still so small that you can't see it beneath the simple Grecian-looking princess-cut wedding dress she's wearing—one that is going to look mighty fine on the floor in a few hours. But I stare anyway. Something she catches me doing a lot lately.

Just like now. A small watery giggle escapes her lips. And I look back up, melting into her soft smile.

I need everyone to get the fuck out of here so I can christen this woman as Mrs. Harding for the first time. Waiting until tonight is going to be torture. My eyes scan the crowd. Getting her away from her dad and brothers, the Three Musketeers, is going to be like a goddamn military operation.

They're staring at us now. Her dad looks choked up. The grizzled old rancher's cheeks flush, and his eyes are full to overflowing. He shook my hand so damn hard that he almost broke all the bones the first time we met. But the "Hurt her and we'll kill you" he whispered in my ear made me like the guy instantly. We were on the same page with that.

Her brothers are a little harder to read. They're all so different but are clearly all good men. My eyes trail over to them. The youngest, Rhett, with a handsome, cocky smile on his face. He just looks like trouble, like a little kid who's been caught with his hand in the cookie jar but knows he'll get away with it. The middle brother, Beau, swipes a tear off his cheek and looks around himself like he's hoping no one saw. He reminds me of Vaughn, charming and eloquent. Possibly the most presentable of the three. Definitely nothing like the eldest, Cade, who is staring daggers at me. He reminds me of myself before I sought Trixie out. Angry. Cold. Distant. You can see the turmoil bubbling beneath the surface. The only time I've seen the man smile is when he's with Violet or his son.

Violet's fingers pulse around mine, forcing me back into the depths of her baby blues as the officiant carries on.

"I now pronounce you husband and wife. You may kiss the bride!"

Fuck yeah, I may.

I tug Violet toward me, one hand instantly snaking out around her waist. I love the feeling of her body pressing into mine, the way she instantly fits herself to me. My left hand skates up over her throat, and I don't miss the way her eyes heat at that. My shy little Violet loves it when I grab her there, but I'll save that part for later. Instead, I cup her jaw and brush her cheek with my thumb and look down into the eyes of the woman who is it for me.

Mine.

"I love you," I whisper against her lips as I claim them. I leave my eyes open just long enough to watch her lashes flutter shut and hear her responding moan as she slips her tongue into my mouth. *No shame.* My chest rumbles with amusement and possessiveness.

This. This is what I've always wanted.

Her arms wrap around my neck as she pulls me down toward her and kisses me with so much passion, it almost bowls me over. I somehow thought she'd tone it down in front of a whole crowd of people, but no. My girl can't help herself around me.

I hear a loud whistle from behind Violet, and I just *know* it's Billie. The whistle turns into the sound of my brother, Vaughn, hooting behind me, which turns into cheers and laughter and clapping. And fuck. I feel like my heart could grow wings and just take off into the sky.

Violet bursts into giggles and tucks herself into my shirt, her fingers sliding down the lapels of my jacket before fisting them and holding me close. I wrap my arms around her tiny body and look around us at all the people smiling. Friends. Family. Friends who have started to feel like family. Whatever Billie is.

She smiles at me, wide and genuine from over Violet's shoulder, where she stands as her bridesmaid. I can't stop the enormous smile that spreads across my face in response. I owe a good bit of my happiness to her meddling, and that's something I'll never forget.

Violet's arms wrap around my ribs as she comes to rest her chin on my chest. She stares up at me with one small tear streaking over the apple of her cheek. "I love you, Mr. Harding."

My thumb rasps over her skin, clearing the tear. I'll wipe away her tears forever. "I love you too, Mrs. Harding."

Fuck, that sounds so good. I'm so fucking happy I don't even know what to do with myself. This is it. This is the life. This is the light.

And I'm so glad I chose it.

"I need a break." My lips brush across the shell of my wife's ear, and I see her smile.

I'm being a needy bitch, and I don't even care. I've been a good boy. I've made the rounds. I've talked with people. Shit, I've even smiled. My cheeks hurt from it. I'm going to have to scowl for a week straight to recuperate. But Violet wanted a wedding, and I'll do anything to make her happy. I would have married her in the middle of a swamp with only the mosquitos there to witness it. But here we are, doing the whole thing with what feels like everyone we've ever met.

"There are still guests here." Violet whispers as she gives me a quick poke in the ribs.

A PHOTO FINISH

I look around the wooden dance floor set up under a sea of string lights. There are too many people here wearing cowboy boots with a suit. Chestnut Springs is something else. I feel like someone dropped onto the set of *Yellowstone*, a show that Violet keeps making me watch with her. She's even told me she had a childhood crush on Kevin Costner. After which she told me I should *thank* him for getting her into older men. I could see her cheeks twitching as she tried to keep the laughter in. Eyes glued to the TV, lips rolling against each other with amusement.

Joke or no joke, I'm still going to punch Kevin Costner if I ever see him.

"I don't care." I let my hand slide down from the small of her back and over the curve of her very delectable ass as we stand looking out over the dance floor. "Plus, I don't want to watch Trixie make her move on Hank."

The two of them are dancing and laughing and looking at each other in a way that feels like too much information.

She snorts. "God. That would be adorable."

"Ugh." I shudder. Trixie has no filter. I can already imagine the lack of boundaries that would come with that. The stories she'd subject me to. A growl tears itself from my chest. "I'll show you adorable." I bend down and scoop Violet up into my arms.

"Cole Harding!" She slaps my chest on a shocked gasp as I turn away from the party. "Put me down."

"Wave goodbye, Mrs. Harding."

She wiggles in my arms and laughs, waving goodbye over my shoulder to the guests who are now chuckling and shaking their heads as I carry her away like a total caveman.

I don't care. I'm done being paraded around. I hate crowds. I don't even know where I'm going. I just want to be alone with my wife.

My wife. That's going to take some getting used to, but fuck, does it sound good.

I walk out into the darkened pasture, pausing only when we get close to an old stone well.

"I want to stop here," Violet says quietly, the humor in her voice seeping away.

I place her on the ground, but she just tucks herself into my side, clinging to me as we both stand facing the well.

"Today is one of the first times I really feel the absence of my mom." Her voice is clear and quiet under the cover of the stars. "I've never known any different, but today I can't stop picturing how my wedding day would have looked with her here."

It's like she reached into my head and plucked out my thoughts. I've been joyously happy today, but the ache of knowing my dad wasn't here to share in that happiness is hard to escape.

"Same" is all I say. I don't trust myself to say more, so I just squeeze her petite frame into mine, reveling in the feel of her palm sliding across my stomach and her head resting against my ribs.

"This is where she used to bring my brothers. They'd bring coins and toss them in. Making wishes and waiting for the sound of them hitting the water."

My chest constricts as she continues.

"My dad renamed the ranch after she died. On one hand, I think it's kind of beautiful. On the other, a little morbid. Like when you're here, you can't escape her memory."

Wishing Well Ranch.

My eyes trace the cedar shake peak that covers the stone well, the vines planted on either side that crawl up the posts propping up the roof. It's like a tribute.

"I kind of like it," I say to her as I reach into my pocket, knowing I have one coin in there from tipping the bartenders tonight. I can vividly imagine a woman—a spitting image of Violet—seated on the edge, surrounded by a small throng of unruly little boys with disheveled hair, spending a sunny afternoon making wishes.

It sounds like heaven.

"Go make a wish." I guide Violet forward and hold my palm out across my body, the metallic shimmer of the coin catching the moonlight as her gaze drops. Her lip wobbles as we approach the wishing well, but she picks the coin up and takes a deep breath anyway. She steps forward to look down into the depths of the dark water. And I stand back, letting her have this moment, watching her slight frame, her glowing hair, the curves on the body that's carrying my baby. *I'm going to be a dad.*

Is there such a thing as too happy? Because that might be me.

She holds the coin up and drops it down into the well, leaning over slightly like she'll be able to see it under the cover of darkness.

When the splashing sound reaches us, I see the corner of her mouth tip up. A small satisfied smile graces her elfin features as she lets out a ragged sigh. She turns around to look at me, and it takes my breath away. Every damn time.

"What did you wish for?" I ask jokingly.

Violet just rolls her eyes at me. "Can't tell you, or it won't come true."

I just chuckle and fold her into my arms again, letting the heat of her body seep in through my tux.

"We need to go get another coin so that you can make a wish," she murmurs against my chest.

I just scoff, lifting her up in my arms again and turning toward our guesthouse. My strides cover the ground as she snuggles up against me, and I realize I'm never going to tire of carrying this woman around. Or other things. I'm never going to tire of all the other things. Other things that I am going to show her so hard right now. As soon as I get this woman behind closed doors, I am going to *thoroughly* other-things her.

I smile into the night just thinking about it.

"Don't need to, Mrs. Harding. I've already got everything I've ever wanted."

"Don't be such a baby."

Stefan has his arms wrapped around Loki's neck and is looking down at the foal like he's a stuffed animal, not a future athlete and animal that needs space to frolic and run.

Read on for a sneak peek of the
next book in the series

THE FRONT RUNNER

Stefan

My heart hammers against my ribs as we walk the tiny colt down the concrete alleyway, small, soft hooves clopping quietly through the barn. I feel like a shmuck. Here I am, joking around and flirting with Mira, feeling all proud of myself for squeezing three dates out of the woman while a horse's life is on the line.

And this might not even work.

I'm usually comfortable with morally gray business decisions, but this time I just feel like a dick. Mira saves lives for a living, and I leveraged that passion for my own gain. Asking for the dates was a shot in the dark, just like it was the first time I did it and every time since. But her turning me down has me fixated. I want to know Mira Thorne in ways she can't even imagine.

Truthfully, I should probably feel worse. But watching her work, so steady and focused, just makes me more attracted to her. I've studied my ass off since starting this venture to learn as much as possible about the business. My closest friend, Griffin—who I bought this place from—is my go-to source for horse information. But orphaned foals haven't come up in our chats yet.

Mira slides the stall door open and takes a deep breath. Her eyes meet mine over the back of the foal, and she gives me a decisive nod before we step into the stall.

I'm nervous. It's so unlike me. But, God, I really want this to work. I don't even care who owns the foal. The truth is, I'd have done this even if she said no to the dates. Plus, I don't dislike Billie Black or the Harding family enough to wish this upon them. Watching my foal die this morning was heart-wrenching. I've come to love these animals, and watching them suffer is torture in a league of its own.

"Hey, mama. Meet baby. He's a real sweet boy." Mira's voice is deep and smooth. She doesn't use a high-pitched baby voice. It's almost like she could hypnotize the horses into acceptance with a tone like that. Or me. I'm a sucker for her sultry voice.

She flicks her head back at me, effectively dismissing me as she holds the small red foal and lets the mare walk toward it. Stepping back into the doorway, I watch raptly. I'm not a superstitious man, but I'm not taking any chances tonight.

I shove my hands into my pockets and cross my fingers. I think I'd cross my toes if I could.

The mare's dark globes for eyes assess the colt, and her ears flick around in confusion as she tries to sniff him. To the colt's credit, he may be weak, but his sense of smell is just fine. I watch his head snap toward her udder, ears pointing exactly in that direction, and spindly legs follow. His back moves right beneath her flared nostrils. They're glistening with the rub that Mira smeared there, but she must catch some small scent of the manure because she gives him a small nuzzle on his bony haunch with her top lip.

I don't miss the small gasp that slips past Mira's lips. She holds her hands up off the foal like he burned her and steps back slowly. Carefully. Like she doesn't want to break whatever momentary connection the two horses seem to have formed.

My fingers hurt from how hard I'm squeezing them across each other. I don't move, even as Mira's body comes to pause only a few inches away from mine.

Within moments, the colt shoves his head beneath the mare's belly and nuzzles at the overfull udder. Trying to figure out something he hasn't quite learned how to do yet.

I glance down at Mira's tense body—raised shoulders and hands fisted in front of her breasts—feeling her heat seep into the front of my body. The only part of her moving is her chest, with the rise and fall of her deep breaths.

The stall is almost entirely silent. Until a noisy suckling noise fills the space. Followed by a ragged sigh from the woman standing in front of me. In wonder, I watch the content mare go back to the hay net before her. Mira's thick black ponytail flops forward as she drops her face into her hands.

The relief pouring off her bleeds into me, and I pull one hand out of my pocket and place it on the nape of her slender neck, giving her a reassuring squeeze. "You did it."

She just nods. She doesn't shake me off; she stands there, soft skin beneath my palm, watching the mare and foal accept each other like life meant them to be together no matter how tragic the circumstances.

"Fuck. What a relief." Her voice is hoarse, but I can't see her face to confirm how emotional she might be. I absently brush my thumb across the base of her skull, and after a beat she clears her throat and steps away. "Let's leave them for a bit." Mira turns to exit the stall but doesn't meet my eyes.

Usually, she covers her vulnerability with a smirk—but not today.

I shouldn't have touched her like that. I'm like a cat playing with his food. But all I really want is for her to see that I'm not a bad guy. I don't always play by the rules, but I'm not a bad guy. I grew up with one, and I refuse to become him.

I move away, letting her pass. Wishing my hands were still on her. I don't know why the woman intoxicates me the way she does. Her eyes, her lips, her cool exterior, the sensual hum of her voice—it's all driven me to distraction since the first time I met her down at the track. Her no-nonsense way of handling me while being perpetually gentle and sweet with the horses was a contradiction that fascinated me then and still does now.

She's an equation I'd love to solve.

Or maybe the broken little boy in me just wants her to treat me the way she does a horse. With love. I shake my head at myself as I turn to follow her. The thought of her softening up for me is the ultimate carrot she could dangle. I want nothing more than to watch her melt.

I don't love Dr. Mira Thorne. I barely even know her. I'm just fascinated though—inexplicably drawn to her. And I'm too damn accustomed to getting what I want to let it go.

"What now?" I ask as she marches toward the lounge area, complete with cushy brown-leather couches, a pool table, and a fully stocked bar.

She straight-up ignores me for a few beats before flopping down onto a couch with a loud sigh. "Now we wait a bit and see what happens."

I follow suit and drop onto the couch across from her, propping my feet up on the table and resting my hands across my ribs. "You look tired."

She hits me with an unimpressed look. "Charming, Stefan."

"Why don't you sleep for a bit, and I'll keep an eye out."

"No." Her head drops back, and her eyes close.

If she's half as exhausted as I am, she must feel like utter garbage. But I don't argue. Mira doesn't give off the vibe that says she wants to be coddled. So, if she wants to be dead on her feet, good for her. I'll support it.

"What's the accent?" she asks without opening her eyes.

"Romanian." I keep my eyes wide open. Truthfully, I can't peel them off her.

"You're Romanian?"

"I was raised there."

"You just look so…I don't know. Not Romanian?"

Yeah. I'm not sure how it took me so long to figure that out either. I'm about to ask her about her family's background, but after only a few moments, her fingers fall open and her pillowy lips part.

She's out like a light.

She looks younger and…softer somehow while she's asleep. More innocent. The sight of it stirs some instinctual part of me, and all I want to do is take care of her. Make sure she's comfortable. That she rests for a while.

I walk over to the large wicker basket at the end of the couch, pull out an Aztec-style wool blanket, and drape it over her gently. She stirs slightly, but only to nuzzle her cheek into the couch.

She looks so damn tired.

I figure I can sleep tomorrow while she'll probably have to work. With one final glance over her sleeping form, I walk back out into the barn alleyway to the stall with the mare and foal. I flip the latch and creep in. My chest warms seeing mom standing and dozing with sprawled-out baby sleeping happily beside her. They're a perfect match. Red and red. You would never guess they aren't related.

I step into the stall, closing the door behind me, and slide down onto the ground near the foal's head. With my back against the wall, I let my gaze travel over his spindly body, warm under the glow of the red lamp hanging above. He looks weak but peaceful.

I'm momentarily transported back in time to the horse I had as a child. The same color as this foal, but not with flashy white legs and face. An entirely different type of horse. But he was mine. He was my reprieve from the hell that was living in my childhood home.

I lean forward and let my hand trail over the sleeping colt's leg to his knee, where the white stocking blends into the coppery brown of the rest of his coat. My body moves of its own accord, coming to kneel beside the small horse. My palm rests over his rib cage, feeling it rise and fall in a steady rhythm. He may not be out of the woods yet, but his breathing is strong. I think he's a strong little horse.

A fighter.

When I move up to his head, cupping the round plate of his cheekbone, he nurses in his sleep. A sweet suckling noise that makes me smile. This guy knows what's up. He's not down for the count yet. And I'm going to make sure he succeeds.

I lean back against the wall, resting my elbows over my knees, vowing internally to make sure this is the healthiest foal anyone has ever seen.

"Wakey, wakey."

My foot wobbles from a kick, and my eyes flutter. The first thing I feel is stiffness as I try to get my bearings. Stiffness in my joints...and in my pants.

Mira's voice filters into my consciousness. Something that is definitely not helping the morning wood situation. "Up we get, Sleeping Beauty. I made you coffee."

And there she is, standing in the stall's entryway, looking a tad disheveled. How I imagine she'd look after a night spent in my bed. Soft and lacking the snarky smirk that's always plastered on her face.

I scrub at my stubble, trying to wake myself up. A small chestnut face moves into my periphery. The foal is looking at me like I'm absolutely fascinating. Farrah is just ignoring me—the weird guy who slept on the floor of her stall.

Mira steps closer, leaning down slightly to hand me the mug of steaming coffee in her hand.

I peer down into the mug. "Cream this time?"

Her eyes flit away shyly. "You didn't seem big on the black coffee, so I tried something else. How do you take it?"

I just don't want you to think my soul is black. It had been a joke when she said it, but I'd let it bug me anyway. I'm inexplicably concerned with what this woman thinks of me.

"This is fine," I reply gruffly, taking the coffee from her, willing my raging boner to disappear. *Hello, morning wood.*

"Okay, get up. I need to check these two over."

I take one thoughtful sip of the coffee before I calmly say, "I can't get up right now."

Mira scoffs. "Of course, you can."

I grin back at her, and after a beat, her confused eyes trail down to my lap and then go wide as she puts all the pieces together. "Oh." She clears her throat. "I'm, uh, just going to get a few things from my truck then." And then she darts out of the barn.

I can't help but chuckle as I bang the back of my head on the wall a few times. That's not the reaction I was expecting from her at all. She acts like a siren, but the mere mention of a boner, and she can't get away fast enough.

After a couple of minutes, I stand and lean back against the wall of the stall. I sip the hot coffee and scan over the mare and foal again. The foal comes closer, clearly curious about the person who spent the night sleeping with him. His soft nose rubbing against my jeans, nostrils flaring wide as he tries to take in my scent. Bulging black globes with chestnut lashes fanning down as he wiggles his lips against my shoulder curiously.

Damn. He's really cute. I reach my free hand out and rub the fuzz of his goofy little forelock between my thumb and forefinger before letting my palm slide down over the wide white blaze on his face. His eyes flutter shut, like he's enjoying the feel, and I can't help but smile at how sweet and trusting he is. How unmarred by the world—by life.

"He's pretty sweet, isn't he?" Mira's voice interrupts the dark turn in my head. She's standing in the doorway with a stethoscope around her neck and her ponytail slicked back harshly against her scalp.

"Does he have a name yet?"

She sips her coffee and shakes her head. "No. I think Billie was pretending to have a hard time coming up with something under the guise of not wanting to get attached. You know, in case he doesn't make it."

It's the perfect opportunity to take a jab at the other woman, but I can't bring myself to do it. "What's his breeding?" I ask, curious about the colt's lineage.

Mira continues to sip her coffee and stare at me. Her eyes flit momentarily to my crotch, and I swear her cheeks pink a bit, but I don't get long to think about that before she says, "He's the black stallion's first foal."

I blink at her. "The one I tried to buy?"

"Yup."

"Jesus. Did you have to tranquilize Billie to get him over here?"

"Don't be a dick. She's been sick over this foal. She hates you, but she wants him to survive more."

Feeling properly chastised, I hide behind my cup of coffee for a moment before changing the subject. "He needs a name. It's important he has a name."

"Why?" Her voice is quizzical as she steps in and holds the stethoscope over the nameless colt's ribs.

"Because he's going to make it. A name ties him to this world. It gives him an identity. Means we recognize his existence."

I see the searching look she gives me. It's quick, but it's there. Full of curiosity.

Every time I ran away as I child, I'd end up with the local villagers who lived nearby. I'd hide out in their homes and listen to their stories, their teachings, their connectedness. That immense sense of community—it all stuck with me. Rather than growing up to be a man who was afraid to fall into my parents' footsteps, I decided it was my goal to prove that I wouldn't. I'd have a wife, I'd have a family, I'd have it all, and I would treat them like gold.

She rolls her lips together but doesn't look up from where she's staring down at the foal. Her mouth moves silently as she counts his heart beats.

"Then name him. He needs all the help he can get," she says as she steps away. "I'll be back later to check on him again. I need to go open the clinic. Can you make sure he's nursing throughout the day? I'm going to do a blood draw when I come back. I'm probably going to bring Billie—she needs to see that everything is good. So can you either keep your mouth shut or make yourself scarce?"

I nod, trying to hide my amusement over her thinking she can dictate my behavior or whereabouts on my property. My gaze follows her decisive movements as she packs up her kit and heads out. I shouldn't check her out the way I am, admiring the roundness of her ass in the pair of dark-wash Levi's she's wearing. But goddamn, she fills them out so well.

Her hand taps the frame of the stall door as she leans back in, tongue darting out over her bottom lip. "And, uh, thanks for the blanket last night."

"Next time I'm joining you." I wink, and she just rolls her eyes.

I should try harder to keep things professional and not let my curiosity about Dr. Mira Thorne take over my brain. I shouldn't think with the wrong head.

But the more time I spend with her, the more of a challenge that feels like. I like a challenge…but keeping my hands off Mira isn't one I'm sure I want to take on. The woman is not my biggest fan, this much I know.

But then I've got three dates to make her want my hands on her body.

A Special Thank-You

I'd like to note a special thank-you here to Kelsi and Jay, both of whom so candidly shared their experiences with me. I know that each individual's experiences with PTSD, adjusting to civilian life, and living as an amputee are vast and varied. What I've written here represents but a sliver of what people are living with on a day-to-day basis, but these two individuals gave me a special peek into their personal histories, and I wouldn't have felt comfortable writing this book without their invaluable feedback. I feel so honored that they both entrusted me with their stories.

Acknowledgments

There are so many moving parts that go into getting a book ready for publishing, and I'm eternally grateful for all the awesome people involved in mine. Thank you to each and every one of you. Even the ones I've undoubtedly missed.

To my husband, thank you for your relentless support. Your pep talks are the stuff of legends.

To my son, who always asks me if I'm "working on my Kelsey Silvers stuff." You are my favorite human.

To my editor, Paula, this book wouldn't be what it is today without you. Your feedback is invaluable, and you are pretty much the ultimate hype girl.

My editor at Bloom Books, Christa Désir, thank you for believing in my very first books. It's such an honor to work with you.

My beta readers! Amy, Amber, and Christy: you ladies are awesome. Thank you for your time, energy, and direction.

My ARC and street team members, I am absolutely overwhelmed by all your support! It makes me a little misty-eyed to think about how much you have all done for me. I'm really not sure how I'll ever thank you all. I send hugs to each and every one of you.

Shannon and Laetitia, hats off to you both for your exceptional eye for detail and time spent poring over my words. I so appreciate your help.

Finally, the biggest thank-you to my agent, Kimberly Brower, for being a constant source of support and wisdom on the wildest ride of my life.

About the Author

Elsie Silver is a Canadian author of sassy, sexy, small-town romance who loves good book boyfriends and the strong heroines who bring them to their knees. She lives just outside Vancouver, British Columbia, with her husband, son, and three dogs, and has been voraciously reading romance books since before she was probably supposed to.

She loves cooking and trying new foods, traveling, and spending time with her boys—especially outdoors. Elsie has also become a big fan of her quiet 5 a.m. mornings, which is when most of her writing happens. It's during this time that she can sip a cup of hot coffee and dream up a fictional world full of romantic stories to share with her readers.

Website: elsiesilver.com
Facebook: authorelsiesilver
Instagram: @authorelsiesilver
TikTok: @authorelsiesilver